I0743003

Pisgah Press was established in 2011 to publish and promote works of quality offering original ideas and insight into the human condition, the realm of knowledge, and the world around us.

Printed in the United States of America

Published by Pisgah Press, LLC
PO Box 9663, Asheville, NC 28815
www.pisgahpress.com

ISBN-13: 978-1-942016-99-1

Fiction

First Edition
First Printing
November 2025

DEDICATION

This is for a sweet survivor. The Russians, the Taliban, two idiots and life's random crapola could not scar you. Anisa, you are the embodiment of all that's right with this dumb old world.

Anatomy of a Shark

A novel by

M. G. Akins

Pisgah Press, LLC
PO Box 9663
Asheville, NC 28815
www.pisgahpress.com

Prologue

Me, formerly innocent me, may have smiled at a fortuitous moment when I was six weeks old, all but sealing my adoption. Perhaps some poor kid next to me soiled his diaper mere seconds earlier and was thus doomed to adolescent life in an orphanage.

Well ... any plausible scenario represents circumstances that I simply cannot account for, seemingly trivial matters, which, in a hard world, can make or break a life. Piddling stuff.

Take names for instance—blue eyes and blond hair and my name is Vinnie. It's not that I was named in bad taste, but my name is illusory. Like all the little princesses in trailer parks named Tiffany. Or like if Fred Flintstone had been christened Herschel—Herschel Flintstone at ease cranking the levers operating a brontosaurus in a rock quarry.

So. Adopted as an infant. Not a perfect start for me, but a lucky one, with imperfect love coined both head and tails. It was life itself that was to be taken for granted, which is normal. I've been told that I laughed, I cried, spit up seriously awful mashed peas, and burped when encouraged. What did I know? I was a baby, doing okay, unaware that I had started out a winner.

My adoptive mother was (and is) a nurturer, all smiles and hugs, accepting my boo-boos as I presented them, disfiguring injuries worthy of great drama. If parenting can be said to be a balancing act, then my mom should be envisioned on her half of the scales pivoting as needed to make my life level.

Even so, being honest, I have to say that as a kid I had this uncomfortable knee-jerk reaction to the manner with which Mom would finish cleaning a gun by imparting a small soft kiss to the barrel, a tradition inviting luck I supposed. Usually dad's gun. Usually about the time other young matrons would be darning watch caps or damning the chore.

Not that my dad had his gun cleaned all the time, not on a daily basis. It's just that some memories become embedded little barbs forever tenaciously alive, no matter how many whacks one takes upside one's head.

Guns. Guns just were. Captain Crunch, Hungry Hungry Hippos, and gun-cleaning kits. My parents, my adoptive parents, never bothered with cute euphemisms for weaponry, never felt a need to knowingly flash a meaningfully cocked finger at a semi-alert listener, nor spell out deadly words in front of my impressionable self as a toddler.

Some of my earliest memories of my dad, a guy who looks like a mean Frank Sinatra, involve him breaking down guns: at the breakfast table; in his easy chair; on the back porch; in the backyard; or on some back-of-the-beyond road trip where unaccustomed dogs and chickens unexpectedly crossed streets, and I trusted that there was a very good reason why I was along. In hindsight, such reason was likely the lack of an available babysitter to be had on short notice. But I could not have known that. No, I was going with the flow of a normal life.

Dad was always an independent sort, openly voicing disdain for all who believed that just because a government made up a bunch of rules that he had to fall in line with any of them, the idiots. Rules were easy to make, he would say—"Make a living, pal; how about that?"

By the time I was getting good at talking, and generally catching on to what the family business was all about, some cutesy symbols did come into play. There would be my parents' discreet show of turning a key in a lock that represented the potential liability that was my mouth. And then swallowing the key. Lots and lots of tossing back symbolic keys.

This was especially true if the prompt was accompanied by sustained eye contact, amounting to an on-the-spot verification of my taking whatever unspoken oath. Such a silent agreement was instantly stored by the prompter as a commanding mental snapshot, dated and stamped, to wit: "I do so solemnly swear not to rat out mommy and daddy."

This was in addition to the usual correctional tweaks my socially responsible/ lawbreaking parents spoon-fed me: respect family; avoid cops; tip well; cameras are everywhere; DNA evidence is a bastard. All normal stuff.

And it was normal stuff. For me, for my world. Forget TV dramas in which mob families are forever attending funerals. Last I checked, there were thousands of people dying every day, needing very little help. Everyone has to take a whiz. No one gets out of life without trimming their toenails. And pretty much everyone's farts do stink, including those who remarkably insist theirs do not.

Whizzing while alive, pissed off while dying—all that normal stuff. Like school, which always kind of sucked, but served as a social contrast, the girls taking the sting of education out while slipping the hook in. You know what I mean.

And the neighborhood kids—ours consisted of a bunch of wiseasses. One did not grow to be magnificently manic by sitting on one's backside playing violent video games. To make it in our neighborhood one had to move physically and keep moving, like a shark, not letting up on the smart mouth or the practiced look we all learned to wear, the one that said "What? I'll take that bat, that cue, that crutch, and pound your stupid-ass brains to mush...." Yeah. Like that.

So, you see, it's like I say, we were quite normal. What was weird was when I reached a certain youthful age and heard, "You're not really our kid, but you know, of course, that you'll always really be our kid." What's to explain? What, my parents were supposed to wait until I grew naturally paranoid, as all kids do at some point, having entertained midnight suspicions which might conceivably be true? My parents had forthrightly beat any such deliciously horrid speculation to the punch.

When it did happen, it was strange. Until that moment my reality had been a uniquely sharpened image fine tuned on life's Etch-a-Sketch. Having learned the truth, the firm lines seemed to have been suddenly, though not indifferently, shaken.

As I got older I understood that this preemptive confession from my parents had not been a trifling matter, not a Thanks-I-Guess moment for poor me to morbidly ruminate upon. My parents did not have to adopt me. They could have adopted a puppy. Or an iguana, it taking all kinds to make this tired old world peppy. And if someone cares to adopt a leprous iguana, then fine, the idiots.

Hopeful people such as my parents, unable to produce their own offspring, and who would like to order a baby, a human one, will, likely as not, have certain criteria in mind, at least in this neighborhood: A very young one, please. Male. White skin, but not too white. And one preferably not resembling a cartoon weasel. Oh—and a decent tally on the fingers and toes. A six-week old smile? Say! That's an adoption bonus.

There have always been much worse families throughout history than mine. No matter how strenuously imaginations are experienced, no flawlessly empathic guidelines can be grasped in aid of understanding the tragedies some kids face, kids who have never enjoyed the breaks I've had. That goes for across town or across time.

That's what I need to share with you, this something I have learned.

And, sir? Or madam? If you are currently holding a gun as you read these words, and there is a child in the room with you, please, put the gun down, gently, well out of harm's way.

Thank you. Distractions breed unintended consequences, and, yes, your kids are watching.

CHAPTER 1

The sidewalks of Queens were crowded enough for me to feel to be a member of the herd without also feeling an urge to cull half of it. I was hoofing it westbound when my phone chirped loudly. I checked the number calling, slowing my pace not at all, having some place to be and not all day to get there.

"What's up?" I said, dodging beef stuck in first gear.

"Possibly the stock market, but who gives a crap?"

It was my boss, or as he preferred to be called, Dad. I allowed a perky young pair of twenty-somethings to pass before putting my back to the bricks, scanning the street out of habit.

"Not me. Something important come up?" I asked, hoping the answer was no. I had things to do, even if those things had nothing to do with the family business and everything to do with my business. I glanced at my watch.

"Important? Not so much unless you're Paulie Pet. Our local connection in booking just called it in. The big ape's in jail, and I need you to bail him out."

The ensuing pause announced that I had not stifled my irritation quick enough, causing dad, Ronnie Renaldi, to say, "What's that? Speak up." Dad's Brooklyn intonations were punchy and to the point.

I was tossing out a smile for Mrs. Sukovitch, a sweet old neighborhood lady who was making me bend down so she could pinch my cheek. I let Dad hear that I was making good with community relations before answering his command. Little Mrs. S. toddled off, leaving behind the smell of onions she had been handling, the odor lingering with the likely red marks on my face.

"Paulie, huh?" I said. "Isn't there anyone else who can go get him?" I gave another look to my watch. I had an appointment, and these real estate elephants had long memories when the economy was good.

"If you think I could get someone else at this particular moment ..."

"*This particular moment in time*" was one of my dad's favorite phrases, coming down hard on the "tick."

"... in time, do you think I'd even be asking you, numbnuts?"

Favorite phrases. Pet names. Speaking of Pet ... "What did Petralucci get tagged for?" I asked, tossing up a warning finger to a known pickpocket, the punk showing me his hands, not wanting any trouble.

"Who the fuck knows? D and D, shaking down a sandwich shop, whatever, but we need him Saturday night, so get him out."

Knowing Paulie Pet, I was betting on the drunk and disorderly, then again, the odds of the Neanderthal rattling the cage of a local small businessman or street vendor would surprise me not at all. And Dad was right, we needed the muscle for Saturday night, a little job I had set up myself.

"How about Dom? He—"

"Vinnie, Vinnie, Vinnie. I tell you once, I tell you a hundred times, eh? Everyone's busy. Except you."

"Yeah, well, you see, I'm just now on my way to see about a new apartment," I explained reasonably.

Silence. I could practically hear the old man's gears meshing as he took in this bit of irrelevance. Looking to flag a taxi, I edged up to the curb. I could make my appointment and still have Paulie out by lunchtime. Early to mid-afternoon at the latest.

"Vinnie? You listening to me? Which came first, kid? The chicken or the freaking egg?"

Well. It was going to be like that, eh? Pulling out all the old chestnuts today, par-tic-u-lar-ly the anti-chicken joke, like I was a perpetual schoolkid.

"Neither, Dad," I replied by rote, curving a hand and catching a cabbie's eye with a hard look, willing him to me across three lanes, "the job comes first."

"And don't you forget it. Tell Paulie to call me this evening. Make sure he's got some money. Done?"

"Done," I answered, pocketing the phone and reaching for the taxi's door as the bucket of bolts squealed to a stop on noisy brakes. A well-developed sixth sense informed me that the taxi's interior stank.

"Where to?" the driver asked, casually inspecting me in the rearview mirror. I was right—stale tobacco smoke, spilled booze, and ground in Chinese take-out.

I gave him the address for the new apartment. Petralucci wasn't going anywhere fast.

* * *

Geez, I hated this place. No wonder lawyers made a killing. Who wouldn't pay to get out of here? And I was only in the lobby.

Whatever cleansing agents were used in maintaining places such as this—jails, courthouses, and aging government buildings in general—all had one thing in common. Well, two things if you granted that the chemicals "naturally" gave you cancer. Beyond that, they lingered, and whatever stench had supposedly been cleaned, clung to that scent. It smelled like fresh bad times atop old bad times, with a sprinkling of ancient food and body odor.

When I had asked the boss about anyone else available to take care of this task, I made the assumption that this included our lawyer. Had to assume, because I was not about to make an issue out of it after Mr. Renaldi, AKA dad, shoved the chicken/egg biz in my face.

"I'm here to make bail for Paul Petralucci," I announced crisply. I was wearing my business face, bland, with a visible hint of commiseration for those having to deal with the Great Unwashed, essentially conveying that I would dearly love to tip the sourpuss in front of me twenty bucks, but would genuinely hate to insult her nonexistent sense of public spirit.

When the scowling woman finished scrutinizing my face, she tilted up her nose to glare through bifocals at the screen before her, taking her time. Both her hair and her face looked shellacked.

"Spell it," she ordered, large and in charge.

I did and waited, listening to the pecked-out keystrokes, breathing through my mouth. I also hated the echoes in joints like this. Years ago, architects believed marble was the only way to go, I suspected on the theory that if marble was good enough for mausoleums, it was good enough for haunts like this. I doubted that even the dead liked it.

"Not here," the woman said, her narrowed eyes proclaiming that she wished the same could be said of me.

I did no such thing as ask if she was sure, though I did go through the spelling a second time after explaining that I had been informed that indeed he was here.

"Okay. Here we go. He's in juvie."

There was a funny twist to the woman's almost-smile that I didn't know quite how to interpret. I supposed she thought herself a wizard for thinking to check with juvenile records.

"And how old is this Petralucci you have listed?"

"That's classified," she snapped, both her words and personality at a premium.

I didn't think so, but much like seeing little profit in arguing with the don, I could see no sense in wasting further time with this refugee from a pickle factory. Nevertheless, I thanked her for her assistance and retraced my steps out of the depressing building.

By the time I had caught another taxi and made it to the big roundup for juvenile justice, any notions of wrapping up this chore by lunch were long gone. On the plus side, I had earlier signed a lease on the new apartment, so no matter how rotten my day was going, I had that working for me.

I was also pretty sure I knew what was going on with this whole Petralucci thing, and I wished that it was anyone other than me dealing with it.

* * *

Well, it wasn't as bad as I thought it was. It was worse.

I posted bail and sat on a hard bench for over forty minutes, keeping my mind occupied with thoughts of a dinner date tonight.

Afterward, I might go shopping at a big box store to take a look at TVs; this one wall at the new apartment cried out for a gazillion-inch screen. My pleasant daydream almost kept me from seeing the unending ushering of young people in trouble, their sizes ranging from 4'2" to well over 6'2". Most struggled to cultivate a few scraggly hairs on their chins, having greater success raising pimples and sprouting a bumper crop of falling pants.

"Vincent Renaldi to the desk. Vincent Renaldi."

This "new" woman was the twin of the clerk across town I had dealt with earlier. I was sure of it. Same meanness. Same bifocals with hellfire glinting from the lenses. Identical inverted smiles frozen in place. They must have been grim children, which explained how they gravitated to this line of work, misery loving company.

By the time I signed the last of the necessary paperwork, I felt a presence behind me. Two presences. My eyes went first to the ugly bruises on the face of Paulie Jr., dad's paid cop in booking getting the I.D. mostly right. Paulie Jr. was a big kid, offensive-end big, and only 15. I focused on the one eye that wasn't nearly swollen shut.

"You okay, Paulie?" I asked while allowing my gaze to drop to the young man's escort, a diminutive young woman with large, expressive eyes, and wrinkles in her beige dress suit, the inside of the elbows looking like accordion pleats.

The kid blew out a pent-up breath that I was afraid would start his recently busted lower lip bleeding again. It was answer enough. I felt my suspected Irish or Viking blood rising.

I extended my hand to the woman with the styled, short brown hair. "Vincent Renaldi."

This woman's hand was warm and soft without being mushy. Her big, dark eyes gave her the appearance of being in need of a hug. A trim figure had me considering it. Two seconds passed as my face was memorized. Four seconds elapsed and she was still holding my hand, which was fine by me. I tried a smile. It was met with a frown, the thin dark eyebrows taking a nosedive.

"Cara Beely, Mr. Renaldi. You went Paul's bail?"

"I did. Is there a problem?" I asked, matching her frown. Obviously Beely worked within the system, at what level I could easily guess. In case I was wrong, I waited to see if her position came with a badge. Several charming freckles held my attention.

"Would you give me five minutes of your time, Mr. Renaldi?"

Outside of a stinkhole such as this I would be tempted to turn the question into a date. Cara Beely's frown was cute. I turned toward Paulie once again, keeping my wince internal. The kid looked rough.

"Paulie? If you'll have a seat over there, I'll get us a ride as soon as I finish talking here. All right?"

Oh man, the boy really did look bad. In addition to two black eyes, one nearly shut, and the busted lip, there were abrasions around the left side of his head and ear as if something, or someone, had had a hard grip on the kid, one impossible to break. I was thinking headlock, and it wasn't the only thing I was thinking about.

Paulie mumbled "Okay" and turned, his big shoulders slouching as he shuffled off to the miserable bench I had just vacated.

Beely and I were silent as we watched him go, witnessing the pain evident in the kid's careful locomotion. He'd had been through the grinder, all right.

Turning slightly more toward me, I guess so Paulie wouldn't be able to read her lips, Beely sought out my eyes, possibly to focus attention away from the boy.

"Are you a friend of the family?" she asked.

It was a yes or no question, but I still did not know the woman's true identity other than first and last name. I was surrounded by walls representing the system of which I had spent the better part of my life bending to my own needs. I wasn't going to give this person any ammunition that may come back to haunt my family's organization.

"Yes," I answered.

"For how long, may I ask?"

"You may, but first, Ms. Cara Beely—who are you?"

The heavy frown broke up, rearranging itself into an uncommon smile, uncensored, marvelously transformative by way of imparting the young woman's true nature once unbound by the constraints of the job, whatever it was. The smile was momentary, but real. The controlling muscles marshalled themselves back into neutrality, a nice trick, the lively freckles settling.

"Sorry. It's been a long day," Cara Beely said.

I was betting they all were, but I kept quiet, waiting for more.

"I'm with Social Services, and Paul is now one of my cases. I've been reviewing his history, quickly, I admit, once I heard that his bail was being put up. This is not Paul's first visit here."

"Paulie," I clarified. Paul sounded like a saintly Beatle.

"Pardon?" Beely said, tugging at implacable wrinkles.

"He's called Paulie. Like his father," I said neutrally.

A cold look crossed Beely's face. It would have been difficult to mistake her expression for anything other than anger.

"Did you know it was his father who pressed charges against his son?" Beely asked, setting her jaw in challenge.

I had to admit that I did not. To myself I had to admit no surprise whatsoever. This was precisely what I was afraid I would find following my ride over here.

Paulie Pet was a beast. He was good to have in your corner when things got tight, but the man was a throwback. Earlier, I referred to him as a Neanderthal, a completely unnecessary black mark against that worthy race. Paulie Pet was an ogre.

"Paulie, this Paulie, Mr. Renaldi, refused to press reciprocal charges, claiming that the incident was a misunderstanding," Beely said quietly. She refreshed her memory with an abbreviated look over her shoulder to see Paulie Jr. with his forearms resting atop his big thighs, his head lowered to hide his features from passersby, staring dismally at the floor.

I kept my mouth shut, my sympathies with both the kid and the do-gooder, but The System was The System, and the less I had to do with it the better. Beely was watching me closely.

Lowering her voice even further and, by doing so, lending it a deadly rasp worthy of a cute snake, Disney version, Beely said "Don't you even care that his father beat him up? If this continues he will almost certainly kill the boy. Is that what you want?"

Those sad eyes glinted, underscoring the message, searching my face for any sign that she wasn't wasting her breath.

"I care," I said, leaving it at that. I had known Paulie Pet for ten years, and his namesake as long. There were siblings, all girls, all younger than Paulie Jr.

The boy was just the right size to stand in as an ogre's convenient punching bag.

I found myself being scrutinized, making me uncomfortable, this situation somehow turning into my problem.

"Look, Ms. Beely, I'm just here to put up bail. I can't make the world play nice."

Long day of frustration, including a bad lunch, all of it went into the thrust of the social worker's arm which ended in a quavering, accusatory fingertip.

"You call that playing?"

Even Beely's freckles now looked angry. "No, Ms. Beely, I do not. And I hate it for Paulie. What would you have me do?" I was not easily ruffled.

And I most definitely was not used to having my hand grabbed. I controlled my flinch when this small woman firmly took hold of my right hand and boldly slapped a card into it. I could not help but notice a lack of jewelry on her left hand.

"Call me. That's what you do, Mr. Renaldi. If you or someone else won't stop this, I guess I'll have to!"

I stared at the cheap white business card before meeting those oh-so-sad eyes again. Unless Beely knew some world class kick-ass martial arts, or could rent a cannon and was willing to assassinate Paulie Pet with it, I just didn't see this little gal stopping anything except me getting on with my day. Let sleeping dogs lie and bury the dead ones. Not one of my dad's sayings, mine.

"Okay," I said, pocketing the card as the current path of least resistance. It was time to collect the kid and go before this got any worse.

"No, you won't," I heard behind me as I was turning to leave.

"Excuse me?" I said, stopping myself from instinctively squaring up.

"I said, 'No you won't'. You won't call. You won't lift a finger, will you? Make bail, sure. Make a difference, never. Thanks a lot, Mr. Renaldi. I was hoping you'd be different."

See? I stayed too long and it got worse. And now I was getting emotional, dammit.

"You don't know me!" I said forcefully, exasperated by being put on the spot in a public situation. From the corner of my eye I noticed Paulie's head come up.

"What makes you think I won't help? Do you think I like this any more than you do? Well, I don't. I've got your card and—"

"And?" Cara Beely quickly fired back, trying, as seemed her nature, to reintroduce some backbone into mankind.

"I'll do what I can," I said, quickly back in control.

One step closer brought the firecracker under my nose, forcing me to stare straight down into the depths of those expansive eyes.

"Promise me," she said as forcefully as I had moments ago, though in her quieted voice.

What? Really? A promise?

"Be a good guy, Mr. Renaldi. Get involved."

"I—I'll try," I said, anything to keep her from pinkie swearing.

A skeptical look had her eyebrows worming their way into an unfathomable configuration. Hope and doubt warred on the young woman's face.

"Look at him," Beely commanded.

Damn, she was a hard-ass. I looked. When I looked back she had a tear in her eye. Honest, a tear.

I nodded and turned, clutching her card, certain that I had caught the trailing end of a sigh behind me. I motioned to Paulie as Beely's sigh wormed its way into my mind.

CHAPTER 2

Moving slow and easy, I led us out of the upper esophagus of the beast and into the harsh light of late June sunshine. Slipping my sunglasses from my jacket pocket, I held them out to Paulie who took them without comment, jamming them onto his wide face, probably ruining them, making them now a $200 present.

The day had warmed up something fierce. Damned if I would not be willing to bet that our sorry excuse for a lawyer was working the back nine by now, the bastard. I shucked my jacket in time to use it as a flag, liking the look of the rolled-up windows of the approaching taxi. We climbed in and got where-to'd.

Good question. I felt Paulie Jr. tighten into a knot beside me. I kept my eyes averted from the kid, thinking fast.

"Ah, just head south for now," I said to the driver. "I'll let you know."

I had crushed the social worker's card in my hand while removing my jacket. Straightening it out, I replayed the highlights of our conversation. It had been unusual.

"Want to get something to eat?" I asked Paulie as a way to feel out the situation, unsure if Paulie eating anything right now was such a great idea, unless maybe it was French fries so that the kid's blood would blend in with the ketchup.

"Sure," the young giant replied in a vocal shrug.

The answer was really a no-brainer. Jail food sucked, notoriously so, and Paulie Jr. was a great big kid. Big kids needed lots of calories. They also ought to get tons of sleep, good dental care, and an occasional pat on the back from their fathers. Maybe the mayor could fix it. Or the pope. Or maybe me, starting with a late lunch. That wasn't so hard, right?

"What do you feel like?" And before Paulie could answer my question I rushed on to say, "Because with the lip, I'm not sure a slice of hot pizza's going to be the way to go."

Paulie's right hand rose. Using a butterfly's touch, the fingertips gingerly assessed the lip. I couldn't see Paulie's eyes, but his forehead crinkled in recognition of his vulnerability. The big shoulders shrugged, accepting the limitation. I believe pizza had been a probable answer.

"Leave it to me," I said, and gave our cabbie instructions. I knew of a nice diner featuring high-backed booths that was quiet this time of day. Perfect.

I slipped Beely's card into my pocket rather than dropping it on the floor, surprising myself.

* * *

The diner's air-conditioning triumphed over the early summer weather. A tinted window in the back corner separated us from the baking sidewalk. I had the tuna. Paulie had everything else on the menu.

I encouraged this, cracking wise with the situation, just enough to get the kid to drop his defenses, relax, and fill his capacious belly. I mean, I was already out $200 on the shades; what was the worst the kid could do, another $200 on diner fare? Watching him eat, I would have to say the answer was yes.

By the time Paulie pushed away I was on a second cup of fairly good coffee. I made a gesture, pointing to my own lip, the teen dabbing a napkin to the reopened injury, a small price to pay for making amends to a stomach that thought Paulie's throat had been cut.

"I'm not going to tell you you've got to go home," I said by way of just putting it out there without a bunch of touchy-feely roundabout trying to get inside Paulie's head. You didn't take beatings like this kid did and feel solid about anything half-assed. What Ms. Cara Beely did not know was that I had grown up with kids like Paulie Jr. Same problems, different generation.

I watched the parade of pedestrians making their way along the sunshine-spanked sidewalk, waiting for the kid to speak, not sure what to expect. Paulie was 15, an awkward age for most anything, let alone making a decision of where to lay his head at night without fear of getting it caved in before he had a chance of putting his hands up.

"I ain't goin' back," Paulie declared.

"Okay." Fifteen was old enough not to be stupid.

Using my cup as a prop, I sipped and nodded, stretching the moment, undecided on how best to pursue this, if at all. Dad and I had planned on using the kid's old man to help with the heist I had planned for Saturday night. In general, to keep the peace and everything on track, I figured Paulie Jr. was right in staying away.

"You got friends you can stay with?" I asked, running down possibilities.

My sunglasses faced me. "Not really. Not like this," Paulie said, indicating his bruised face. The diner was quiet enough to hear the A/C whisper.

"Yeah," I said. "You got relatives?"

The same huffing of breath I'd heard at juvie was trotted out, accompanied by a slow shake of the head and a mumble.

"I'm sorry. I didn't catch what you said."

"They got relatives. I don't," Paulie said with mild heat.

The computer between my ears didn't get it. "What do you mean, Paulie? Who's 'they'?"

Following a minor shake of his head, Paulie was staring out the window. I could see the right side of his face, his purpling eye. I would bet he could use some aspirin.

"Paulie?" I nudged.

The teenager drew himself away from the table to lean back in the booth. "I mean 'they' got relatives, not me. I was adopted."

Whoa. A hard chill came over me, twin grips squeezing my upper arms. "I thought—"

"Yeah, Paulie Jr.? Right?" Paulie said, cutting into what I thought, as if he had used a knife.

Oh, hell. The kid really did not need to explain it, didn't need to say another word. Yeah, I got it, all right. Still, Paulie, no matter how brave he was, probably needed to talk this out. Without costing another dime, listening wasn't going to make my investment suffer; besides, I was feeling guilty, like I owed this kid.

Paulie's younger sisters were all years apart from his age if my memory was correct. And now that I thought about it, the only thing Senior and Junior had in common, physically, was their size, which by itself had led me to assume a father-son connection. But this wasn't about blood, unless we were talking bad blood.

I cleared my throat. "I was adopted."

Paulie's head oriented on me, his eyes apparently searching my face, seeing no reason that Vinnie Renaldi would lie to him.

"No shit." Paulie said, obviously stunned nearly speechless.

"None," I confirmed.

"Your old man . . .? Paulie's right hand made a definitive fist.

"Never," I answered truthfully, not in the head anyway. My old man had this thing about kicking me in the ass. Used to. "I was adopted as a baby. You?"

The young man's affirmative headshake elicited a perceptible wince.

Definitely needed aspirin. I couldn't think of how to follow this up. "Hey, look at me, I turned out great!" did not seem appropriate.

I stood and made a sly show of patting my pockets. "Damn. Left my wallet. Can you get this?" I whispered, tapping the check and glancing at the exit as if I was contemplating bolting, as I might have when I was Paulie's age.

The kid's big head canted to one side, and a busted smile informed me that my fledgling joke never made it off the ground.

Paulie said, "You went my bail," meaning there was no way that I was broke, the kid naturally understanding our gang's preference for cash.

"Oh, yeah. In that case . . ." I grabbed the check and walked it toward the counter after laying down a tip, the hustler in me double-checking that Paulie didn't nab it.

I had stuff to do. Not important stuff, just stuff that didn't include babysitting, if a 6′2″, 230-or-so-pounds of fifteen-year-old could be called a baby. Honestly, I did not know what to do next. I thought of the distressed card I had pocketed, which led me to consider the rumpled suit Beely had been wearing, and what may lie beneath it, likely not rumpled at all.

No. What was I supposed to do was call if Paulie got beat up again? And I certainly knew what happened to kids taken away from their families. Foster homes at best, and with Jr.'s size, not likely. I couldn't let him live with me. There was bound to be some law, some statute, against harboring a kid without his parents' knowledge. Some little something called kidnapping.

"There's one," Paulie stated, snapping me out of my reverie.

Huh? I looked around, squinting in the glare. Paulie was raising a hand, thought about whistling and prudently elected to forgo the resultant spray of blood.

Taxi. Great. Got us a ride and no place to go. For a guy used to problem solving, this figured to be damned interesting.

* * *

Not strictly necessary, I stopped by my parents' house anyway, letting myself in using my key and my signature knock. I wouldn't want anyone to get the wrong idea and shoot me.

"That you, Vinnie?" came a call deeper within.

Who else rapped out Shave and a Haircut and added an extra six bits? Familiarity bred contempt, true, but it also warded off bullets.

"Yeah, Mom, "I sang out, sniffing the air.

"Come in here a minute, "came Mom's persuasive voice.

Easily done. I could have wafted weightlessly on the wonderful aroma stretching from the kitchen. I entered a scene from my childhood, the only difference being the silvered bands of hair above Mom's ears like racing stripes. That and the fact that no one was any longer worried about me spoiling my dinner.

Well, well, new window blinds over the sink. Looked like raspberry bleed. I noticed them because Mom was pointing them out like a game show model wearing daisy-patterned oven mitts.

By the way of hello, Mom said, "Just came out of the oven." Not the blinds. "They're hot."

Cinnamon buns. An ill-advised minimal amount of caution was required, burning several of my fingers, because it must be proven that the buns were never too hot if they were fresh-baked.

"Milk?" Mom said with a knowing smile.

"Sure, Mom. Thanks, "I said, scorching my lips with hot icing.

In walked Don Renaldi. The first time I called him that, *don*, he kicked me in the seat of my pants after asking me to pick up a nonexistent quarter under this very table. I never called him Don Renaldi again, to his face. The don wears size 12.

"Everything straight?" Ronnie Renaldi asked, walking to the head of the table where a plated hot bun was whisked between his spread forearms, steam flattening in Mom's wake.

Rather than getting fussed at for spewing lava crumbs, I finished my mouthful. Pastry any fresher would have to be eaten inside the oven.

I began my report by saying, "It wasn't Paulie Pet. It was Junior."

"Why didn't the creep tell me?" Dad groused.

He meant the paid police officer we had in booking. I didn't have an answer for that, except that maybe you got what you paid for.

"So, you did what? Got the kid out?"

"Seemed like the thing to do, Dad."

My dad does this thing in which he turns his head to the right and places his stare at a 45° declination. Mom always called it "The Zone." As a kid I simply declared, "He's doing it again."

When my old man snapped out of it, he said, "So, it's still on for Saturday night?"

I blotted my mouth free of the weak, no-percent-fat milk. Oh, maybe the watery mess possessed a tenth of one percent fat or something equally ridiculous.

Over the years I have repeatedly accused Mom of trying to live forever. Her reply was always, "So far so good."

"Yes. No changes, "I answered, short and sweet. We were pros, planning jobs and following through in steps.

This pleased the don. As far as he was concerned the subject was closed.

"What about your apartment?" Dad asked out of curiosity.

Mom had just seated herself. At Dad's comment she said, "What about your apartment?"

"His new apartment," Dad informed, picking at his bun as if unsure that the incorporated raisins were not baked-in bugs.

"New apartment? Vinnie, you're moving? I thought you liked your place," Mom said, frowning at the unexpected news.

"I do, Mom. I just wanted a change. I've been in that apartment forever it seems." Change was good unless one were a comet-crossed dinosaur.

"So? You took it?" Dad asked, spearing a raisin to bring it closer for inspection.

"It's still iffy," I said, leaving it at that, which was much easier to say than to explain that, as we spoke, Paulie Petralucci Jr. was sitting in the vacant apartment —vacant save for a beanbag chair and a giant screen TV, both brand new.

* * *

"It's me," I said for clarification, feeling foolish.

Okay, so I gave the kid my spare phone, too, separate number. And I wasn't calling because I didn't trust Paulie Jr., but, well, he was 15—he couldn't be trusted.

"I figured," Paulie said robotically.

"You need anything?" I asked, playing an easy hand.

"Well . . ."

"Just kidding. I'm sure drinking from the tap sucks. Try not to eat the carpet before I get there. All right?"

I was at my old apartment, getting ready to go out. I had a date with Deborah Delvecchio. DeeDee. Dee was fun, but has a thing about punctuality, stressing out over appointments missed at the hair salon where she slaves. It carried over, this anxiety that time and people must mesh predictably. If I was late she would get all pouty; and I really wasn't in the mood for pouty.

Paulie laughed about the rug and swore it would be fine. All the same, I needed to safeguard my security deposit by either killing a moose or raiding a grocery store.

There was a local business that made deliveries. My account was good there so I phoned in my order. I told Paulie to let the guy in when he showed, and not to worry about a tip. I even had the presence of mind to tell the kid that the frozen stuff went into the freezer. I just assumed all kids were clueless nowadays.

Mission sort of accomplished, I was ready to make DeeDee happy, take her mind off the world of blended tints and highlight rinses, leaving her free to make me happy. It was a very simple progression of logic. Unless I was late.

"You said se-ven!"

"Traffic," I said.

It was now all of half past, and boy could this girl pout. The upside was that when she stamped her foot for emphasis on the spitefully pronounced "se-ven!" her boobs jumped nicely. I looked up to see her lower lip thrust forward in imitation of a three-year-old. Just for that I was going to fuck her brains out.

"Man, it's hot out there," I said, deftly changing the subject.

A roommate scurried around a corner and was out of sight before I could identify which one she was. There were two more lurking about. You did not want to see the bathroom. I gave DeeDee a consoling hug, her unresponsive arms hanging limply by her sides.

Finally, a small smile flickered into being. "Sorry. It's been a long day," DeeDee said, sounding familiar, like it was contagious.

"In that case, do you want to go somewhere quiet?"

"Why would I want to do that?" she asked seriously.

"Never mind," I said, glancing at her hands where a sparkle caught my eye. Keychain. Oh no.

"You ready? Let's go!" DeeDee said, jangling her roomie's keys, the girl who fixed computers or something and hardly ever went out. She was well over halfway homely and hated everyone, the one with humongous panties forever hanging on the shower curtain like caution signs.

Dee couldn't drive for shit. And she wasn't a listener—directions or the color of changing lights. Luckily, I had made out a will years ago.

"You want me to drive?" I asked hopefully, reaching for the keys in case Ms. Delvecchio suffered a moment of weakness.

"Silly! Let's go!"

We went.

* * *

The Breakers was a nice seafood restaurant without all the kitschyness of nets, glass floats, and stuffed seagulls. Paintings of beach sunsets were all the reminders I needed not to expect lasagna when I opened the menu, and thankfully the menus were not shellacked onto oars, like it mattered if the oars were short.

Dee was bubbly and babbly. The gal needed her own TV show to share all her breathless reality. I was nodding politely and sipping scotch, because I hate scotch and could really make it last. I had started tuning out DeeDee a minute ago, something within my own reality scratching at the back of my skull, wanting out.

"I said," 'Who did you vote for?' Aren't you listening?"

Vote? The last I recalled, Dee was ragging on one of her roommates, something about the lack of respect. How much respect could you expect crammed four deep into a two-bedroom apartment like budget-conscious Guatemalans. Not that there was anything wrong with budget-conscious Guatemalans. Thinking quickly, I took a mulligan, saying, "It's been a long day."

"You poor thing," DeeDee said, patting my knee, glancing around, running her hand higher, grinning like she was oh-so-naughty.

"Before our meals come, do you mind? I need to use the restroom," I said, showing the smallest of grimaces to lend credence to the lie.

"Shoo. And hurry back. You know I hate sitting alone."

I stood, gave her a peck on the proffered cheek, and stole away toward the little 'buoy's' room, some idiot slipping, recklessly allowing this singular, overworked pun. I pulled out my cell as soon as I was around the corner.

"It's me."

"Right," Paulie Jr. said, confirming this small fact.

"I just remembered—you don't have a blanket or anything. I'll drop by later tonight and bring something. Okay?"

"All right. Thanks," Paulie said, voice raised one notch to express gratitude and residual puppiness.

"I want you to call your mother and let her know you're fine."

"Okay," Paulie agreed, obviously into minimalism.

"But you can't say where you are," I reminded.

"I know," Paulie said, making it sound like he knew.

"You all right?" I asked.

A pause over the connection. I peeked around the corner to see Dee tapping a spoon atop her napkin, bored. The bottom lip was out, kind of sexy.

"Yeah. I'm okay. I was just wondering, when do you think that delivery guy will be here?"

"What? The guy should have been there an hour ago."

Silence.

"Paulie?"

"Yeah?"

"You haven't gone anywhere, have you?"

"No, sir."

Sir. Crap. "Call me Vinnie."

"All right. No, no one's been by, and I've got the TV on low."

Somewhat answered. Good enough.

"I'll take care of it. Just stay there, okay?"

"All right."

"And I'll be by later."

"Okay."

"Right. Ah, later," I said.

"Later," Paulie said a bit awkwardly, not entirely comfortable interacting civilly with an adult for any protracted length of time.

I hung up and dialed Martini's grocery.

"Martini's. Jacob speaking."

"Jake. Vinnie Renaldi. How ya doin'?"

"I'm just fine, but, where were you? My delivery guy says no one was home. You know I've got to charge you for perishables. In this heat, we can't restock anything that—"

I cut him short. "Fine, Jake, fine. I'm sorry about that. What address did I give you?"

Rustling papers, phone shifting, a blown-out sigh.

"Here we go. Um, same as usual. Your place, right?"

I was going to have to take the fall for this one whether or not I had given Jake the new address. I couldn't assume it was his fault.

"I'm sorry, Jake. No, it was meant to go to a different address. Have you still got the list?"

"Right here."

I rattled off the new address, telling him there would be someone there to take delivery. "Bump your man an extra twenty for me, Jake."

"Consider it done."

"You're a pal, Jake. See ya."

When I got back to the table I could tell that something was wrong.

"Our waiter is waiting to serve us," DeeDee stated severely.

"It's his job, Dee," I said, trying a grin.

When I received a roll of her eyes? with the lip sticking out? I was thinking that perhaps Paulie would be getting his blanket sooner than expected. I retired the grin, casting about for our waiter.

It had been a long day.

Has been. Wasn't over yet.

CHAPTER 3

I guess that because I had acted as if I were not going to get any, I got some. Dee was lightly snoring when I tiptoed from her bedroom. Her room roomie, it appeared, was off into electronic dreamland.

"Hi, uh . . ." I said to Dee's R.R. on the sofa, watching TV with the lights off. I could not recall her name, not that either of us cared. A hand lifted from the depths of a large bowl of popcorn to flutter hello/goodbye without her eyes ever leaving the screen.

Out on the sidewalk, I called a taxi and began walking in the direction of my apartment, old version, telling the dispatcher his driver would recognize me as being the guy whose ass was dragging.

I had the cabbie wait outside my place while I loaded clean sheets, pillow, and a blanket into a garbage bag, also clean. Hesitating, thinking, I added a new toothbrush, new bar of soap, and a bottle of shampoo, only slightly used; it wasn't as if I had put my old suds back in it.

Almost out the door, I rushed back to the bathroom and snagged a bottle of aspirin, 100-count, less one or two headaches. Anything else I was forgetting could wait until tomorrow. Surely all these good deeds were not going to go unpunished.

I enjoyed the look of my new building as we neared, the exterior all white, with clamshell balconies. There were nice plantings surrounding the digs, and proper amenities within. The place had everything I had been looking for except a black and blue teenager. Now it was complete.

Up the elevator and down my hallway, all was quiet. I listened outside my door and couldn't hear a thing. I let myself in.

The kid had left the range light on in the kitchen. Other than that the apartment was dark, the TV off. Paulie was using the beanbag as a pillow, his big self, sprawled on the floor, shoes off and paired neatly by the balcony door.

Back in the kitchen, I opened the refrigerator. Wow. It resembled my mom's fridge, everything neatly placed exactly where it should be. Non-perishables were aligned on the countertop as if for inspection, and a good thing, too, because I would much rather stock the cabinets according to my own personal whimsy. Good job.

Returning to the great room, I quietly removed the bedding, figuring to drape the blanket over Paulie and leave the rest nearby. I had the blanket settling over the kid's bulk when POW! I saw stars.

"Whoa, whoa, Paulie, it's me, Vinnie!"

"Oh, shit! Aw, man! Geez I'm sorry! Here, let me . . ."

And here Paulie commenced to pour forth a nonstop stream of apologetic mea-culpas, which I tried to wave off but couldn't, and for all I knew the considerate purging may have been therapeutic. Paulie even gave me a hand up from where I had been knocked flat by a pretty impressive from-the-floor left hook.

"I'm fine, I'm fine!" I said, laughing. "You're all right, Paulie; I ain't mad, okay? Calm down."

The poor kid looked as guilty as having punched Santa Claus, which, in a way, he had. Pressing my shirt tail into service as an instant blotter, I made my way to the bathroom to find Paulie hovering in the mirror behind me.

"Do me a favor. There's soap and stuff in a bag where I went down. Bring it to me, will you?"

"Sure, Vinnie. And I sure am sorry. I didn't mean to . . ."

I waved the talk off and jerked a thumb in the direction he needed to be heading. Then I checked the damage. Well, I wouldn't be making out with Dee the next couple of days.

"Here," Paulie said, safely out of reach.

Taking the bag, I fished around for soap, telling Paulie that I would be out in a few minutes.

The shirt, a good one, and now probably ruined, had caught a line of drips down its front. My lip wasn't ruined, just cut against a tooth on the inside, no biggie.

I rinsed up with little improvement, shrugged at my image in the mirror, and trucked down the hall to find King Kong on his hands and knees attempting to remove bloodstains from eggshell-white carpet.

"Leave it, Paulie. You've got to use cold water or it'll set worse," I said, something of an expert on the subject.

The kid looked like a ghost, his pale face framed in steam rising from the hot water his one shirt was soaked in. His bad day just would not end.

"I . . . I . . ."

"Forget it, Paulie. You were trying to do good, and in my book that means something. It's not that big a deal. They've got crap on the market now that'll take out blood, ink, all kinda shit. Nothing on TV?"

This last question threw him, changing gears unexpectedly, the wet shirt in hand forgotten.

"Be back in a second," I said.

I returned with two bottles of Sam Adams, Paulie having touched nothing in my fridge that he could get in trouble over. The look on the boy's face was worth a mint as I handed him a cold beer: unalloyed gratitude.

Now, how best to drink a beer with a busted lip?

Easy. You turn it up. The beer, not the lip.

* * *

The night was warm. Standing outside on the balcony was a good choice, lacking furniture. The beanbag had been a give-away with the purchase of the TV, and the kid and I weren't that chummy.

I don't smoke cigarettes as a rule, but then again, I live my life breaking the rules every day. Bumming one from the kid, at this par-tick-u-lar moment as Dad would say, seemed the right thing to do, as with sharing the beer—a physical ice breaker. I just wished that my lip would quit bleeding. And that I could stop coughing. These coffin nails were terrible.

"You want to tell me what you and Senior got into it about?"

"Not really," Paulie said.

"Yeah?" I said, pushing my torso off the railing to look the kid in the face. Enough ambient light suffused the night to make it easy. "There's lots of things we don't want to do. Just tell it in your own way."

I mean, if I was going this far out of my way, then I was damn sure going to get the story. Again, as with most of this sad affair, I could pretty much guess the cause, Paulie Pet being a mean drunk; all the reason in the world, and no reason at all, was the way I was reading this.

"He had his hands on Sandra," Paulie said stiffly.

So much for pretty much having guessed the cause. Two and two equaled, "Sandra being your sister?"

"Yeah. The oldest."

Something in the boy's voice had me thinking that a smaller man than good ol' Paulie Pet would be wearing a toe tag this evening.

"We talking touching, or are we talking more?" I lifted my bottle and realized it was empty.

"More," Paulie rumbled like a large oil furnace kicking on.

I made sure he saw me nod before turning away to take in the view. It really was nice, Queens laid out like a bumpy sheet of velvet studded with the brilliance of street lights and the shifting dance of traffic lights, with the huge glow of Manhattan to my left. Somewhere out there someone wound out a crotch rocket, making me wonder at the cause, good times or bad. I thought about Paulie's dad and what he deserved. I wasn't real sure that I even cared to bring this matter to the don's attention, though to do so would be protocol.

"The lousy bastard," I said, letting the relative quiet stretch. Then, "Want another beer?"

"Yeah."

"Don't go anywhere," I said, turning to go inside.

The kid snorted. Kinda like a laugh. Kinda.

CHAPTER 4

There was nothing I liked about alarm clocks other than loving to hate them. Hardly ever used them. Waking naturally was the way to go. Unless the phone beat you to it.

Getting the preliminaries out of the way, I heaved a few sighs before answering. "Hello?"

"What are you gonna do? Lay in bed all day until the sun shines up your ass and gives you heartburn?"

"Good morning, dear Father," I growled back through a yawn. I smacked my lips and checked my watch, fairly certain the sun couldn't find my ass at a quarter 'til eight.

I got back to my place, my furnished place, late last night, having stayed up late with Paulie until I just had to get some sleep. I never should have answered the phone.

"What's this 'dear Father' crapola? I need you over here, Vinnie. We gotta set up for tomorrow night."

"Cell phone, Dad."

"What? Oh, yeah. Whatever. Get your ass over here. And bring some cream cheese for your mother."

I was trying not to laugh at the tough old mob boss forgetting Uncle Sam was always listening, even when they said they weren't any more, maybe especially when they said that, but not forgetting what Mom needed in the kitchen.

"Got it," I said. "Anything else? Some butterscotch chips? Maybe some of those candy sprinkles?"

"Smartass. I'll see you in twenty minutes."

Right. Only if you're looking at my college graduation picture on the mantel, I thought, rolling out of bed to hit the shower. I felt like crud, confirming it in the mirror. A hot shower and a strong cup of coffee would fix that.

I considered calling Paulie, then scolded myself for thinking like a helicopter parent—though maybe that wasn't the worst model I could emulate since the kid looked as if he had been in a helicopter crash. What I did do was call some local movers to pack up my current, livable apartment stuff, and transfer it to the new crib. Local movers would know the name Renaldi, and were unlikely to treat my things roughly, with stealing being so far out of the question that, if it were possible, they would do the job and keep their hands in their pockets at the same time.

After setting up the deal, I made my way to a small business tucked between a dry cleaners and a tattoo parlor. The little joint had class, putting all those fancy schmancy coffee shops to shame. Hot espresso in hand, I stopped for the cream cheese, and while in the store, bought Mom a gift assortment of gourmet cheeses, tiny wheels all decked out in wax and foil like Christmas in June.

"Where you been?" the boss demanded when I walked into the house.

"Ran out of gas," I said smiling, nodding to Tony Funicella, my dad's left-hand man if I was to be considered his right, and I was. Tony nodded back in that dark and serious southern Italian way he had. The man was born and raised in Brooklyn. I think he practiced his badassness in the mirror. Good man, though, no matter what.

"Dom," I said after turning from Tony F.

Dom Bartelemeo gave me his signature salute, snapping two fingers off the brim of an imaginary hat. Dom was younger than Tony by fifteen years, closer to my age. I looked Dom in the eye, keeping the smile working. His other eye was on my mom waltzing in from the hallway, both eyes never having moved. Dom was overweight, and one walleyed son of a gun, my mom says due to being shaken as a bambino, though my dad swore that the condition ran in the family, explaining that Dom's grandfather was the same way, with Mom chiming in that the grandfather had probably been shaken too.

Mom, brown eyes twinkling, came up to me, accepting my gifts and planting a peck on my cheek, using the move to whisper in my ear, "I heard about Paulie Jr. Let it ride for now, you understand?"

She backed off, still smiling as if thrilled with the cheese, meeting my eye as if I should now swallow a key. When Mom said "You understand?" you understood. I presented her with the barest of coded nods.

As Mom left us, my attention traveled to Paulie Pet over in one corner, his ham-sized fists gripping the knobby ends of an antique armchair, the hands completely covering the wood. I dipped a nod to Petralucci without letting my chin rise back up to complete what would have been the proper form. And he knew it, eyes narrowing.

No doubt he knew by now that it had been me who had bailed out his kid.

Just as he would also know that Junior had not shown up at home yesterday, or last night, though Paulie Jr. did say he had called his mom to let her know that he was all right.

I ignored the sour look on the man's face. If he took a swing at me I'd shoot him, if my old man didn't beat me to it. There was heavy stubble on the man's face, surely pleasing my dad not at all. Dad liked his crews to be clean shaved, well-dressed, and looking to fit in anywhere needed on short notice.

Paulie Pet was about ten years older than me, call him late thirties, and big in every way. Big head atop big shoulders, tall and heavy and naturally muscled. Guys like Paulie Pet didn't need to work out, unless using his kid as a speedbag counted. He had dark hair and dull eyes which would fool you. The man was quick enough in his thinking, and you would be a chump to believe the big guy was physically slow—dangerous as a water buffalo.

"What's up, kid?" I heard from my left.

I turned to see Uncle Mike, not really my uncle, all of my adoptive "real" uncles being dead by natural causes—bullets slung by law enforcement or rival gangs. Uncle Mike was a small, wiry guy with these funny, large-spaced teeth that made me think of a laughing horse. I had known Uncle Mike forever. Everyone else called Mike Spinoza "Spoons" on account of his uncanny talent of playing spoons, musically you understand, like nobody's business.

Maybe you wouldn't believe it to watch him sitting still, but to see Mike Spinoza work a pair of spoons in complicated blurring rhythms, was to witness a work of fascinating beauty. I used to worship the guy, and will always be terribly fond of Uncle Mike. He used to always bring me presents when I was a kid: cap pistols, bad-ass squirt guns, *Guns & Ammo* magazines.

"Well, let's get this out of the way," the don said, everyone being here who needed to be, not all the gang by any means, only those with a role for tomorrow night.

We all trooped into the dining room, taking seats around the highly polished walnut table. Centered in place was a pot of coffee and full cups atop heat-resistant pads, Mom having done her part. She was now free to attend to more important matters, such as whatever may include cream cheese and/or an oven.

Dad poured himself a half cup, already having had two or three cups full if beginning his day in typical fashion. He said, "Vinnie."

This was my cue to shock and awe. I slipped a manila envelope from an inner pocket, my jacket carefully tailored, constructed of lightweight, reinforced material for enterprises such as this morning's. Inside the pocket I was able to carry somewhat bulky items without telltale visible bulges or outlines, because

I never left to chance who might be watching.

I started with Tony F. across the table from me, sliding him the first photograph, a long-distance exposure showing a short row of cheaply constructed storage units. A red Sharpie had marked what was to be our target: the second unit from the right-hand side. Also included in the picture was the smallish parking lot and partial view of the surrounding chain link fence. A slim portion of the street beyond was shown, visible between the end of the storage building and a cluster of trees at the lower right of the perspective.

Tony studied the picture briefly without commenting, frowning in that way he has, before passing the photo to Dom on his left. I slid the next photograph I had taken toward Tony, slowly, respectfully, this shot from up in those same trees, giving the viewer a good angle of the units' front, but including the left end of the structure and the continuation of the same street beyond.

Dad sipped his coffee, watching the familiar scene play out, all faces relaxed, business as usual. He heard Mom sneeze in the kitchen and called out a blessing.

From the corner of my eye I saw Paulie Pet take a look at the first picture, figuring the angles, the possible exit points, and where he would make a stand if the heist turned south on us. I had an urge to pick up the chair under me and break it across his big fat head, but my mommy had warned me that I had to play nice. For now.

I tossed out the next photo and began talking. "The Dezzes are getting careless. And cheap. I had no trouble renting a unit two down from our target. The unit between the two is occupied, and the one on the end I didn't want for obvious reasons," such as visibility from the street.

"Dezzes" was dad's moniker for all the local Puerto Rican gangs, as in certain crime families, such as the Hernandez, Fernandez, Mendez, what have you. Dad also said that political correctness was for politics; this was business.

"Security?" Tony asked.

"You see that fence?" I responded, grinning.

"That's it?" Tony added, livening up his cadaverous features with the ghost of a smile.

"Yeah," I told Tony. "The Dezzes did have a guy try living inside, but he couldn't take the heat. Inside those units, the temperature will climb to 130° when it's 90° outside. They check it from time to time, but really what they're counting on are two things: moving the merchandise soon, and a lock on the door."

"What are we after?" Uncle Mike asked, suspicious of the job being too easy. The Dezzes were into trafficking a lot of dope, and were not known to shy away from extreme violence.

"Cigarettes," I said, rubbing the fingers of my right hand together. "Name brands. Wall to wall." Retailing $13 per pack.

"How big are these units?" Dom asked. "Ten by twelves?"

"Right at," I said. "The goods were boosted straight off an eighteen-wheeler. The Dezzes were actually clever, luring the driver away for five minutes with some bullshit story. Whatever it was, it worked. But they won't sit on the stash too long. That's why we move in tomorrow night."

"How do you know it's in there?" Paulie said.

I kept my gaze on the next photograph in hand, holding it up before turning to meet the sullen stare of Paulie Pet.

"Because I've been inside the unit next to it. That unit is used for storage by a family who has no need to document how much dust is collecting on their junk. By the way, they've got some nice junk if we've got the time," I said, making the ogre smile and making me want to bust his teeth out.

I had known and disliked this guy for so long that I was almost glad I now had a legitimate reason to hate him. On the other hand, he had been useful to us, just the same as a bad-tempered mule may profit a farmer, even as the farmer grew more vigilant when rounding the critter. I got that analogy from Uncle Mike who has a country mouse cousin.

"This photo is proof," I said, thumping the glossy.

Tony F. took the picture and grinned. I had busted my way into the family's unit, entering through the rented vacant unit. My assault on the block wall was some of the sweatiest, dirtiest work I had ever done, the sledgehammer I had used producing an excellent cardio workout.

I had stayed in touch with an associate who remained outside as a safeguard against my indelicate breeching. Once inside the family's unit, I had drilled a small hole through a mortar joint near the ceiling. I then inserted a thin flexible cable ending in a fisheye lens, scanning the interior in ultraviolet light, the seepage of light under the unit's roll-up door sufficient to make out the boxed cartons of cigarettes mostly filling the space, confirming the intel.

"Good work," Tony praised, looking to gauge the boss's expression, Dad sitting all smugly pleased, hiding a smile with the rim of his cup.

"Looks good, Vinnie," Uncle Mike said, pulling a cigarette from his shirt pocket without lighting it because he knew Mom would have his balls if he did.

"Right," I said. "So, here's the plan. We go in at four in the morning. The place will be cooled off. We pull up to the locked gate, cut the lock, and relock it with a matching lock as soon as our truck pulls in.

"By the time I'm backing the truck up to the unit, the roll-up door is being cut and it's Chinese fire drill time, hand-to-hand-to-truck. I figure two guys on the floor of the unit, one to lift the boxes, one to take it from him and hand it up to the truck. That'll be Dom and Paulie.

"Spoon is in the back of the truck tossing the boxes to Tony who stacks. I'll be in the driver's seat, and Dad will be outside the fence at the trees looking out for us. If anything goes down we'll bust through toward dad's position, use the truck as a shield if that's convenient. Dad will have a backup vehicle. We do this right, and hustle, we can be in and out in ten minutes tops."

The guys were back to looking at the photos and each other, pondering the possibility of anything I had left out. I could practically hear Uncle Mike calculating the price of a carton, a case, a truckload. It was a gook lick.

"Sounds good. How'd you find out?" Tony asked.

Dad broke in to say, "They're too cheap to pay their guys not to run their mouths. Things got overheard. We bought the information from a guy selling. It's secondhand. This can't get back to us."

In other words, what Dad was saying was, "What they don't know can't hurt me or you."

I poured a cup of coffee, yawning, wondering if Paulie was sleeping late or still drinking my beer, maybe adding his puke to my blood on the once-pristine carpet. I hoped not. What would the movers think?

The movers! Paulie didn't know they were coming.

Thankfully, no one had any questions beyond what time to round up, and who was carrying the bolt cutters, and a question to confirm the lack of alarms. These were professionals; there were no nerves on display. I looked up to see Paulie Pet watching me.

He should. He damn well should.

Chapter 5

Just when I thought all our business was completed, Tony F. pulled me to one side for a private critique. Though I was not expecting a one-on-one with Tony today, it was far from extraordinary. Tony's nature was mature, solemn, and he often dragged me aside for beneficial advice, whether or not I felt it warranted.

Usually these tête-á-têtes resulted in my gleaning some imparted nugget of wisdom, some aspect of oversight that I had either neglected or had been blind toward. On such occasions I felt like the grateful student to Tony's wise professor. The problem was that I could not blow off Tony to make a phone call. Rudeness of that sort took a long time to heal. It wasn't worth contemplating.

By the time Tony F. had made clear his tactical point, that two additional operatives for tomorrow night's heist, one atop the storage units' roof, and one inside the unit I had rented under a false name, both acting as safeguards, nearly an hour had passed. Tony could nauseatingly break down a situation, in this case a guy on the roof tossing off hand signals like a third base coach, and the guy in the unit downloading satellite intel or some such nonsense. All were good extreme points if I wished to share out another two portions. Mine and dad's big cut would have suffered, as would Tony's own, but that he didn't mention. Our six guns versus whatever stumbled blindly into the works? I liked our odds just fine.

When I could finally break away, thanking Tony for his enlightenment, I was tugged into the kitchen to sample mom's fresh cannelloni. Mom, whose head came up to the top of my shoulder, was holding her wooden spoon high, her left hand cupped underneath it at the level of my chin to catch drips, upturned eyes expectantly on mine, mouth parted in anticipation, uttering, "Uh? Uh?"

Sometimes in life there were no yes/no answers guaranteed to satisfy your needs. I already knew when Mom was going "Uh? Uh?" that I was sentenced to sit down to at least two plates of an early lunch. That same spoon holding a sample was hovering far too close to my skull to make any answer other than "Fabuloso!" unthinkable.

So, being reasonably sound of mind and body, and preferring to keep it that way, I ate, smiling and chatting about nothing of any great significance, watching as a couple of strands among mom's silver streaks above her ears came loose, floating in defiance of gravity with every small movement of her head. All in all, it was a nice way to massacre another full hour once Dad joined us. I never did figure, or ask, what Mom needed the cream cheese for, fearing the explanation would further prolong my stay.

Escaping with a covered dish and a promise to refrigerate it the very minute I got home, I collapsed into the waiting taxi and whipped out my phone.

"Hey, it's me."

"'Sup?" Pauli Jr. asked.

"Look, I forgot to tell you that I've got movers coming over today and—"

"They're here."

I frowned at the passing scenery, thrown forward coming to a red light because I wasn't paying attention, which was rare. I blamed it on a bellyful of cannelloni. I needed a nap.

"Oh, okay." There was nothing to do now except to roll with the development. "In that case I'll be right over," I said, touching my tongue to the inside of my lip and tasting blood. Great.

"Okay. I—" Paulie said, ending abruptly.

I waited for Paulie to finish what he was about to say. When that didn't happen, I said, "Go ahead."

"Ah, nothing. See you when you get here."

Hm. Curious, but no big deal. Could be anything, from him getting weird looks from the movers because of his colorful condition, to maybe his feeling guilty over attempting to help, and breaking a lamp, or even not knowing how best to express himself in requesting some essential item that he lacked. Interesting, because so far, I was batting zero in the cause and effect department.

I had the cabbie make an about-face. Checking my watch, I figured I could possibly squeeze that nap in right when it was time to turn in tonight.

* * *

Who said that good help was hard to find these days? Not me. The movers must have rolled this morning as soon as I had disconnected the call.

This was superb, considering that I had not lifted a finger to help. There had been loose change scattered atop my dresser when I left my old apartment this morning, dirty clothes lying about, junk everywhere in both the kitchen and bath. Come to think of it, there were still dirty dishes in both the sink and the dishwasher and, well, did I hear one word of complaint over the phone from these guys?

Nada. It was part of the incidental fortune of having a name, for what it was worth, which was cool. Still, to maintain my notorious infamy, I would tip well.

Not a problem. I've got money in the bank—make that banks, plural—and solid investments, all untouchable. Plus, a hefty payday tomorrow night. I would try not to let it all go to my head.

I rode the elevator up to my new apartment, genuinely excited about a fresh start, even if I had an invited, yet previously unenvisioned, teenage roomie. All I needed now was to get Paulie Pet into crisis counseling, and for hell to quit messing around and freeze over.

Empty boxes were stacked neatly in the hallway between my front door and the next door closest to the elevators, a hand truck parked beside them. My door was ajar, so I made myself at home. Exertions were heard coming from the rear of the apartment. Paulie, still wearing the stretched sunglasses, met me coming down the short hallway, another empty box in hand.

"Everything's coming together, huh?" I said, allowing him room to pass as I continued on, wanting to check that the furniture was arranged to my liking, better now than later.

"Um, Vinnie?" Paulie said to my back.

I hit the brakes and pivoted, waiting for Paulie to speak.

"Ah, well, see . . . I, uh, wanted to say something sooner—"

I was listening, but again had to flatten against the wall as one of the movers, a thin dude with bulging veins on his forearms, fairly breezed past carrying a dinged-up toolbox in one hand and sporting a red toothpick in the corner of his mouth. On his heels followed a young girl who couldn't be much older than Paulie, and I was guessing to be the mover's kid sister hustling up summer spending money.

The guy said, "Hey, how's it going?" and the girl barely met my eyes, saying "Hi" while lugging an armful of bubble wrap and tape-tangled packing paper. I "Pretty good-ed" and "Hi-ed" back, waiting for the hall to clear before again meeting Paulie's eyes, waiting to up my batting average from zero point zero, the big kid unable to zig every time I guessed that he would zag.

Clearing his throat, Paulie said, "That was Sandra."

A lack of my usual six to eight hours of sleep, combined with an out of left field kind of day, caused me to expend several long seconds processing Paulie's short snippet of information.

"What? Sandra? As in your sister, Sandra?"

Paulie's head bob was as good as an, "I'm afraid so."

It wasn't easy to get me flustered, even though I was still hitless in predicting Paulie's behavior. I held up one finger, saying, "I'll be right back."

Leaving Paulie in my wake, I stepped into my new bedroom and whistled at the change. "Wow. You guys work fast!" I said, beaming a smile.

One of the two guys setting my box springs into place looked up briefly to return my smile, while the other guy was already slipping to the far side of the room to grab the mattress, an attitude exemplifying the concept of a fast work ethic.

Now this second guy looked my way. "You're Mr. Renaldi?"

I extended a hand. "Yeah. Good job."

"Thanks." The name tag, again in motion, read "Roberto."

"Just one thing?" I said. "Would you please switch the head of the bed to over here? And put that dresser in its place?"

Yes, I should have requested the change twenty-two seconds earlier.

"Won't take but a minute," Roberto said.

Literally, one minute.

"How about the rest of the apartment? We've got your kitchen stuff unpacked and on the counters. Same with the bathroom. You may want us to rearrange the front room. If you've got a minute, we'll go check."

This guy, Roberto, was so efficient that I wanted to hire him. But who was I to lure him away from a legitimate living for a split of my ill-gotten gains? This fellow bolted my bed together; I was the one who had to lie in it.

I followed Roberto into my great room, my living room, and my home entertainment headquarters—all the same room. Paulie and his sister were on the balcony, both glancing over their shoulders as my ears burned. It had been a couple of years since I had last seen Sandra. I recognized the face, but the youngster had sprouted and filled out, totally transforming from a gawky girl into an attractive young lady.

Nodding to the pair, I put it out of my mind for the time it took to supervise a few adjustments of my furniture. I invited the three movers into the hallway to settle up, tipping each guy two hundred bucks. Believe me, you can buy goodwill.

With the movers gone, I grabbed a beer from the refrigerator. I reentered the front room to see what next needed to be accomplished. I killed a minute mentally sorting through a to-do list of framed pictures, books, knickknacks, etc., waiting for Paulie to reveal his unconventional houseguest behavior. He wasn't long in getting the hint to exit the balcony.

"You remember Sandra? She remembers you from the Christmas party a couple of years ago," Paulie said nervously.

Good. The kid was no longer wasting time. And seeing as how his sister was here, uninvited by me, I now understood Paulie's earlier awkwardness. He was on shaky ground and he knew it.

Sandra was growing tall. Though still quite young, her size characterized half of Paulie Pet's genes. Thankfully, she took after her mother in the face. Unfortunately, she also took after her mother in the development of her upper body, no more than 13, yet with the breasts of a fully mature woman. Many young girls would consider this a blessing, but I was certain that Sandra's view of her "gift" was one of a burden, if not an out-and-out curse with a predator such as her father around.

Her handshake was demure, and to a degree embarrassing for her, not for me. Sandra's sad brown eyes dropped to the floor.

"I called home again this morning so our mom and sisters wouldn't worry. I hope that's okay," Paulie said thickly, something practiced in his delivery. With a nod, I encouraged him to continue.

"Sandra answered the phone and said that it, uh, happened again. Last night."

The poor girl blushed deeply and hung her head, crying silently. I really didn't need to hear the rest. How could Paulie, having heard the latest bad news, and himself sitting in a place of safety, refuse to have his sister share his breathing room, even if it was not his right to offer? I had never had siblings, that I know of, but had I, and my and Paulie's roles were reversed, I shudder to think that I would not offer the same assistance, come holy hell or high holy water.

"It's okay," I said in reassurance, reaching out to touch the crying girl's shoulder before reconsidering and staying my hand, my adult male hand, in time. And the way I saw it for now, time was the major factor that would begin to set matters right.

"You hear me, Sandra? I said it's okay. I don't know about the law on this, but there are more important things. For now, don't worry. I just want you to call your mother and let her know you're safe, not where you are. Okay?"

"Yes, sir. Th-thank you," Sandra said, sniffling.

She broke down again, crying hard. Paulie wrapped a big arm around her shoulders, tears of his own tracking below his shades.

As hard as this was, I had to ask, "What about your other sisters? Are they in danger?"

Paulie frowned and said, "They're too young. At least I think they're too young. Sandra?"

Face red and crumpled, long brown hair in disarray, the girl looked up as if underwater to say, "They would tell me if he was after them. It's just me right now. But no more," Sandra said before erupting into a cruelly wrought wail which sprang from unbearable depths, surely unimaginable to anyone not so suffering.

"Well, for what it's worth, it's over now. One way or another, it's over. When you're composed, call your mother," I said. "If your dad answers, hang up. Again, do not say where you are, all right? I'll be in the kitchen putting things away."

I walked off, remaining calm on the outside, leaving them to console each other, a chore I was neither suited to nor experienced in. My beer tasted bitter. I poured it down the drain and finally remembered to put mom's cannelloni in the fridge.

Everything in its place, right?

There was a strong possibility that I might have to kill that son of a bitch, a graveyard being the right place for the likes of Paulie Petralucci.

<h1 style="text-align:center">Chapter 6</h1>

There were some things best not put off. When it came to dealing with the boss, I did not need to be told repeatedly that business came first. Yeah, it was supposed to be, "Family first," but when family and business were one and the same, my dad had a point. I laid my rap down upon the door of the Renaldi mansion and let myself in.

Actually, that was a jest. My parents' house was nice without being at all ostentatious. One of the first lessons I was taught was that it was okay to live well, but that it was the nail whose head stuck up that got pounded down.

"Well, that was quick enough!" my mom quipped, a pair of gardening gloves occupying her left hand as she accepted the return of her glass casserole dish, or tried to.

I gave her a peck on the cheek and started for the kitchen to set it down myself, Mom sensing more than a need for my timely reuniting of cookware and owner.

"Where's dad?" I asked far too innocently.

We both smiled. Had Dad known that I was coming back on the same day, he never would have been caught thus, taking a nap, his image of always being on point tarnished by pillow lines on his face. Being larger than life came with a wicked price to pay.

Psychic Mom sweetly said, "Something's troubling you. Coffee?"

"Why not? Thanks," I said, sliding into a chair at the small kitchen table, the same table I had bumped my head on a thousand times growing up. If I cared to peer under its top, not only would I find my name scrawled there in a variety of childish fonts, but drawings as well, of dinosaurs and mythical beasts, every one of them a poor rendition of a lopsided dog with lots of teeth.

I allowed the quiet to settle easily as coffee was poured. One of the neighbors' lawns was being mowed, creating a comfortable background noise of middle-class stability—the gentrification of ozone depletion. Mom settled across from me, eyes level to go along with her overall disposition. She encouraged me to begin talking by saying nothing. The distant mower shut off as if wary of being scrutinized.

"Paulie Pet's out of control. First it was beating up Paulie Jr. Now he's sexually assaulting his oldest daughter. He's a liability, Mom. I know that he's worked for Dad for years, but irreplaceable he's not. Now, before you say anything, I want you to know that I heard you loud and clear this morning."

Mom laughed. "It was a whisper, sweetie. 'Loud and clear'!"

Sure. I had to go along with her lead, engaging in a brief chuckle.

"Something's got to give. I wanted to tell Dad that. After this job tomorrow night, there is no way I can work with the guy," I said.

"Why don't you let me be the one who decides that?" the don interrupted.

I half turned. "Nice nap?" My knock had most definitely disturbed his slumber.

"What nap? I've been in back going over some figures. What's this about you refusing to work with Paulie? Since when do you start refusing anything?"

Damn. Woke up like a grumpy old bear. "Last I remember, Dad, we turned our backs on pedophiles," I stated, standing my ground.

"Who's a pedophile? Paulie Pet?" Ronnie Renaldi growled.

"Got it first-hand. Dad, a guy like this'll bring heat on us sooner or later," I said, wary of the boss's mood.

"Says who?" Dad said. Boy, working those figures in back sure had gotten under his skin.

"Says I about the heat. Says his oldest daughter about the kiss-and-don't-tell crap."

Mom was watching the two of us closely, carefully keeping her face neutral, maintaining her own counsel for now. But just because she didn't care for what she was hearing didn't mean that when it came to a tie-break she wouldn't side with Dad no matter what.

"And you know this how? You're over at Paulie's in a closet or something? Got video?"

"The kid isn't having anyone on. No way is she faking, Dad. A professional actress she's not, okay?" I said, willing to go along with the old man's sense of fair play, being devil's advocate to a guy who wasn't here to defend himself against strong allegations, one who had helped fill the family coffers for years.

"What are we really talking about here, Vinnie? A bit of slap and tickle, or worse?" Dad said, still on his feet, the red crease on his face comical at the wrong time.

"What are you grinning about?" he barked irritably.

Now was not a good time to prove my dad a liar when it was a thirteen-year-old's honesty in question, not his.

"Nothing. Sorry. But to answer you, yes, Dad, this is serious. Obviously, Paulie's wife is afraid to interfere, something I can't respect, but I can understand it. Paulie can be damned intimidating."

Which is one reason that the guy made such a good slab of muscle to have on hand. Paulie Pet never flinched from orders, never questioned beyond the pragmatic, and displayed a natural enthusiasm when heads needed thumping. I understood my dad's reluctance to turn against one long in his employ.

At the same time, I also knew that Dad held no sympathy for any child molester. And another thing, and one that stung—he knew better than to question my judgement, knowing that I would not come to him like this if I did not consider the issue to be of major importance.

Finally, Don Renaldi had a seat, sharing a look with my mom. She pointed to her own cup of coffee and got a headshake in return.

Drawing a deep breath, Dad said, "Look, I don't know how bad is bad, and neither do you no matter what the girl says, and don't give me that look, Vinnie. Kids, they exaggerate. Now, I ain't saying that the girl's lying. Where there's smoke, there's fire, okay? But I can't throw the guy under the bus on this alone. Who knows, if I get more information that's liable to change."

Seeing the disappointment on my face, he threw up his hands, waving them in the air, what I called, "Going all Italian" on me.

"Now, look you, Vinnie! You gotta learn that sometimes we gotta let family matters ride themselves out. There's things you don't know that'd curl your hair, all right? Not all the people we got working for us are angels, *capiche*? You think your cousin Carlos is a saint? That boy's sins would try the patience of the pope! Do I hold all his filthy habits and behavior against him? And Tomasso? Do I single him out like I'm a frigging cop? Tomasso may be a piece of shit where his own family is concerned, but he does his work when I say, and he keeps his mouth shut. What more do I need from a guy, eh?"

"Dad—"

"Don't 'Dad' me, Vinnie. And put your eyes back in your head where they belong. I take your point, okay? You satisfied? I hear you, kid, but sometimes you gotta stand aside, let people work these things out for themselves."

Aw, shit. Mom was nodding her head. I wasn't sure when the last time was that I was this angry. There was no doubt that it showed, especially in my eyes, but I've been taught well. I didn't go off. I kept my emotions internal the best that I could, giving my dad respect.

I nodded. "All right, Dad. Mom, thanks for the coffee. I've got to go."

It was not good, this walking away with injured feelings, but better this than a scene I would regret, and one I did not have a chance of winning. Besides, there was a saying I like quite well: If you wanted something done right, do it yourself.

I set my cup in the sink after rinsing it, gave Mom a goodbye kiss, and told Dad I would see him tomorrow night.

"Make a couple of passes by the job later, just for the hell of it," Dad said, making the order sound like a suggestion.

"I'll do that."

"We good?" don Renaldi asked stone-faced.

"Of course," I answered with the only answer that would do. "I'll see you later."

I let myself out, my fire banked but not extinguished. There was a bad taste in my mouth, and a stench in the air. The shit I put up with to keep the peace.

* * *

It was telling of my foolhardiness that I did not realize the full depth of the situation I had created until I was on my way to the new apartment, my new apartment of which I had maneuvered myself out of livable space. I couldn't tell Paulie's sister that she had to sleep on the sofa, because that was where I had planned on installing him.

The apartment was actually spacious, for a one bedroom, anyway, but all three of us living there seemed wrong. And leaving the two of them there alone, unsupervised, or unattended, or whatever, seemed just as wrong. Sending them to a hotel or motel was out of the question. I didn't want these kids anywhere Paulie Pet, or the law, might get to them.

Crap.

I opened the apartment door, greeted by a rich savory odor. If it was take-out, it was righteous. I had left the kids some spending money in case they needed anything, it having occurred to me that there always existed the possibility of an unforeseen emergency. I was impossibly green at this—good at being adopted, but clueless now that I, myself, had shouldered that same responsibility.

TV on, Paulie was slumped in the beanbag although there was now plenty of seating available. Another case of adoption I reckoned. I would be getting all psychoanalytical if I suggested that Paulie felt safe to be enclosed within the beanbag's embrace, an inanimate hug, but I won't even mention it.

Positive that I had neither been seen nor heard, despicable me tiptoed toward the kitchen. It was not that I enjoyed scaring people, it was that I liked surprises, especially ones that I could eat.

Sandra had made herself at home, and I wasn't complaining, or all that surprised. Nothing quite conquers worry better than constructive activity. Even in these times, good Italian girls are encouraged to learn the old styles of cooking, and, sure, boys, too, and if they do not it will be a poorer world for the loss.

"Something smells great," I said, dropping out of stealth mode.

"Oh. Hi. Thanks. I didn't think you'd mind if I made something. I'll clean everything up. Promise," Sandra said.

There was little doubt that the upcoming cleanup would take some time, not that I had misgivings as to the girl's sincerity. Every eye on the range was occupied, and something was in the oven. Used bowls and pans were scattered here and there, pretty much every piece of cookware I owned which was habitually devoted to the collection of dust. My raised eyebrows raised a question. My smile anticipated Sandra's answer.

With an exactness of carriage containing both pride and joy, Sandra needed no further prompts, saying, "Scallopine alla Marsala, and a little antipasto, and oh no!"

The something in the oven was fetched up quickly.

"*Amaretti*," the young lady announced.

Even Mom just calls them macaroons, *Amaretti* being proper.

"Good grief, Sandra, you're hired!" I exclaimed, which resulted in the kid beaming ear to ear, earned praise being a tad more beneficial than unwilling submission to rape. A few hours in a safe environment had given Sandra the ability to muster self-esteem in a fight for normalcy. Wait a minute—"The wine I had—"

"Wasn't exactly the best for marsala, but I've used worse."

I kept my smile from enveloping my ears, the girl's pride being of a humble sort, which was good, and I was glad to see that it was so. Maybe I would have the kids call me Uncle Vinnie.

"And the veal? Delivery?" I asked, curious.

"Oh, no, no. I couldn't spend your money on something I can do for myself. The store wasn't far," Sandra said, turning back to the sauce and whatever her antipasto was.

Though I appreciated the gesture of saving me money, it was the fear of some wrong someone seeing the refugee coming and going that gave me alarm. Then again, what was the alternative? Tell two young teenagers they must hide out to protect my paranoia? I was certain that either teen could outdistance Paulie Pet in a footrace; and I would like to think that even Paulie Pet wasn't stupid enough to violate my home.

And just as soon as I considered this, the prickly matter of The Law, and Parents' Rights, nailed me. It might be time I consulted our lawyer, that depending on if the slickster could be tracked down between 19th holes and grieving widows.

"You called your mom?" I asked Sandra.

A timid glance and a small "Yes," was answered with a frown.

"She's behind you on this? Your need to get out?"

"Sorta. She said it isn't right me running away and only thirteen. I told her it wasn't right to be groped by my father and she shut up. I'm not sure she's on my side at all."

Right. No Mother of the Year nomination worries here. I was trying to think of what to say without sounding superficial.

"One way or another it'll work out," I said weakly, better than nothing at all. "Can I help in here with anything?" I said, hoping the answer would be negative.

"Nah. I've got this," Sandra said, quickly checking every pot before facing me again.

"Mr. Renaldi?"

"Vinnie."

A small blush. "Okay. Vinnie? Thank you for this. I know we can't really stay here, but thank you for giving us a break."

"Well, Sandra, you're welcome. I, ah, don't pretend to know what to do, so let's play it by ear and not worry too much about it. It's summer, you're out of school, your mom knows you're safe I hope—"

"She does," Sandra reaffirmed.

"Right. So . . ."

"Vinnie?"

"Yeah?"

"I had to use some of the money for personal stuff. I hope you don't mind."

"Not at all. I'm going to check on your brother. Keep up the good work!" I said far too cheerfully, happily at odds with my life being turned upside down.

Personal stuff. Geez. If anyone had predicted my taking care of a couple of kids, my thinking would surely had turned toward balloons rather than tampoons.

* * *

The meal was great, Sandra demurely playing the role of hostess, with me cracking jokes at every opportunity, getting laughs, even at the sacrificial price of humoring poor Paulie with his beat-up face. I got a lot of mileage out of Paulie's wearing the sunglasses at the dinner table, watching TV, or taking a nap, though I would be the last to imply that he could not. When fun time was over I had a decision to make.

"Do you guys think you'll be okay here by yourselves tonight? I've got a date."

Assurances that nothing I did, or could ever possibly do, would bother them in the least, were immediately followed by pledges of not burning down the place, and not inviting drunken teens over to loot the joint. They were thirteen and fifteen, not exactly babysitter fodder. And not exactly grown either. Yet, I was sure that adversity such as these kids have been through had propelled them toward maturity.

That problem solved, I showered and shaved, the same as I would have had I a real date this evening. I had a date with surveillance on a sleepy row of storage units, figuring to make it an all-nighter.

Before leaving, I made it clear not to expect me back until tomorrow, shocking no one. This was just the way that fun Uncle Vinnie rolled. All of the above was laid out so that when I told Sandra she should use the bedroom, both she and Paulie would feel less awkward.

The pair had likely discussed this between themselves, working out who got the sofa and who was going to sleep on my recliner. But this was better, the best solution I had for now.

I had to make a hasty exit to escape the profuse thankfulness heaped upon my ego-swollen head. Good kids. Locking the door behind me, I rattled the knob in check as a not so subtle reminder.

Having plenty of late June sunshine to work with, I set out to revamp my mode of transportation. My old neighborhood, not far away, was crowded. Whatever I had wanted—deli, liquor store, drug store, restaurants—I could walk to within two blocks.

Who but a putz drove two blocks? The other side of that same coin was that I spend a lot of time across the bridge in Manhattan. Own a car in Manhattan? For what? You paid a cabbie the same dough you'd have to shell out for gas, maintenance, insurance, parking, and incidentals, and you came out ahead.

But now I had a nice underground parking garage with space for two vehicles, costing me not a dime more. It was my intention to fill one of the two spaces today.

On Long Island, car dealers were hopping around lots like fleas, itching to sell or lease to who- or whatever. Flashy I did not need, never forgetting the maxim of the pounded nail. I wanted something with power. And a nice big trunk. Old School. Stylish, yet something your average Guido, blond variety, would look at home in.

I flagged a taxi and went cruising used car lots, having a great deal of fun, prepared to write someone a check for the full amount on the spot.

Well, the full amount less what haggling I could negotiate. All these guys were a bunch of crooks. If my old man knew I was buying a car without asking him to tag along so he could show off his intimidating shopping skills, he would be pissed, so I wasn't going to tell him. If I did, he would be haggling down to the last half dollar with the sun long gone, along with my good mood.

"Let's try this one," I told my cabbie, a nice Pakistani grandpa with bad breath and good taste in leaving the radio off. "Don't go anywhere," I added, climbing out as the old-timer patted the air in place above his steering wheel.

I got jumped by a Long Island sand flea when I was no more than three strides from the taxi.

"Good afternoon, Partner!"

Oh, really? This was that place? It was impossible to mistake their TV ads— roping in high prices and putting the spurs to all that is rotten in the world of used car corrals. The dude was from Dallas. Dallas, North Carolina.

"Let's take a look at the Chevy," I said, already walking.

"Oh, good eye! She's a beaut, all right!" the sales hand informed me, ready to pop the hood to show me how good the beast's teeth were.

The closer I got, the more I liked what I saw. I wasn't sure of the model year, but it was a vintage Nova, circa '70 was my best guess. The car was all black, with flared skirts to accommodate large rear tires surrounding subdued chrome rims. Revealed under the hood was a very clean reconditioned 350 H.P. engine will all-new chromed fittings that gleamed in the afternoon sunlight.

I smiled without pretense and rounded toward the driver's door, the salesman scurrying to open the door for me with all the courtesy his fantasy of a big fat commission could impart.

Ah. Original steering wheel. The interior had been reupholstered to specs, instrument panel likewise. I checked the odometer, frowning. 38K? I said it out loud, incredulously so.

"Thirty-eight thousand miles? One hundred thirty-eight thousand," I scoffed.

"Ha, ha! Nosiree! That there's 38,000 oh-riginal miles, my good man! Guaran-teed! The car's only known two owners. The last guy that had 'er fixed 'er up like this and fell on hard times. His loss is your gain!"

Of course, it was possible. It was also possible that Santa Claus held Canadian citizenship, and that me and Paulie Pet were destined to become the best of pals, growing decrepit to sit side by side in rockers at the old wise-guys' home, jawing about the good old days.

"You really like your job. Don't you?" I said, giving this dude a look perfected by time. I was switching charm gears, the used car salesman backed off, smiling, saying, "How about a test drive?"

"All right."

"Be right back!" the sucker wrangler called over his shoulder.

I used the nano-delay to let my cabbie know that I still wanted him to hang around, handing him some good faith money. The oldster patted the air again in understanding.

Cranking up the Nova, I was pleased how she fired right up. Uh-oh, I was already romancing the bitch. Pipes sounded good. The engine rumbled totally in sync. Quarter tank of gas. Suicide range on the speedometer. Sweet. I narrowed my eyes as I buckled up, grinning like the devil as my sidekick swallowed hard, one hand in contact with the dash in case this bronc should buck.

I eased out of the lot into traffic, observing the speed limit, monitoring the car's handling, listening for noises that should not be there. I experimented with the radio, the A/C, heat, wipers, the frigging horn as I cruised past my parent's house, sort of hoping Dad was taking care of paperwork or whatever else he cared to call a nap. I opened her up only once, warning the southerner riding shotgun in advance, and that only briefly, both the flooring and the warning.

Her.

Well, I was all in except settling on the bottom line. I rolled the Nova back into the lot, and parked her where I had found her. Climbing out, I ponied up what I owed the patient cabbie.

"How much?" I asked the dude.

The number the salesman tossed at me was a little high.

"How much for paying it off right now?"

A lower number. "Is that the best you can do?" I asked.

"It is."

"Drop another $200 and I'll take it."

He did.

I have a badass, black 1971 Nova. She was mine, and I'll never call her a bitch again.

Chapter 7

I've mentioned that all my uncles have departed this "mortal coil" in typical family fashion, taking one for the team, sometimes a lot more than one. Sad, but their passing still left me with a wealth of cousins, most of them female, though a few of them guys, a couple who are rock solid.

As I drove I hit my speed dial, looking out for bored cops who didn't have anything better to do than harass someone who can readily talk, drive, and chew gum at the same time without an issue.

My old man owned a legitimate business in lower Manhattan near Chinatown off East Broadway, a redistribution warehouse that supplied restaurants, offices, and other commercial enterprises, using imported overstock bought at bargain prices and resold here at profit. It was a money laundering bonanza, and was where my cousin Dino could be found on weekdays.

Dino was two years younger than me and was the antithesis of his untrustworthy older brother Carlo. No one was sure where it had all gone wrong with Carlo, how his attitude and judgement had become as rotten as his luck. But Dino, Dino was good people.

"Dino! Vinnie. You busy?"

"Eh. You know. Fill out this form. Fill out that form. It's great work if you like that sort of thing," Dino said, faking a yawn.

Dino sounded stupendously bored. My cousin was not the kind who liked that sort of drudgery. But to work his way up in the family business he would suck it up, and in doing so was guaranteed to move up the ladder, even if it was one lousy rung at a time. It was the right outlook. Even I had to work summers at the warehouse as a teenager. The don declared that such donkey work built character and all that junk.

"I was hoping you could spare yourself for some cruising," I said, careful to keep the conversation general. "Tell whoever your boss is that it comes from me. What do you say?"

Me, I was vice-president in charge of marketing. Or maybe it was advertising.

"Okay. Sounds good. Where are you?"

"I'm about to get on the Manhattan Bridge," a straight shot to East Broadway from Brooklyn. I had made good time into town, breezing past the early outbound commuters. I was having a blast driving my new, old wheels, playing the radio and feeling like a kid again, surfing my hand out the window.

"Wait. You're driving?"

I laughed. "You bet! I'll see you in the parking lot. I'll be the cool cat in the killer black Nova. Old school, Hoss."

"No shit," was Dino's comeback.

"Nada. So, we good to go?"

Dino chuckled, assuring me that we were, indeed, good to go, the sooner the better.

Cool. I hung up, cruising across the big bridge. It was a beautiful day and I was in a fantastic mood, gassed up, rolling the speed limit with my temporary tag, but that was all good. I didn't feel a need to go fast to be happy.

* * *

Leaning against the left front quarter panel, I threw up a hand when I saw my cousin exit the office end of the huge warehouse. He was walking as if the warehouse were chasing him and possibly gaining. It was Friday afternoon, a good time to smile and keep your back turned to what you were escaping.

"What's this!" Dino called when he was still fifty feet away. He walked fast, coming up on my right side and, hand-slapping my shoulder before backing a couple of steps to inspect my chariot, letting loose with an obligatory low whistle of appreciation as if the Nova were shucking her panties.

"She's sweet, all right. Let's go for a ride," I said, shoving my cousin to one side because he was trying to get behind the wheel, both of us laughing, playing King of the Hill in a flat parking lot.

"What about my car?"

"Leave it," I said.

"This ain't the best place to be leavin' cars at night."

I gave Dino a look." You got insurance, right?"

"Yeah."

"So, what's the worst that can happen? Your piece of shit gets stolen by some truly desperate person, and in a few days, you get an upgrade. Someone would be doing you a favor."

Dino shrugged, climbed aboard, and started again with the low whistling.

"How much you pay?"

"You don't want to know," I said.

"Yeah? Probably got sawdust in the transmission."

I nodded as if it was likely. "Yeah. Probably. I thought we'd stop at a bar and let the traffic clear out."

"I'm with you," Dino said easily, messing with the radio, a navigator's prerogative.

"Right. Your choice," I said, laying him back in the seat as I floored the Nova.

Dino whooped his joy and freedom. "Okay, hang a right. Make like you're headed for the Brooklyn Bridge."

My navigator led me to a block of restaurants and bars packed with people of a like mind, large herds of Friday evening animals at the local watering holes, gleefully exchanging wampum for a chance to unwind before heading to whatever horrors awaited them at home. Many would make it no farther than this tonight because, seriously, one thing does lead to another, which in turn leads to another.

We craned our necks looking for an open slot of the telltale brake/backup lights that meant a space was about to open up.

"End of the row," Dino said, jumping from the car in case another driver looking to park approached from the opposite end, claiming the spot bodily and willing to defend it until I pulled in.

Locking up, I took one last glance at the car's sexy lines, and the way the late daylight made the polished black paint glow.

"I'm trying to think if I've ever been here before," I said, taking in the front of the familiar looking stand-alone building. A very happy young woman with green and yellow hair, holding a large red Solo cup, was braying laughter at her companion's wit, preparatory to entering the bar.

"You have," Dino said. "About a year and a half ago? Around Christmas? You and me and whatshisname that works in shipping. The place was called something else then."

I was grimacing and rolling my eyes, drawing a blank. "Did we have a good time?" I absolutely had to ask.

Dino reached for the front door and hesitated. "Almost had us a real good time, but someone blew it when we had a game of naming what animal everyone most resembled. Geez, Vinnie, all you had to do was lie!"

I was laughing as we entered. We weren't here to score tonight, but I was willing to bet that on that December night in question, that even if a girl had been really pretty, I had been too much of an ass to behave myself, a rare occurrence. Since I recall nothing, and had likely blown it for Dino and What's-his-face, I had probably been a handful just getting home. Okay. I would make it up to my cousin, no problem.

We undertook a quest to find a place to park ourselves, practicing the equivalent of scanning for backup lights. We hit lucky on two stools centered at the first bar we approached, listening to the grumbling of two guys on our heels that were a little too slow. Dino and I looked at each other, keeping the victory grin confined to our eyes, not looking for trouble.

Following my lead, Dino also ordered a beer. We were here to kill time, not get hammered. A small kitchen in back was good for hot bar food which we took advantage of. Shoulder to shoulder, we tuned everyone and everything out.

"I'd appreciate it if you kept me company tonight. There's a score I'd like to keep an eye on. Do a few cruises is all. The rest of the time we can stop here and there for a beer or whatever, shoot pool, mess around."

"Keep your ass awake you mean," Dino interpreted, grinning, cool with it, touching his glass to mine. "Cheers."

"Yeah, pretty much. We can sleep tomorrow, right? That way I'll be fresh when we go in tomorrow night."

"We?" Dino asked, having to talk louder now, the sound system having been cranked up a notch on the theory that louder music generates higher profits. I had a marketing professor in college who swore this was true.

"Yeah. One handful," I explained, meaning myself plus five others. "Sorry. I'll make sure you're in on something nice before long, bro."

"I'd appreciate it, Vinnie."

"Speaking of nice, you still dating whatshername—"the girl with—" I said, pantomiming with cupped hands.

"She's in Europe on her father's dime. She sends postcards."

I nodded, unconcerned. It would never work out between them. Dino says maybe he'll get married when he's forty, definite on the maybe, and there was no way the girl on vacation was going to hang around that long. Save the postcards for your old age, that was my advice for Dino.

"Aunt Gabby's okay?" I had to ask twice over the noise.

"Mom's mom. Worries about everything: the state of the world, my immortal soul, Powerball, Carlo, my sisters, you name it. I saw her last week and she goes, 'Dino, ya gotta keep your 501k diversified; it's important.'"

Dino was using his falsetto momma-mimicking voice.

"Five-oh-one k?"

Rolling his eyes once up toward heaven, Dino said, "Bless her heart. She had been listening to some investment guru on NPR. Now she thinks she's a financial swami."

"But she's doing okay?" I asked again. I liked my Aunt Gabrielle, a really sweet lady who had this retro look with the '80s hair and Princess Di makeup, as if she was stuck in a time warp, but making up ground in other areas. She "Twitters" on X. Whenever we lost Uncle Lorenzo she decided that she had to buckle down and watch out for her future security, as if Dad would ever let her sink. Never, no way. But it was healthy for her, gave her one more thing to worry about.

Dino flipped a hand. "Mom's mom, and I'm too thin, and you can never be too careful about sexually transmitted diseases."

"For sure. Want another?" I asked.

"Beer? Sure. I'm a little on the dry side. Been a long day."

What? This was now our national slogan? I tossed up two fingers after catching the bartender's eye. We were still waiting on the hot wings. I checked my watch, figuring to spend another hour before we made our run back across the bridge. Dino was turned around now, watching the action because one never knew when lady luck, or at least her phone number, was going to fall into one's lap.

I paid for the beer and had a very un-Vinne-like thought. I wondered how the kids were doing, which was pretty wild, me raising Paulie Pet's kids. What was really going to be wild was when I told Dino what was going on.

Chapter 8

You gotta be kiddin' me!"

"No. Really. The way I saw it, I'd feel like a jerk if I brought that kid back to his home. You know what Paulie Pet's like. Might makes right. My word against yours. King of the freaking castle."

"King Kong," Dino said, firing up one of his Marlboros, another thing Aunt Gabby worried about.

"Right. He's an asshole, but somehow he's got these great kids. Seriously. Regular angels," I said, automatically looking out for cops as we headed back east.

"Go figure," Dino muttered, soaking in the news.

My cousin was flicking ashes, hopefully most going out the window. We had stopped at three beers apiece, and who counted hot wings? We were wheeling through Brooklyn, looking for an auto parts store that we both spotted at the same time.

A fine New York sunset put New Jersey on fire as we walked the aisles. I popped a breath mint, holding the roll out for Dino. We were here for accessories, laughing at the gaudy and appraising the merely tacky. Dino wanted a clip-on mirror for the shotgun side's visor, not for vanity, but for a second pair of eyes on what was behind us on the street. That sort of thinking I liked.

"And you don't have a place to sleep? Dude, that is totally messed up."

"Yeah." I shrugged, not sweating it

Dino looked at me like I was crazy. Maybe I was.

"You ain't worried he'll do somethin'?" Dino asked softly.

"Paulie? He's stupid but he isn't that stupid. Plus, he might suspect, but he doesn't know. And, if he did try something, Dad would gut him and he knows that," I said, ignoring the look of mild terror stamped across the counter clerk's face as he rang up my purchases.

Dino said nothing more until we exited the store, not one for letting strangers know his business, whether he thought he would ever see them again or not. Same with me, but I was a bit distracted as of late.

"Don't count on it, Vinnie," Dino said as we eased up beside the Nova, in no hurry. "Paulie Pet's temper ain't going to let him count to ten before he swings on you."

"So, let him swing already. I may be a criminal, but that doesn't make me a bad guy," I said, showing Dino my grin.

"All right, tough guy. I'm just sayin' be careful. I know you're doin' this because you feel you gotta but, Come on, Vinnie, Paulie Pet's kids? Huh? What, Hitler's kids busy or somethin'?"

"Frigging Hitler?"

Dino stood by his door and shrugged, eyebrows lifted. "I couldn't think of a big-time modern-day evil person for an example. All the top terrorists got names I can't pronounce."

"Who can?" I said, unlocking and climbing in the Nova to unlock Dino's door, and to hang an air freshener from the rear-view mirror.

Dino gave it a thump to send it twirling, the representation of fruit an orange blur. He asked, "Where next?"

"The job."

"Cool," Dino said.

I nodded and started the engine as Dino cranked up the jams.

* * *

"Tony wanted to put a guy up on the roof," I said as we drove past the storage units, going just under the speed limit.

"I could do that," Dino said, seeing the dollar signs from the score, imagination taking no actual work.

"Coming up on less than twenty-four hours, we don't jiggle the switch. Tell you what I'll do. I'll hold out a few cases for you for helping out tonight. How's that?" I said, enjoying free gift giving.

"Cases? Hell, that would be great, man."

The cost per pack was high. I was going to lay enough free cigarettes on Dino that it would surely take a good two or three months off his life. It was the least I could do.

"How do you know they're still in there?" Dino asked.

"I don't yet. It's a daily thing. I'm going to pull in here," I said, rolling in to park at the near end of an aging strip mall. This was where Dad would be parked tomorrow night. Across the side street was the short tree line flanking the storage units' eastern fence.

Standing at the edge of the walkway in front of the still-open stores, we waited in plain view, casually talking, waiting for a near perfect break in traffic from all directions.

"Come on," I said. Dodging the shine of streetlights was a game we had been good at since we were kids. We raced toward the trees on a jagged transverse.

Safe from any eyes, I drew a compact set of cased binoculars and focused on the target unit's lock. I handed the glasses to Dino. "See the rough spot on the edge of the lock? Up near the hasp?"

Focusing and squinting, Dino said, "Yeah. Barely."

"They haven't removed the lock. When they make their move, they'll take it with them. It appears to be evident that they've had that lock a long time."

"I don't see how you could know that's true," Dino said.

"Human behavior. It's obvious. Let's get out of here."

One second later I grabbed Dino's shoulder, hissing, "Cops!" which was as good as saying, "Duck!" Which we did. The wash of security lights from both the mini storage and the strip mall petered out before reaching the line of trees, making our position relatively secure.

I had slipped on my lightweight black watch cap as a matter of course when Dino and I were crossing the side street, blond hair being a liability in my line of work. We kept our faces averted to prevent any small reflection.

The patrol proved to be routine, just a pair of cops talking baseball, women, bitching about the job, looking around, but not too hard—the usual.

When they were gone we decided to go with my idea of cruising bars to kill time, one beer per, impossible to get in trouble like that. I would have thought so.

* * *

We began our pub crawl with a sports bar, shooting eight ball, and nursing our beer while ignoring the crowd of mostly guys who, for whatever reason, thought this was a hoot. We didn't stay long.

Opting for adventure, we chose to hit joints we had never set foot in before. Large or small, old or new, it didn't matter, as long as the experience was new to us. Some establishments were worthy of only a rough glance, Dino and me walking in and out in under a minute when the clientele was too old, or too quiet, or too anything other than fun. There was no such thing as too fun while bar hopping.

We hit pay dirt with a mid-size club named Spotz, a theme bar featuring a galaxy of stupid mini spotlights set into the high ceiling. A computer algorithm kept up to half the lights blinking on and off to the beat of the music, with all lights changing in waves of color and intensity, wretched if one were an epileptic or had a bum ticker. But the band was hot, well worth the cover charge, and the females were plentiful.

I led the way. It beat trying to talk, which you could all you wanted, but unless you read lips or were a dork who would actually stand next to someone and text, forget it. Pointing to the beer of a guy at the bar as an example, I raised two fingers for the bartender to interpret.

We took our overpriced beers off to one side of the dance floor, watching the band and the dancers, letting our ears bleed freely, far too close to the speakers.

As I sipped my beer Dino attracted a gal who I guessed to be pretty drunk, because out of nowhere she leapt on Dino, locking her arms around his neck and her legs around his waist, her short skirt slinking to her waist. This all happened in the space of one second, with the next several seconds spent by the leaper attempting to vacuum Dino's spleen through his throat. If Aunt Gabby saw this she would be highly concerned.

As for myself, I was laughing like crazy. Me, I was considered to be okay-looking, on the rugged side, but Dino had been born with dark, pretty-boy Italian looks that got the girls' hearts and libidos racing. When we were out, it was always Dino getting hit on, with me entertaining peripheral attendants.

Girls literally threw themselves at my cousin. So did their boyfriends, their boyfriends' fists anyway.

Dino never saw the guy coming. Darn well never heard him coming. Dino, gentleman that he was, had reacted on impulse, slipping his hands under the girl's derriere to support the unexpected load. The nut caught my eye, making these comical eye rolls at me as if asking, "Why me?" or possibly, "Help!"

The pissed off boyfriend was fast storming up from the girl's blindside. He plucked the amorous leech off Dino, using a well-muscled arm, doing so almost as fast as he threw a right cross at Dino's face.

Intent on his wandering girlfriend, and the current object of her lust, the fellow had paid no attention to me as a possible wingman. I caught the incoming punch inside the crook of my arm, robbing its power.

The crowd cleared only as far as the interest of those behind allowed, the music not letting up. I knew, however, that it was only a matter of seconds before the club's security goons would be on us.

Dino, mouth wet and shirt hanging askew, computed what had just taken place, and punched the boyfriend hard in the nose, breaking it. Blood sheeted down the guy's shirt as his hands flew up to his injured face.

And, as if cued, here came the beefy tees. Security.

Again, I led, prompting Dino by tugging on his unbloused shirt, dropping my beer, Dino's beer long gone. Four strides into our escape a big fellow planted a hand on my chest and said something lost to the music.

I mouthed, "We're gone," holding up both hands in a gesture of peaceful cooperation.

Now, here was the problem. These security guys got paid to stop trouble. But what they really got off on was starting trouble, more moronic than ironic.

The .45 automatic was out of my waistband before the guy knew I was resisting. That right hand parked on my chest was a mistake. Most guys were righthanded, as was I. I clocked the ape with the flat of my gun, sending him to the floor. When I turned, Dino was dancing with a second security dolt.

What the hell, I stepped in and clobbered that guy, too. Grabbing Dino by the shoulder, I lunged through the crowd to beat any other security to the door.

We almost made it. One really big guy in a stretched t-shirt blocked our way. Unheard, I sighed, pointed the gun at his belly, keeping it close to my body and low. The gun was not visible to anyone more than three feet away and looking for it. The big guy raised his hands, shaking his head in recognition that I held the winning hand.

I pushed Dino ahead of me, out the door and into the night past another security guy clueless to what had happened. I headed right, opposite the direction of where I had parked, Dino following without question. We raced away toward the end of the building. I could feel eyes following us, as expected. If our watchers talked to the cops they would give them our direction of travel, as I intended.

In relative darkness, away from the parking lot's lights, we circled the building. From my back pocket, I slipped my watch cap on now, gun inside my waistband once more, racing, having fun with the adrenaline still boosting me, Dino right by my side.

Arriving clockwise to the far corner, we came again to the parking lot. Hunched over, we slipped our way among the parked vehicles, working our way to the Nova. One of the first things I had done upon buying the car was to remove her dome light.

Inside the car, keeping low, we watched the security guys out front looking around. I started the engine and pulled out, having backed into the slot in the first place. The headlights remained off until we hit the street.

"You all right?" I asked my cousin.

"Depends on if the crazy bitch has herpes or somethin'," Dino said.

I laughed. "Women."

"Yeah. Women," Dino said, shaking his head as he removed a crumpled Marlboro from his crush-proof box.

"Tell you what . . ." I said.

"What?" Dino replied, lighting up and blowing out a stream of smoke and released tension.

"Seeing as how we didn't get to enjoy even one beer back there, we'll have two at the next place. Deal?"

Dino leaned closer to bump fists. "Deal."

* * *

Every couple of hours Dino and I would home in on tomorrow night's project. Or, if I cared to view it in another light, tonight's project, it now being Saturday morning. Nothing had changed according to the unvarying tale of the untouched lock, untouched as far as I could be sure of without going through the hassle of first entering the unit I had rented, then the place adjacent, then employing the snake camera, all risky activity subject to outside scrutiny. The story of the lock was good enough for me, a guarantor of human nature, both the Dezz's and my own.

We ended up at a round-the-clock restaurant, lacking half the clientele's juiced wakefulness from pulling a coffee-sustained all-night drunk. Our limited alcohol intake had been boringly social, but safe. The cops would have been proud had they known.

I dropped Dino off at his unmolested car as the sun was coming up, telling him that I would call when I had his smokes.

"And thanks a lot, cuz. Had a good enough time, but next time we'll do it up right," I said, stifling a yawn.

"Likewise for me. Ciao," Dino said, looking spent, up twenty-four hours now. Even the cigarette dangling from his lips looked sleepy.

Okay. Back to Queens. I had to crash so I could be rested up for tonight. Yet first I needed to figure just where that crashing was going to take place. Good Uncle Vinnie did the right thing, stopping by a store to throw a bagful of breakfast items together, including cereal and milk. Maybe one of Paulie Pet's kids would name their firstborn after me.

I wasn't surprised to find both of them up. I received a short wave from

Paulie glued to both the beanbag and the screen. Sandra bounded from the kitchen to give me a hand, taking the bag from me.

Actually, what she did was took over, freeing me to take a shower. I had eaten a couple of hours earlier, but bacon, eggs, hash browns, and toast figured to make a second, painless deposit. Keeping my eyes open was a fight.

"If you guys will forgive me, I've got to crash. You need anything out of here, Sandra?" I had not spotted any panties tossed into a corner, or tampoonies cluttering any wastebasket.

"No, I'm good, Vinnie. We'll be quiet," she said sweetly, sounding like a kid on her best behavior, which I guess she was, and for good reason. Behind her, Paulie nodded, backing what his sister said.

I smiled and got one in return when I quipped, "Goodnight" with the sun brightening the cloudless sky seen through the balcony door.

When my head hit the pillow, my lungs emptied with the last breath requiring effort. I was anxious for eight to ten hours of uninterrupted sleep. A smell, from either very faint perfume, or soap from Sandra, was on my pillow. Good kid. But this was screwed up. And I didn't know what to do to fix it. For now, I would sleep on it.

Chapter 9

By six o'clock that evening I'd had another shower and felt much better, with plenty of time to show up at the don's house. The kids were watching TV. Sandra asked if I would like her to fix me something to eat.

Overriding the eternal quest for food was the bizarre feeling that I was watching an episode of *Bonanza* in which the supposedly well-to-do Cartwrights wore the same clothes every episode for years, like a sumo wrestler's lucky, unwashed jockstrap/diaper gizmo. Of course, the kids' stay had not been nearly that long, but the clothes Sandra and Paulie had on were the same ones that I had been seeing since their arrivals.

Well, heck. They hadn't said a word. Nor would they unless I did something about it. They were willing to suffer this inconvenience rather than return to Paulie Pet's little shop of horrors.

The bruising had not gone down worth mentioning on Paulie's face, though the level on the bottle of aspirin had. With time, Paulie's youth would speed the healing. Still, I was afraid that this inactivity was killing his spirit. Perhaps I could inflict mortal damage upon two hypothetical birds, using but a single stone.

"You guys want to come with me," I said, making it a statement rather than a question.

Paulie said, "What's up?"

"We're going to the mall," I announced.

Sandra smiled. Paulie tightened up his sunglasses and struggled out of his beanbag's clutch.

Thinking back to my own childhood, I cleared my throat and asked, "Ah, anyone need to use the bathroom before we go?"

Yeah, it felt weird, but darn if I didn't get two takers. Five minutes later we were on the road.

"Nice car," Paulie said, riding shotgun.

I glanced in the rearview to see Sandra looking side to side, glad to be outdoors again, uncomplaining of the breeze from the open windows blowing her hair around, holding it in a loose ponytail, her free hand brushing away loose strands.

The nearest mall had about everything any other mall did, so that was where we went. Locking the car, I asked the kids where they usually shopped for clothes. Yes, it would have been smarter to ask before leaving; still, I got several answers. Putting the question differently, I asked if there was one store that they both could agree on.

Paulie didn't care. Sandra said to follow her. Paulie Jr. and I obeyed as far as entering the store of her choice, where she politely asked me what I was willing to part with.

She did not put it like that. The kid was embarrassed to ask, and had I been thinking clearly, I could have saved her the pain. What Sandra actually said was, "What should I stop at?"

I didn't get it, then I did, smiling. "Keep it under a thousand dollars," I said.

Her eyes got big.

Too high. "Um, under $400?"

Still, she looked at me sideways. I was practically a stranger and a guy, though I had made it clear that I just wanted them to feel safe, no strings, especially walking a thin line representing maleness after her father's inexcusable behavior. I got scrutinized before getting smiled at.

Eyes twinkling, Sandra chirped, "Okay!" and took off, leaving me to wander the men's department with Paulie.

Paulie shopped like a guy should. If it caught his eye and fit, fine. Shirts, pants, underwear, socks—done in fifteen minutes.

For the following hour we wandered around, looking at this and that, with me noticing how Paulie's attention lingered on gaming consoles and such. I wasn't heartless, but I could not see myself stretching this improv adoption to such a length. My new apartment had been seen by myself as a flash destination—half inspiration, half desperation.

There was no telling how many laws I was running afoul of. For now, though, I felt morally justified. Screw Paulie Pet and screw his wife, too.

I was having Sandra call her mom every day, and so far, I had heard of no plea, no begging related by Sandra for the two of them to return home. It might be a good idea to begin squirreling away a college fund.

When, finally, we had Sandra in tow, glowing with her shopping experience, I suggested snagging some take-out, allowing the kids a choice between chicken sandwiches and chicken sandwiches because my time was now running close. I still had plenty of time before the actual heist, but it was important to show up early at Don Renaldi's house.

Chicken sandwiches and specialty cookies bagged up, I steered us homeward, installed the kids with a minimum of care, and left, seeing no cause to rattle the locked door.

* * *

Knowing it would make a good showing, I supplemented last night's surveillance with a quickie drive-by before showing up at my parent's house. The same recognizable lock had still been in place. I was neither the first nor the last to arrive at Chateau Renaldi.

Seated around the dining room table was everyone participating in tonight's action except Uncle Mike. It was after 10 p.m., and from the looks of it, the gang was on their second pot of coffee. A deck of playing cards sat to one side, along with a scorepad, where at least one game of Rummy 5,000 had been tallied.

Happy that I had not arrived too early. Dad was ruthless at cards and would cheat every chance he could. If caught, he would explain, "It's a game, stupid. The object is to win."

Relating my observations from the previous night, leaving out my and Dino's exploits, I added that I had just made another pass, and that everything looked good, earning me a nod of respect from dad. Mom, in for a minute to check on snack orders, commented, "How sweet."

I saw Dom Bartlemeo chuckle quietly, one eye on me, the other on mom, a fantastic field of vision approximating 300°. Which made him a spectacularly good lookout man.

Paulie Sr. had both Popeye-esque forearms spread atop the table, his big head immobile, staring into his coffee cup. I wondered if he had a hangover. Maybe he was having a vision. At least he had shaved today, though the heavy stubble sprouting since would qualify as two day's growth on another man.

Tony Funicella was cleaning his fingernails with the tip of a knife and looking bored. I always thought Tony would have made a great mortician. He damn sure had been a frequent contributor to that profession, making his bones early in life and coasting on the reputation ever since. Normally, the threat of siccing Tony F. on someone was sufficient inducement to that party's straightening up damned fast.

And Dad, Dad was as cool as ever, rested and professionally expectant at the same time. He was using his coffee cup as employment for his hands, time spent waiting just one of those things taken in stride. I noticed that he had nicked himself shaving, the residual off-white from a styptic pencil showing low on his throat via the open collar. I caught myself staring at the representation of blood lost.

When a knock on the door sounded, Mom was on it with speed. It was always fun to watch how dad's hand would leisurely drop to his lap. From there it would reach to touch the nine mm handgun secured in its specially constructed draw installed just above belt buckle height beneath the table's top.

I doubted that anyone else seated at the table, even these veterans, knew what Dad was doing. Then again, some were obvious at being on guard, such as Paulie Pet with one hand doing The Napoleon inside his jacket. What a bunch of nuts. I would recognize Uncle Mike's knock anywhere, anytime.

Paying out compliments to Mom, Uncle Mike breezed into the room, smelling lightly of aftershave and shoe polish. The guy had the shiniest shoes of any man I have ever known. Mom accused Uncle Mike of using the polished toes of his shoes to gain a reflection of what was under women's skirts. The accusation was always denied. Uncle Mike just had his old-fashioned ideas of what was spiffy, a word he liked to toss out a lot. A nice car was spiffy, as was anything I executed with flair as a kid.

"You got the trucks?" Dad asked, both hands atop the table as if one had never left.

"Ready to roll. Got 'em stashed down at the car lot," Uncle Mike said, depositing one set of keys in front of Dad and placing the other set in my hand.

The car lot Mike referred to was owned by a family connection. One of the keys on each ring would unlock the lot's metal pole gate.

As a ritual, Uncle Mike passed around a box of medical gloves, everyone around the table taking however many they cared for, at least two. I took three pair, hating sloppy hindsight, it having been drilled into my head early on in my career that evidence was a dirty word.

I had the keys to the truck in which we would load the merchandise. Dad's "truck" was actually a van large enough to accommodate the entire crew should the need for an alternative getaway arise. I stashed my set in my front pants pocket, patting it in place as I had been taught—thorough, no carelessness.

Going on midnight, Mom asked if anyone cared for some cookies fresh from the oven. I saw Paulie smirk. For myself, I could not think of a more genteel setting prior to pulling a job. The only thing that could make it better would be a cold glass of real milk, and a baseball bat to wipe the crumbs and that stupid smile off Paulie Pet's face.

* * *

I was behind the wheel. Tony F. was riding shotgun. Dom, Paulie, and Uncle Mike rode in the back, hanging on to wall straps in the musty, humid, dark confines of the U-Haul truck appropriated for the job.

The truck had been eased away from a gas station in Jersey. Thin, precut appliques were unrolled and pressed in place in less time that it takes to tell it, transforming the moving truck's iconic logos into the bland exterior of an ordinary truck. Cops looking for the familiar would not be looking for this vehicle.

Using walkie-talkies, I made sure that Dad was in position before pulling up to the storage unit's gate. Tony cut the lock; I rushed through. A replacement lock was secured in place. There was no traffic to witness our entry. So far so good at this, our most visible, and therefore most crucial, moment.

I backed the truck up to the targeted storage unit's door as Tony was already cutting that lock, having slapped the side of the truck in passing, alerting those inside to open up, the door rigged to do so.

A double click over my walkie-talkie was dad's signal that all was clear. I kept the truck idling, my eyes everywhere. All was dark beyond the security lights' reach, all calm, my .45 resting in my lap.

* * *

Hardly moving a muscle over the past three hours, Dino Puljoli smiled at the sound of the truck's stopping outside the fenced gate, then pulling through. Those below used no voices, a smooth operation. Without turning his head, he carefully scanned what he could from his prone position atop the mini storage's flat roof. There was no movement along the parking lot's visible perimeter, nor did he expect any.

When his cousin had told him that the notorious Tony Funicella would have put a man on the roof, his mind had begun to wonder if his own desire to be a part of the simple operation was all that crazy. If things did go bad, and he was in a position to help, he would be a hero and most likely be promoted instantly, praised for both his intuition and his initiative.

And, if not? As in that he was almost certainly not needed, then where was the harm? He would simply wait until the Renaldis and their crew left before slipping back over the fence and going home, mentioning his adventure to no one, ever. Dino was sick of office work. Any opportunity to shorten his time at the warehouse was a chance that he was willing to take.

Dino checked his watch as sounds of cardboard being handled rose up to his perch mere feet above the guys loading the cigarettes. No matter if he was a help tonight or not, he was thrilled just listening to the sounds of his cases being loaded aboard the truck. He was dying for a smoke right now, and could almost taste the freebies, his no matter what.

Uncomfortably motionless atop the rough tar roof, with hard-edged pebbles digging into his knees, pelvis, chest, and elbows, Dino was grinning.

* * *

The sound of light thumps grew less distinct as the cargo space behind the cab of the truck filled from bed to ceiling, front to back.

We were five minutes into the operation—by my calculation halfway. I knew that I had mentioned that there were items of interest in the storage unit next door, and now I wished that I had kept that information to myself . . . some negative association . . . I didn't know how to describe it, but I had this feeling, not a good one, and not one—

"Get out of there! Now!" erupted my dad's voice, flooding my system with adrenaline, freezing me in place no longer than a second.

Sure that the boys in back had heard the same transmission over their own sets, I was throwing the truck into Drive as gunfire broke the silence of the night. I stubbornly held my foot on the brake for a count of five before flooring the accelerator, knowing that whoever wanted to hop a ride had now had their chance, just as had been discussed in our planning.

Breaking away, I heard a mysterious thump, a crashing thud, as something or someone landed atop the roof of the truck's cargo section. It had to be one of our guys or I most likely would have been a dead man already.

A round smashed into my driver's side mirror as a barrage of return fire could be heard coming from the truck's open bay, our crew countering the surprise attack.

I couldn't spare a glance, my focus saved for straight ahead, picking my emergency exit between two trees on the other side of the rapidly approaching fence, hoping Dad was well on his way to our backup van at this near end of the strip mall across the side road. Or in place, but out of my way, returning fire if he considered that the best option.

A five-foot-wide grass border separated the parking lot's curb from the chain-link fence. Concentrating on the widest gap between trees, I was committed, the front of the truck centered on one of the fence's metal posts. I was screaming, "Hold on!" to little use over the roar of the engine at full throttle—and the booms, bangs, and pops of continuous gunfire.

The truck's front tires banged violently, launching us upward off the curb, carrying the cab airborne to connect with the fence in a short but loud screech of ripped metal fencing and gouged metal truck sides. My vision blurred with the jarring impacts.

Trees flashed past on either side of the truck. I felt the resistance, knowing I had scraped one hard, then I was free, fighting the wheel to the right to bring our crew in back out of the perceived line of fire.

My passenger side window exploded, safety glass pelting me in the same instant that I felt something hot whisk by my forehead. The truck rocked hard to a halt.

I snatched the keys and walkie-talkie and tumbled out my door, putting thin metal and packed tobacco between myself and all the flying lead. Taking a quick inventory, I was scrambling back inside the cab, low across the floorboard to find my gun on the far side—two seconds and a million miles away.

The grating confusion of gunfire continued. It was either race to the iffy safety of our getaway vehicle or join in on the fun. Running risked exposure. Delay risked severing this long link I've enjoyed with respiration.

Over all the chaos, I heard the sound of shoe tread slapping on pavement. Wait—both away from me and toward me. Shit.

Keeping low, gun in hand, I quickly checked its action, not needing more surprises. For the moment, I was protected by the bulk of the truck in front of me and, on my left, by the open driver's door. Unseen from my position, someone was firing from atop the truck. Whoever it was, was in an extremely vulnerable position. I began rounding toward the rear of the truck when the sound of running feet was nearly upon me.

I calculated where a torso should appear now and fired. A split second later an arm whipped around the corner of the truck, unexpectedly low, the enemy shooter in a crouch. In the half-second that followed I had fully contemplated what it meant to be a dead man, when from my right came an eruption of gunfire, sounding like a full clip loosed, catching my assailant as he was bringing the gun to bear on me and blowing him backward, peppered with lead.

I spared a quick, stunned look in the weak illumination to see Paulie Pet changing out clips, yelling, "Let's go!"

No fooling. I turned to run when a body dropped beside me. "Dino!"

"Run!" Dino screamed at me, his normally sedate eyes wild and scary.

There have come times in my life when I would gladly give every worldly possession I own in trade to slow down events long enough to get some sensible answers, everything for a brief time out, like now, because not much of this snafu was making sense, other than the fact that we had somehow been expected, or near enough not to matter. Frigging Dino, out of nowhere, was propelling me across the street as bullets sprayed from in front of us and behind us.

The van's side door was open and those inside were yelling for us to jump in, a most excellent invitation.

Jump, hell; Dino and I dove in headfirst.

* * *

"Go, go, go!" half our crew was yelling as the van got under way, rocketing out of the parking lot in a squeal of tires. I could hear Dad at the wheel but couldn't make out what he was saying. Sirens were approaching. Someone's ankle was under my head.

"Everyone down flat! Away from the windows!" Dad shouted as the van's speed dropped dramatically.

Seconds later the sound of sirens approached and screamed past us, with yet more on the way.

"Stay down!" Don Renaldi ordered, allowing the van to show only a driver doing the speed limit.

I worked one hand free to wipe sweat out of my eyes, my cousin crammed with me into the tight foot space. "Dino?" I whispered so only he could hear.

"Dammit, dammit, dammit!"

That was the response I got from Dino. I figured that I would give him a minute to calm down before I tried to talk to him again. This would likely be right before I fucking strangled him, having this really bad feeling, the ass end of the bad feeling that had been toying with me earlier.

I smelled blood. And sweat.

Any tears would have to wait until tomorrow.

* * *

We ditched the van at a preselected location, all loading into yet another van, Uncle Mike being carried.

"Let me," I said, shoving my way to kneel by Uncle Mike's side as knees and elbows pressed into me. Doors were shut with a minimum of noise, and we began moving again.

We couldn't risk an inside light, dammit, but I was catching glimpses of

Mike Spinoza as streetlights' shine gained and receded like an urban tide.

I ripped open Uncle Mike's bloody shirt to find not one entrance wound, but three. How the man was still alive I had no idea. Tearing off my own shirt, struggling in the close space, I pressed it to two of the chest wounds, telling Dom to apply pressure to the third. Uncle Mike's hands clutched my wrists in a weak grip.

"Leave it, kid. I'm done for," Mike rasped.

The hell with that bad advice. "Give me another shirt!" I demanded as another flashing streetlight painted Mike's face a frightening shade of blue.

My left hand was bumped with an offering from Dino. There was neither time nor room to turn Mike over to treat the dreaded exit wounds. I was fearing the worst and cursing the dark, unable to maneuver freely with Dom's bulky assistance locking me in place. Frustrated, all I was able to do was continue pressing against Mike's wounds, pressing so hard that I feared I may be cutting off the injured man's ability to draw breath.

"He's got to have an emergency room, Dad!" I said, my voice too loud, my labored breathing too incongruent over the monotonous whine of the van's tires on pavement.

"No, Vinnie."

"What?" I said, feeling outside myself as if locked in time darkly between uncaring streetlights. It was Uncle Mike, Spoons, talking to me, his voice a gentle whisper, as if he was exhausted and falling asleep. There was not a word from dad, or from anyone else for that matter. The whine of the tires was an insult.

"No hospital, dammit. Don't be stupid," Uncle Mike wheezed before I felt him go slack.

"Uncle Mike!"

In the Renaldi tradition, I forced myself to calm. Hands still in place, I lowered my ear to Uncle Mike's open mouth and felt nothing, heard nothing. The next dimensionless streetlight showed me his eyes, staring into mine, a knowing look locked in place.

"He's gone," I murmured to Dom, backing off and twisting hard to peek over the bench seat, see where we were. Turning back, I found Dino staring at me, eyes wide with comprehending fear and dawning shock.

The shock I understood. It was the oncoming fear that I believed Dino was realizing all too well, if I was reconstructing this debacle correctly. Yes, it was for damn certain that Dino should be tasting fear right now.

I gazed down at poor old Spoons. My uncle I called him. I closed his eyes, a creepy feeling washing through me as I had never done such an act before.

Using a blood-soaked shirt, I covered Mike Spinoza's face and looked up at Dom inches away.

Dom quietly said, "Damn."

* * *

Dad pulled the van around to the backyard. Everyone jumped out, unloading Mike. Dad and Tony sketched out the situation for Mom, she having flown out the back door within seconds of our arrival. In another minute, no more, Dad, Tony and Paulie were driving away to ditch the van.

Before moving Mike any further, Mom ordered a plastic tarp to be fetched from the carport, which I did, getting the creeps again. The sound that the plastic made was horrible, synthetic and cold.

The two things that kept me going were my ingrained professionalism and knowing that Uncle Mike would have found it necessary to perform the same duty had it been me lying on the grass. We took risks, and we all understood that the time for mourning a loss was not indulged in until the safety of those remaining was secured. Any other way, as Mike implied, would be stupid.

"You two. Strip," Mom said, talking to Dom and me, needing to get rid of blood evidence.

"Dino," Mom said in a harsh voice. There was a hard look in her eye. "Trash bags in the carport on the tool bench. First—take off those shoes. Now, go."

Keeping his mouth good and shut, the man who should not be here, Dino, took off for the carport, Mom's edged voice behind him instructing him to touch nothing other than the box of trash bags.

When Dom and I were soon stripped, Mom inspected the soles of our feet as we covered our own nakedness the best we were able to with the clothes in hand. Of course, we then had to abandon them on the grass at our feet.

Mom nodded, all business. "Okay, inside to the showers. Get going. I'll have coffee ready when you get out. Dom, what size pants?"

"Forty-eight's fine," Dom tossed over his shoulder, his naked bulk quivering and quaking as he mounted the back steps, at any other time embarrassing, tonight just another day at the beach.

I was climbing the steps behind Dom as Dino flew back with the trash bags.

"There are gloves in my back pocket, Dino," I called, trying to be helpful. "And keys are in the front pocket," which would not burn. "Check Dom's pockets, too."

Dino made short work of the chore, donning gloves and bagging separately what would burn and what would not.

"Grab the other end," Mom told Dino as I lingered on the back deck, watching as Mom reached down to grab Mike's tarp-wrapped feet.

She glanced up to witness my awkward pause.

"Move it, Vinnie."

* * *

As the sun was rising, Paulie Pet pulled into the backyard with two of our crew in a plain black hearse. They swiftly loaded Mike's body, leaving one moment after the rear door closed. Elapsed time on site was forty seconds.

Dad was on his second cup of coffee, standing in the living room and peering through a one-inch division of the curtains. Dom had been told to go home, Tony as well, leaving only Dino in borrowed clothes, standing at attention, waiting for my dad to speak.

All vehicles involved in the heist and getaway were now burned and abandoned, same with our clothes. Blood evidence from our bodies was down the drain. All that was left were words. Words did not happen by themselves, and it wasn't up to me to make them appear, even though the interminable wait seemed like torture.

Don Renaldi permitted the silence to lengthen, his gaze vigilant upon that narrow opening onto the breaking day, the first day in his adult life he had ever known without Spoons there when needed. He was more than certain that his nephew behind him viewed this harsh quietness solely as a prelude to punishment, if not punishment in its own right.

As had his boy, Vinnie, assumed. He, too, had been quick to judge Dino guilty, although, to be sure, not one word of his doubts had he voiced aloud. There were usually two sides to most stories; many times, there were more—parallel truths, and it would be prudent to bear this in mind.

Dino Puljoli was Don Renaldi's dead brother-in-law's youngest son. With the blood kinship came an obligation that Renaldi had long considered as being met. He had been conscientious to bring the young man along the path of family business slowly, even painfully so, in no hurry to get the young man killed, for Ronnie Renaldi did not operate on a principle of greed. Securing a modest fortune was good business, not greed. And whatever risks occurred in gaining a comfortable future must be weighed against an even greater good—family.

Renaldi brought the coffee cup to his lips, blowing without thought across the rim of the lukewarm beverage, sipping, birthing, and burying various scenarios while also resurrecting Michael Spinoza in his memory. One thing was clear: Dino had taken it into his thick skull to invite himself to an affair that he had no business attending, which was bad enough.

What was unclear, and perhaps never would be resolved, was what had led to the shootout. Dino being spotted, alerting the Dezzes, seemed the likeliest possibility, but certainly not the only one.

Yet, if the Dezzes had made Vinnie coming and going, even as discreetly as he was sure Vinnie had been, certainly they would have acted before last night, removing either the interloper, or relocating the cache of stolen cigarettes, not waiting for a move to be made against them.

And if countersurveillance had been employed, either in the form of a manned post, or through the use of video/listening devices, or even low-tech motion sensors hidden within the storage unit itself, it all came back to the same bit of illogic—why leave a valuable asset so vulnerable?

This had hardly been the first time that Renaldi had ripped off the Dezzes, considering them fairly low in the smarts department. But what if this had been a setup? What if the cache had been sacrificed as payment for past offenses? the Dezzes possibly adding two and two and coming up with his name?

Also, there was another answer, the simplest, that the Dezzes had been ready to move the goods, and the timing was coincidental to their own plan, neither impossible or implausible.

There was much to consider, and Spoons just as dead no matter the truth. And even at that, he and his gang had been lucky. The frigging Dezzes couldn't shoot for shit, and that was a given. Assholes using automatic rifles, spraying their shots high and wide. The Dezzes were fortunate to hit anything on purpose.

So, what was he to do with Dino? Renaldi thought the matter over, knowing he couldn't shoot the kid. That wouldn't bring Spoons back. Gabrielle herself, Dino's mother, would drop dead with grief should anything happen to Dino. Plus, he liked Dino. Everyone liked Dino. Just not so much this morning.

Ronnie Renaldi turned from the window, his features level and nonthreatening, though not warm, coldly neutral and searching for the truth before his tongue began to wag, contemplating what he could see for himself. Yes, the kid was guilty as hell, but the guilt was tempered by regret and crushing contrition. Not only had Dino fucked up his heist, he possibly cost a favored member of the gang his life.

And for what? A lousy bunch of cigarettes. Sure, it was a good haul, would have been quite lucrative, but still just a lousy bunch of smokes.

"What's the matter with you?" Renaldi said for openers, advancing one step.

"You taking stupid pills? Is that it? You watching too much TV, huh? Too much Hollywood bullshit—you think 'Hey, what fun! I know what I'll do! Invite myself to the party?"

"Yes, sir. I'm sorry," Dino said, looking his uncle in the eye before again lowering his eyes to the carpet.

"Vinnie says he let you tag along the other night to keep him company. I don't even have to ask to know that he didn't invite you. Am I right?" Renaldi stated, aware of the contradiction.

"Yes, sir," Dino said, no choice other than toughing this out.

Renaldi took another step, the frown on his nephew's face growing into a mask of paranoia, the kid having the worst day of his life, the dummy.

"What? I don't pay you enough already, Dino? Is that it?"

"Yes, sir. I mean, no, sir!" Shit! "I mean, yes, sir, you do."

Wow! The kid was jumpy as a frog in a frying pan. "What am I gonna do with you, huh? You know if your momma finds out about this she's gonna lose it. Your momma can't handle little things, let alone her youngest responsible for Spoon's death."

Okay, maybe that last bit was going too far, Ronnie thought, but then again it may be exactly true. If for no other reason than the kid knew better, he deserved the guilt trip.

Dino hung his head, his world crashing down about his ears, and there was nothing he could do to stop it. He had screwed up, earlier envisioning only positive outcomes and little risk. The hindsight was a mental flail of anguish.

"I'm sorry, Uncle Ronnie."

"Shut up, you. I want to hear your stupid mouth I'll open it with my foot!"

"Ronnie . . ." came my mom's low call of warning, just that and nothing else, a reminder that he was dealing with family.

I kept my eyes on the swirling woodgrain of the table, hating this, but hating losing Uncle Mike worse. I was bone tired and the day was going to drag, drag, drag.

Renaldi took two more steps, bringing him nose to nose with Dino, forcing his nephew to look into his eyes and witness the pain and betrayal there, not allowing Dino to flinch and look away, making him soak it all up like a sponge drawing on a spilled bottle of poison.

"Dino. Why?" I heard my dad say softly. "The money?"

The quaver, however controlled, noticeable in Dino's reply, was a result of his anguish breaking its barriers due to the breech in dad's revelation of feeling.

"No, sir. I was there on my own as backup. Vinnie mentioned that Tony F.

would've put a man there on that roof, and I thought it was a good idea. And, if nothin' happened, I'd go home and keep it to myself. I am so sorry, Uncle Ronnie. I never thought—"

"You never thought!" Renaldi nearly shouted. "You never thought!" he repeated. "And if something did go down, which it most certainly did, just how do you keep your own guys from shooting at you, when you're not supposed to be there? Huh? So, if you start shooting, the likelihood is that you have both sides shooting at you! Christ, boy!"

Thankfully, Dino kept quiet. I do believe that had he attempted to defend himself at that par-TICK-u-lar moment, my dad would have raced behind him to kick his ass.

I began to rise from my seat, and Mom restrained me by settling a hand on my arm, shaking her head. Bowing to her wish, I lowered myself to wait out the confrontation, the next room again silent. I imagined my cousin still at attention, with his knees about to give out, and who knew what going through his head.

A half minute later the slurp I heard was grating, just awful, the one sound of my dad slurping coffee, whereas normally he sips. Hard to describe, it was so wrong.

"Vinnie, get in here."

A half-dozen paces brought me to the threshold, another three to stand by my cousin's side. I kept my eyes on dad. Never had I seen the old man look this old. Lack of sleep, combined with tragedy, combined with grief, all had taken their toll on Ronnie Renaldi.

And now this guilt by association, made to stand side by side with Dino as if I had encouraged him, seeded his imagination by asking him to ride along with me.

His severe look lasering between the two of us, his bloodless lips compressed into a hard, white line, my dad was as scary as a smoking volcano.

"Vinnie, I want you to drive by the scene, low profile, and report back what you see. Take Dino with you."

To Dino, I asked where he had parked last night. Dino told me, wisely adding no more.

"All right, Dino. I want you to listen and listen good. You go home and you stay there. You don't go out for Chinese, you don't go get laid, you don't go to work tomorrow or until I tell you. You sit in your apartment until I say different. *Capiche?*"

"Yes, sir."

I was thinking funeral, wondering how Dad was going to work out Uncle Mike's funeral, and if he would allow Dino to pay his respects. If we could have a funeral without questions raised. Dad was smart. He would not let the law know the truth, and he wouldn't play too cute by being foolishly creative.

"Give your aunt a kiss and get out of here," Dad told Dino without looking at him, looking at me.

When my cousin exited the room Dad said to me, "This is all on Dino?"

I nodded.

Though my cheek got patted, I was afraid to turn away lest I got that size twelve in the seat of my pants.

Chapter 10

I don't blame you if you hate me, man," Dino said, slumped in the passenger seat of the Nova.

Cranking the car, and pulling out of my parent's driveway, I thought about Uncle Mike cracking jokes and giving me presents and advice, reminding me on the sly about respect, and about how you had to give it to get it. In my imagination I saw his big horse's teeth fanned out as he laughed at a joke, usually one made at his own expense. I thought of how those same choppers bit down on his lips when he played the spoons, making them disappear. There was this one time when I asked Mike why he did that, and he said, "What?" puzzled, "Do what?"

Dino was staring straight ahead when I glanced at him. "I hate what you did, cuz, but I don't hate you, okay?"

A huge breath gusted the windshield. "Man, I fucked up. Ain't nothin' I ever do gonna make up for last night."

True. I kept my mind on driving, doing the speed limit and watching my mirrors. Dino lit a cigarette and got quiet, blocks and time passing by. Tired as I was, I was too emotionally jacked up to be concerned with it. Chores needed completing . . . chicken and the egg . . .

The cop presence at the scene of the shootout was prominent, there still being evidential processing involved due to the huge amount of spent ammo and other signs of mayhem. Crime scene tape ringed the area like a second fence. The stolen U-Haul was right where I had left it. We all had worn gloves, so any trace evidence found would be minimal.

As we passed the busted fence I saw where the truck had scraped bark from one of the trees. Spilled cases of cigarettes littered the fence line, many shredded by gunfire, an excellent argument for tobacco causing death.

In the storage units' parking lot were two ambulances, lights off. I casually turned my head as we passed, making out two stretchers, one form atop each covered with a red-dotted white sheet. Not surprising and not the whole story, the survivors having long ago limped away or been carried to emergency rooms.

"Paulie Pet saved my life last night," I said. To my own ears this statement had a dreamlike quality.

"I saw. You were between me and the shooter. I couldn't fire. Paulie took him out," Dino said in this funny sort of way, in a younger voice.

Passengers and drivers alike in either direction was rubbernecking as well, though much more obviously than my covert posture, making me think that a second pass would not be out of the question. I almost did just that, but changed my mind, not wanting to push what little luck I may have remaining. I was to drop off Dino and report to dad. Doubling north two blocks, I parked beside Dino's car in front of a 24-hour laundromat.

Dino didn't budge. He just sat there in my car, unmoving. Finally, he looked at me and nodded. His right hand reached for the door's handle and froze. He wanted to talk, needed to talk, and I was willing to listen, but, for myself, I did not know what to say. Honestly, I was unable to think of anything that would help. Well, maybe one thing. "Dino?"

A big sigh. "Yeah?" Dino looked across to me, and when I did not immediately answer he again faced forward to watch a middle-aged woman folding sheets, with what was probably her granddaughter beside her staring at a dryer full of clothes spinning in a colorful circle, the next best thing to a TV in the long, boring room.

"You need to wipe down and throw that gun away. Wipe it down good, okay?" I said. Dino was wise to prints, but I had to make sure of all loose ends, Dino having stashed his piece in the backyard before Mom saw it.

"Yeah. All right," Dino muttered.

Man, I did not like the sound of that. I said, "Better yet, hand it over." CYA. CHA. Cover his ass.

"I'll do it, Vinnie."

My hand was out and my cousin was in no position to argue. He would either have delayed the task, which was no good; forgot about it, even worse; or gone on to shoot himself, which would have been a silly crying shame.

Reluctant to do so, he parted with the gun. Using my shirt tails, I broke the piece down where we sat, wiping everything free of possible fingerprints, bullets included. Removing my shoes, I yanked off my socks and dumped the gun's components inside them, the contour of one sock looking as if a python had swallowed Dino's .38.

"See ya, Vinnie," Dino said, opening the door and sliding out.

"Dino?"

I waited for him to lean down and meet my eyes through the open window. Dejection plastered his face, worrisome, but natural given the hard spot that he was in, something to be endured like a man.

"I'll be by to see you tonight, okay?"

"Sure, Vinnie. Okay."

His heart wasn't in his words, but he wasn't crying, which I would not have put up with, and he wasn't babbling which would have been almost as bad. He was just hurting, and there wasn't anything but band aids for that.

"Pick up a bottle. But promise me you won't open it until I get there."

Dino nodded, face blank. "All right."

"I'm serious," I said.

"Damn. Okay, already. I promise. Shit."

Better. "Later then," I said.

"Later."

I took off, watching Dino in my rearview, making sure he got in his car. Checking traffic, I pulled into the street and stopped, lunged across to the passenger door, opened it, and tossed the weighted socks into a storm drain. Eyes on the mirror, I got the Nova in gear and got going.

I called the don and relayed all I had seen. He asked about Dino.

I was glad my old man did that. I was glad that he asked about Dino. That might have been the most important lesson I learned that day. You certainly took care of your dead, but, more importantly, you took care of your living.

* * *

I was positive that this was what an incorrigible hound dog felt like dragging his pecker home after being out three nights in a row, albeit without the attendant morose past joyousness.

The kids silently regarded my haggard face and rumpled clothes. With exceptional control, they dialed down the circumference of their wide eyes and waited for the zombie to produce the first utterance. Too tired for false explanations, and owing none, I forced myself to say, "Good morning."

"How about some breakfast?" Sandra said, hoping to be of use, and erring on the side of caution against forced cheer.

"How about we hold off on that until I get some sleep?" I said, squeezing out a small smile for the girl who smiled back and nodded, leaving well enough alone.

Heading for the bedroom, having figured that a precedent had been set for sleeping in shifts, and little else, I noticed Paulie rising from his beanbag station, sunglasses off. But that wasn't all I noticed. On the sofa was a stranger, a new kid and the first violation of my trust.

Paulie was opening his mouth to speak, to explain. I was sure that it was a wonderful story, colorful, and not without merit, but right now it was bad timing of almost the worst sort. I held up my hand.

"Save it. We'll talk when I'm rested," I said, leaving it at that.

Something in my voice, my manner, must have communicated a semblance of reasonableness, all three faces nodding acceptance, the newest one bruised.

Place was beginning to look like a fight club.

* * *

I woke up disoriented and semi-surly as half-remembered dreams dissipated, disturbing images of starving people hell-bent on cannibalism, city dwellers with no thought of escaping outside their steel and concrete confines to discover a possible reprieve.

Trudging to the bathroom, I stopped at the sink, staring into the mirror. I found myself frowning, the entirety of the previous night coming back to haunt me. Not yet thirty and I felt I was getting old. And crazy.

In the shower I replayed what was real, nightmare enough. Though lacking cannibals, there was sufficient terror stored in my memory to keep me awake the rest of the day. Checking the time, I amended my previous thought to: what was left of the day. I had best get dressed and see if the headcount inside the apartment had increased while I slept. For a one-bedroom apartment, I was sure getting my money's worth.

The kids were watching TV. I had to suppose that they had been doing little else other than watching TV for days now. I had to get a handle on this, find something constructive for the kids to do. But, first, introductions and, possibly, admonitions were in order. Solomon I was not, yet I believe I possessed at least enough patience to listen before drawing a sword, either as stagecraft or war craft.

"Good morning," I said for the second time today. At least Sandra was appreciative of my puny attempt at levity.

Paulie almost bowed. I nearly laughed, but did not. Paulie said, "Vinnie, this is Chris Lewis. Chris, this is Vinnie."

I gave Paulie a look, one I was sure he had no trouble interpreting, letting him know that even if he had a good reason, he had nonetheless violated my trust by bringing someone else to the apartment without my permission.

Whatever this was about should prove interesting. Paulie gave me a small grimace of recognition, his bruised face shading darker.

As I waited for an explanation, the new kid, who had been standing stiffly by the sofa, offered me his hand. I shook, inspecting the shiner that the kid sported. Upon closer scrutiny, I also noticed the ghostly impressions of previous bruising around both cheeks and eyes. Maybe I was still dreaming and the urban cannibals were morphing into teenage walking dead.

"Chris," I acknowledged, omitting any, "Good to meet you," disallowing any familiarity to develop until I had the story, of which I was still waiting. I turned back to Paulie while noting that Sandra, perched on the edge of the sofa, had twined her fingers into a knot.

"Sandra needed something from the store this morning, and I went to get it," Paulie said, finding a starting place.

I was switching my attention between Paulie and the stranger, this Chris's looks screaming out his Irish heritage—freaking flaming red hair and a score of freckles dappling nose and cheeks. Bright blue eyes shone with intelligence and something else, a wariness I was beginning to become accustomed to, sadly so.

"I met Chris here on my way back. He was, uh, in the hallway outside," Paulie related uncomfortably, as if embarrassed to recount the nature of the two youths' meeting.

The fact that Chris had been met practically on my doorstep was a turn I found alarming, serendipity of the oddest kind. I waited to hear more, my stomach rolling with hunger.

"He said that he'd seen me and thought maybe we could talk, seeing as how we had so much in common," Paulie said before swallowing a lump in his throat.

"Whoa. Wait a minute. What do you mean you had seen Paulie? Where?" I asked Chris, not liking this part of the story.

"End of the hall. Last apartment on the right. I . . . ah . . . saw Paulie through the peephole," Chris said with a sadness in his voice that took me by surprise. "His sunglasses were off."

That the kid was having problems, there was little doubt, but I can attest to the fact that in just being a boy, a shiner was a given occupational hazard. In every neighborhood was found that stripe of troublemaker assertively declaring, "I can take you," true or not, lacking only a realized outcome of proof or reproof.

Yet, in this stranger's voice I knew that I was hearing more, much more. And for Paulie to jeopardize his own shaky foundation here, informed me that he had likely done an honorable thing, not that his probable good deed showed the keenest of judgement. That was for me to decide, though as far as drawing a line went, hell, that piece of chalk went missing several days ago.

"You live at the end of the hall, this hall," I said, making sure all everybody's chilluns were on the same sorry page.

"Yes, sir," the new kid stated, still standing as if formally at attention.

This apartment/condo hi-rise was new and fairly expensive. Chris seemed not to be a creature of material neglect. But material wealth without emotional support was like a beautiful ice sculpture, admirable in its own right, yet supremely cold and superficial. I had reason to suspect this kid's odd hobby of peeping.

"And you just happened to see Paulie walking by. Happened to notice that he was, ah, colorful?"

"Yes, sir."

Chris Lewis was a husky kid, but not tall like myself or Paulie, or Sandra for that matter. His was a mug right out of the 1930s, a kid seen portraying a tough in a street scene from a black-and-white movie of that era, the kind of kid wearing a flat cap and no coat in the freezing outdoors, blowing on busy hands while laying out a jaded rap. Yet this boy was soft spoken and well mannered. In that regard he just may fit right in. All my kids were well behaved.

I raised my chin. "Looking through the peephole something you do often?"

"Yes, sir."

Can't say I was expecting that, nor did I doubt the news. "Want to tell me about it?"

"No, sir."

Good grief, the kid was throwing curveballs.

"But I will," Chris Lewis said, drawing me in. It was the right call because I had to know what was going on, my help being, as yet, an unknown. I was in enough of a messy gray area taking in Paulie Pet's kids, and that thought nearly threw me off my feet with the recollection of mere hours ago—Paulie Petralucci, a man I despise, saving my bacon.

The boy cleared his throat, and this time his look went to Sandra, causing me to observe her reaction. She met my eyes, her own brown eyes holding a plea I could almost read verbatim. I felt like sighing but held it in.

"That's where I'm made to go when I'm being punished," the boy said, instantly coloring, his Irish face blooming beet red, embarrassed by the confession.

Okay, I could see why he had been reluctant to tell me, the humiliation evident. The kid wasn't Dennis the Menace sitting time-out in a corner; he was nearly grown.

"How old are you, Chris?"

The blue eyes dropped away as he said, "Sixteen."

Christ on a hobbled horse. I encouraged him to continue by asking about the black eye.

"Disobeying a direct order."

I blinked. "Excuse me? What does that mean? Is your dad in the military?"

"No, sir. He's a cop."

Holy McMoly!! I stared at Paulie as if seriously considering an experiment to see if the big kid could fly the seven stories to the sidewalk below.

"It's all right. His father doesn't know he's here," Paulie said, and immediately flinched from my unrelenting, bug-pinning stare.

"No, it's not all right, Paulie. You trying to get me up on kidnapping charges for real? A cop? You understand how little it takes to make a kidnapping charge stick even if you're not guilty?"

I had to calm down. I had just made all three kids recoil from my blast. Turning my back, I strode into the kitchen and grabbed a cold beer. Breakfast. Screw it. When I stomped back the way I'd come the three were at the door with Chris's hand on the knob, saying goodbyes.

Crap. "Hold on. Where are you going?"

"I don't want to cause any trouble, sir. I'll go," Chris said, opening the door and stepping out.

"Geez!" I launched myself past the startled Petroluccis to snag the near-stranger by the shoulder. One quick look down the empty hallway and then I hauled the kid back inside my apartment, shutting and locking the door. Incredible. Now I really was kidnapping.

"Did I tell you to go?" I asked Chris.

"No, sir, but I don't want any trouble."

We were clumped at the door. Three pairs of eyes were on mine. Half of those eyes were bruised, which ought to be funny, but wasn't. Same number of bruised eyes as bullet holes in Uncle Mike. The next time I opened the door I would be checking for cannibals and the cops.

"Look kid. Chris. I'm not unsympathetic. Really, I'm not. I just don't know what to do. I mean, I'd like to help, but come on, your dad's a cop."

"Stepfather."

The last was said in a low voice. I asked the kid to repeat it.

"He's my stepfather," Chris said. "And he's a psycho."

Well, shit. Of course, he was. This was absolutely perfect. Paulie Jr. and I were adopted. Sandra had a child molester for a father. And now we had a redheaded stepchild. I was being punished for something, had to be.

"A psycho," I echoed; some particular items begged repetition. "A psycho cop."

"Yes, sir."

Wait a minute. "Your mom works?" I asked.

"No, sir."

Even with the money I've saved, which is a considerable amount, and even figuring my investments which are substantial and well managed, I still had to think twice before signing a lease on this apartment. These units were expensive. Now, I know what NYC cops make, and there was no way a cop on a single paycheck could afford this place.

"He works a second job?" I pried.

"No, sir."

Huh. By gesture I herded my ducklings back to the front room, waiting until they were all seated. Wanting to do right by these kids, and sticking my wet finger in a live light socket were two different things.

I struck a pose equidistant from the three and asked Chris, "What's your stepfather's rank?"

"Sergeant," Chris replied, fingers locked together. Clearly, he was nervous about this temporary reprieve, his mind on the gravity tugging him toward the bleak hallway and what monstrous black hole was at the end of it.

Forget it; a sergeant's pay didn't cut it. That sum wasn't nearly enough to swing the lease or monthly payments if psycho Dad signed on to purchase the condo. Yet, somehow, clearly, Chris's stepfather had found a way.

I needed more information. Hell, even if I did have to kick the kid out, I was gaining valuable intel that could save my hide.

The kids watched me drain half my beer. Paulie looked like a giant raccoon. "Did he come into some money that you know of? Like an inheritance? Hit the lottery? Anything like that?"

Chris met my gaze and shrugged. "Not that I'm aware of. But he doesn't talk to me about anything. If he does it's about what he wants me to do. Or not do. He likes for me to be quiet."

Ah, yes. The psycho would believe that kids should be seen but rarely, if ever, heard.

"What about your mom?" I asked. "Anything there? She get a lot of money from a divorce?"

The kid revealed a simple smirk, 1930s version. "No, sir. I'm told that my real dad's a junkie."

Okay. Junkies are big spenders, but just on dope.

"Nothing else—no money coming in from the stuff I mentioned before? For your mom, I mean."

"No, sir. She sits at home or goes shopping. It's what he wants," Chris said.

And what the psycho wants, the psycho gets, I thought. I was fearful of this being all too easy to sketch out, mental well-being aside. I did not just have a cop living down the hall from me; I had a psycho cop who was crooked and beat his stepchild. It was like hitting the anti-trifecta.

If this was karma at work it was both the instant and the bad kind.

"Does your mom know you're here?" I asked.

"Here? No, sir." The husky kid looked gratefully at big Paulie who was playing the stoic, silently prepared to get tandemly lost at my command. This plain sucked.

"And do you and your mom get along?" I probed further, turning up the balance of my beer and feeling like piling on a dozen more.

After getting a "no" I said, "Do you mind me asking why not?"

The kid's color was rising again. He toyed with the ridge of one ear before absentmindedly touching a spot under his bruised eye, stalling. He said, "I believe it's because I'm adopted. She's not my real mom. My dad married her and left us and she adopted me. Don't ask me why."

Okay, I won't. But I would love to ask her. I felt as if all seven floors had just been yanked out from under me, and that I was free falling, out of control. This couldn't be happening. I had to adjust my census: make that three effing adoptees here, and one molested child. Ain't no way that I was buying a lottery ticket today.

What to do, what to do?

"You, ah, have any plans?" I asked, afraid that the kid was going to answer in the negative.

"No, sir. I thought maybe I would just go walking around."

"Walking around," I echoed, dumbfounded.

"Yes, sir."

Kids. Even those transplanted here have got to know that you just do not go "walking around"! Geesh.

"Maybe that's not such a good idea," I said, feeling safely understated.

The kid shrugged.

"You do this before?" I started to finish by saying, "Run away", but changed it to, "Walk off?"

"Yes, sir. It really pisses him off, but sometimes I just have to go. I'm right there at the door where I'm made to stand. I think he does it on purpose. I think he wants me to go out and not come back."

And I had to think that Chris was probably right, but I couldn't say it. The kid was in a fragile situation as it stood. I looked at my watch, and at the sunlight growing dim outside.

I pointed to my landline phone. "If I let you stay here again, I mean, tonight, you've got to call your mom, your stepmother, and let her know that you're okay."

From the way Chris looked, a great weight had lifted, one he had carried far too long.

"I've got somewhere to go, but I'll be back tomorrow. Until then, you stay here and do not go out that door unless the place is on fire, in which case none of you had better come back," I said, winking at Sandra who appreciated even this smallest easing of tension.

Chris was reaching for the phone on the end table beside the sofa when I added, "Keep it short," just in case the psycho had cop buddies tracing the call. Shit, it was a landline and I believed the odds were long that the psycho police sergeant was looking for this kid, but the whole thing was freaking me out.

Short it was. From this end of the phone call it seemed that there had been scant sign of the mother protesting Chris's small declaration. Stepmother.

"I'm trusting you two," I told Sandra and Paulie, "To make sure nothing happens here. And I mean nothing. *Capiche?*"

I got "swore to." Sheesh. I felt like my dad.

"I'll be back," I informed one and all, half threat, half promise.

<h1 style="text-align: center;">Chapter 11</h1>

I had told Dino to get a bottle of booze. Figuring misery did indeed love company, I stopped on my way to secure another, thus making certain all bases were covered.

A joke. I was playing a one-man infield. I didn't have squat covered.

Dino lived in an apartment built above a garage. It was owned by an absentee landlord who had the unattached house rented out as well. It was a perfect fit for my cousin who had a good place to park his car, and plenty of privacy. Some people naturally fell into good deals, getting breaks without really trying.

And other people easily fucked up falling off a log. It reminded me of something Uncle Mike used to say. "Kid," he would always begin, calling me kid even when I was grown, "you ain't gotta be told not to stick your nose where you know, you damn well know, it don't belong."

Troubled teens. My cousin. Uncle Mike . . .

I had called my parents on the way over to Dino's, making sure I wasn't needed. I was double-checking, because in mournful situations such as we were in, people were going to say that they were fine when they were about anything other than fine. I was thinking about Mom and just where her breaking point was. Perhaps I was afraid to know if one existed, and maybe I was concerned for having my nose bloodied trying to find out.

Both Mom and the don told me that everything was taken care of. Reading between the lines, I would have to imagine that a plausible cover story for Uncle Mike's demise had been laid down and strategically backed—whatever legalities had needed handling, handled. Whatever signatures had to be on file were by now. Funerals happened. Unexplained disappearances never go away. It was easier to tell a few lies now than it was trying to perpetrate a mystery. Told to be available the next day, I promised I would.

It was likely to be a stupid promise, at least that was what the bottle in my hand whispered to me as I mounted the outside steps to Dino's place. I would be sure to get good and drunk tonight so that I would look and feel my best tomorrow. It worked for Arlo Guthrie. Maybe it would work for me.

On a hunch I tried the doorknob. Open. The timing was lousy or I would have kicked Dino's ass for that slip alone.

In an imitation of knuckles, I called out, "Knock knock!"

"Who is it?"

"Ha ha," I said, entering and shutting the door behind me. I allowed my eyes to adjust, standing in the kitchen/eating area, there being no dining table. Instead, there was a bar counter serving that function.

"Geez. You got it dark enough in here?"

"No," came the answer.

I heard in my cousin's voice that my work was cut out for me. The theme of tonight's party was going to be "Paint it black"—window, hearts, whatever slathering it took to suck all the remaining life in this place right the heck out.

"If I stub my toe I'm suing," I called louder than necessary, able to see just fine in the gloom. Above the kitchen sink I manipulated a pull shade to provide a bit of illumination from a streetlight outside. Entering the second half of the big room, which was a continuation of the kitchen, I hit a light switch, wishing I had not.

Becoming one with his recliner was my pal, Dino. Dino had been a bad boy, breaking his promise. Oh, he had kept to the apartment, all right, but the poor fellow had broken the seal on a bottle of bourbon some time ago.

"The hell, Dino. I thought you were going to wait until I got here."

Dino blowing a raspberry was a nice touch, going well with the prevailing ambience.

"I'm on house arrest. Who cares?" Dino rationalized.

"That's not the point, cuz. I was hoping we could do this together. There's no way I'll catch up to you before you pass out."

"Whatsa matta? Chicken?" Dino slurred.

In Dino's state this was supposed to be funny. His following chicken imitation was a strong clue that he was beyond caring. I grinned at him until he ran out of clucks and squawks.

"You eat anything today?" I asked, looking around, finding not a single potato chip bag carelessly flung aside which Dino will do even sober.

"No, Mother, I haven't. You hungry, get somethin'. You know where everything is. Myself, I'm goin' to have another drink." And, so saying, Dino lurched from the recliner to the kitchen.

I stepped aside before following, itemizing the contents of Dino's refrigerator while he concocted another bourbon and Coke. At least he used ice, even if he took it easy on the Coke. Repressing a shudder, I pulled out some fixings to make sandwiches, figuring to force feed the guy. Besides, I was about to starve.

"What'd you bring?" Dino said, lifting my contribution from atop the counter, hauling it out of its brown paper bag.

"Tequila? Hoo-hoo!" Dino crowed, recklessly reviving.

I grimaced. "Hold on, cowboy. You mix tequila and bourbon and you'll die."

"What's with you, man? This here's a party."

I had to let it go. To Dino it was a party. To me it was the start of Uncle Mike's wake to come. And I was certain that when Dino had begun drinking today it had been the same. But the alcohol intake had brought on a degree of forgetfulness, and, I swear, it would not be me who turned the clock back at this hour. There was no harm in letting Dino hoot and carry on. He was hurting, and this was how he had chosen to deal with it. Fine.

Quickly, I made sandwiches, cut everything in halves, and placed them upon a large plate, pushing the plate at Dino who had found new life atop one of the stools along the counter.

"You're going to make someone a good wife one day, Vinnie."

The jerk was grinning ear to ear. I bumped his free hand with the plate. "Eat," I said, leading by example.

It worked. I got three halves down him before he pushed away to step outside, lighting a cigarette. I joined my cousin on the small square platform at the top of the stairs, both of us leaning on the wooden rail.

Night was closing in. Insects were buzzing and thrumming in the line of tall shrubbery separating the property from the street, the trees on the western boundary blocking whatever remnant of sunset there was. The coming night was humid, and I couldn't say why, but somehow that aspect seemed perfect.

"Fourth of July comin' up," Dino said.

In one cabinet I had found a small clean glass which now held two fingers of tequila. "I'll drink to that," I said, because no matter if I made a toast or not, nothing was going to stop Dino from getting blistered tonight.

"I usually go to the beach," Dino said, leaning hard on the rail.

"Yeah, I know," I said, knowing where this was going.

"Not this year," Dino said, "this" coming out as "thish."

"What are you talking about, Dino? Because what Dad said, you don't know that."

"Yeah? Well, I gotta make plans, right? Gotta make reservations."

"Dino? Don't get all worked up. Take it one day at a time," I said, having so much fun.

"Shit! You should hear yourself!"

I let it slide. I looked away to the tall bushes, their tops and sides trimmed neatly, their shadows blending with other shadows, losing that cubic definition. The insects cranked it up a notch.

"Let's go inside before I catch West Nile," I said. And when Dino didn't budge I added, "Plus, I need a drink," knowing he would follow.

I mentally patted myself on the back for how I maneuvered Dino back into his recliner as he held onto a fresh, full drink. An odd chair nearby was useful as I scooted up close so that hardly any space separated me from my cousin. This was a technique I had seen Dad use with guys like Paulie Pet when they were in danger of going off like cheap fireworks while deep in their cups. It's easier to push a man back in his chair than to knock him down once standing with a full head of steam up. The bottle of tequila was at my heel, tame for now.

"What're you so quiet about?" Dino asked.

Rats. I had meant to keep up the patter, trick Dino into burning up his reserves so that he would pass out all the quicker. I really wasn't up for this—bad company keeping bad company. Party, my ass.

"Just thinking, man. Frigging Paulie Pet saving my life last night. I can't wrap my head around it. You know what I mean?"

Dino paused before saying, "It's his job, Vinnie."

"Well, yeah." It wasn't as if I could reasonably gainsay that bit of logic.

"Anyone would've done the same thing, man. He just happened to be the one there," Dino mused, eyes on the outside door, far away.

And here Dino went into a long spiel about how he would have done me that boy scout favor, but the angle was all wrong, which I knew, I remembered; we had already discussed it. I waited until he wound down. It was okay. This was good. Dino was talking, getting the replay out in the open, some of it anyway.

"We got what? Two of theirs?" Dino asked, recalling the scene of our earlier drive by.

"Radio said three. With two more wounded.," I stated, having caught that bit of news on the drive over here.

"Well, that's something at least," Dino said.

I didn't respond. This wasn't a stupid video game. The heist was supposed to have been clean. All the jobs I set up were clean, as clean as I could possibly make them. I was careful like that. I studied a project, worked the angles, tried to account for the worst that may happen, and did what fine tuning I could to eliminate any remaining risk. Last night's fiasco blew my excellent batting average all to hell.

I poured a shot of tequila and slammed it back, passing the bottle to Mr. Tough Guy with the fingers making gimme motions. Fine. But if he puked, he was going to be cleaning the mess up, not me.

Dino took such a large drink of the liquor that he actually belched. Walking dead man seated on a recliner.

For the next half-hour I laid off the booze, while Dino got stiller and quieter. When his eyes closed for good, I figured my work here was done. Almost. I straightened the place up, and even gathered a light spread from Dino's bed to settle over him before letting myself out.

My original plan had been to spend the night, but now that Dino had crashed I felt free to roam, nursing only a slight buzz. Leaving the tequila at Dino's, I climbed into the Nova with no destination in mind.

Right then I would have given a great deal to have somewhere to go, anyplace at all, if only for a few hours. I nearly headed back to my apartment, but, no, that wasn't where I wanted to be.

I turned the key and drove, going nowhere.

* * *

"You on the big phone?" I asked Sandra. Codes were cool.

"Yes," she said, answering from the same private number on Paulie Jr.'s borrowed cell phone.

"Everything good there? All present and accounted for?"

"Yeah. Is there something wrong?"

A loaded question if ever there was one.

"No, no. I just needed to talk to Chris again for a minute," I said.

"Oh, okay. Hold on a second."

With nothing better to do, I counted to one. Didn't get to two.

"Hello?"

I didn't blame Chris. I would be wary, too. This kid had been walking on ice so long that all his survival senses were super acute.

There was a cop car behind me, probably calling in my temporary tag. I slipped in a breath mint, wondering if somehow all the planets had aligned like a trick pool shot.

"Hey, Chris. Listen, everything's okay. I just wanted to ask you a little more about your stepdad. All right?"

"I guess so."

"I'll take that as a yes. What's his name? I'm assuming that you're still carrying your father's last name."

"Yes, sir. I am. The three of us all have different last names. His is Eddy. Alfred Clarence Eddy," Chris enunciated clearly before mumbling some weighty afterthought sounding suspiciously like "dickhead."

As long as I was assuming, I'd assume that this last was a pet name for the psycho stepdad. I had to give my pause an extra beat to keep the smile out of my voice. "Can you spell that last name for me?"

"E-d-d-y."

"E-d-d-y. Got it. Oh, and Chris? What's his rank?"

"He's a sergeant."

"That's right. You told me," I said, double-checking. "And he's how old?"

"Forty-eight."

"All right, Chris. That's all I need for now. I just thought I'd check it out. You know."

"Sure. No problem."

"Okay. You take care and I'll see you soon," I said.

"Yes, sir."

I punched out of the call, hands free, thinking that if this cop pulled me over my day would be complete. I was probably borderline with the tequila, even though I felt sober as a judge still in grammar school. My attitude was—screw this cop.

But it was the one who lived at the end of my hall that I was really worried about. Alfred Clarence Eddy, 48. I had meant to ask Chris how long Eddy had been on the force, but I was on my way to get that answer and more. Guessing that Eddy had been with the NYPD since he was a mere stripling psycho, I had to wonder about his ranking.

Some people did not want the responsibility that came with promotion. Others were too stupid to pass the test. And still others got busted back down all the way to foot patrol. At 48, with a career going even half right, anyone on the force could reasonably expect to either retire or move up in rank.

Hanging a right brought me to my parent's house. The cop stayed with me. I was expecting a blip from the siren any second, this cop's curiosity itching to be scratched. There were plenty of knuckleheads bored enough to pull you over just because they admired your car and wanted a better look at it.

I slid into the don's driveway. That must have been good enough for the law tonight, the cop continuing down the street, trolling for bigger fish to fillet.

Mine was not the only car in the driveway. Dom and Tony were here.

Thankfully, Paulie Pet wasn't or I believe I'd just leave. I dreaded seeing the guy again, a mixture of disgust and gratitude wreaking havoc with my psyche.

Posting my signature knock, I gave it five seconds before using my key, Mom nearly at the door when I opened it.

"Well, Vinnie, come on in. Are you all right?" Mom said, giving me a light hug.

"I just came from Dino's," I said, ending any questions before they began about liquor on my breath.

Keeping her voice low, Mom asked, "He okay?"

"Not really. Okay enough, I guess. He got drunk and passed out."

"Well, that's good for now," Mom said, the meaning clear: If Dino was asleep he couldn't cause any trouble. "I'm glad you're here, Vinnie. They're in there like a bunch of old tombstones, and about as talkative."

I gave her a smile and asked if she had anything light to eat, pushing the right button. If I made it to 115-mom would still be feeding me, by hand if necessary. But, by then, she would be putting paper clips and rock salt in the cookie batter.

"You go on in and I'll bring you something," she said, a hand lingering on my cheek.

Good ol' mom. I detected the lingering scents of gun oil and allspice.

"Vinnie," Dad said as I entered the dining room, expressing his curiosity.

"Thought I'd drop by." I nodded to Dom and Tony.

"Sit down. We're planning Spoons' funeral."

Which would explain the bottle of vodka on the table, half empty. I sat.

Even knowing that right now wasn't the best time to bring up the subject, no one else was talking so I figured why not? What I had on my mind would give them a break from this planning, though I was interested to hear what spin had been decided on—had Uncle Mike been killed in a car accident? Boating mishap? Fell off a nature trail? Mugged and shot by a dope fiend was what I was guessing.

"Dad, I need to check a guy out. Turns up I've got a cop living down the hall from me. Guy by the name of Alfred Clarence Eddy," and I spelled the last name.

"This cop giving you some beef?" Tony asked, looking more like an undertaker than ever tonight.

"Not at all, and I aim to keep it that way. To be forewarned is to be forearmed," I said.

"Say. That's good," Dom allowed. "Who said that?"

"Some dead guy," I replied, watching Dad give a half shake of his head and leaving it at that. Like the cop tailing me a few minutes ago, he had other fish to gut and I wasn't showing up on his radar.

Dom shrugged. Tony, though, was writing Eddy's name down. Looking up, he said, "I'll let you know tomorrow."

"Thank you, Tony. I appreciate it."

Dom poured me a shot of vodka, and Mom waltzed in with a bowl of zabaglione. I was running a real risk here of waking up tomorrow mirroring Dino.

I raised my glass. "To Mike."

We had a drink. And a few more. Another bottle appeared and we planned a funeral. It was going to be beautiful, that is if any of us were sober enough to show up.

CHAPTER 12

I woke up with my clothes on and my shoes off. Could have been worse. Could have been the other way around. I dimly remembered plonking down on the don's sofa last night.

My watch informed me that I could still catch breakfast at some greasy spoon, but my stomach vetoed any such nonsense. There was a good chance that the kids had burned the apartment building to the ground by now, so I just might want to check on that.

Now that my brain was waking up, I recall Dad mentioning doing some homework on an outstanding score. And I had a viewing, and a wake to attend this evening. And I needed to get in touch with DeeDee. And I had to pee. Where did it all end?

I left a note saying I would be back early this evening, then let myself out. There was a clinging mist falling that promised to get its act together, form a trillion committees, and rain like hell. The distant thunder was my biggest clue. Great. Just great.

By the time I arrived at my building I had a good start on a shower, lacking only suds. I had squelched through the dry cleaners, the deli, and the grocery store, dripping. Perhaps when I passed sixty I would be smart enough to have brought an umbrella. Or a hat.

Parked in the underground garage, I imagined that the kids would be sitting around the apartment watching TV. I was willing to wager that if our society took away all the TVs and PlayStations, took away all the unsmart phones, we would have warp drive and teleportation in three years. Less. As it stood, TV did make one helluva cheap nanny.

All my grand postulations proved faulty. When I entered the aerie, there was no noise other than the faint sound of rain falling on a slant onto the patio, heard through the closed glass door. I began a search for bodies and a note.

There were no bloodstains to be found other than the initial one left by myself when Paulie Jr. slugged me that first night. That fast-talking guy on TV swore his product would take out any stain from carpet, but he neglected to tell me how to remember to get some.

Ah—a note under the phone.

"Dear Vinnie—"

Maybe my mom dropped by.

Nope. It continued—"We're all going to the library. Be back soon, Sandra."

I felt like such a rotten parent, having wrongly lumped my kids together with the couch potatoes of America, or, in Paulie's pigeonhole, the beanbag potatoes.

The library. On foot in the rain. I had no idea where the nearest library was. I could go out looking for them after querying my computer, or I could get my shower taken properly.

First, I stashed the groceries and sorted out my dry cleaning. Next, I grabbed a restorative bottle of juice from the fridge and called DeeDee. She loved it when I called her at work.

"Damn, Vinnie, I'm really busy. Can't this wait?"

There. What did I tell you? Girl was crazy about me. "Well, it's good to talk to you, too, Sweetpea."

"I'm sorry. It's Monday, and I hate Mondays. And it's raining, and I hate rain. And I've got Mrs. Jacobs in the chair, and I—"

"Hate Mrs. Jacobs?" I helpfully supplied, a stab in the light.

"How did you guess?"

"Psychic. Look, I was thinking of you, and wanted to see if we could—" I began.

"You woke up with a hardon this morning, right?"

"Something like that."

"I don't know, Vinnie. I've got to go. Call me."

"Sure, Dee. Bye."

Huh. All of a sudden, I had kids who would rather read books than watch TV (practically un-American) and a girlfriend who would rather tease me than please me (totally American).

In the shower I allowed the water to run hot and long, wondering if it was possible to drain a tank at a place like this. Thirty minutes later the answer was still no, and I was tired of being wet.

I heard noise in the apartment, thinking *Please don't be the Dezzes*. I was born naked, but I didn't want to die that way.

"We're back!" Sandra called, obviously the de facto spokesperson for the trio.

"Out in a minute!" I yelled back. Either a minute or another thirty, the indoor shower being beneficial, but I was not making what I would call significant progress with my recuperation. I didn't see how the old dudes did it. They have probably been pickled for years and only needed the occasional top off.

I dressed in black and checked myself in my closet mirror. Perfect. The only items missing were a hoodie and a scythe.

The boys were in the front room not reading books. Maybe one of the coffee table's legs had been short. I found Sandra in the kitchen playing den mother.

"How about some fried chicken?" she said with a great smile.

Homemade. Cut up a naked chicken and fry its ass. Very cool. "Hey, that would be great," I said, the very idea getting my stomach back to thinking positive thoughts. If Sandra were forty years older I'd get her to adopt me.

"Need any help?" I felt obliged to ask, receiving a big fat no. Gratefully, I slinked away to stand in front of the balcony door, watching the rain come down as if India had misplaced its monsoon. I turned, and it dawned on me that all the kids were dry.

"I'm taking it that you guys didn't walk to the library," I said in a casual way. On TV I saw some wannabe flying squirrel turn about twenty revolutions in the air on a bicycle, nailing the landing when I was convinced he would nail his head into the ground. The boys didn't blink.

"No, sir," Chris said. "We drove."

Normally, I was unflappable. This morning's out-of-whackness I blamed on the tequila, the vodka, the rain, the long shower—basically, anything liquid. To hide my confusion I said, "You drove."

"We took my stepmother's car," Chris informed me.

I do believe I witnessed Paulie straining not to look at his new friend.

"And your m-, your stepmother, she was okay with that?" I asked, expecting anything other than the truth.

"I don't know. I suppose. I didn't ask permission if that's what you mean," Chris said.

Score one for the redheaded kid.

"She doesn't drive much, and never in the rain. It was a perfect time, and I'm a real good driver."

"Is that right, Paulie?" I asked for the hell of it.

"Made me wear a seatbelt to go three blocks," Paulie muttered playfully as Chris looked on, wearing a neutral expression.

"You're sixteen," I said. "You do have a license?"

"Yes, sir."

No, I was not going to ask to see it. As soon as he had said, "We drove," I admit that I had assumed that Chris meant, "drove a stolen car." Funny, huh? I had no doubts that Chris Lewis used turn signals, did no more than the speed limit, and had first checked the tires for proper inflation.

But the young devil who was me at sixteen had to see this through, this minor grilling of the suspects. Anyone would tell anyone else anything. Didn't make it true.

"So what kind of books did you get?" I asked, laying down trumps.

"*Magnetic Resonance Signature in Byfeeds / Enhancing Gain via Local Energy Sources and Why We Should Be Concerned*," Chris said, adding, "I know it's a long title, but the guy who wrote it is kind of a dork."

I slid my gaze to Paulie to see if I was being had. Paulie looked ready to yawn. Chris was watching the stunts on TV and glancing back to me, uncomfortable in that having asked, I appeared to either not like, or not appreciate his answer.

"Right. I've been meaning to get that one. What's the guy's name . . . it's right on the tip of my tongue," I said, giving myself a ton of leeway.

"Charles Van Ostenburen," Chris said. "You can borrow it if you want."

Only if one of those coffee table legs truly goes lame. Upon seeing the book, I had to rethink. Said coffee table leg would have to be amputated above the knee. Chris's library book would make a terrific doorstop, and an even better booster seat. Damn thing would choke a blue whale. When Chris got off the sofa and put Van Ostenburen's heavy reading into my hands, I mugged as if a hernia had developed during the handoff.

"It actually goes beyond what the title suggests," Chris said.

"Do tell, do tell," I mumbled, thumbing through the lengthy table of contents. "You like computer stuff, huh?"

"Yes, sir. I'm a little lost without my computer, so I thought I'd do some catching up."

"Catching up," I drawled instead of shutting up.

"Yes, sir."

"I've got a computer," I said. "In the bedroom."

By the unmasked look on the kid's face, what I had in my bedroom was an elderly dinosaur needing the mercy of euthanasia. Now that I was searching, I saw that Paulie did have a book for himself. It was lying on the floor on the far side of the beanbag. The cover had a spacewoman in a bikini. She was brandishing a ray gun, blasting a swarm of menacing alien rats. I nearly fainted with relief.

"Did you call your mom today?" I asked Chris.

"Better than that, I went to see her after Al went to work."

"That's what you call your stepfather? Al?"

"Not to his face, no, sir."

I kept my smile in check. "And she's, ah, not worried? That you've been away?"

"Not really. I told her it was safe and all, and that no one was drinking or doing drugs, and she said that was okay, but not to wear out my welcome."

Such concern. "And did she mention your stepdad? Him hitting you?"

Chris gave me an odd look, puzzled. "No, sir."

I had given up on Chris calling me Vinnie. His "sirs" were inspired, beaten in, I supposed.

"Later, we'll sit down and talk about it. But if you're sure your m-, stepmother is okay with it, then you're welcome to stay here again tonight," I said, afraid to have the kid think that I was taking him in for ever and ever. I did notice that he had changed clothes.

"Thank you. I appreciate it more than you know."

Sixteen, and he spoke as if he were thirty-six. I smiled and excused myself to the kitchen where I understood fried chicken and little else. I had a seat and found myself staring at yet another book. I spun it around to read the title.

"French," I said.

At the stove, Sandra said, "I've got French III coming up this year and want to get a head start. You know, so it will be easier once we get into it," and turned back to poking the chicken.

If the kids wanted to play Trivial Pursuit, I was teaming up with Sandra and Chris against Paulie. But at least I understood Paulie. Me, I took Spanish and hated it, getting good enough grades to order a taco and say thank you for it. Computers you turned on, clicked stuff, and paid the bill. Further than that, except how to plug one in, I would leave for others.

Which left me, well, not feeling old or stupid, but certainly feeling as if I were on the outside looking in. Whatever. I was good at what I did and, speaking of which, I needed to follow up on a lead to a lucrative score, seeing as how the home team was down a run.

Sorry, Uncle Mike. I meant no disrespect.

* * *

The "soup" in the chicken soup should not be considered essential, as chicken alone was known to cure every illness. I was living proof, a revived man, fortified with hot chicken and cold milk. I even choked down some broccoli, but that was because Sandra, the French-learning chef, had added cheese.

Next, having ascertained that Paulie had called his and Sandra's mother, I had locked the puppies in the kennel, bidding one and all adieu, putting my Nova "dans la rue." The fried chicken came with a French lesson free of charge.

The rain had slackened but not stopped. I liked the way drops beaded atop my car's wax job. Considering the start to my day, I liked everything I saw around me: crowded traffic, gray skies, and some crazy guy giving everyone the finger. That was what good fried chicken would do for you.

My destination was an address in Manhattan, not all that far from Dad's warehouse. But first, on impulse, I swung by Dino's. I wanted to make sure that in his drunken stupor he had not tried to slash his wrists with a butter knife.

For every forty-six raindrops I dodged making my dash from the car, I encountered forty-seven. At the top of the stairs I pounded on Dino's door.

"I don't know who that is, but if you don't stop hammerin' on my door I'm gonna beat the mother-lovin' daylights outta ya!"

Ah, good. He was awake.

"Vinnie? What the hell?" Dino called as he peered out at me with bloodshot eyes behind the lifted curtain in the door's window. Locks clicked and clacked.

I was horse laughing my cousin as immediately the locks clacked and clicked the opposite way after Dino had figured out that the door had been unlocked and he had locked himself in.

"Ha," Dino grunted. He finally opened the door to let me enter, without returning my smile.

"What time is it?" Dino growled.

"Seven o'clock," I lied.

"Seven o'clock! Are you out of your mind!" Dino hollered, his day off to a nose dive.

"Oh! Did I say seven? I meant twelve o'clock."

Dino turned and gave me a dirty look. His hair was all over the place and his wrinkled clothes made him appear even rougher. Dino unshaven was funny, but one of his socks was halfway off, and this I found funniest of all. I grinned and pointed to it.

"Fuck the sock! What're ya tryin' to do? Kill me? Geez, I got a hangover!"

"Sit down and I'll fix you something for it," I said, Mr. Calm.

Not needing a heap of persuasion, Dino did just that, collapsing onto one of the stools and draping himself bonelessly across the counter, looking like a gigged flounder.

I poured the miserable fellow a shot of tequila and slid it in front of where his nose was buried in the crook of one arm. Dino stared at the shot, and then up at me, the shooter.

"You're a funny guy, Vinnie Renaldi. A real funny guy."

Yeah, maybe not, but I did coax a grin from the sourpuss. He pushed the poison away and stood to ransack the refrigerator, coming up with a quart bottle of orange juice, opting for full-blown indigestion. I winced, watching him chug the juice in an attempt to put out the fire. Wiping his mouth, he looked at me, almost as if he were lifelike and not the desiccated husk I knew him to be.

"What?" he said.

"What what?" I countered.

"The fuck . . ." Dino muttered. "What's up? You come by to torture me, or is there an actual purpose to this harassment?"

"'Purpose to this harassment'? Dino, that's poetry."

He threw the capped o.j. at my head. I ducked, and then turned when I heard a crash of something out of sight and also made of glass.

"Good arm, sport. Take a shower and get dressed. We're going out."

"You—you're crazier'n hell. Goin' out's ass! You heard Uncle Ronnie! You think I'm gonna fuck up my only chance? Forgeddaboutit!"

I sadly gazed upon the ghost of the former outgoing Dino Puljoli. I shook my head.

"What's happened to you, Dino? Where's the fun loving, devil-take-the-hindmost kinda guy I used to drag out of bars by the ear, huh? You used to never take shit from nobody, no way, at no time. Am I right? And now what? You're scared to go riding around a little? Look outside, bro, it's a beautiful day!"

Ha. Made him look. The kitchen window was rain-streaked from the drenching gusts outside. He burped rather liquidly and looked a little greenish.

"Your old man—" Dino started.

And I flattened his protest, "Isn't here, isn't going to be here, and even if he was, so what? You aren't smart enough to think up an excuse that you have to be somewhere? Shit happens, Dino. You gotta get back in the game, kiddo."

As far as productive booster speeches went, this one was nice and short. It served to fine tune Dino's outlook toward the positive end of the dial. He wandered away to reestablish his ongoing campaign of laughing in the face of impending lung cancer, his smokes lying on the floor next to the recliner.

Dino fired up and blew out a prize-winning plume of Carolina's finest before frowning at the Marlboro in his hand, as if it could be at fault for the rotten taste in his mouth, being only partially correct.

"Come on, cuz. You can smoke that thing in the shower. We need to get moving," I said, adding, "Chop!" and snapping my fingers.

Dino gave me a look. "Someone spike your cornflakes this morning?"

"It was fried chicken, I'll have you know."

"What?"

"C'mon, Dino, move it! We're burning daylight here!" I said, watching the dismal doubt creep back across his face as he contemplated the nastiness outside.

"Daylight's ass," he muttered, yet moving in the right direction.

I cut on the TV and flicked channels for a couple of minutes before turning on Dino's sound system. He had sunk a lot of money into the equipment, nothing but the best. When the volume was cranked up you could start stuff sliding across Dino's counter top if it was clean, all that heavy vibration.

My back was turned, discovering what I could do with a couple of plastic cups, when there arrived a silence so abrupt that my ears were ringing and changing pitch. Dino was shaved and dressed, his dark hair wet. A new cigarette dangled from his lips.

He said, "Payback's a bitch, you know."

I smiled. "You ready?"

"No. What I am is crazy. Where we goin'?" he said, tucking an altogether different gun into his waistband.

"You'll see."

Unwilling to be badmouthed and shamed out of lameness twice in the same day, Dino shrugged and pulled up the collar of his windbreaker, ready to do whatever it was I had in mind. Like me, he didn't bother with an umbrella, hat, or frigging galoshes.

Besides, hats weren't cool unless you were in a band.

We were in a gang.

Dino said, "Let's do this," without knowing what the heck he was about to do. No wonder I loved this guy.

Inside the stuffy Nova Dino baked and relighted his freshly damp cigarette, filling up the interior with one monstrous exhalation. I was waving smoke around to no effect, trying to shoo it through a tiny gap in the window as the rain redoubled its efforts. Uh-oh—this was Dino's payback.

"You know that shit's going to kill you," I said, annoyed.

The rain was coming down hard, thunderous in the enclosed space. I peered through the smoke to see Dino watching my entertaining smoke-ridding antics.

"Vinnie," he said, "if I'm lucky these things will kill me. But I gotta be lucky just to live that long, eh?"

I cranked the Vinniemobile. "Good point," I said.

Chapter 13

Historically, hurricanes did an admirable job of keeping most New Yorkers off the streets of Manhattan. Likewise, blizzards with white-out conditions, and wind chills approaching minus forty, were likely to produce similar results. Other than those two exceptions all the sane and semi-sane pedestrians were to be seen on a daily basis bracing searing heat, numbing cold, and pouring rain without a second thought, people scattered all over like minnows scurrying before a net.

Unless you were lucky. Maybe Dino and I had talked it up in a good way. Across the warehouse parking lot that we were watching was a tractor-trailer with numbers matching those stored on my phone's notepad, and there wasn't a soul, doomed or otherwise, in sight.

Crossing my fingers, and praying to the patron saint of crooks, ol' whatshisname, I hauled ass away from that site to park at the first parking deck available. We caught a quick cab back to the corner of the warehouse. What had begun as initial surveillance had just turned into something else.

Paying off the cabbie, I told Dino to follow me. The information was good. This particular bone had been tossed Dad's way by a grateful, yet fussy, high-ranking boss. If we scored we only got a cut, but a portion of a fortune was okay with me.

Right now, backed up on the loading bay, our target truck was either being loaded or getting ready to be, perfect for us. I told Dino what I wanted him to do. Dino did not like my plan at all. I told him that I would be right there, practically speaking.

"But what if the guy checks?" Dino argued, the rain not dampening his sense of self-preservation. "If it was me driving the truck, I know I would!"

"Well, sure, Dino, that's a possibility. This is a gamble. That load wasn't supposed to go today if my intel is correct. They're in a hurry, which means that they're rushing the loading and the driver to get it on the road. It's now or nothing."

Dino looked skeptical. His doubts were understandable. This was not one of my patented, nearly foolproof plans. No, this was pure judgement call, and sometimes simple was best. Dissecting a golden goose to see what made it tick was a supreme brain fart.

"C'mon," I said, staying close to the side of the warehouse, getting soaked again but not caring. It wasn't as if this were January.

No one was around. The ramped bay just below the rolled-up warehouse door was wide enough for two trucks, but only "ours" was backed into place, fortunately on the near side toward our position. We could hear a forklift loading the trailer. A gap between the truck's left side and the huge bay door frame was a foot in width.

Peeking around into this space, I could see no one inside the comparatively well-lit warehouse, only hearing the forklift's whine deep inside as its operator made run after run.

"I'll check the cab. If someone comes, yell at the top of your lungs, 'The British are coming!' And then run."

Blinking rain, Dino gave me a tense nod.

I sighed. The poor guy was used to filling out paper forms. Dryer. Safer. And not half as rewarding as today's action was sure to be. In hindsight, I realized that I really should have grabbed Dino a small order of fries or something on the way over, because he wasn't looking so hot.

"I'm kidding, man. Relax. I'll be back in a flash," I said, winking.

Dipping my head around to peer through the gap, and seeing no one, I bolted for the driver's door, climbing up and in, ready for a pit bull or a mean trucker's wife with a baseball bat. Or both.

Scanning, ready to throw down and/or run, I was met with emptiness and the sleepy sound of rain pinging off the cab's roof. Quickly, I checked the cab's sleeping compartment which was the crux of my improvisation. To my utter joy it was empty, yet nice and rumpled. Fantastic. The driver was not a neat freak.

Using the cab's large mirror, I watched the narrow gap of warehouse and listened for the muffled entrance and exit of the forklift in the trailer behind me, feeling the jounce and shift. Counting down to silence, I sprang from the cab and flew to the side of the building, either the rain or circumstances keeping this parking lot free of activity. Dino was glad to see me, expectant now and a tad nervous.

"Keep your phone on vibrate," I told him, seeing that he still looked frail.

"Got it," Dino said in a firm voice.

"As soon as I buzz you, acknowledge with a text. Then secure your phone and make your presence known. Get a steady hold on something in case he tries to make you tumble by jamming the brakes. All right?"

"Right," Dino said, swallowing a lump of fear-flavored mucus.

"Don't worry. I'll be in my car right behind you."

Dino frowned, but did not argue such faint aid.

"Okay, so, you've got your gun on him but out of his reach. He's driving, cuz. He can't turn and jump you. Carefully, climb down into the passenger's seat. Do not allow him to touch the radio or use the phone—anything of that sort. When you see my lights blink, tell the driver to pull off at the next exit. Then I'll get ahead so he never thinks to connect me to you, so he can't get my tag. You see?"

"I believe so," Dino said, his frown redoubled.

Hm. "Okay. If he is stubborn, jam the gun right behind his ear and tell him that as long as he does exactly what you say that no one will get hurt. Right? Only if you feel you have to. Otherwise, keep your distance. Cool?"

Dino was moving his lips, repeating my instructions. The plan was simplicity itself. I gave him a minute, a short one.

"Got it?"

"Got it," Dino confirmed, Adam's apple yo-yoing.

"All right, once more. Your phone vibrates. Text me. Steady yourself. Announce yourself and caution the fucker. Get in the passenger's seat. Keep the gun low and tell him to keep his hands in sight on the wheel. Look for my lights. Next exit, follow me. I'll take it from there."

"Okay. Vinnie?"

"Yeah, cuz?"

"I think I'm gonna throw up."

He did look as if he might.

"No time," I told him. "Relax. You get to lie down at first while the loading is still going on. Take it easy for a while. But, whatever you do, Dino, do not sneeze and do not fart."

Dino nodded at the sage advice. I grinned, adding, "And do not puke. Okay?"

"All right, Vinnie," Dino said, silently swearing to never mix bourbon and tequila again.

I patted my cousin on the shoulder, the same method I used to calm him down when we were kids up to something and me the instigator.

"Ready?" I asked, my steadying gaze traveling between Dino's bloodshot eyes.

"Yeah," Dino answered, biting dry lips.

"Now, should the driver discover you before pulling out of here, put the gun on him and get out if you feel like it, or take him for the ride. Your choice."

"Geez, I'm nervous," Dino confessed, a raindrop on the end of his nose swaying side to side.

I did some extra shoulder patting. "You'll be fine. I've got to get to the car so I can follow." I peeked back into the foot-wide gap. Still clear.

"Go!" I hissed over the patter of the rain.

The look in Dino's eyes! Wow. If this heist panned out, and we both didn't go to prison, I was going to tell the story of the look in Dino's eyes until long after we were cackling old men. I continued to watch the warehouse as Dino scrambled up into the waiting cab, shutting the door with a soft whump.

An instant later I was running in the rain to get the Nova, counting on Saint Whatshisname to be worth his Holy Salt and not let me down.

* * *

The remains inside a carryout pizza box were spitting out virulent fumes that were all but visible. And if they were visible, Dino decided that they would be green, puke green. He shoved the box as far away as he could, which in the enclosed space wasn't far at all. Breathing through his mouth, he fought down another nearly runaway liquid burp, and busied himself by pulling the berth's comforter over himself.

Coming and going, the forklift rumbled as Dino searched for a favorable position, one that upon casual inspection would show him to appear as nothing more innocent than a lump of the super fluffy comforter, a lump ready to spring into action. He tried lying on his side, and found to his dismay that if he was thus discovered he would be lucky to even pull the trigger, let alone point a gun.

Not that Dino was at all anxious to shoot anyone. He had not the least bone to pick with any trucker, and would apologize if he got the chance should he have to pull the gun. Unless he had to actually shoot the fucker.

Rejecting all other possibilities, Dino chose to sit on the edge of the bunk, all the way to the right, ready to blend with the wall once Homer T. Southbound climbed aboard.

Feeling as if the evil pizza fumes were congealing inside his brain, Dino closed his eyes and tried to let the dancing raindrops upon the metal roof lull him into tranquility. Fifteen minutes later he was all but asleep when the sharp sound of the driver's door opening startled him into full wakefulness.

Scrunched hard as he could into the near right corner of the sleeper compartment, Dino held his breath as a clipboard sailed onto the berth, landing softly at a high angle atop the rumpled comforter.

A click and a loud exhalation announced that the trucker had lighted a cigarette. Dino, one step away from following suit, suppressed the urge, settling for a spell of deep, noiseless breathing, hungrily taking in the second-hand smoke, even if he caught a stray whiff of poison pizza as a consequence.

The big rig's engine erupted in a surge of life. The cab lurched, caught, and bucked as the two halves of the semi found conjunction. Gears were slapped into place as Dino held his position, one hand on the ceiling, and the other on the corner of the mattress, with both feet braced on a narrow sliver of floor.

By the time driver and stowaway were beyond the city grid and on the highway, Dino had relaxed enough to fit a cigarette to his lips, unlit, cold comfort the best he could do. Carefully, he snuck a peek at the driver whose face could be seen at a severely oblique angle.

Son of a bitch! It was a woman! A mean looking hard woman. She wore a gimme cap, and her hair was pulled back into a ponytail through the gap above the plastic sizer. The brown and gray ponytail created a lifting bulge over the roundness of the woman's grizzly bear humped shoulders. Damn woman was wearing a tee shirt revealing biceps as big as Dino's thighs.

Dino gripped his gun tighter and bit down hard on his filter.

* * *

I didn't have time to waste waiting on a passing taxi. I ran the quarter mile flat out to the parking deck where my noble steed was ignobly stabled. Utilizing a page of windblown newsprint, I scoured a rich oil stain on the concrete, transferring the grime onto my temporary tag as insurance against events to come.

By the time my shaking hands were attempting to fit my key into the door lock, I was overcome with dread that what malady I thought I had shaken was making good on its threat of a matinee showing. I was going to involuntarily withdraw my fried chicken from the good luck bank.

Fighting the nausea set off by my sprint, I jammed the key home into the switch. I was cranking on the wheel and gunning the gas the second the engine caught, roaring in a double circle toward the exit in a squeal of tires. I slammed to a stop to pay my fee, telling the attendant to keep the change. I recklessly roared into rainy day traffic that had best get the hell out of my way. Horns blared and tires barked, and so did the people around me in a variety of tongues.

I got their meaning just fine.

When I careened around the final corner before the warehouse, the eighteen-wheeler was pulling out. Breathing hard, I eased up on my forward rush to fall in behind my target, three cars back. I had not had time, or glances to spare, to spot Dino on foot if he'd had to abort the mission.

There was nothing to do now other than retame a wild chicken, and wait for the semi to gain the highway in Jersey. An almost-smile played across my face as I thought about Dino, about getting his paper-pushing feet wet. Scared spitless during the shootout two nights ago was one thing. On his own, with the score resting heavily on his shoulders, was something else again. I really should have encouraged him to pee in the parking lot while he had the chance.

Twenty minutes later I punched Dino's number. After I received his text reply I felt much better.

The text read, "1 4 the money. 2 4 the show . . ."

I liked that. He showed class.

Welcome to the minors, kid.

* * *

The vibration felt like the unexpected handshake of a rectangular electric eel, one that was instantly powered down as Dino's heartrate jacked sky high, the cigarette filter between his incisors all but guillotined.

Dino's thumb slipped executing the text message, causing him to retype. Boom, he sent the note, not feeling a fraction of the bravado that the message implied. "Ready" did not equate to "steady." Nevertheless, it was time to "Go."

Phone in pocket, Dino braced for the unknown with his left hand and leaned through the sleeper's opening. Going for a big surprise, Dino rammed his gun's barrel harder than intended into the lady trucker's head, a dangerous ploy, and one not at all necessary for his introduction.

"What!" yelped the driver.

Dino held on as the big rig rocked left and right.

"Easy! Don't freak out and you won't get hurt! Dammit, keep your eyes on the road. That's a gun against your head in case you don't know."

The woman was breathing hard, really hard, but the truck had straightened after several vehicles had made their displeasure known, the semi's jinking having nearly caused a pileup.

"What do you want?" the driver asked in fear. She was catching nothing more than glimpses of Dino's torso in her peripheral vision. But it was the weapon pressing painfully against her skull that captured the majority of her attention, with just enough left over to control the truck.

"Why, your full cooperation, of course. I get that and we have a happy endin'. How's that sound?"

"Good. Sounds good."

It was strange, this feeling of having conjured the essence of his cousin Vinnie, and how that borrowed persona had claimed him so fast. Dino considered the abrupt change in himself odd, yet welcome, gaining insight into his cousin's sense of control.

"Okay. My name's Richard. What's yours?"

"Duh-Diane," she said with a tiny stutter.

Dino wished he had a ski mask, a bandana, something. His new friend did not look the sort to be wearing pantyhose with which he might conceivably improvise. Even if she did, it would mean Diane negotiating her humongous self out of them and driving at the same time. Dino didn't believe that he would be able to handle the sensory overload that the pizza box miasma and Diane's pantyhose over his head would create. As an alternative, Dino messed up his hair. Then he altered his features by screwing up his face, putting on the mean mug.

"I'm climbin' down. You keep your foot off the brake. We don't want an accident, do we?"

"No. I'll be good," Diane said, ready to swear to it.

In a flash Dino was riding shotgun, saying, "Keep your eyes on the road. Look at me again and I make you pay for it," his inexperience making him dangerous in that he was apt to overact in a corrective situation.

Diane wondered what was wrong with the guy's face. It was all twisted, distorted as if he had been sucking on a lemon and had been slicing an onion at the same time, maybe sucking the onion as well. At least the gun was out of her face.

Dino spared a glance out of the large right-side mirror, seeing nothing of Vinnie, the angle set for the driver. With one hand to the back of Diane's seat, he looked at the image in her mirror, all to no use. He brought his phone from his pocket and texted, "cant c u. call instead of flash."

Ten seconds later he had a response.

* * *

Smiling at Dino's change up, I punched in a text telling him to take the next exit. I was thoroughly familiar with the territory, this stretch of Jersey being one long rundown realm of old redbrick buildings, aged shopping centers, and parking lots in varying states of disrepair. One more eighteen-wheeler around wasn't going to make a bit of difference.

When the truck curved onto the exit ramp I blasted around by using the paved breakdown lane, my eyes as much focused on my rearview as they were straight ahead. Past the stop sign, I pulled into a nearly deserted parking lot, huge by today's standards, a throwback to when this segment of interstate highway was a major manufacturing hub. Vehicles were parked at the far, southern end where remodeling had led to a few businesses taking advantage of cheap commercial real estate.

I waited for Dino's taxi to meet me where I had parked at the dilapidated northern end, having time to pull my black watch cap from the glove compartment and settle it low, down to my eyes before exiting the Nova. Using hand signals, I instructed the driver to back into the down-sloping loading ramp of a derelict warehouse. All the time I kept an eye on the lot's entrance for any curious cop. The rain was letting up.

"Leave it running and get out. No one is going to hurt you, mister," I called over the idling diesel, keeping my gun tucked away, shirt tail covering.

The driver climbed down and I immediately barked, "Put your hands down!" Sheesh! "Come over here, eyes on the pavement!"

Oops. Not a mister.

"Lady, this will be over soon. All we want is the cargo. You will get your truck back. No violence. You understand?"

Diane nodded, keeping a close eye on the scuffed toes of her boots.

"Okay. For the moment, I want you to stay right there." And to Dino I said, "Watch her. I'll be right back." Dino's shoulder got slapped to show my approval.

These old places were valuable to someone at the rate of pennies on the dollar, just not to me. A couple of kicks beside an old lock and the rusting chains fell away, along with the old lock and hasp, rotting wood all that had been holding together a set of double doors.

"Up here," I commanded, entering the body of the dinosaur.

Dark. Really dark, all windows boarded up. As my eyes adjusted I found plenty of discarded relics with which to truss up our obliging trucker. I used twine for the hands, securing them genteelly behind the back. The cowboy boots were removed before loosely tying the ankles. I kept glancing at Dino who was at the opening, hawking for me. A few lengths of old electrical cord were wrapped around the woman's thighs and torso and I was done.

I admired the woman's uncomplaining courage. For all she knew we were animals. Even if we were rapists of the most desperate sort, this poor lady was as homely as a badly used elephant seal—a poor way to talk about someone's momma, I suppose, but this, I had promised, was to be a factual account.

Taking a break from his hawking chores, technically a rookie mistake because trouble would find you much quicker if you dropped your guard, Dino asked, "You're not gonna gag her?"

"Why? Look around you," I replied, my outstretched hand sweeping through a full circle.

To our captive audience I said, "Ms.? I apologize for ruining your day, but I know that the warehouse you loaded at has insurance coverage. And I will release your truck in good condition after a couple of hours. Not only that, but I will not gag you. If you will be smart enough to wait here and not wiggle away I will phone the police and tell them where to find you—just as soon as I have taken care of the load. Do you follow?"

"Yes. Thank you."

"Eyes down, please."

"Sorry," Diane said. "I ain't never been hijacked before."

I shot Dino a smile.

"Okay. We're outta here. If you're stubborn, I suppose you could wriggle like a worm, and yell a bunch, and maybe get loose sooner or later, but you might hurt yourself in the process. My way is safer and easier on you. You have my word."

That made her laugh.

"Really," I said.

"Sorry," Diane said to the floor. "Couldn't help it."

I patted her beefy shoulder and tucked a loose strand of hair behind one ear.

"Let's go," I told Dino. "I've got the truck. Keys are in the car."

I remembered to wipe the gunk off the Nova's temporary tag as best I could. Dino followed me back to my dad's place of business where I quickly rounded up some helping hands, speed always a key factor in covering tracks.

Dino, right by my side, was positively glowing. You never knew when you got out of bed, or sofa, just how excellent the day would turn out to be.

CHAPTER 14

"Diapers?" Dino said.

I, too, was particularly gobsmacked at this particular moment. We had cut the seals, rolled up the trailer's door, and were confronted with palleted cases of brand-name crap catchers, wall to wall and stacked very tall.

I tugged Dino aside and told him to shut the hell up. Our warehouse deals in all kinds of goods. Yes, mainly restaurant equipment and office supplies, but it was a warehouse and warehouses did not give an undiapered crap what was put into them. Most employees here had no clue that Ronnie Renaldi's business was other than legit, and for that reason it was tug Dino to one side, or slap him to shut him up. I could damn well see for myself that we had a truckload of diapers and not the latest smartphones I had thought we were procuring.

Finding a suitable area to offload the cargo was not a problem. As light as the pallets were, the forklifts made short work of the truck's contents. A good thing, too. I could not get rid of this rig fast enough.

"Follow me," I told Dino.

Driving the tractor trailer, a skill I had learned as a teen right here in the warehouse's parking lot, I was pulling out and ignoring Dino's latest text asking, "We RNT going back there R we?"

The way that I saw it, it would be as easy to bring the driver back to her truck as it would to be to ditch it outside the city. Besides, it was also a matter of righting a wrong, implementing some assbackward chivalry. In no time, I had the trailer backed into where it had been a couple of wet hours ago.

"Dino, quick like, hop into the truck and wipe down anything we might have touched." I handed him a mini bottle of glass cleaner and a clean cloth from my trunk, telling him, "I'll be back in five minutes."

My cousin shrugged and got busy as I reentered the old warehouse to find the driver right where I had left her.

"Eyes away, please," I called from a distance. "I brought your truck back. Empty, I'm afraid, but this will save you time looking for it, all that red tape.

When we leave, you will still need to call the cops to square it with the insurance people. Okay?"

"You're not exactly my idea of a robber. Not that I'm complaining," Diane said, face averted.

"Yeah, I get that a lot. Okay, I'm going to untie you and ask that you walk to the far end of the warehouse before I leave."

"All right. But my feet are going numb. Bad circulation."

"Damn. Sorry about that. Here we go," I said, employing my trusty pocketknife, making short work of the binding cords and twine. I handed the driver her boots.

"Eyes closed. Give me your hand and I'll stand you up."

I had to put my back into it. At first, she was wobbly, so I steadied her until it became evident that she wouldn't topple.

"That way?" she asked, peering toward an unseen far wall and not at me.

"Yeah. All the way to the back if you will."

Slowly, she began walking. As the circulation came back she picked up her pace.

"Would you do me a favor, please?" I asked.

Without turning, she said, "Love to. What?"

I gave her a chuckle, which I believe she was after now that we were sort of pals.

"Tell the cops I was driving a white car?"

"My truck's really out there?"

"It really is," I said, glad that it really was.

"And no damage?"

"A little lower on fuel is all. I'll leave you a hundred dollars on your seat to take care of that."

"It damn sure ain't cheap," Diane said with feeling.

"Right. So. About the cops?"

"White getaway car. Three guys," she said.

"Four," I bid.

"Four," she concurred.

"Hispanic males," I added, going for broke.

"I like you, fella. Hispanic hombres it is. Make it two hundred dollars and I'll throw in names I overheard. You know, Pepe, Jose—"

"Hernandez, Fernandez, Mendez," I tossed in, helpfully sticking it to my enemies.

"Matter of fact, hold on a minute," I said to her back as I dug into my wallet.

I pulled out three hundred dollars. Walking up behind her I flashed the money over her shoulder.

"Take it. And, thank you. It's truly been a pleasure."

She laughed and said, "Thanks, Pepe," as she was walking away.

What a nice lady. If she wasn't so old and ugly I'd ask her out. Or maybe look her up someday and hijack her ass again for old time's sake.

"Any time, señora," I called, walking fast the other way.

* * *

I returned Dino back to his place in good shape, telling him that after I found a buyer for the diapers he'd get paid. How hard could it be? Babies weren't going to stop pooping anytime soon. The payoff just wasn't going to be as profitable as the expected zillion-dollar score would have been.

Dreading having to inform Dad that I had screwed up, I simply postponed the matter. I would let him holler at me later, even let him kick me in the pants if he figured I deserved it. Of course, by now I had easily ascertained where I had gone wrong, and there was no excuse for it, not even an Olympian hangover. I had been at the right warehouse, and I had identified the correct trailer. But I had not been thinking clearly, a gaffe that should haunt me for some time.

Trailers made good full boxes as well as they made good empty boxes, day in and day out. Just because the right trailer had been identified did not mean that our desired freight was early. I was early. After such an error there was no consideration of a second attempt. The cops would make the probable connection and have a laugh.

I briefly entertained a daydream in which I lobbed an anonymous tip to the Dezzes about a sure thing. With the cops clued in, it would be like a run-in with a buzz saw. Plus, Dino had told me about the gun he had discovered when wiping down the lady's cab.

Right now, I had other concerns to busy myself with, pulling into the mall to get a permanent tag for the Nova. I had already spent most of my afternoon after the diaper run getting my car a new paint job. Do not think that I trusted that lady trucker to lie to the cops.

Maybe she had, but in my line of work, being a nice guy is all good and well, yet being too trusting had a way of coming back around to take a bite out of your ass. My sweet baby was now an interesting Forest Green, still dark the way that I wanted her, but no cop would call it black, as in, "The getaway car was black." Business done, I made tracks.

Quite a number of vehicles were at Goldoni's Funeral Home in Brooklyn, Uncle Mike's old stomping ground. I parked next to dad's car, mine gleaming in comparison. Uncle Mike would have called the paint job spiffy. It was hard to believe that Spoons was lying inside dead.

Dino had wanted to come, but as far as anyone knew he was still at his place with his tail between his legs. It had done my cousin a world of good to get out today, curing a monster hangover and growing a thicker hide at the same time.

Inside Goldoni's everyone was rattling around, talking lively enough for sure, everyone having a good story to tell about Uncle Mike. There wasn't any booze in sight, though the atmosphere was polluted with all the boozy good wishes on everybody's breath.

I blindsided mom, kissing her cheek. Dad made a show of placing a paternal paw on my shoulder as a booster shot of intestinal fortitude, meaning well, but playing out a role nonetheless, the b-list don holding court.

Dom, Tony, other members of our gang, and assorted cousins, the usual cast for an event such as this, were dressed up, escorting aunts, sisters, nieces, and dates. Yes, dates. Some of these clowns would do anything to make an impression.

After making a few comments about how Uncle Mike would have appreciated the turnout, I separated myself to view the guest of honor, something I could not put off.

Coming up to the casket surrounded by large standing floral arrangements, I saw that no expense had been spared. The box itself was a top-of-the-line number, burnished steel or titanium for all I knew, fitted out with all the bells and whistles, polished oak handles and whatnots. We humans have been tossing a lot of wealth into the ground for millennia. Traditional stupidity I would suppose, but that was where the materials had come from in the first place, so, no great harm done. A lot of wasted effort, but no harm done.

Damn. Uncle Mike looked good. Too good to be dead. The Goldonis had done a superb job. I liked the way his hair was combed neatly for once, sprayed in place probably. Some well-meaning soul had placed a pair of silver spoons in Mike's right hand.

Son of a gun. The spoons got me. I found myself recalling all the good times, and there were tears in my eyes. Someone came to stand on my left. I didn't look up.

"He oughta not be dead."

I whirled. Paulie Pet held a dangerous look in his eyes. The big bastard stepped into my space, looming over me. I wondered if I was seconds away from getting into a tussle right here in Goldoni's, right over Uncle Mike's body. Taking a step back, I just nodded. It was true. Uncle Mike should not be dead.

Time slowed during which I began to open my mouth, to say something to Paulie, let him know that I appreciated me not being dead. Those hard eyes bored into mine. Now was not the time. And later was never going to be any better.

"What you did the other night . . ."

"Fuhgeddabouwdit."

Not likely. I nodded. It was done.

"You'll be at the wake?" I asked because there was nothing left to say. Other than being appreciative of my continued oxygen/carbon dioxide exchange, there was a small matter of my still wanting to massage Paulie Pet's scalp with a tire iron.

"Yeah," Paulie said.

I nodded again as if we had just concluded a meaningful dialog. Which, for Paulie and myself, I guess we had.

"See you there," I said and turned back to Uncle Mike, giving the cold cheek a last kiss.

"Goodbye, Uncle Mike," I said and walked away.

"He was a good soldier."

I stopped and looked back at Paulie Pet.

"Yes," I said. "Yes, he was."

Petralucci's jaw muscles were jumping with the grinding of his teeth. I spun on my heel and left, past my parents, past my cousins, friends, and associates, out the door to find some fresh air and allow my stomach to unclench.

* * *

The rain had stopped. That was the first thing that I noticed. Evening traffic passed on the street with tires throwing out a shush of spray like comet tails. Red taillights mirrored disturbed, elongated reflections trailing in their wake, beautiful in its own way. Humidity made itself known, invasive and clinging, like walking into a nonstop wall of spider webs.

Abundant lighting from inside the funeral home cast a golden glow across the rounded tops of the building's perimeter shrubbery, all greens turning sepia and black as the illumination dissipated toward the sidewalk where I stood.

I briefly thought of just leaving, going home, but, no, I owed it to Uncle Mike to attend the wake.

"Vinnie! Smoke?"

Then again, had I kept walking to my car I could have altogether avoided Mario. I had seen Dino's older brother inside Goldoni's, and had successfully dodged him before now. My meager luck for the day had all been used up.

"You know I don't smoke, Mario," I said, working hard to keep the annoyance I felt out of my voice. It was a given that Mario had not forgotten. This was a lame ploy to get me talking. He wanted something. So did his brother, but Dino was willing to work for what he got. Mario was a bum.

"Yeah, yeah, that's right," Mario said, lighting up and standing far too close, like we were running short of space outside.

I took a step to my left and pivoted, making it impossible for Mario to reinvade unless he wanted to make this look like a bad dance.

"So, what's new with you, Mario? You working?" I asked and watched for signs of squirming. Mario was my age but looked older. The booze and the dope had caught up and long passed his youth, leaving this shell in place to mark time until death, accomplishing nothing. In the lack of success blame was everywhere except where it belonged.

"Ah, you know, man. A lick here and a lick there. Life's good. What about you? Stayin' busy?"

The cigarette got sucked on hard, as if there was a time limit. I shrugged. The last thing I was going to do was talk shop with Mario.

When Mario got high, which was most every minute of every day he was awake, he was liable to run his mouth. He knew better, of course, but it was such a habit with the guy that he would never stop. There would be a surprised look on Mario's face one day when he got the third eye, someone, somewhere, sometime simply making a statement—enough being enough.

"Shame about Mike, huh?"

"Yeah," I allowed, making me wonder if he had heard something about his brother's involvement. When Mario went fishing for information this was the sound it had. I had no doubt that he bragged to all his doper friends of how he was in the loop. And, truth be told, he once was, years ago until he could no longer be trusted to show up, to stay awake, to stay shut the fuck up.

"You know, Vinnie, I might have something big going on soon. Figured maybe you'd like a piece of it."

I wouldn't trust this guy as far as I could throw both him and the whole of this building behind me. My fresh air began to lose its appeal. Yet, the part of me that was amused by the nerve of bull-shitters and habitual liars decided to stay tuned.

"Yeah? What's that, Mario?"

Believing that he had secured a nibble on his line, my cousin looked sly as he tried to set the hook, not that I believed for a second that there was anything to whatever he was about to lay out. There were people in this world who could not permit themselves to admit that their actions were transparent, that their house of cards was all they had left to shelter their self-esteem.

Hair coiffed to allow an old school curl to fall across his forehead, Mario had the same Italian good looks as his brother, but Mario's look was overdone, too retro, doing nothing to negate the lines on his face that should not be there for another fifteen years.

He said, "The cops are getting ready to take down the West Side Boys. Gonna be a free-for-all after the roundup. I'm talking about all their operations left unsecured. No one left minding the candy store, man!"

What the hell? I stared into the bloodshot eyes, Mario grinning large as if he had just let me in on the biggest secret in the history of the universe, or one so huge that no one could blame him for blabbing. The cops taking out the Boys? In one fell swoop? Not bloody likely.

"I'm telling you, man, it's gonna be easy pickings. We can hook up and score big time, man!"

He had crept back into my space, forcing me to look into his eyes which were, well, red, but also shining with excitement, figuring that I just had to jump in on this, his say-so being good this once.

"The smoke . . ." I said, backing off again, waving a hand.

"Aw, man. Sorry," He apologized, then leaned in again anyway, apology done with.

"So? You in? I'm telling you, Vinnie, this is a once in a lifetime opportunity. Big time, man."

I blew out a breath. "Who told you all this, Mario? The cops?"

The storm cloud racing across my cousin's features was ugly. And as soon as it arrived, Mario's animal cunning let it blow away, replacing the injury with an expectant smile, needing me for his own reasons. Big time.

"Damn, Vinnie, really? The cops? C'mon, man, you know me better than that! Not me, man, but yeah, the cops are the ones leaking it. I just heard, that's all."

Something was wrong here. Unsettling, there was a ring of truth to Mario's rap.

"No can do. One, Mario—cops. No way I'm getting involved, good or bad. And two—the Boys aren't stupid. Reckless? I'll give you reckless, but the Boys are on point. Reckless is not the same as stupid. Those fuckers are crazy as hell.

I appreciate it anyway, Mario," I said as a salve to soothe the blood relationship, and as a wedge into opening a path out of this uncomfortable conversation.

Mario box-carred his cigarette, flipping the short onto the lawn where it landed upright, refusing to die, a red coal now and looking like a littered dog turd come daylight.

He held up his free hand, saying, "All right, all right," turning his head and eyeing me on a slant as if to suggest that he could not believe someone would walk away from such a lucrative deal, pitying the fool.

"If you change your mind, call me."

"I've got to get back inside, Mario. You take care of yourself."

"Yeah, me, too. I'll walk with you."

Halfway up the sidewalk I halted, Mario two steps ahead before he realized I had stopped.

"I just remembered. I've got to get something I came out for. I'll see you inside," I said, almost hating myself for feeling a need to resort to such an immature tactic to dislodge this leech, but better this than more awkwardness later.

Mario looked as if he would follow me to the Nova that, thankfully, he was still in the dark about, probably thinking that I was heading for Dad's car, which previously would have been in character. A frown crossed his face as he considered that he was reading this scene correctly, that he was being ditched, before electing for his ego to intervene, going with my less hurtful spin on reality.

"Right, man. Catch you inside."

I nodded and headed for the parking lot, thinking "Not in Goldoni's you won't," hoping like crazy that Mario wasn't going to follow the crowd to the wake.

Fat chance. There would be free booze.

It seemed to me that I could almost see Uncle Mike shaking his head. And grinning like hell.

CHAPTER 15

Smalley's had been no less than a charmed haven for me all my life. As a child I had come here with my parents, if such was the case that it was easier to tote me along than not. Smalley's was a bar that existed as bars are intended to be . . . dark, secretive, and filled with old wood that would last until the sun went red giant on us. The punched tin ceiling was cleaned occasionally of its accumulation of smoke residue, and I would love to see the Mayor Almighty make an issue out of it—the smoke, not the tin ceiling.

Smalley's. Lots of liquor bottles on thick glass shelves, the long backing mirror little more than a distorting effect, the joint too dark and the shelves too cluttered for anything ethereally substantial as an entire reflection of either bartender or patron, and no one had ever come into Smalley's to stare at themselves. High-backed deeply cushioned booths added another earthy layer of privacy, and the handcrafted stools holding station at the long, solid bar were as good as islands on an ordinary evening, everyone's business their own.

This neighborhood institution, this cloistered bar, was an excellent place for deal making, and an ideal spot for idiots such as Mario to see what the old days were like when you could smoke like a chimney as long as you didn't run your mouth at the same time. If Mario did show up it wouldn't be for long, bet on it.

I was early, nodding to James behind the bar. James was a wide man, not tall but thick, with a naturally bald head, not the shaved crap today's wannabe tough guys felt compelled to work at. James might be late sixties, but might well be older, and it wouldn't do to ask. The guy had been behind the bar since I was a little doofus.

When I approached the blackened, highly polished bar, James looked at me as if he had seen me just last night, when the last time I had been in here had to have been five, six months ago. Too damn long.

"A short one," I said, going with beer, there being no way of dodging shots of firewater once the gang arrived from Goldoni's. I would sip and keep my own company.

James pulled my beer, a good Irish stout, and perceiving that I was yet in a talking mood, moved down the bar to do something else, anything else. Smalley's had long been a neutral bar between the city's Irish and Italians, a whispering haunt where quality whiskey and beer were common ground enough for all. You started trouble here, you were banned for life, believe it.

A few old-timers were scattered among the booths, talking low in an ageless manner. It was so dark in the bar that when the front door opened, the close ambient streetlight was bright by comparison. Vampires and dum-dum Goths would love this place, but either had better not walk through that door. Half the old dudes in here were carrying. I did not need to check to know. Me, I always carried.

The stout was good, heavy and dark. I would use it as a chaser once the merriment began. My dad didn't know for sure when wakes became a tradition with the Renaldi clan, and I use the word clan for a reason. Not that Uncle Mike was a Renaldi, but, being a part of our gang, he understood that when his time came there would be numerable toasts made to his memory right here, lacking only the body for a bona fide wake; but concessions had to be accepted so that hard lines would not be drawn.

For myself, I considered the practice of celebrating the deceased most civilized, perhaps one of the finest traditions mankind's mind could conceive: immortality on the lips and past the lips. Cheers.

A paler glow shone briefly throughout the bar, the slight increase in luminosity announcing new arrivals. Fractured reflections of several individuals broke up and partially reformed across gaps along the lengthy mirror's irregular clean spaces, dark and anonymous save for a minimum estimate of height and a rough guesswork at number. I maintained my forward gaze, listening, preparing to have my small reverie become as shattered as the ghostly images floating behind me.

"Vinnie? What's this?" Dom said from beside me, referencing to my choice of refreshment while squeezing my shoulder. "James? Whiskeys. We'll let you keep count."

And that was pretty much the story to come, no one counting shots, and no one worried about tomorrow. Uncle Mike did not get a tomorrow, so we would live tonight as if we did not get one ourselves.

One hour into the evening, I found myself in a booth with Tony Funicella and my mom opposite me. Dad had wandered off to address some minor issue with a lackey, still politicking, keeping score of who was here, and perhaps more importantly, who was not. For once I was glad that Dino had stayed away, and that I had not insisted on being hardheaded.

"Your cop's dirty," Tony F. said once I asked.

Mom watched my face for how I took this news of my new neighbor, concerned but unworried. She was wearing a black pantsuit tonight that I had never seen, and which flattered her, highlighting the white paint of her wings, as well as contrasting with her healthy glow from working in her garden.

Tony F's appearance on the other hand seemed as if Goldoni's' staff was down by one, caught up in the general move here to Smalley's.

"I'm not shocked," was my answer. I had a strong buzz and the night was still young. Either I faked a few toasts tonight or slept it off wherever I fell.

"He's been on their Internal Affairs radar numerous times. Used to be a lieutenant," Tony said, speaking in a monotone against the growing roar of the wake, Smalley's at the moment being livelier than it had been in some time.

"It fits with the way I've got him pegged. Got a bio?" I asked. Had I asked for a curriculum vitae, Tony would have made certain that Mom knew he considered me a smartass and not past spanking. If Uncle Mike had been the fun non-uncle, then Tony F. had been the stern disciplinarian, as if my dad had not been serious enough.

"Guy was a freaking marine," Tony said after another shot of whiskey was raised and annihilated following the latest paean eulogizing the late, great Spoons Spinoza. "The usual jarhead crap. Tough guy then, gonna be a tough guy cop. Story is that he put his mitts on an assemblyman's son, busted him up. Then it's suspicion of this and suspicion of that. Dope, prostitution, gambling—not handling, shaking down."

"Well, I knew there was no way he was living at my digs without something going for him. He's not connected, is he?"

"This jerk? Nah. Way I hear it, he operates out of some good ol' boy loyalty bullshit. He's got his time in, but you can't make the squeeze if you don't carry the stick no more. He'll retire when the higher ups have had enough. Until then, he's seen as useful, knows his way around if you know what I mean."

"Sure, I do. Thanks, Tony," I said. "You need something? Mom?"

Both said they were fine, and not for the first time did I wonder if there was anything between these two. Nothing I could put my finger on, and the odds were long against it. Yet, at gatherings, they gravitated toward each other, like magnets, or binary stars. Something else—if it was true, then I did not want to know, period.

I caught sight of Mario in the back of the crowd and told Tony what he had said outside Goldoni's.

Tony F. stayed quiet for a long moment, looking at me and away. Mom used the time to sip a whiskey, no shots bolted by her, and no peer pressure felt to cause her to do so. She would give her own respects to Uncle Mike by not getting shitfaced.

Finally, Tony turned his funereal countenance my way again and said, "There's some talk."

"And the Boys are heads up with it?" I asked, thinking back to the way Mario had been so frigging sure of himself.

"Can you imagine that they're not?" Tony said, having a wonderfully economic way with words. Sometimes.

I pushed out my cheek with my tongue, reflecting, pondering why now, and why the city would suddenly get a hard-on for a gang whose violence, though legendary, was strictly business. Why would the authorities push it?

"No. I believe I see your point," I told Tony. "Where are you going to go, right?" Meaning that the West Side Boys were not likely to run away. Run where?

The slimmest of smiles broke across Tony's face for his gifted pupil. His chest swelled with additional stale air, rendering the old wardrobe nearly lifelike.

And Mario wanted to be in the middle of a war? Shit. That's what being stupid would get you—killed.

My mom laughed. I turned in the booth to see that Dom Bartlemeo, having procured a pair of spoons from James, was doing his best imitation of Uncle Mike. Lips wrapped under and above his teeth, eyes closed like he was straining to take a dump, banging the spoons against his chubby thighs and the heel of his off hand, poorly. It was just the thing for the moment.

I forgot for a spell that people wanted to go out of their way to get killed, while killing themselves in a million little ways on a daily basis, forgot my own ineptness—scoring a load of diapers rather than top-end electronics, and, most importantly, forgot that the last time we did something like this Uncle Mike was playing the spoons, not Dom.

Chapter 16

It was stupid of me, I admit it, but I drove home anyway. My reaction time wasn't the best, but I wasn't seeing double, concentrating, up on the wheel, radio off and muttering encouragement to myself. I had probably escaped Smalley's just in time, imagining those left behind dropping like stunned flies.

Parking my car was real fun, not. The trip to the seventh floor was like that of a sailor first stepping off a small ship after a long, rough sea voyage. Letting myself into my apartment, I was grateful not to have hardwood floors, the plush carpet deadening my clumsy steps. The place was dark except for the small glow of light above the range. Complete quiet reigned.

I froze as if another tiny bulb had winked into existence above my cartoon self. Imagine: I drove all this way, taking appalling chances with life and limb, mine and others', risking jail, only to come home to the realization that I had no adequate place to lay my spinning head. There was a decent chance that it would be funny tomorrow, or later this morning I should say, but right now it just plain sucked. I briefly considered spreading myself out upon a patch of vinyl kitchen flooring, and rejected that bad idea as grossly undignified. Damned tempting though.

Sighing, I made for the bathroom and peed, feeling a bit better. Checked my face in the mirror. Shouldn't have done that, I looked terrible. Headed for the kitchen remembering I had forgot to flush. The hell with it.

Sixty seconds later I was back at the hall door with a cold beer and a pack of cheese, quiet as an inebriated church mouse. A million miles later I was reunited with my car, sitting behind the wheel in the basement parking lot, radio on and working a mouthful of cheese.

When I woke up, the radio was still on. The wrapperless cheese was sitting on the dash like a mini white seesaw, teeth marks grinning at me like a home-schooled dental impression. I straightened in my seat, my heel knocking against the beer bottle. Taking inventory in the rearview mirror revealed zero improvement over the last check. My next mistake was in taking a large bite of the air-aged cheese with zip to slake my thirst.

I looked at my watch. Band. My watchband. Darn thing had got itself spun around. I respun to see 9:17. Good. The kids would be up by now, watching toons and eating Fruity Pebbles.

That's funny, I thought upon opening the apartment door. There came no sound of animated mayhem, no popping of anything frying in the kitchen, not the slightest peepage of existential teenage angst-related commotion.

"Honey! I'm home!" I tried, door remaining open as a point of instant escape.

Huh. No groans from within accompanied my dulled and throbbing wit. I stepped into the front room. No one. I walked past the kitchen (no one) and down the hall.

"Sandra?"

Nothing. I knocked on my own bedroom door, waited a few seconds, and tried for an answer again. Gun leading, I opened the door, my disturbed imagination ready for a bad paint job on the walls.

There was nothing out of place except missing children. The bed was neatly made. Everything, the whole place neat, was Sandra's doing, but there could not be found any sign that the kids had even been here last night.

Which meant a couple of things the way I saw it. For one, it appeared that I most likely could have slept in my own bed last night, dammit. And another—even for as short a time as I had sheltered these kids, it seemed unlike them to abandon their refuge without saying something to me.

True, I had been gone most of yesterday and all of last night, but that didn't make me a bad parent, did it?

Crap.

I began yet another search for a note explaining that the kids had taken a trip to the library in Alexandria, Virginia, or Alexandria, Egypt. A tour led me to inspect the refrigerator, coffee table, end tables, nightstands, dining room table, medicine cabinet, knickknack drawer, any- and everywhere. Nada. Rethinking, I rushed back into the bedroom where my corroded memory nudged me. The red light was blinking on my answering machine.

One of my bad feelings had me by the throat. As much as I did not want to, I stabbed the playback button.

"Mr. Renaldi? This is Chris Lewis. I'm afraid that Paulie and I have been arrested. Sandra is out trying to gather money for bail without going to either her parents or mine. If you, sir, could provide that service, I can and will pay you back. I apologize for this abuse of your generosity. I am also concerned that the Petraluccis' father will find out first. Either way, thank you."

What in the hell had these kids got themselves into? Dope? Shoplifting? Chris taking his stepmother's car? Paulie taking Sr.'s life? Could be most anything, except the latter. I needed to wake the hell up.

So. Chris mentioning Paulie Pet finding out whatever there was to find out didn't worry me half as much as did this bad mental image I had of a thirteen-year-old girl without resources attempting to raise bail. Unless she signed on as a sous chef at a Parisian restaurant, and got a large advance on her first paycheck, I would say her options were sorely limited.

Hm, Paulie's trouble with Sr. . . . What about Chris's trouble with his stepdad, a cop. A psycho cop. A dirty psycho cop. Crazy and bent.

Hangover set aside, I ran through the situation, ready to rush to—where? Dammit, Chris had not said. He had also neglected to say what they had been arrested for. Okay, bail implies jail.

I picked up my phone and began to connect with information when I clicked off. Setting down the phone, I dug into my wallet to find the straightened, once rumpled, card of Cara Beely, the guilt-tripping, social-working, sad-eyed beauty who had chiseled open my head the last time Paulie had been picked up.

Wait. I didn't know if I needed to check with jail operations or juvie. Confused, I punched in Beely's number.

"Social Services."

Just that. No name, no, "How may I help you?" Service my ass.

"Yes. Cara Beely, please."

"Hold one moment."

"I . . ." started to say, to declare that I would rather not hold. In my experience, when someone asked me to "hold one moment," what they meant was half of forever.

"Cara Beely. Who's calling, please?"

Ah. Fifteen seconds of forever. "Ms. Beely, this is Vincent Renaldi. I'm calling about—"

"Oh, yes, Mr. Renaldi," Beely said as if my name had been on the tip of her tongue, cutting me off, but what the heck, she had said "please," putting the service back in social. "I was hoping you would call. Paulie said there was a chance you might."

Paulie now, not Paul.

"You've talked to Paulie," I had to assume.

"Oh, yes. We had a very interesting and long conversation, Mr. Renaldi. As a matter of fact, you might say we had a revealing talk."

Uh-oh. Paulie Pet's kid ratted me out.

"Oh? Really?" I forced myself to say, mainly for lack of anything clever or of substance. With this burden of a hangover, two in a row, I found myself operating at around 14-percent capacity. I needed six hours of sleep and another bite of cheese. Maybe a couple of beers.

"Oh, yes," Beely said, being either entirely too cheerful, or a good-looking smartass. "Albeit in a, mmm, generalized way, so to speak."

Ah! Paulie Jr. had not finked on me. Just had made allusions, that is if Beely was playing this straight.

"All very interesting I'm sure, Ms. Beely. What exactly have the boys got into trouble over?"

"Trouble? I guess that's one word for it. Try grand theft, Mr. Renaldi."

I would try not to blow my cool was what I would try. "Grand theft, eh? And what is the bond set at?"

"Hasn't come up yet, Mr. Renaldi. But I should think if a body wishing to post a bond were here within, say, another hour or so, a figure might possibly be available by then."

"I see. Is my information correct? Was there a second juvenile arrested with Paulie? On similar charges?"

"My, you do have good information. One Christopher Lewis. A rather uncommunicable boy. Polite, but tightlipped would be the best way to put it, I believe. I kind of like him, Mr. Renaldi. But, between you and me, these boys seem to be walking into an inordinate number of doors, wouldn't you agree?"

Ms. Beely was a comedian. I was looking for a simple yes or no. "Picked up on the same charge as Paulie?"

"Like digging goldfish out of a tank," Beely said.

"I take it that's a yes. Grand theft."

"Bingo."

Rather than ask, I took that as a yes as well. "Ms. Beely, either I or my lawyer will be down within the hour. Um, same place as before?"

"Why, yes! Small world at that. And, if it's no trouble, Mr. Renaldi?"

"Yes?"

"If it is you who shows up? A large cappuccino with extra whipped cream and sprinkles would be appreciated. Bye!"

I stood staring at the phone in my hand for several seconds. My day was not off to a spiffy start. First, I would brush the cheese paste out of my mouth. Second, a shirt without wrinkles would be nice. And third, I needed to unlimber my fingers because I was going to strangle both those kids.

* * *

These benches in the waiting area at the juvenile justice center looked as torturous as they felt, lacking only milky varnish, splinters, and protruding rusty nail heads to make their evil presence complete.

After I had given my name to the—to use the term loosely—"lady" at the counter, I doubted, instantly so, that she would be with me "in a minute."

Now, I had been wrong before, and recently, I'll admit, but the so-called "lady" and her "minute" and the social services telephone operator's "moment" were light years apart. There was no "light" moment to speak of and, blazingly ironic, time travel could not be invented, or reinvented, fast enough to suit.

And another thing that I would like to get to the bottom of was just what precisely we Renaldis were paying our lawyer for. His office said that he was out. I made it known to his secretary that his continual "out" could cover quite a bit of territory: outside, out and about, out of town, or an out I could currently use a dose of—passed out.

Our guy's secretary, receptionist, deceptionist, or whatever the hell she was, asked if she could take a message after totally ignoring my attempt to pin down her slippery definition of where Mr. Big Shot Lawyer was. I told her no, no message, but thanks anyway, explaining that if he was never around when I needed him, that I guess I was just out of luck.

Being a graduate of the Secretary School of Sarcasm, she remarked how clever that was of me, to which I told her to kiss my ass and hung up. I had no illusions, sure that this little exchange would come back to haunt me. I was certain to get chewed out for heisting diapers and mouthing off to our mouthpiece's telephone squeezy.

I certainly felt foolish babysitting this large coffee I had picked up for Beely, cappuccino, hot chocolate, whatever. Not wanting to waste time, I had bought myself a coffee to go as well, a nodding concession to both the new day and my need to rehydrate. Initially, I had no intention of drinking Ms. Beely's concoction, more milkshake than coffee, for crying out loud.

Throat still parched, and tongue swelling, I lifted the lid and grimaced at the drying out white goo that some time ago had been whipped cream with sparkly colorful crap floating atop it, but was now looking a lot like styrofoam shot through with last New Year's confetti. Close to death, I tried a sip. All I got for my trouble was a terrible start to softening up by beard for a much-needed shave.

I wiped the mess off and sadly studied the offensive cup in hand like a dim monkey clutching a handful of grapes that now would not fit through the neck of the jar. In the fable I believe that the monkey eventually figured it out. Me, I was still sitting on the butt-numbing bench, frowning, when the cup was snatched out of my hand, problem solved.

"Hey, thanks!"

From long experience in cautioning myself not to be surprised, I watched as Cara Beely magicked a plastic spoon from her suitcase-sized purse and stirred the shit out of the coffee-shake before sipping. She made a moue and wrinkled her nose.

"It's not hot," she said.

I made a show of looking at my watch. The liquid party-in-a-cup may no longer be hot, but I was.

"Really?" I said. "That's a puzzler. It was an hour ago."

"Bad day, Mr. Renaldi?" Beely said with far too perky a grin on her wide-awake face.

Bad day, long day—what was up with this social person? Whoa. Careful. She might be a carrier.

"Not at all," I lied, smacking my mouth to keep my tongue from sticking to the roof. "Got any gum?"

"It's possible," she said, sitting down beside me and handing me her cup to hold as if I were her personal assistant.

Waiting. Waiting. Still waiting.

"How much longer?" I asked, done in by the bench and the exponential nastiness that arrived following twenty-four hours since any previous shower, and tired of spitting dust balls.

"Patience. There's a lot in here," Beely said, going in deep, using one hand and wrist to dam a tide of miscellaneous items as she dug around the lower geologic layers of her shipping container.

I had a sick feeling that I would soon be picking lint and ancient whoknowswhat off any piece of fossilized gum unearthed from that seaman's trunk.

"That's not what I meant," I said. "The kids? How much longer do you think I'll have to wait to find out what their bail is?"

"You mean you're still . . . oh, here you go! How's that?"

The dubious stick of spearmint had one end crumpled as if someone had mistaken it for a pogo stick or a test dummy for front end collisions. An unholy discoloration stained the wrapper's other end. Could be coffee. Could be worse. I said thanks. I was desperate.

"Let me go check. I'll see what I can do," Beely said.

She had taken several steps before abruptly turning back. Her big eyes grew somewhat bigger, damn near bugging out as she said, "You have plenty of money? These two will be a teensy bit more than the last one."

Beely was holding her finger and thumb a half-dozen molecules apart. There was some sort of inverse square ratio implied, no doubt. I told her that I would just play it by ear. I got okey-doked.

Damn gum was so historic that it had fallen into fragments once bitten. At least it caused me to salivate. I tried to use my freshly moisturized tongue to corral all the bits and pieces to work them into a cohesive whole. This could take some time. Luckily, I seemed to have too much.

Bored, I tuned into The Beely Show, the star's heels together were beginning to lift off the marble floor. Her wheelless barrow was perched ungainly atop a shallow ledge of counter, in danger of collapsing government property. Firm fingertips were seen gripping the counter's edge to guide a boost, going up even further on tiptoe to look the demon behind the counter in the eye, still at a disadvantageous angle but doing her best. Nice form.

Busy chomping into shape one from many, I continued my study of Ms. Beely. She was wearing a pastel peach dress with subdued white piping today, the hem knee length, but with her exaggerated attempt to overcome a personal altitude deficit, her dress in back was riding up her thighs, admirably so. I followed that line, lingering on the hips, and that was where my gaze was frozen when Beely suddenly twisted her torso, catching me throwing my tongue back and forth at a feverish rate while staring at her ass. Heh heh.

She did this thing with her fingers, forking them at me, and causing my eyes to rise to the height of her own before reversing the fork to her own narrowed eyes. I tried to smile without losing track of stragglers.

In another minute she was walking back toward me.

"I, ah, was admiring your dress," I said in defense of my being busted. "Vera Wang?" I asked gummily.

"Wally World," Cara said, ignoring my lust. "They'll be ready in a few. It seems that there was a question of how much to set bail because of the estimated price of the merchandise."

"Ah, merchandise?" I asked.

"The Rolex watch the boys were attempting to sell."

"The Rolex," I repeated stupidly.

"Mm-hm. The boy's age aroused suspicion. The jeweler called it in and a detective dropped by as the boys were stalled. I may not have some aspects entirely correct, but it seems that according to this Christopher Lewis, he did not know that the watch was stolen merchandise. Since he doesn't have a record the judge reduced bond for both of them."

"They weren't trying to pawn it. And they weren't acting as if they were trying to fence it. They were trying to sell it outright?" I said, fitting the pieces.

"I don't know, Mr. Renaldi. But what would a sixteen-year-old boy be doing with a Rolex?"

"Good question, Ms. Beely, and one I would like an answer to."

The crap gum was turning into ooze, easily the worst gum experience of my life. Beely was watching me the way a robin studied a bug before pouncing. Could be the rugged unshaven look I had so carefully cultivated accidentally.

"What?" I said.

"Oh. Just wondering. How do you know Christopher?"

"He's a friend of Paulie's. From what I gather they met only recently."

"Oh?"

"Yeah. Seems like a good kid."

"Yeah? Mr. Renaldi, you have a lot of friends Paulie's age?"

"What! No!" I spluttered. "I mean, not like you mean."

"And how do I mean?"

I counted to four, as close to ten as I could get. "Look, Beely."

"Call me Cara."

What! "I am not that way—" I began.

"And what way is that, Mr. Renaldi?"

"You know damn well—"

"May I call you Vincent?" Beely interjected.

"Would you please—"

"Depends on how you ask," Cara said.

The little woman was running circles around me. I quit trying to make sense. It was like attempting to claw your way out of a rip tide; all you did, if you were stupid, was to flail around with zero forward progress until you were spent.

Beely was smiling real big. Maybe I had made her day.

Slowly, I said, "I am not a child molester."

"Didn't think so, but still, it's nice to hear you say it. Paulie won't come right out and say it, but I get the impression you've been a good influence. Have I got that right?"

Being careful, unsure of my legal footing, especially since I seemed to have a lawyer who I shall classify MIA: Mostly Invisible Asshole.

"I hate to see kids getting hurt," I said.

The big eyes softened, still amused but human, very human, very dark and deep. I was either going into a trance or falling asleep.

"You have very nice eyes," Beely said.

"I was about to say the same thing."

"You were about to say you have nice eyes?"

Loved to play with words, this girl.

"Would that make me shallow?" I asked, working my mouth like a dog chewing grass.

"Oh, yes."

"Then I meant yours."

"Ah."

"Hm," I kinda said.

"Renaldi. Vincent Renaldi to the desk."

The ersatz "lady" was staring a hole through me. Ten paces away. I could have heard her clearly without her use of the public-address system.

"You look like a big spender," the counter devil said with a smile like a mule chewing on briars and liking them just fine, another Uncle Mike-ism. "Bond for both?"

I glanced over the paperwork. Reduced, Beely had said. The courts were a racket. It was all right, though. I planned on taking it out of the boys' hides. Then again, there must be a perfectly logical explanation.

Out came my wallet. From long habit I kept it stacked with hundred-dollar bills, plus whatever paper change accumulated until I cleaned it out. I could feel Beely's presence behind me, slightly to one side, just out of my field of vision, watching the money being counted out.

Maybe I would have the boys scrub my kitchen and bathroom with toothbrushes. But, no, I had a feeling that Chris's stepdad had likely beaten me to that one, the jarhead psycho.

"Be just a moment," the lizard lady told me with pleasure, reptilian eyes sparkling, wanting to cackle like a lady chicken lizard should. I wondered how many people over the course of a year attempted to dive over the tall counter to get to her.

I collected my receipt, traded goodbye sneers, and turned to find Beely looking at me funny. The dough. Had to be the dough.

"What do you do for a living, Mr. Renaldi?"

"I thought it was going to be Vincent and Cara," I said, lobbing the ball of fuzziness back over the net into Beely's court.

"Okay. Vincent—"

"Vinnie," I amended. "Vincent" conjured images of bandaged ears and classic B-horror.

"Vinnie," she tried out, letting her interrupted question stand.

"Restaurant resupply and office furniture. I'm in sales and distribution." Or was it vice-president of human relations? I can't remember, but Beely didn't know that.

"Really? You don't look the type."

"And what type is that?" I asked innocently enough, putting a spin on the ball.

"Touché, Vinnie."

Somehow, unfelt, there must have occurred a significant seismic event, the floor jiggling somehow to bring the two of us closer together without conscious movement. I could smell her perfume, her shampoo, her dumpster on a strap. It was all very intriguing.

"Do you like—" I started to say.

With the perfectly lousy timing of a typical teenager, Paulie Jr. hooved into view, followed seconds later by Chris, both looking a trifle worse for recent events. No smiles were on display. I noticed a fidgeting, a sense of the boys knowing that they had got lucky, yet had to be wondering at what price.

"What kind of bird doesn't fly?" I said, trying the old jailbird joke on the boys. I got a smile from Paulie and a truly puzzled expression from Chris. Green as grass.

"You were saying, Vinnie?"

Something in Cara's voice caused the boys to look suspiciously between the adults, as if they had just walked in on us naked.

"Um, whatever it was must not have been too important," I said, faking forgetfulness. Really, I was a one-woman-at-a-time kind of guy, and I still needed to repay DeeDee for her latest rebuff, make her cry uncle, and more.

"Well," she said, appraising her caseloads on the hoof. "You two please stay out of trouble. Okay? You're going to be grown up soon, real soon. You do not want to be in the adult jail system, do you?"

"No," both boys said.

Using a skeptical look, that of a pro, Beely said, "All right. And, Vinnie? Thanks for the coffee."

"My pleasure."

"Almost," Beely said, turning on her heel and tossing a finger twiddle over her shoulder.

I telescoped my focus, smiling. Then changed gears, frowning. "You two ready?" I growled.

Yes sirs. Like twins.

I started for the exit, the delinquent ducklings falling in line.

What had I got myself into? These kids had already been on the nightmare side of tough love, if you wanted to get extremely loose with the term. And I was kidding about "strangling," about "taking it out of their hides." What was needed here was someone smarter than I was. I needed someone, needed to find someone, who fit that description. Swing a dead cat or something.

* * *

"We didn't know that the—" Paulie began to say once we were in the parking lot, but I cut him short.

"Where's Sandra?"

Still walking, but slower now, almost stopping, Paulie opened and closed his mouth without a sound.

"Great. Where do you think she could be?" I asked, shooting the alien mass of spearmint onto the sidewall of a tire where it would probably still be a month from now.

"She mentioned your aunt," Chris said to Paulie and clammed up, totally unsure if I was going to pick up where his step-monster had left off.

"You know the number?" I asked.

Paulie said, "Not right offhand. I can get it though."

"At your house, you mean?" I asked.

"Yeah," he said in a way that labeled everything a major drag and rigged against anyone under twenty-one.

We were at my car. "Hang on," I said, hauling out Beely's card, and going through the transfer.

"Cara Beely. Who's calling, please?"

"We talked earlier today. You may remember me. Tall, blond hair, used to have a fat wallet. The guy who is not a child molester?"

That last earned me a nervous smile from the boys. I made a goofy, fierce face back, as in, no, I wasn't that, but I was really pissed, really. It was easy to sense the boys' momentary relief. I would untangle this knot soon enough. Until then, I was trying to bear in mind that however almost grown, these were still kids and basically stupid.

I enjoyed Beely's laugh much more than her gum. "Have the boys already got into trouble again?"

"Give it a half hour," I said. "No, but I have a favor to ask. If Paulie's sister calls or comes looking for them, would you please see that she hears that I had them released? Maybe ask that nice lady at the counter to help?" I forced out. "Her name is Sandra."

"Actually, it's Lucinda Warren."

"The sister," I said, grinning.

"Same last name?"

"Yeah."

"Warren?"

Good grief! What, was Beely a disgruntled English major? It would explain the poor career choice.

"Would you stop that! Sandra Petralucci. She's only thirteen, and from what I understand, the unfortunate girl is trying to come up with these knuckleheads' bail."

The k-heads in question looked away.

"Not good. Not good at all. Okay. I'll most definitely post a lookout for her. Anything else? I'm out of gum, but I think I have half a roll of LifeSavers here somewhere."

"I'm going to pass on that." Threats! "Thanks anyway, and, ah, thanks for showing an interest," I double-entendred.

"You're welcome. And I'm concerned about the boys, too," she fired back, on point. "By the way, I owe you a coffee."

Flirtatious. Forward. Witty. Good-looking. And an effing government employee. "You're a good egg, Cara Beely. I appreciate it."

"De nada. Take care, Vinnie."

"Thanks, Cara. Bye."

From the looks on their mugs, if the boys weren't already in so much hot water right now, both would be freely making smacking sounds about Beely, and taunting about us sitting up in a tree, k-i-s-s-i-n-g.

I shook my head and told them to get in the car, Paulie calling shotgun.

Once I was behind the wheel I asked Paulie what his aunt's full name was, dialed information, got it, and told him to call. He still had my spare phone and whatever other property was on his person upon arrest, minus the frigging Rolex. Supposedly, the watch had been Chris's. I had yet to get that story, hoping it wasn't a fairy tale.

The aunt had seen Sandra yesterday evening, but had not given her any money for bail. I wasn't surprised. Sandra had not stayed.

"I assume she's taking buses?"

"I'm sure," was Paulie's answer.

"Okay, sport. I'm heading to the apartment. Hopefully, she'll call. She doesn't have a phone, does she?"

"No, sir," Paulie said.

Back to "sir" again. Okay. Respect was good. So was truth. Maybe Sandra would be banging around in the kitchen when we returned. The boys said she had the spare key. Maybe I was worrying too much. I wanted to think that I was far too young to turn into my Aunt Gabby, professional worrier.

I cranked up the Nova and wheeled us out of the depressing parking lot. Fishing under my seat, I found this morning's beer bottle, and had Paulie toss it onto the miniature border of grass near the street.

In the rearview mirror I caught Chris's eye. "You want to explain all this, Chris?"

Well, this time he did say, "Yes, sir," but that was due to a combination of fear and ingrained manners. No way did he want to explain.

The red-headed kid turned his face from the passing scenery of traffic to meet my eyes three times before making a lock. His black eye was a mockery of all that society professed, an ugly badge that would sink into the young man's heart in an illusion that it faded from his skin.

"I could see that our time at your apartment was running out. We needed money so we wouldn't have to go back home. The Rolex was real, not a knockoff. I thought I could get enough for it to get a room somewhere."

As far as logic went it wasn't bad. What was bad, was the series of assumptions Chris was operating under. True, I could not indefinitely shelter the kids under my roof. Also true, had the jeweler not suspected the Rolex of being stolen, the sale could have earned the kid enough green for a room, some cheapo something okay for a short period, without taking into account other basic necessities of life. Chris was articulate enough that his demeanor would serve to deter questions, even if he did look like Howdy Doody in the flesh, with a black eye.

"Anyone say anything about kicking anybody out? Paulie?"

"No, sir."

That's right, Paulie. Keep it simple, and just agree with any fucking thing I say.

"Chris?"

"No, sir, not at all, but—"

"Save your 'buts'," I told the backseat, seeing a break in the traffic ahead, stomping the accelerator for the joy of it, and because I was just a smidgeon pissed off, feeling perfectly entitled to a spot of reckless endangerment.

"I understand that your situation is precarious, Chris, but trying to sell stolen goods was a little harder than you expected, right?"

Ha. Open mouth in the rearview. "Save it," I said. "The watch was stolen and you knew it. Did you steal it?" I figured I knew the answer, but let's see.

"Technically? Yes. But only thirdhand."

Hmm. I believed him, but still… "I'm waiting," I prodded, easing off the gas and looking across to see Paulie grinning real big, sunglasses in place. I do believe the bruising was beginning to lighten a tad.

"Al has a small floor safe. My stepmom had gone shopping, so I helped myself. He doesn't know that I have the combination. Besides, there's so much crammed in there that I doubt he'll miss it," Chris said, a true edge to his voice.

"And you got the combination how?" I asked, finding myself at ease with the conversation, the topic at hand.

"I read a couple of books," Chris answered in a manner which forced neutrality into his voice, the pride evident nonetheless.

Reading is fun-damental, as politically correct educators would have it. The kid had boned up on combination locks. Smart.

"Well, the damage is done now," I said, giving Chris a glance, no lectures on stealing from me. I was more the kind to hand out pointers.

"No cash, no Rolex, and now a court date. Not to mention all the money and aggravation you've cost me. Got any other bright ideas?"

"A few," Chris said when I had expected another "No, sir."

"Let me rephrase that, Chris. Any good ideas?"

"No, sir. Not really."

That was more like it. The young man was possibly just bright enough to work his way up to a supermax cell by the time he was twenty-two.

"Okay, quiet time. I've gotta think," I said.

What I really had to do was sleep, for Pete's sake. I was running on fumes, the wimpy helping of caffeine from my earlier cup of coffee never coming close to making a dent in propping me up. I had a funeral to attend, and if I wasn't careful it would be my own. My eyelids felt weighted. Even so, I spotted a fast food joint a block ahead that I didn't entirely despise.

"All right. You screwed up. Congratulations. The thing here is that you fucked up when there was no need. I understand why you did what you did, but, hey, what's the difference when you get caught, right?"

By now there was zero doubt in my mind that the boys had talked plenty, with Paulie letting Chris know what his adoptive father did for a living, and therefore Paulie Sr.'s connection with yours truly. If Chris understood that, and if he was as bright as I believed him to be, he would listen up and understand that school was now in session.

"Rolexes, anything high end, is likely to have an I.D. number, sometimes two—one number from the factory and possibly another for personal insurance purposes. I suppose the jeweler removed the watch's cover to have a look?"

Chris gave me a belated, sorrowful nod.

"If someone has the dough to buy Rolex-type crap, you can bet it's insured, not a 100% guarantee, but count on it as a rule of thumb. So, if this someone has the piece get stolen, they're going to file a police report for two reasons: for their insurance coverage, and for revenge against the thief.

"Now, if you're the thief, you go through the bother of eliminating I.D. numbers on merchandise and maybe botch it, or you fence the damn thing, and fast, for a fraction of the retail price and walk away, your business complete.

"You do not waltz into some frigging jewelers you do not know and blindly ask for cash. Especially when you're sixteen. Are you hearing me back there okay, Chris?"

"Loud and clear, sir!"

Fucking marines. "Okay," I said, turning into Wendy's to order from the side menu.

Food in hand, we tooled down the street. At the apartment I told the boys that if they left the place to just keep walking. And, also, that I had to crash. And that if Sandra called and needed a ride, or help, to wake me. But that anything else, including WWIII-IV would have to wait.

For Chris, anything and everything was clear. And loud. And it was still "sir." Paulie was a weak echo, as unsure of life as ever.

Chapter 17

Two hours of sleep. Two hours of sleep. I could not get the cramped fact out of my head. Dead on my feet, I jumped in the shower, shaved, and dressed so fast that I was woozy.

The ex-cons were in place, watching tv. Sandra had called, leaving a number for me to call back. I asked the boys if they had called their mothers. Moms. Step-, adoptive, whatever. I was very tired.

Paulie admitted that his mom had told him to come home, and the same went for his sister. In an unexpected outburst, Paulie declared, "I'll go to jail, or hitchhike to L.A., or anything, but I ain't going back there!"

His tone was not petulant, it was defiant. The big kid was determined to grow up in the hard, harder, or hardest way, as long as one of them was a-way.

"And they do not, absolutely do not, know you're here. Right?" I said, a bitch of a surprise the last thing I needed.

"Right," Paulie replied, his breathing high and tight in his chest.

With the desperation of wanting instant adulthood, there was yet fear in his eyes of losing his position on the beanbag. So much for Paulie. "Chris?"

Chris Lewis laughed. Well, it wasn't a real laugh, more of a self-deprecating snarl. He held out his hand for what I now call Paulie's phone.

Seconds later Chris said, "It's me."

There was a pause, then listening as Chris stared at the floor, at Paulie, at the muted TV.

"I am."

A shorter pause.

"I will. Bye," Chris said, omitting any possible reciprocal endearment, not that I was expecting one from either end of the connection. As young people sarcastically said these days, "Good talk," meaning anything but.

Dialing the number from Sandra, I rolled a hand for Chris to start talking to me, quickly, I hoped. It was okay to be late for your own funeral, but not someone else's, especially Uncle Mike's.

Chris talked while exhaling a sigh. "She asked if I'm eating. Duh. And to let her know if I plan on staying away for good."

Despite his hardened shell, the kid was unable to keep the hurt from his face. So, that pretty much settled that.

"Hello? Vinnie?" Sandra said after I made the call.

"Yeah, kiddo. I heard you were running around town trying to make the world a better place, and at the same time trying to get these two desperados out of the hoosegow."

This elicited a giggle.

"Where are you. Are you okay?"

"Yeah. I'm fine. I'm at a friend's apartment. Her folks are at work. Thank you for getting Paulie out of jail. Can you believe what they did? I—"

No matter how tired I was, that was funny.

"Hold on a second?" I said.

"Sure."

I began moving off, saying, "Boys? Do I really need to say it?" My eyebrows were up around the ceiling.

"We'll stay right here," Paulie said for both of them.

I saw that I could force them to pinkie swear, but blood oaths are so much better. "Uh-huh. You don't, I'll kill you." Another step, it and my voice softened as I said, "Just kidding. Gotta go."

And with that I told Sandra I was back. I closed the door on my way out, rattling the hell out of it.

"I couldn't come up with the money for them, but I never really thought I could. Give me a month and I'd figure out a way, but—"

"Was your aunt mad?"

"No, not really. A little surprised, I guess. She knows what my dad's like, just not about . . . you know."

Dammit. I did. Poor kid couldn't say "it" unless it was absolutely necessary.

"Paulie says that he's not going back, period. But, Sandra? Honestly? I do not know what to do for you."

Dispirited, she started to say something and I rushed in to make myself clear. "That does not mean that I won't do my best to help."

I was thinking about Beely, and about my ignorance of the law in these matters. My fear of what the law would do, and my distrust that the cog of social services might have already begun to grind the kids away and apart, was pulling me in different directions. Just because Cara Beely was nice did not mean that she could wave a magic wand and keep the machinery of government at bay.

"I'll probably have to go back," Sandra said in a tone I did not want to register. "I'll just have to sleep with a knife or something."

I was at my car. Up the ramp, I merged into traffic fast as I could, whipping my steed lane to lane, willing to chance a ticket. A knife! I mean, damn.

Busy, I had to put Sandra on hold. "You there? Okay, look, I've got a funeral to go to. You'd met Mike before, hadn't you?"

"Yeah. I liked Mike."

Everyone did. Hell, I would bet that if the Dezzes had met Mike, they, too, would have liked him. Still would have shot him all the same, yeah, but with respect.

"Can you stay with your friend a few hours more?"

"Sure," Sandra said, "but you don't have to come get me. I'll be all right."

The kid had guts, I'd give her that. "Ah, you know, until we figure out what's best? Why don't you just stay with your brother again tonight. We'll talk. I can pick you up after the funeral."

"Hey, thanks, Vinnie, but I can take the bus."

I blew out a breath, running a red light with plenty of room to spare. No cops, no problems.

"Okay, then. I'll see you later."

"Okay. And, Vinnie?"

"Yeah?"

" What would you like for dinner?"

This kid was too much. "You still got money?"

"Not enough for bail," she laughed, "but some, yeah."

"Then surprise me. And, uh, thanks. Take care."

"Ciao, Vinnie."

I hung up and felt good. And felt bad. It was a tough old world, filled with people who just didn't care, takers, takers like myself. Well, almost filled. In small crevices there existed a special glue holding the whole rotten mess together, a few truly good souls such as Sandra and Beely.

What an alarming thought, this honest stab of pinpointing where I fit into the moldy mold. I did not fall in lockstep with any one religion. Heaven sounded like a nice, yet achingly boring mythical set up, and the concept of hell just plain stupid. Yet I did believe in souls. One could say I was a firm believer in puzzles. It would probably require the industrious use of a hammer to set my own piece in place.

Cheery thoughts right before the funeral. I patted the steering wheel of the inanimate Nova and floored her.

* * *

It was the end of June and the sun couldn't make up its mind whether to start its July run early or not, balanced right on the edge of unbearable. Effing suits, effing summer-weight suits. Sounded okay in a pleasant air-conditioned shop, and tailors are nice people—they wouldn't lie, would they?

I now understood what a roasted ox felt like, dead and burning at the same time. Thankfully, I didn't believe in hell. I would have to remember to tell Dad that one. The man himself was standing still as a block of granite at the gravesite, sunglasses on, arms crossed and mom's left hand in the crook of his right arm.

Mom had on a black hat and veil that had to be trapping in the heat like a sonofabitch, yet I never saw her once lift a handkerchief to her face to blot tears or sweat. Composure. Grace. Endurance.

Myself, I was sweating buckets. Every mother's son who had at least one elbow to bend at Smalley's last night looked like death on reheat, mopping red faces. Halfway through the service I saw one of the gang take a knee.

The earlier service had been fine, church-wise that was, the A/C on nice and high. And the priest knew his business, letting those assembled shoulder the work load.

Dad told an old story I had heard a dozen times of how Mike had carelessly mistaken a hundred-dollar bill for a ten spot when he had told a hotdog vendor that he was in a hurry and could have the bill if he made his dog pronto. And when the hotdog vendor, wanting no regrets, unfolded and held up the hundred-dollar bill as a last chance question, Uncle Mike, egotistically taking the high road, had said, "Make it the best damn hot dog you ever made in your life," letting the guy keep the change.

Yeah, it was all fun and games inside, with Uncle Mike up front all nice and cool with his silver spoons tucked in one hand and me discreetly sucking on Tic Tacs as I sat with my parents.

Then there was the long-ass drive to the cemetery. What I wouldn't pay for a cloud! Nothing big, a small one would be just fine. We take clouds for granted when, honestly, clouds were our friends, though this observation was probably just the incipient heat stroke talking.

Then it was over. I did not like the handful of dirt I held. Too much clay, I ventured to guess. Something. Really, I didn't know squat about dirt other than

I didn't much care for it. Clouds on the other hand . . .

I scattered my dirt and crossed myself because I was expected to, no big deal. I hated the way that a scrap of too bright artificial turf was draped over the waiting mound of burial soil. What did people feel they had to use before artificial turf was invented, green tablecloths?

Glancing around, I noticed no police presence, nor saw any reason for there to be such. I found it sad knowing that some of the old guys like Tony F. would feel better if they bore the same burden of scrutiny as did the big bosses in town, when the comfortable truth was that our gang was but a single cog in a large machine.

Personally, I liked the lower profile. I most certainly tried not to shoot at anyone other than an occasional Dez, and only then if one of them was shooting at me or one of mine. And it really wasn't fair considering what lousy shots they all were.

Uncle Mike was a tragic accident. Well, his death was, I meant. The guy who shot him had probably been more surprised than Mike. Even had Paulie Pet not peppered the Dez rounding on me, chances were that he would have missed.

No. That was a delusional lie. I had been point-blank dead meat.

Right now, Paulie Pet had his hand on the back of dad's shoulder, resting lightly to be sure, yet should not be there at all. They were off to one side, Paulie's head bent, talking in what appeared to be a monologue. The sensitivity on my bad-feeling gauge was pushing the needle to the peg. Something was off with Paulie's stance, as was dad's absence from a single pairing with Mom who looked frozen in a distanced leg of the triangle. Paulie Pet knew about me running a daycare. I didn't know how he knew, but he knew. Damn, I thought, damn his eyes and all the rest of him.

Right or wrong, I just wanted this day to end, positive that Cara Beely would have something relevant to add to such a sentiment. I was thinking of calling her when my phone vibrated. Dusting off my hands, I tore my eyes away from the earth raining down upon Mike Spinoza's casket, and walked away to seek the shade of a small but fortunately placed tree. I checked the caller's I.D.

"'Sup, stranger."

"I thought you were going to call," DeeDee said.

Crap. "Sorry. I had a wake to attend last night, and the funeral today. It's been busy."

"Oh? Who died?"

See, I never told Dee anything of substance. As far as she was concerned I worked for my dad at the warehouse, was well paid, and never mentioned this one freaking big mole between her breasts.

"Friend of the family," I said.

"Oh. So, what are we doing tonight?"

Well, shit. I had planned on taking a shower, eating early, and then crashing for about eighteen straight hours.

Rats, I couldn't even do that. I had promised Sandra that we would talk. At this point it seemed that our talk might be very short.

"Sweetpea, I'm all in. What about tomorrow night?

"But I want to go out tonight!"

Was that a whine? Silly question. If it needed to be replayed and studied, it was.

"Baby, I'm sorry. Really. But I'll make it up to you. Promise." I mean, Dee was nice and all, despite the ugly-ass mole, but there was no way. . . .

"But Trina's got her dumbass boyfriend coming over and I'll have to stay in my room!"

Tragic. "I feel your pain, Dee, but I'm not kidding. I'm so tired I can barely keep my eyes open, okay?"

"You're turning me down."

The hell? "DeeDee, I am not—

"Either you change your mind or you can forget about calling to try and make up."

I had to smile. Tired as I was, this was genuinely funny; if you wanted to really piss me off, try making demands.

"I'm sorry you feel that way, Dee. Have a nice life."

I hung up, stashed the phone, and inspected my fingernails. There was a little dirt there, but DeeDee could vouch that I cleaned up just fine. Well, if we were still talking.

"Vinnie?"

"Hi, Mom."

"Share your shade?"

I grinned and made room, the little tree having to work harder to shelter both of us. The veil was still in place, but not for long, Mom looking left and right. People were leaving for the comfort of A/C, iced drinks, and cool pools. July promised to be a beast. The hat and veil started to come off but needed help with a pin.

"Thank you, Vinnie. This heat," she said.

"Pretty bad," I allowed, waiting. If my mom had really wanted to cool off she would be waiting on Dad in the car with the A/C blasting.

"Vinnie, Paulie's got this notion in his head that you're keeping his kids with you at your new apartment. Where did he get such an idea?"

It was good to know that my posture-reading skills were still accurate to a fare-thee-well, and not so good to learn that someone had blabbed. At this point it hardly mattered who. By the look on mom's face, any evasion on my part would be ludicrous. What did I expect? That this minor secret, my playing Vinnie The Humanitarian was going to go forever undiscovered?

"Confession time, eh?" I said with a weak smile.

Mom looked sweetly stern—soft eyes and a backbone of steel.

"When I went down to bail out Paulie, and it turned out to be Junior, the kid had been beaten to a pulp. By Paulie Pet, okay? The kid didn't ask to stay with me. I just couldn't send him back, and now he insists he'll never go back. And, Mom, it's not the first time."

"It's not your business, Vinnie."

"Mom, I love you, but I'm a grown man. I've made it my business."

The chin came up and the nostrils flared. It was a good thing that I added how I loved her. A few deep breaths later, Mom smiled.

"And his daughter, Sandra?"

"Paulie's been after her. Sexually, Mom. Would you send her back?"

I believe I had just come within a whisker of getting my face slapped. This time it took somewhat longer for mom's composure to reset itself, all wordless.

"Paulie Pet is a pig, Vinnie, but that's nothing new. He's useful, and he's loyal, and the man saved your life the other night. Didn't he?"

Well, I had this part figured wrong. I had thought that I would be going toe to toe with Dad over this once the dam broke.

"Didn't he?" she repeated.

"I'm afraid so," I said, sounding lame in my own ears.

"Afraid so? Afraid so? Why, you . . ."

I waited for the slap to arrive, not really caring. Maybe I wasn't the most moral man walking the planet, but I was not about to forgive Paulie his wrongs because he had saved my life. Doing that would not make the situation balanced.

"Mom?" I said with softness, needing her to understand me, the boy, the baby she had taken to raise as her own, and the man I had turned out to be.

"I'm listening."

Yes, dear mother, you were, and being a bit cold on the hottest day of the year thus far. Fine.

"Mom, I understand about loyalty. But what about Paulie Pet's loyalty to his own family, huh? Yeah, Paulie stepped into a responsible position when he took out the guy who was going to pop me, and I call that the right thing to do. And had the situation been reversed I would have done the same."

I was speaking to the side of her face, her gaze on the dwindling line of cars, or maybe a point far past them.

"And now I am stepping into a position of responsibility because he will not. Mom? Mom, look at me."

Shoot. My mom did not like to be preached to. It was difficult for her to accept that there might be overriding trumps on this deal. She squared up to me, tearing her long-distance survey away to burn me up close. I've seen Dad look this way, and had no idea who was copying whom.

I spotted Dad among the knot of suits. Even from far away his look stated clearly that it was time to go. Again, I met mom's stare.

"Look, I can't pretend to know what's best, but I do know what is worst for those kids, and that is being forced back home to be pulverized and raped."

Mom's jaw was locked hard.

I kissed her cheek, a fleshy stone.

"Dad's waiting."

Without further communication between us, I was permitted to escort her to Dad's side. Silently, I turned and left.

Chapter 18

I avoided slumping to the floor of the elevator for the ride up to the seventh floor, but it was a close call. Trudging through the open doors and into my hallway my jacket was slung over one shoulder and my shirt tail was out. I slowed my tortoise sprint as the first apartment door on my left swung open and a big man backed into the corridor.

Broad shoulders supported a bowling ball with a crewcut. This guy was sporting a summer-weight jacket, too, unrumpled, and looking to have cost twice what mine had. We were even to each other when he turned quickly, sensing my presence. Hard, dark eyes combed my face before searching up and down my length for any threat.

I looked away, face impassive, still moving slow though listening for movement behind me, waiting to hear what had to be Chris Lewis's stepfather heading into the elevator car I had just vacated. At my door I casually turned my head to see the monster staring. There was no attempt to disguise his scrutiny of me.

Undoubtedly, the guy was a jerk. I mean, ordinary guys don't sign up to be cops anyway, but this guy appeared to be a fully-fledged asshole.

This, I did not like. This, I did not need. And me, with a one-year lease.

Ignoring the psycho, I entered my apartment, ready to drown myself in the shower and sleep forever.

Crap. Forgot about Sandra. Maybe I could borrow my bed for a few hours, until sundown, say. I would apologize and then go away. Days were sunny and life was funny.

"You look tired," came a voice from the kitchen doorway.

Sandra had heard me come in. Obviously, she had chosen to take the bus and, just as obviously, she was hellbent on outdoing herself in the kitchen. Something smelled delicious. I smiled. Tiredly.

"Yeah. I'm going to take a shower. You don't suppose I have time for a quick nap before that's ready?" I said, hooking a thumb in the direction of the kitchen.

"For sure. It won't be ready for some time," Sandra fibbed, having no problem with keeping the meal warm. Her largest obstacle would be keeping her brother and his appetite out of the kitchen.

"Great. Smells good by the way," I said, once again trudging. Once again stopping.

"The boys are home, aren't they?" I couldn't hear the tv.

"Yeah. Chris is teaching Paulie how to play chess."

Ah. That would explain the slight grinding noise coming from the big room. . . Pauli Jr.'s rusty intellect in motion.

I nodded, slowing as I passed the archway. The boys were bent over the board atop the coffee table. When not in use, the chess set rested upon the middle shelf of a glass and chrome étagére in one corner. The set was a gift from a gal I had dated last year, a student at Columbia who got fed up with me beating her at her own game, so to speak.

The shower was superb and my mattress superb. I must have conked out moments after lying down. When I woke it was dark. Dark was good. Dark was comforting, but also disorienting.

I found myself staring at my digital clock. I was in a foggy mental state, trying to decode a.m. from p.m. Good gravy, logically it had to be after five in the morning! I had slept nearly eleven straight hours. My bladder confirmed this working hypothesis.

I dressed and tiptoed in socks down the hall. In the dark I saw a glow greater than the metropolitan light pollution through the open curtains of the patio door, the earth spinning up a new sunrise.

There was one lump on the sofa, another in the easy chair, and one on the carpet with a beanbag for a pillow. Okay, problem solved, and I had to surmise that for three kids who could not stomach the idea of going home, this apartment beat the heck out of the alternatives.

Curious, I quietly made my way to the kitchen, wishing there was a dimmer switch for the refrigerator light. Tempted to toss several covered somethings into the microwave, I decided that it was awfully early for young'uns on vacation to be awakened early. Poor Paulie still needed the better part of two tons of restorative beauty sleep.

I settled for a hasty cup of instant coffee, walking it back to the bedroom where I stripped the sheets and made up the bed with a clean set. There was a growing pile of laundry in my hamper that demanded attention.

Making up my mind, I gathered it all up and, maintaining stealth mode, snuck it out the door and down to the car.

The morning was bright, promising to be another scorcher, but for now the air temperature was relatively cool and refreshing. I drove with the windows down, catching a fine wind and so-so news. The weather forecast was surprisingly good. For the west coast. Here, it was going to be aitch-oh-tee.

I dropped the laundry off at my dry cleaners, then wheeled the chariot to the grocery store. Mentally, I brought up the contents of the fridge, not what was there but what I saw missing—believing that it just may pay to invest in a cow. I did still have that extra parking space.

When I returned, I boldly leaned my head close to Chris's apartment, listening for signs of life, my ear pressed to the door after checking that Chris's favorite hated peephole was undarkened, as far as I could tell. Nothing was stirring, I would have to ask Chris about his stepdad's schedule for obvious reasons, and some maybe not so obvious.

Inside my apartment, Sandra was working a spell involving the physical transformation of chicken eggs. The boys were still sound asleep. A shy smile accompanied the girl's quiet movements as she helped me put away groceries before serving me breakfast, which was pretty darned good. Some people, no matter how simple the task was purported to be, could not properly cook an egg, any make or model—me, for example. These were excellent, these eggs. I would be sure to leave a big tip.

Across from me Sandra ate daintily as we shared the morning newspaper, occasionally talking to the tune of more coffee? more toast? like that. It was a good start to my day. I felt renewed and invigorated, though I still owned the same number of problems as yesterday. My phone buzzed. I was searching for an app with which my phone would civilly clear its throat in a suggestive manner.

I took leave of Sandra, holding up a finger as if putting her on hold. I stepped down the hall to the bedroom.

"Good morning," I said. It was dad. As if I had not seen this coming.

"Vinnie. Come over this morning."

No preamble. No questions.

"I'm on my way in five minutes," I said. I was going to brush my teeth whether the don liked it or not.

"We gotta talk," Dad added, unnecessarily, I felt.

I said, "Okay. I'm on my cell right now."

"Oh. Right. Your mother wants you to bring some cream cheese."

What? Again? What was she doing with all the cream cheese? I would ask, but I figured that the government didn't need to know any more than I did.

"All right. Anything else?"

"Just get your ass over here."

Plain enough. "Message received. Over and out."

Right when I thought our tense conversation was over, I heard Dad call me a smartass. Nothing new there.

I brushed my teeth and combed my hair. Added a touch of cologne. It was important to be presentable when reporting to one's executioner, all the difference between a painless death and something messy.

"Don't know when I'll be back, but I'm still looking forward to having some of that dinner from last night," I said brightly now that I saw the teenage male contingent stirring.

"Good. It's—"

I stopped Sandra right there. "Hold that thought. Remember, I like surprises." I also liked to earn grins.

The closer I got to Rancho Renaldi, the less true it became about me liking surprises. It was heating up outside, and I had to wonder if the same would hold true when I walked through the don's front door.

* * *

On the feasible assumption that I was about to have my head handed to me on a platter of baked goods, I delivered unto the matriarch a brown bag containing not one, but two packages of cream cheese. Last minute brownie points were those freshest in mind.

"Your father's waiting for you in the backyard," Mom said.

Were I a smoker I'd have asked for a long cigarette following a slowly eaten last meal, and then used a requested blindfold to blow my nose. Sure, it was possible that I was being overdramatic, but I didn't think so. I've heard that Argentina had some good rentals this time of year. I fixed a careful smile on my face and stepped outdoors.

I used to have some excellent adventures here in this backyard when I was a kid. My cousins and I would play at being pirates, soldiers, cowboys, pretty much any occupation with pretend weapons of mass destruction, although our cannon sounded much the same as our six-shooters that actually held about a hundred rounds. If we were playing cops and robbers I would complain if I had to play the cop twice in a row. Childhood could be cruel.

The old tire swing still hung in the property's far corner; the oak tree it depended from was of decent size, but had appeared enormous when I was small. Next to the tree was our old picnic table, a sturdy redwood piece decorated with bird droppings that Dad ignored as he sat on one of the faded benches, one elbow strategically positioned atop the table. Dad's coffee cup was half empty, and I believed wholeheartedly that neither of us this morning would call it half full.

Ronnie Renaldi was wearing shorts. I have always thought that my dad looked ridiculous in shorts. A bulb of knee and a wedge of phosphorescent white leg showed twixt the top of the pulled-up-high white socks and the hem of the long, navy blue, Mrs. Renaldi-purchased shorts.

Yesteryear, long ago when Mom would badger Dad to take me to the beach, he would sit in a rented lounge chair under a rented umbrella, dressed as he was now, never taking off his shirt or his shoes. He always carried, using a shoulder rig, which explained the shirt, but Dad was a bit, no, a lot funny about his feet. Everything did not reside in the land of the explicable.

Mom's garden was looking good, the tomatoes in healthy production, and the eggplants looking unearthly as ever. Birds, butterflies, and bees, the backyard was alive with everything good. And then there was the don, staring at me as if he could not believe what would come up in a backyard these days.

"You're slipping, kid," was how Dad chose to open up.

"Is there anything specific you wanted to go over?" I said, unwilling to offer free fuel with which to burn me at the stake, or the gas grill.

"I would say that at this par-tick-u-lar moment, what we have here is a multitude of specifics."

Dad pronounced it "mull-tee-tood." He presented his left hand, palm up, and from there proceeded to grasp his index finger and bend it toward the good earth. "One—" he said, and now you could see where I got my list-making skills from "—you can imagine my surprise when I was informed that we had a buyer for nine kazillion cases of diapers."

"Hey! That's good," I said, having nothing to lose, and both of us expecting me to say something smartassed, and I do so hate to disappoint the old man.

"Vinnie, I agree."

And he rattled off a number that indeed was good. Premium diapers weren't cheap, boyo, and a tractor-trailer load added up to a butt load.

"Ordinarily," he added. "I would agree, ordinarily."

"Yes, well, you see—and it's really sort of funny how it happened—I think you will be able to appreciate the mix-up. Those numbers you gave me—"

I was talking to a hand. Seemed that it was useful for more than just counting to one.

"The number of the trailer or the number of the date, kid?"

"That's the funny part," I said.

"Nothing funny about losing a million dollars."

"I hear you," loud and clear as a certain redheaded stepchild might put it. "I don't mean funny funny." If I were onstage just now this would be a lone cricket moment. "It's one of those hindsight things."

"Hindsight thing, huh? Oh, you mean like me telling Dino to keep his keister parked in that garage apartment of his, and you're taking him out the very next day to rob a diaper truck? That kind of hindsight?"

"When you put it like that it is kind of funny," I said, and shouldn't have, and now it was far too late to take back.

"What is it with you thinking that everything's a joke, Vinnie? Losing a million-dollar score? Ha ha. Hilarious. Making moves behind my back with Dino? Going against my wishes? All that funny to you, Vinnie?"

"Right now, no, sir."

I could not prove it, but I believed there had to be some genetically fused odd wiring between my brain and tongue.

"You're damned right no, not now! And why is that? Because you gotta answer for shit, that's why! All fun and games until your tit's in the wringer, huh, kid? And now, on top of all this crapola, you wanna play house with Paulie's kids? Geez, Vinnie! I didn't believe you could be that dumb!"

Oh, yes, I can! I wanted to say, along with at least a dozen wisecracks but, thankfully, there is that part of me that, through training, has been conditioned to shut up, take it, and show some respect. I kept my mouth shut.

My phone vibrated. I ignored it, not easy, but the boss needed my full attention, and he finally had it. I for damned sure didn't like being called dumb. I preferred the term "stupid."

"I explained it to mom, and I'm sure she told you what I said. It isn't as if I set out to do this. And I saw nothing but insurmountable complications once I made that first decision not to deliver Paulie Jr. back to his house. But I'll tell you what—I feel like I've saved one life if not two."

Figuring I was making sense, I saw no reason to stop at that.

"Remember that guy? I forget his name. The one who used to bug Dom to try him out? It was some ass-backward son of a third cousin's best friend's mama crap, and we said okay, give the fucker a shot, and he turned out to be a child molester. What'd you do?"

"You know what I did."

Boy. When he got like this he gave me the creeps. I did not believe that the whack was performed personally, though at least one version of the story had it that it was an execution at Dad's own hands. But first, the rumors concerning the guy's guilt were verified, and man was it ugly. I had serious doubts that the guy was still alive, but, if so, then he's been holding his breath for years.

"And what makes this different?" I voiced.

A second finger got tugged to the center of the earth. "That was confirmed. This ain't," Renaldi said.

I kept my cool, but dammit, it was hard. My phone buzzed again, further trying my patience. Locating and discerning what was dried and what was fresh, bird-shit-wise, I leaned across the picnic table and said in an even tone, "I believe her, Dad. No way do I not believe her. And it's not just her. Paulie Jr. says the same thing."

"Well, he would, wouldn't he?"

"The fuck is that supposed to mean!"

Well, shit. I was doing good keeping myself in check there for a while. Dad began turning purple.

"Whoa, whoa!" I said, both palms up and out. "Dad? I apologize, okay? I'm sorry I shouted. I meant no disrespect."

Right words, wrong judgement of the birdshit. I lifted my right hand to wipe it on my pants, watching as dad's face calmed down to a more natural alarming color.

"The kid's been stealing from Paulie. And I believe him, okay, tough guy?"

Theft would explain a lot, if it were true. For what it was worth, I have witnessed Paulie Pet put his fists through walls, windows, and doors just because the mood hit him. I haven't known Jr. one on one for long, but the story didn't jibe, not that I wouldn't ask the kid in no uncertain way when I got back.

"Dad? I really can't speak on that. Right now, it's like whose word do you take, whose story sounds true?"

"You take my word, that's whose word you take! Christ, Vinnie, what is the matter with you, eh? Alla sudden you got shit for brains? Wanna get mixed up in something that doesn't concern you? These are Paulie Pet's kids. Not yours. I'm sure you meant well, but, fuck, Vinnie, come on here! Let it go! I'll talk to Paulie, get him to calm down."

Yeah, yeah, yeah. Right. And everybody goes back to normal, and I just put it all out of my head. Simple. If I did that I would be seeing those kids' faces in my sleep for years to come.

Besides, even if I did tell the kids that they had to tuck their puppy tails and skedaddle on home, they wouldn't do it. Maybe Sandra, but I've got some serious doubts about that. Paulie Jr.? No, I believed what he had said. One way or another, he would take his chances on the streets or in jail. I could see right now that it just got a whole lot tougher being fun Uncle Vinnie.

"Okay?" the old man said with a little of the old softy back in his voice; and when I laid the term "old softy" at the don's size twelves, you could be sure my meaning was different than yours. Dad's idea of kindness was to not rip both your ears off and kneecap you instead.

There was nothing I was going to accomplish here unless Mom needed me to make a run for baking powder or bullets.

"Paulie ain't blood, Vinnie, but he's next to it. *Capiche?*"

I capiched, all right. Paulie was a trusted member of our gang, blooded and Fed-proof. Collateral damage happened, and thems the breaks.

"You're defending a child molester."

"Careful, Vinnie. I'm warning you."

I blew out a chuckle—call it a chuckle, whatever.

"I've always respected you despite what you may think, Dad. You know? No matter what. Even as a kid—sent me to my room, take away privileges, tell me I can't see someone because you don't trust their people, tell me I'm working at the warehouse, tell me what school to go to, one thing after another all my life, and I was fine with it all. You had my respect. Always.

"But this thing, Dad? This thing with Paulie Pet's kids? It goes beyond all that. See, it's not about you; that's what I need you to understand. It's about those poor kids. And maybe you're right, maybe it isn't my fight, but I'll fight all the same.

"Paulie Pet wants to rape his daughter? Fine. He can break down my door to do it, though I would strongly advise against it."

There was some part of me on the drive over here that never really expected things to go this far. That part of me, I saw now, hadn't been very realistic. This was what I had feared, and . . .

I could almost hear what was coming next. It would be what Ronnie Renaldi felt he had to do.

"Boy, you do not pick and choose when to pay your respects, and when to toss them into the gutter. You may think you're all high and mighty with your college education and your bleeding heart, believing children's tales, but I'm giving you an order to send those kids back, right now today, or your own yap is gonna force me to give you your marching orders. Do what I say, or you're on your own. I won't lift a finger to help you, and you won't be welcome in this house any more.

"Are we absolutely clear on this, Vinnie? The kids go or you go. You're already fucking up bad enough as it is, Mr. Huggies; you want to make it worse? Be my guest."

Wild. My entire body felt as if it were on fire, a buzzing sensation in my veins, across my skin, my stomach a giant, hard knot, and my head light and hot. I could feel fate. And destiny. And karma. And more than I could possibly describe, all imploding on my position in the space between one heartbeat and the next, and there was no turning back. I would be less of a man if I did. I would rather die.

"Thank you for the adoption and all that, Dad. I appreciate it. But now I've got to go my own way." I stood, turned, and walked off.

"You're making a mistake, son!"

He never called me son. I kept walking.

"You hear me, Vinnie?"

I did, just as well as I could hear the imagined sound of flesh pounding on flesh, or a young girl's sobs going unheeded as her father abused her.

As I approached the house I saw Mom framed in the kitchen window, her face a mask of horror, very unlike her. She clutched at my arm as I passed through. Without being rude I disentangled myself and kept going. There was nothing she could say. The boss had spoken.

And the boss's son had just quit the only job he had ever known.

CHAPTER 19

I drove. In a mood. Just drove. I ended up along the waterfront, looking across the East River at lower Manhattan, the Nova parked a block away. There I found a bench and sat down, replaying the scene in the back yard, hearing the old man's voice, his—the only—reality.

On a strictly black and white basis I could see his point. Life was not that clearly defined, nor should it be expected to be. I couldn't explain why my dad would choose to ignore what I was telling him. It was absurd. Maybe he resented me in some way. Maybe this had been building forever and I had never really noticed.

The man damned sure had his pride, and the bad thing was that a man standing on pride alone cannot step to one side or another without falling. Stubbornness. Intractability. Old-school dumb shit.

There was a small run-down grocery and package store across the street behind where I sat on the weathered concrete bench. Kids were hanging around out front, sitting hipshot on their bikes while eating popsicles. I handed them a couple of bucks as I entered the store, saving them the hassle of asking. They just nodded, kind of slack jawed. I purchased a tall can of beer which the clerk wrapped in a form-hugging brown paper bag. I exited the store, eyes forward, walking back to my bench.

I looked around for cops and snapped the tab, turning up the ice-cold beer and chugging it, breaking my frown and the stranglehold of the heat.

The water smelled funny today, funnier than usual. I set the minimally camouflaged beer by my feet and remembered the calls I had received earlier and ignored. Oh boy, I saw, checking the calls, that it was my phone, or rather, Paulie's.

"Yeah? That you, Vinnie?"

I supposed Paulie had to ask. "Yeah. Is something wrong? I was busy earlier."

"Um, yeah. Uh, my dad, he came by beating on the door."

Well, that didn't take long. While I was talking to dad.

"You okay? You didn't let him in, did you?"

"Hell, no! But your door's gotta be fucked up. Sandra was crying and yelling at him to go away and—"

Paulie's voice got lower, real low, saying, "and Chris was freaking out, and I didn't know what to do, so I got a knife out of the kitchen and was just standing there waiting for the door to smash open."

Damn. "Pretty good locks, huh?"

"Duh-huh!" Paulie said and gave a little laugh. "I'll say. And then we hear him yell, 'This ain't over! You hear me? You think this is over? This ain't over!' And he stomped off. We think. I'm just guessing your door is fucked up. None of us has opened the door since, just in case he's off to one side in the hall, waiting."

Double damn. "All right. Stay put. You did good, Paulie. Let me handle this. I'm on my way."

"Okay, Vinnie. Um, sorry."

I hung up and drained my beer, this time without looking for cops. I fast-walked back to my car and got moving. I could be back at the apartment in ten minutes this time of day. I didn't have a clue how I was going to handle this, but handle this I would.

Perhaps Paulie Pet felt that he had Dad's blessing on this. He had certainly got the address somewhere, but the big idiot wasn't thinking clearly. I no longer gave a rat's ass about my dad's blessing.

Actually, it felt good to no longer be walking tightrope along that tired old fence. I meant what I had told Mr. Renaldi. It was time to be my own boss.

* * *

"It had to be Evie," Sandra said.

I was inspecting my front door, fingering the dents in it. Paulie Pet had been kicking hard up around the locks. The door was made of metal, as was the frame. Double-bolted, the ogre would have had to do a lot better than he had. I hoped his feet were sore.

"I'm sorry. Who?"

"Evie Tunbridge, the girl I spent the night before and most of yesterday with. I'm usually not too hard to find. So, if my dad called, she would have told him everything she knew, but that's only because she doesn't know, uh, about, you know, everything. Some stuff, but not about, you know," Sandra said, her eyes focused on the door.

"Hey, it's okay. Your father can be rather intimidating," I said.

"You ought to have heard him," Chris said, his voice small in the aftermath of the arrival of a second brutal psycho into his life, a new unknown terror, the dents in the steel door an undeniable calling card.

"Pretty loud, eh?" I said to keep all three kids coherent, keep their minds from wandering too far. They were nodding their heads yes, translating dents into broken bones.

Well, this episode settled one thing. Seeing as how no cops were called, my other unmet neighbors, if home on this floor at the time of Paulie's attempted reunion, were true New Yorkers, not a one lifting a finger to help or report. And another thing I had been meaning to ask. "Your stepdad works days, Chris?"

"Yes, sir. Either making out schedules or riding patrol. Been that way for about a year now," Chris said.

A year. When he got busted back from lieutenant. I kept mum about what I knew. "All right. Well, done is done. Everyone back inside. And Paulie?"

"Yeah?"

"Lock the door, would you?"

"Count on it," the big kid said. He had been forced to bring a knife to a gun fight if it came down to it. That was worth something.

"You two give us a minute. Paulie? In the kitchen."

When we were seated at the kitchen table I got right to the first matter that could not wait.

"Now is not the time for bullshit. Something I heard. Had you been stealing from Paulie Sr.?"

The bruised face contorted and Paulie squirmed, not looking at me.

"Yeah. But only because he was so damn cheap."

Great. Just fucking great. "Often?" I asked.

"What? No! Just the one time, I swear! I wanted to go to this movie with some friends, and I hadn't asked for anything in a long time and . . . well, I mean, I hadn't ever taken anything from him before, but, yeah, I took it. I know I shouldn't have, but he's such a tightwad."

I was getting good at this, keeping these spontaneous smiles from my face when dealing with this kid.

"Well, you're right about one thing—you shouldn't have taken the dough. How much we talking here?"

"Twenty."

"Twenty, you say. That's it?"

"Yeah."

It was the kind of short, solid answer one must not ignore. It was glum, and it was the truth. "You what, get an allowance?"

"I wish!" Paulie declared in such a sincere fashion that I was beginning to renew my anger toward Paulie Pet.

"Never?" I asked.

"An allowance? Nah. Every now and then he'll be drunk and throw some money around. Ball it up and throw it at us when we least expect it and laugh., but it's not something you can count on. I've had him give me money and hit me at the same time."

"Son of a bitch owes me a front door," I mumbled, making Paulie smile.

"Okay, just so we're clear here, it was the one time? The truth."

"Stealing from his wallet? Yeah."

"And what? This was recent?"

Paulie pointed to his face.

"Okay, okay. Got it! Now, one last thing, and I really hate to ask, but I've got to be one hundred percent clear on this." I dropped my voice to a whisper. "Is he only putting his hands on Sandra or has he raped her?"

The fidgeting started up again, the face tightening up before Paulie straightened in his chair and leaned toward me the way I was leaning across the table toward him.

"She says she's stopped him in time, but I say he has."

I gave Paulie a minute to get his emotions in check because he had more to say, his jaw tightening.

"I . . . I think it's because she's trying to spare my feelings. I haven't seen that happen. I can't be everywhere or awake all the time, but I have seen the rest. The bastard."

It fit. "All right, Paulie. Let's go talk to the others for a minute."

I followed Paulie into the front room after I snagged a beer from the fridge, doing a double-take, conducting a quick head count on the bottles to make sure I wasn't contributing to the delinquency of minors. Hell, maybe that should be further contributing.

Chris was on the sofa, watching me expectantly, waiting on some sort of axe to fall. Sandra had been on the balcony and now came inside, closing the door behind her.

I stood tall, taller, unbowed by recent events. "What happened here cannot be allowed to happen again."

Ooh, I got some looks—abandonment! Kicked out! Traitor!—none even all that conscious. Naturally, the kids were on edge.

"Whoa," I said, "don't misunderstand me. I believe that turning you over to your families would just be handing them a license to continue as before. What I want each of you to do is pack up everything you have here."

I looked at each of the three in turn and smiled. "Which should take about ninety seconds."

The return smiles were uncertain, yet trusting.

"We're going to take a ride, and then I'm going to call your dad," I said, looking at the Petralucci kids, "and tell him you are no longer here, and I have no idea where you have gone." I winked. "A little white lie. Let's move it!"

Ninety seconds was about right. When we were in the car Sandra let me know what temperature, and for how long, to reheat my requested leftovers, and told me not to use the microwave, because microwave ovens were for fast food, not real food. She started to let me in on what the mysterious leftovers were, and, not for the first time, I stopped her.

"Surprises, remember?"

A smile.

"Everyone buckled up?"

Nods and compliance, even after a groan from Paulie.

I caught my own eyes in the rearview, surprised, a rotten day turning out like this. I turned the engine over and made it roar.

* * *

I did not inform my wards of my doubts that I could accomplish what I had in mind on zero notice. What they didn't know couldn't worry them. Pulling into my recently vacated digs, I told the three trusting young souls to sit tight, AC running, as I headed for my former apartment complex's office.

"Hi, Ms. Brownlee!" I fairly sang out with all the enthusiasm I could fudge while playing out this skit. Ms. Brownlee was the lady to whom I wrote out checks for rent. Used to, and would again if. . . .

"Something's come up and I need the apartment back," I said in a rush, giving her a hopeful grimace, one that I hoped conveyed my apologies while also acknowledging her unquestioned sainthood.

"Oh? That's too bad!"

"Aw, shoot!" I said, meaning it. Darn and drat.

"I rented that out just today. But I do have another one bedroom the next building over. Will that do?" she said, looking over her bifocals, and craning her plump neck.

"Ms. B, that will do just fine! Thank you. I'm wondering; I won't have to pay another deposit, will I? I never got back my—"

"I'm already on it," Ms. B said, setting her grandmotherly fingers dancing over her keyboard, chained glasses resting on the last half-inch of her blessed nose.

"No, that check has not yet been made out and I'm sure I can transfer the fund. Would you like to see the apartment first, Mr. Renaldi?"

I gave her my best smile. "As long as there's no black mold or residue from a meth lab, I'll trust that it's fine. Same price as before?"

"Well, you're lucky. Next month prices go up for everyone a little. You didn't hear it here."

As a dyed-in-the-wool expert, I zipped my lips and swallowed an imaginary key, making Ms. B happy. I wrote a check for the rent, received keys, and signed papers, including one that was a requisite admonition against keeping pets. Everyone kept pets, but signed the papers. Fortunate for me, the kids were nearly housetrained.

Stepping outside the office, I was on the phone to get the electricity turned on that day. Water was included with the rent, as were bad neighbors, and any unvacuumed toothpicks and straight pins in the carpet.

Back at the car I smiled as I swung behind the wheel. With a flourish, I swept an outstretched hand above the dash, proclaiming, "Your new home."

Getting under way, I concentrated on driving as the teens were going fractionally apeshit, saying, "What! Where!" heads swinging left and right and in danger of flying off their stems.

Fluttering a wave to some indeterminate point behind us, I said, "Back there," driving them to needless frustration, fun as hell.

Everything I needed next was secured at the busy retail center where I used to shop. I parked in front of the store and handed Sandra some cash.

"Get some basics, food wise, but don't forget toilet paper and all that junk. If the boys and I get done shopping first I'll come help. If not, the car will be right here close by." I removed the trunk key, handing it over.

She had not moved. Behind us a horn honked.

"What are we doing?" Sandra asked.

I had thought it was obvious. "You want to go back home?"

"No."

"You want to get taken away by social services? Live in an orphanage or possibly a foster home?"

I received from three points on the compass one "No, sir," one "Hell no," and one, "No way."

Right. "And you cannot stay at my place any longer for fear of you know who dropping by unannounced," I said, catching a nod from Chris in back.

And I still did not know how many laws I was breaking, this go around or while they had been at my apartment. My current guess was: plenty.

The horn honked again. We were sitting in prime real estate in front of the store's no-parking fire lane that others wanted to abuse beside us. The nerve.

"So, get scootin'. Unless any of you have a better idea."

"You're a really nice guy, Vinnie. I don't know how I can ever repay you," Sandra said, exiting the car with tears in her eyes.

I circled to park near the front of the store. "Guys? You're with me."

The rental place we walked into was convenient . . . and that was about it. I didn't know how long I would have to hide these kids, but, for now, it was back to one step, one day at a time.

Sure, the bill was going to be large, but it wasn't the money; money wasn't a problem. The stupid diaper thing alone would net me thousands after the big boss's cut. No, the problem was going to be getting the kids to understand that this new apartment was to be a refuge, not a place to put down roots.

Bed. Sleeper sofa. Recliner. Table and chairs. TV. I told Paulie that I would find a way to get his beanbag over here. The damn thing might fit in my trunk at the price of being somewhat de-beaned.

Lamps. Nightstand. Coffee table. End tables. If I'd had time I could have bought quality second-hand furniture for the same price as one month's rent on this crapola. But, hey, my kids weren't going to rough it. Either I was all in with securing their safety and comfort, or I was all mouth.

We beat Sandra's time, but not by much. Duplicate keys were cut, with all four of us standing around listening to the grind and whiz. It was weird.

By the time we arrived back at the kids' new playhouse the lights were on and, thankfully, the A/C as well. The teens wandered the small apartment as if in a dream. Their home away from home came with pitfalls they were innocently unaware of. Waiting on the furniture to arrive, I thought about what was needed for me to say—a bore, sure, but the kids needed rules period.

"All right, you guys. Here's what I'm thinking. Paulie, you're a big fellow, so I don't believe anyone is going to question you on being old enough to be on your own. And Sandra, you're, ah—" Shoot.

"Well-developed for my age?" Sandra supplied good-naturedly, a wry but supporting smile letting me know that it was okay to say what needed to be said.

"Exactly. So, the two of you should fit in fine. Now, Chris, even though you are the oldest, you look younger than these two. Follow me?"

Chris was at parade rest. "Yes, sir. You're suggesting that it would be a good idea for Sandra or Paulie to run errands if need be, but I should keep a much lower profile."

I worried too much. "Chris, you are going to go far in life, and I mean that. But, sure, this is just common sense here. Keep exposure to a minimum. This apartment is a hideout. If people see all three of you during the day, every day, they, someone, will grow suspicious, and we don't want that, okay?"

All three were on board, so far.

"Great. So, the pool? Not a good idea. Young people in an apartment complex love new blood to move in. Way too many questions. And I'm afraid that it will be the same for most anything fun you can think of. You are hiding in plain sight, but hiding nonetheless. Understand?"

Perfect agreement.

"Okay. Now, this is only temporary. You have to understand that as well. What I'm doing here is giving you a breather, and a chance to find out what I can do that will be best for all of you in the long run. I'm trying to make you realize that a day may come, and sooner than later, when you will either have to move quickly or forever. I hate it, but believe me, for now this is the best I can do.

"And one more thing. Two things, actually. One: you cannot tell your friends, or anyone you meet, or anyone who freaking asks, period. You must not forget that. One slip and this is gone. Seriously. Okay? And, two: if it ever comes down to me getting arrested for helping you guys, please don't say I kidnapped you. I would be an old man before I ever got out of prison."

All three in the secret club laid down promises, and would even have sworn an oath had I demanded one. I settled for them saying that they could never do anything to hurt me after all I was doing for them.

I felt grand. I felt that I had beaten The System.

"Vinnie?"

"Yeah, Sandra?"

"I need at least one frying pan."

"What else have I forgot?" I mumbled to myself.

"Okay," I said, brightening, "here's what we're going to do. Who's got a pen?"

No one. I would have to ask for paper next but we didn't have that either, so, crap.

"Paulie. You stay here and let the rental people in with the furniture. You two come with me."

In another hour the kids had it all, including frying pans, cereal bowls and spoons, and Paulie's beanbag chair. They had everything except parents who gave a shit.

Okay. Some things you could live without if you had to.

* * *

Driving back to my place, that thought kept ringing around in my head. Some things, I had been thinking, you could darn well live without. Such as parents. Orphans did it. The millions of children raised by wolves managed the trick. But that wasn't it. There was something elemental I was missing. . . .

I nearly jammed on the brakes without thinking. Or, rather, because I was thinking. I had been relying too much on Sandra's maternal instincts to fill in the gaps, such as forgetting that a kitchen needed kitchen stuff. But bedrooms needed bedroom stuff, and the kids a few miles behind me had a bed and a sofa-bed, and I had already made it clear that Sandra got the bedroom and bed, yet unless I did something about their current state of affairs, they all would be using spare shirts for blankets.

Getting turned around, I found a discount store, picking up sheets, blankets and pillows fairly cheap. This led me to wondering what else I was omitting. If it was only big Paulie Jr. I could have fixed him up with a small TV, a large bag of chips, a roll of toilet tissue, and the beanbag, and he would have been good to go.

Impossible. I couldn't wrap my head around it, trying to anticipate every little thing. Dental floss, toenail clippers, band-aids, salt and pepper shakers, salt and pepper, coasters, fucking Flintstone vitamins.

It was only after I had dropped off this latest trunkful that I truly saw the light, figured out what that last item was that I needed to complete the list, the ol' cherry atop the cake.

All I lacked now was for the shit to hit the fan.

Chapter 20

"You drunk again?" I asked.

Dino filled his top-of-the-steps doorway, bleary eyed, wearing only underwear and stubble. I looked past his shoulder to spy food items and dirty dishes lining the counter.

"What? No. I was asleep. What are you doin'?"

"Unless you've got a really ugly girl in there you're ashamed to let me see, I'm just standing here getting soaked is what I'm doing," I said. It had begun raining again. And lightning. I pushed my way past Dino, ugly girl or no.

"What are you doing sleeping in the middle of the day?" Clearing a pizza box from a stool, I had a seat, inspecting it first.

"It's . . ." Dino looked at his watch, having already gathered a rough estimate of the time of day from the heavy gloom outside, "after eight, man. Hardly the middle of the day. I stayed up late last night watchin' TV."

"Let me guess. A Gilligan's Island marathon was on and you couldn't tear yourself away," I said, taking inventory of all the crap on the counter. "Company?" I guessed.

"Vivi was over. Left sometime after midnight."

Vivian Binderstaff. I always made fun of her name, but never in front of her. Dino was waiting on me to crack wise now, I could tell.

"So, ah, did she, um . . . ?"

"Have to go to work this mornin'? Yeah, smart guy. Leave Vivi alone."

"Geez, what a grouch."

Dino took in my grin and shook his head.

"Let me get dressed, man, "he said, heading for the rear of the apartment.

"You letting the garbage air out before you bag it?" I said, taking a tour of the bachelor HQ/pig sty.

My cousin ignored my sarcasm. I began tossing refuse into the nearby empty trashcan, unable to understand some people at all. If you wanted a rat and roach problem, this was a really good way to go about it. I bagged up the mess and ran it out to the large city containers outside, dashing back indoors before a bolt of lightning nailed me, what with all the luck I was having today.

"What's up?"

Dino had returned, running an electric razor over his mug, oblivious to the exquisite results from Vinnie's Immaculate Maid Service. Fine. I had something that should capture his attention.

"You're not going to believe this. I got fired," I said in a straight-faced monotone.

The razor clicked off. Dino held the device midair, staring at me and frowning.

"Fired? Whatddayamean fired? You can't get fired, Vinnie." And he clicked the razor back on and waited for whatever punchline I was working toward.

"And told not to come around the house anymore." I would let that percolate between Dino's ears as I headed for his refrigerator. "You want one?" I asked, helping myself to a beer.

"Um, sure, I guess."

When I handed Dino a beer, I still had my face blank as Vivi Binderstaff's mind. There was no punchline. He could read that, the earlier frown deepening.

"The hell's going on, Vinnie?"

I twisted off the cap and shrugged before outlining how things stood between me and my old man, and how I had relocated the kids. Dino was looking at me oddly, not that I could blame him.

"So, lemme get this straight. You no longer work for Uncle Ronnie, and Paulie Pet's after you, and you've set up three little kids with their own apartment. That it?"

"In a nutshell."

Dino scoffed. "In a nutshell. Damn, Vinnie, what's it been? A day and a half? You've been awful busy, haven't you? What're you tryin' to do? Start a war?"

"Don't be dramatic," I said, attempting to take some of the hard edges off this block of granite I was shouldering, without success.

"Me dramatic! Look at you, Mr. Fired Boss's Son! Damn, Vinnie! What the hell are you gonna do?"

Egad! My cousin was a lot more upset than I was. Do? Well, that was it, wasn't it? That was the thing. Back to the nutshell. Being confident that I was in the right didn't put bread on the table. I would be making my own way, whatever way that would be, and do just fine.

"I'll think of something," I said.

"Like what?" Dino set aside his razor and lit up, so at least now the place smelled like a fresh ashtray rather than a stale one.

"Dino, it's been me who's been doing most of the planning for the past couple of years. All I gotta do is hire some new talent."

My cousin just had to turn his head exactly as he did so he could squint back at me at a critical slant, making a silent skeptical point.

"It's a free country, Dino."

"Bullshit, Vinnie. You can't just carve yourself out a slice of pie in this town."

"Why not?"

Dino smoked and tried another sideways look. He started pacing. While he was at it, he started mumbling. "Don't talk crazy, man. You gotta answer to people. You know that."

"I got fired, Dino. I don't have to answer to bupkis. Besides, it's a rather large town in case you haven't noticed."

"With some rather large kingdoms, Vinnie. You were a prince. And now you're a—"

"A nothing, Dino? Is that what you were about to say? That now I'm a nobody?" And, seeing the look on my cousin's face, I laughed.

"Dino! I'm not mad at you! I'm not even mad anymore at dad. Paulie Pet— him I've still got issues with, but even he isn't that big a deal. Believe me, I get what you're saying. The last thing on my mind is stepping on toes around here. But, dammit, this is a big town, and there's plenty of room to move without bumping into the wrong people. Think, Dino! The family ain't everywhere, dude, nor can they be. Okay? I'll be fine. Just have to be careful, that's all."

The cigarette got mashed, and the beer turned turtle, and Dino got himself in front of the window over the sink to gaze upon the gathering darkness, the rain still falling, harder if anything. He was thinking: If there is one guy who can carve out his own turf, it's Vinnie. To hear Vinnie tell it, he's "born to it." Knows more ins and outs than guys twice his age.

"So, cuz, whaddaya say?" I said brightly, snapping Dino out of his twilight daydream.

Just as Dino was turning, lighting struck with a quarter-second thunder count. He was staring open-mouthed as if I had planned the strike and ka-boom for effect.

"Whoa. I hope that wasn't my car," I said, coming closer to stand by Dino's side. As one, we backed away from the window a precautious few feet. The rain came down like it meant business.

Raising his voice, Dino ventured, "You sayin' what I think you're sayin'?"

"Look at it like this—you're already on the shit list, guilty by association, right? You're sick of paperwork. And now you can't even do that until Lord

Renaldi gives his blessing. You're feeling like you've gotta stay stuck here, and it's driving you crazy. Am I right?

"It's only been a coupla days," Dino said in weakness, lacking enthusiasm, stating nothing greater than a lousy remembrance of a lousy couple of days.

I enacted a parody of a hump-shouldered guy dragging his feet and talking like a drooler. "'S only bin a coupla weeks, man. I'm be fine. An' I lub my job, too. Weally. I catchya later, I gotsta watchda TV. Has anyonebody seens da remote? Doh! Dere id is!" I stumbled to the sofa and plopped down bonelessly, sagging and oozing into an imaginary comfort zone, tucking that hand not holding the remote into the top of my pants, a la Al Bundy.

"Ha ha. You're a riot," Dino said, rolling his eyes.

"Uh-huh. Sure I am. I'm just telling you how it is. I don't want you to be surprised if you become Dad's favorite whipping boy. He wouldn't understand all the psychological reasons why he would be torturing you to get back at me. To him it would just make sense. Not good sense, but his sense. You following me?"

"Aw, fuck," Dino said upon reflection, knowing it was true. Would be true.

I smiled encouragement and said, "Thatta boy."

Making a goofy face, Dino silently mouthed back, "Thatta boy!" returning the favor of live theater. Hey, this was fun. I only hoped that really wasn't my Nova out there that got nailed by the lightning.

"Wait a minute. If I say yes, what happens? I gotta call up Uncle Ronnie and tell him I quit?"

I had already thought about all this on the way over.

"Not necessarily. You could wait until he called you. While he's thinking that he's making you sweat, you're already one up. You then say that you've thought about it, and decided that the warehouse job wasn't right for you. Thank him for the opportunity, and then leave it alone."

"Just like that," Dino said, snapping his fingers.

"Just like that," I echoed, able to channel Supreme Confidence. It went hand in hand with my Supreme Bullshit. If you could not think on your feet in this life, all kinds of good stuff were going to pass you by. "Never a dull moment"—that was my new motto.

"I don't know, Vinnie. I think I'd feel better if I just made a clean break. What do you think?"

Think? Why, that my sly plan was working perfectly. "Up to you, cuz. I can see it either way," I said with a green-means-go light in my eyes.

Dino's phone was on the counter. I had found it under a Dixie plate of dried ketchup smears and chicken tender crumbs. I tossed it to him.

He was at war with himself; that was easy to see. Yet, as I saw him looking around his crib, with the rain coming down, I could tell that the walls were closing in on him, and that his sense of isolation being open-ended only helped with his decision.

Speed-dial. Bam.

"Aunt Teresa? Hi. This is Dino."

I watched in fascination as the beginnings of my puppet mastery played out.

"Aw, okay I guess. And how are you doin'?" Dino kept his eyes on the floor as he drew on his Marlboro.

"Yeah, it's really comin' down here, too," he said.

Man. Dino and my mom talking about the weather. Another few seconds and Dino was going to pop like an over expanded balloon.

"I know what you mean. Say, Aunt Teresa? Is Uncle Ronnie there? I need to speak with him for a minute if I could. . . . Sure, I'll hang on."

Dino looked up at me. "She's getting him," he said as if I had not been able to follow.

I nodded in sympathy, paying attention to how Dino kept his nerves in check, something I had cataloged the other day when I had put Dino in the sleeper compartment of that truck. Nervous. But he hadn't backed down then, and after moving along this far, he would not back down now. Not that this unpleasant chore wasn't extra hard, this being not just family, but his boss, his uncle, the local don.

"Uncle Ronnie? Dino here."

I polished off my beer, seeing in my mind's eye where Dad was likely standing, in the kitchen, gaze set between the darkened backyard and mom, frowning, wheels turning.

"Yes, sir. I am. But that's not why I called. I'm goin' to try somethin' different, Uncle Ronnie, and this is me sayin' I'm not goin' to be workin' at the warehouse no more."

There. He'd done it. Guts. My cousin had guts. Though he was looking a bit pale.

"Right. And I'm sorry about that. I appreciate it, Uncle Ronnie. . . . Yes, sir, I'll tell Mom hi. Bye."

Dino punched out, breathing faster, the adrenaline catching up to him. He stared at me.

"I did it. Damn, I really did it. Sonofabitch. I gotta sit down."

Ha. I brought him another beer. My kid cousin had just enough left in the tank to clink bottles with me.

"What was that you were talking about when you said 'I'm sorry about that'?"

"Huh? Oh. Ah, your dad said that my quittin' was for the best 'cause I was costin' him big money."

Right, the don acting as if this was all in his favor, when I knew that it had to be stinging him on a personal note. I was not doing this, this orchestration, out of spite. Pulling Dino all the way over to my side was not calculated to hurt my dad. That aspect was a necessary resetting of the board.

I had not been tricking Dino when I had predicted that Ronnie Renaldi would use him as a doormat in the aftermath of recent ill-omened events. This way, I pulled my cousin out from any blowback right in time, and gained for myself a loyal employee, my first.

"Geez, man, I really did it. What now?" Dino said, taking a long drink from his beer.

"Now, cuz, we go out and celebrate. My treat."

It was amazing how major change came about as quickly as that last bolt of lightning, transforming a half asleep, moping Dino into a wide-eyed energized kid again. He sprang from the sofa saying he was going to change clothes, talking animatedly to me as I waited, the metamorphosis lightening my heart. I loved this nut.

As Dino was still jabbering away, I called a taxi, unwilling to spoil a night with a buzzed driving charge. When he danced out of his bedroom he had one burning question.

"Vinnie? Does this mean I get to be your lieutenant?"

"It damn sure does," I said, giving the nut a big punch on the shoulder, gasping right after as I fought my way out of a bear hug.

"Sorry about that, boss!" Dino said, punching me back hard on my shoulder.

Ow! I rubbed the shoulder. "Rule number one: Never hit the boss."

"You're right. Sorry," Dino said, waiting until I nodded that all was forgiven before slugging me on the same shoulder, harder than before.

I gave my newly commissioned lieutenant a worried look, afraid I'd created a monster.

"You and me, Vinnie, we got no rules!"

We laughed a bit hysterically, nothing major, but it was infectious. By the time the taxi arrived we had another beer apiece and were primed for whatever came our way.

I guess Dino was right. From now on we would be making our own rules. And then breaking them for the hell of it.

As long as I agreed.

<h1 style="text-align:center">CHAPTER 21</h1>

Someone was doing a really annoying imitation of a hammer-headed woodpecker on my front door, for how long I didn't know. The damned persistent noise had awakened me, otherwise there was no way I would be up at—I looked at my bedside clock—6:15!

Oh, this was bad news, because, one: there was the unforgiving fact that I had not crawled into bed earlier than 3:00 a.m., and bad news for the woodpecker because, two: I was getting ready to smash its beak.

I jumped into pants that had been lazily discarded onto the floor a few short freaking hours ago, threw on a shirt from nearby, and stuffed my gun into the waistband at my back as a precaution against having it in hand and therefore be tempted into inserting a spontaneous third nostril into the bird's beak.

Quickstepping down the short hallway, there was nary a teen in sight, the space having an empty feel to it, more than a simple absence of bodies. This was the first time since getting the apartment that I had been alone inside it, and now there was someone at my door figuring to reorder the new order.

When I was still ten feet away, the peckerwood changed tactics and began kicking the poor door.

Had to be Paulie Pet.

"Open this door! I know you're in there you little shits!"

I could not get the locks unbolted fast enough to suit me. I was betting that my new neighbors were ecstatic having me move in. One second later I knew this for a fact, because just before I threw the door wide I heard Paulie Pet bellow, "Whatchu lookin' at?" and at least two doors slammed.

As soon as I opened up, Paulie rushed inside like the biggest kid at the Easter egg hunt. His wide face was red, and his great bulk was heaving with deep breaths. The maniac actually had his teeth bared and was, actually, snarling. He was in the middle of the big, front room before he finally rounded on me, having yet caught sight of any beloved children.

"Where are they! Whatchu done wid my kids!"

As I did not answer within one one-hundredth of a second, Paulie was off racing through the place, looking behind the sofa and recliner as if this were a game. Well, one thing was for sure, I was having a blast. Nothing spelled out good times better than a hangover, a serious ongoing lack of sleep, and an 800-pound gorilla playing twenty questions in my front room, said ape all but beating his chest and slinging feces.

"Yo, Paulie! Dude! They're not here," I said in a clear voice, standing in the middle of the room where even the dimmest vision could see that there were no kids hiding behind me, or painted to blend in with the walls.

I remained right where I was, giving Paulie plenty of time to check under the bed, inside all closets, and even my dresser drawers by the sound of it. But Paulie was a poorly reasoning gorilla, having neglected to search the kitchen trashcan and the sitcom space under the sink.

He came storming back into the big room, his chest laboring with his frenzied exertions. I could smell the liquor on his breath from four strides away. Paulie Pet had come loaded for bear, and things were not working out as he had planned.

"All right, where are dey, asshole?"

I believed in taking the high road in fretful situations like this, and was a better human bean for doing so.

"In case you forgot, I told you when you first barged in, that they are not here. And now that you have verified that fact for yourself, you may leave."

"What'd you do wid 'em, Vinnie? You tell me!"

"Calm down, Paulie. I haven't done anything with them. Dad told me yesterday that they had to go, and that's what I told them. I gave them cab fare. They didn't go home?" I said.

And here was the funny thing—sometimes, when I lied this well it made me feel as if I have innocently failed to answer my true calling in life, like I could have been a celebrated actor, or a dick-headed politician.

"You're lyin'!"

"Now, Paulie, that ain't polite. I was informed that you were upset, which I can see. Clearly. I was told they had to go and, as I've said, they're gone. So, if we're done here, I have really got to get back to bed. I mean, do you know what time it is?"

His giant mitts outstretched, Paulie made it into his second step toward me before I had my gun in both hands, lowering my aim from his belly to his left kneecap, and he has got really large kneecaps, so I couldn't miss.

"Your play, Paulie."

"You son of a—"

"Uh-uh-uhh!" I uttered in warning. "You're drunk, and you're in the middle of my apartment threatening me. Paulie, if I were you I would seriously reconsider my options, if you know what I—"

"Everything all right in here?"

I only tore my eyes away from Paulie after backing up two judicious steps to my left to see Psycho Cop in the entryway, gun drawn on me, but keeping a close eye on Paulie as well.

"Who da fuck are you?" Paulie spat, his fingers opening from clenched fists and closing again, over and over to frame his aggression.

"Police," Alfred Clarence Eddy said. "You," meaning me, "lower your weapon."

"This is my apartment, officer," I explained while lowering my gun and backing off an additional two steps toward the balcony door.

"Okay. I've seen you in the hallway. And you, mister?" my gun-toting neighbor asked Paulie. "Do you live here as well?"

"This dog turd has my kids!" Paulie Pet blurted, answering the cop in his own compelling way.

"Is that true?" Eddy asked, rather suspiciously, I thought.

"Absolutely not, officer," I answered evenly, wishing that Chris Lewis had employed any description of his stepdad other than "psycho."

"Is this man threatening you?"

Eddy was again speaking to me. I had to get this cop out of here. "It's a misunderstanding, officer. This gentleman here was just leaving."

There was a chance, a very good chance, that this situation could go south quickly. It all depended on how stupid Paulie Pet was going to be. I had given him an out. All he had to do was take it.

Indecision on the cop's face was as evident as the drying dab of shaving cream low on his neck from when he had been so rudely interrupted in the midst of his morning ablutions. Paulie's theatrics had obviously been heard all the way down the hall, through a metal door, and into the psycho's bathroom, possibly even over running water.

"And you, sir. I want you to slowly set the gun on that end table . . . good. Now slowly step away and have a seat on the floor over there," Eddy said, pointing with his weapon where I was to sit, placing me away from any furniture, yet well in sight and weaponless.

With one hand in Paulie's back, Eddy used the hand not holding the gun to frisk Paulie, dangerous and foolishly risky. Nevertheless, he came up with Paulie's piece. Keeping his eyes on Paulie, he backed away until he could easily cover us both.

"You got a permit?" Eddy asked Paulie, setting Paulie's gun beside mine.

"Fuck your mother," was Paulie's less than keen response.

"I want you to spread your feet apart . . . farther, sir, back the way I had them. Wider. Now, keeping your hands on the wall, inch backward with your feet until I tell you to stop. Good . . . a little more . . . stop."

Eddy handcuffed Paulie, then led him to sit on the sofa before frisking me.

All this was, by far, not by the book. Eddy had already committed so many procedural errors, that if things had gone badly, his ass could, and would, be toasted upon investigation. The guy, a pro, did not seem to care. He should have called for backup the minute he drew on me. Whatever. It wasn't my business to tell him his business.

I submitted to the frisk. Hell, I didn't even have shoes on. It took very little time and I was out nothing.

"And you?" Eddy asked me. "You have a permit for the gun?"

"Yes, sir. In my wallet in the bedroom."

Now Eddy had yet another meaty decision to make, and another chance to compound his mistakes. I watched him calculate the danger of either having me go retrieve the alleged permit, and possibly a second weapon for all he knew, or going with me, leaving the excitable Paulie unattended, a no-win situation.

"You can show it to me in a minute. First, I want you to tell me why this man," Paulie, "would think you had his kids," Eddy said, looking between the two of us.

Going with a new premise, that a half-truth may travel much farther than a whole lie in the here and now, I said, "Because they were here yesterday, wanting a place to stay."

Eddy frowned. "And you allowed them to stay?"

"I was trying to do the right thing, officer, but I told them they could not stay." Well, after several days. Technically, it counted as the truth.

"And where are they now?"

"Beats me. As I told the gentleman on the sofa, I gave them cab fare and wished them luck."

I saw the cop narrow his eyes. I never should have tacked on that last part about wishing them luck.

"Let's take a walk, big guy," Eddy said in addressing Paulie. He waited for Paulie to stand before grasping the cuffs' links between Paulie's wrists which were behind his back. Guiding Petralucci down the short hallway, Eddy said to me, already motioned into the lead, "Nice and slow, sir. We'll have a look at that permit.

So, this was Eddy's improvised plan to cover all bases. His supervisors would be mortified. Then again, from what I knew of his record, he was an outlaw cop and an ex-marine, or, as any marine out of service will tell you, he was a marine, no "ex" to it.

I made sure to walk at a slow and calm pace. From atop the bedside nightstand, I lifted my wallet in a like manner. Thankfully, I had moved the kids yesterday, otherwise this drama would have never proceeded to this point. We were nearing a resolution, however temporary. Removing my gun permit, I handed it to the cop who, so far, had not revealed his full-blown psycho persona. Alleged F.B.P.P.

The permit was good. I have never been arrested, either as a juvenile or as an adult. As far as Eddy knew, I was a model citizen, unlike Eddy himself, because there was no way he lived in this building on a straight cop's pay.

After studying the paper, Eddy announced, "Okay, everyone back to where we started," dropping my permit atop the rumpled bedsheets before jerking at Paulie's restraints as if he were steering an ox.

I should have seen it coming. Paulie jerked back.

Eddy, sensing the threat, leveraged the cuffs higher as a deterrent against misbehavior, but Paulie, whether fueled by alcohol, or because he hated not being the one doing the bullying, spun hard to his left, carrying Eddy with him, forcing the cop over a well-thought out stiff leg maneuver, with Eddy's center of mass pivoting into a hard fall.

In front of both characters by one advantageous step, I rabbit-hopped through the bedroom doorway into the hall as Eddy, from the floor, caught Paulie's giant foot slamming down toward his face. Using both hands and dropping his gun to do so, Eddy grasped Paulie's foot—heel and toe—and savagely wrenched the thick ankle. I heard bone snap like dry kindling. Paulie roared as he crashed beside the cop.

It was over as Eddy was on his feet in a flash, pocketing his gun and hauling mightily on the cuffed hands to manhandle Paulie upright in one move.

Shit. If I had not seen it I would not have believed it credible. This guy wasn't just strong, he was on some other level of strength beyond fitness. Paulie Pet weighed a good 315 to 325 lbs., and the cop stood him up in a dead lift as if hauling a sack of potatoes upright.

"Up front! Move!" Eddy barked.

Eddy might have been talking to Paulie, but the command was good enough to get my own feet in gear, leading the way. I turned as I heard a large crash, Paulie theoretically having trouble negotiating the bedroom doorway, his boulder of a head bouncing hard off the doorframe with a little help from the cop.

Between Paulie Pet and Psycho Cop, my doorways were like magnets to be abused for the fun of it, though presently I thought I would gladly absorb the loss rather than the impact, grateful it wasn't me all but hopping on one foot.

Paulie was in serious pain, had to be. That snap I had heard meant that the gorilla was probably hobbling with the ends of the bone at the break grinding against each other. The fellow really did need a vacation anyway, a quality time-out, one that would allow that doorjamb-width welt on his forehead sufficient time to heal.

"Mind if I use your phone, Mr. Renaldi?"

The ruckus had not caused Eddy any trouble recalling my name from my gun permit. "Help yourself," I said, downplaying my role as courteous host.

He nodded at my ability to continuously supply correct answers. To Paulie, Eddy said, "You are going to sit there and be quiet. Aren't you?"

"Fuck you, you pussy piece of shit," Paulie managed to squeeze out from between clenched jaws, not sitting.

It really wasn't Paulie's best effort at retort, but, hey, one must factor in the level of pain and the degree of humiliation. The important thing, to Paulie, was not to let the arresting officer forget that he was dealing with a tough guy. Still, I say good for Paulie. I mean, you have got to stay in character, can't go all dish-raggedy once cuffed.

Eddy fluidly spun Paulie and gave him a light push, depositing the surprised ogre neatly centered upon my sofa whence I detected the second loud crack in three minutes. No bone this time I was afraid. No, that was wood, dammit.

Using my landline phone, Eddy contacted his brethren in blue, reporting the facts as he chose to interpret them, requesting an ambulance for the A-hole resisting arrest, and jabbering a lot of mind-numbing code that I found vaguely amusing.

Just wait until I told Dino all that he had missed. He was going to wish he had come back here last night instead of allowing this drop-dead gorgeous redhead to have her way with him at closing time. Wherever the hell we'd been.

"Officer?" I asked without raising my hand first.

"Yeah?"

"Okay if I make a cup of coffee?"

"Fine."

"Anyone else?" I asked civilly, including the mastodon with the snapped ankle.

"If it's no trouble," Psycho said.

"Not at all. Cream and sugar?"

"Black."

Of course. Had Eddy gone for cream and sugar I was certain that Paulie Pet would again have called him a pussy, and rightly so.

Paulie kept giving me dirty looks. And to think—had he not saved my life he would have missed out on all of this. I briefly considered advising Paulie to elevate his ankle, but in the end rejected doing so on humanitarian grounds, Paulie Pet not being remotely human.

Psycho Eddy was all business between sips of coffee as the paramedics and a pair of patrol officers responded. Paulie was splinted, tolerated, and loaded onto a gurney, the paramedics going purple in the face giving Paulie the ol' heave-ho. Me, I was committing it all to memory so that I could relish exaggerating every nuance of the experience as the coming happy years rolled by.

When the hustle and bustle finally cleared it was almost nine o'clock, and I was pretty much wide awake, dammit. I poured another cup of coffee and thought about repercussions, seriously considering breaking my lease. The damned apartment was cursed. It seemed that no matter what, I could not spend time here alone.

I inspected the outside door again, and called the super to replace it, thereby forfeiting my security deposit. While changing out the doors I would ask him to take a look at my splintered bedroom doorjamb. And maybe get around to asking if there was such a thing as a sofa repair person who made house calls.

Chapter 22

Paulie Jr. had been cautioned not to take calls from anyone other than myself. The phone in his possession had a number separate from my second cell phone, one known to only a handful of people, mummy and daddy dearest not included. Still, I had to wonder, not for the first time, how wise this gifting had been on my part. There were so many ways to trip up . . .

"Hi, Vinnie."

"Paulie, you doing okay over there? Need anything?"

"Uh. Hang on. I'll ask."

Ha. He was deferring to the domestic goddess. It was a shame that anything bad had befallen this pair of siblings. At the same time, I knew that it was a comfort to each knowing the other was safe, even if half the team would self-malnourish if it wasn't for Sandra's good work.

"Sandra says the few things we need aren't much and that she can walk to the store to get 'em."

Um. "Has that happened yet? Going outside, I mean."

"Just to get a coupla sodas at the pool."

"During the day?" I asked.

"Last night. I was careful, Vinnie. Right there and back, I swear."

Poor kid. "Well, that's fine. Meet anyone?" I figured that if I didn't ask I wouldn't know, Paulie unlikely to be wary of any causal encounter. He answered me that he had met no one.

"And Chris? Is he okay?"

"Chris? Yeah. Um, hold on."

Discussion time.

"Vinnie?"

"Right here."

"Yeah, Chris was wondering if there was a library close by."

"You can't use the phone to find out?" I asked, puzzled.

"Chris says your phone doesn't do stuff like that," Paulie replied.

Yeah, for good reason, I did not say. You've got too many goodies on a smartphone, you were an easy target to trace. With cell connections, the dumber the better.

"You can't call information?" I said.

"Oh. Hold on."

Ai yai.

"Vinnie?"

Sigh. "Yeah, buddy?"

"Chris said he didn't think of that."

Darn budding geniuses always had a difficult time with shoelaces and common sense in general. I mean, here was a kid, Chris Lewis, who had singlehandedly taken on Psycho Cop one on one. Lost, sure, but took him on all the same—I'd had the full story. He might have had a screw knocked loose.

"Well, then. Anything else?"

"I don't think so. Sandra says to say 'Thanks.'"

And that was all the reward I needed. If I wasn't a gangster I'd probably be a pretty nice guy.

"Okay. You guys take care and I'll be in touch. Everyone call their moms to let them know they're all right?"

"Yeah, and Mom is pissed," Paulie said.

Probably. Pissed, with selective hearing and vision, combined with inadequate overall judgement. Probably pissed that the truth was coming out and she would look bad. This family was so top-heavy dysfunctional that I doubted if any single member would know where to realistically start to try to fix things.

Which brought my consideration around to Paulie Pet. I had yet to inform the kids about what went down earlier, and I was unsure why I was withholding that news. I seriously doubted that Paulie Sr. would be in jail or handcuffed to a gurney for long. Dad, or someone else, would spring him, possibly even our elusive lawyer.

"Well, Paulie, you know you can always go back home any time you choose, right? I'm not telling anyone what they have to do, okay?"

"I understand. But my mom did say something about calling the cops."

Oh, boy. I really didn't think that either she or Paulie Pet would jump in that deep. They would have to know that their monstrous parenting skills would come to the fore, resulting in legal action against them. But I knew the kids' mother. She had issues, her weakness against Paulie Sr. being her greatest.

"One step at a time, Paulie. All we need to do is get your dad to see the light. I'm working on it."

I understood the ensuing silence, Paulie having outgrown absurd fairy tales years ago.

"Anyway, like I said, I'll be in touch. Bye."

"Bye."

Well, that was that. Now all I had to do was keep the cops out of my business, and sit down to an enriching heart-to-heart with Paulie Petralucci.

What could possibly go wrong with that?

* * *

The West Side Boys operated out of an infamously sleazy bar off Canal Street near the Holland Tunnel. If you did not have business there you were not welcome. The Boys looked out for their own, making sure that once you were in prison your life was as good as it could get with money, drugs, tobacco, and food. It was assumed that sooner or later most everyone did get busted for something, the Boys not being the low-profile sort. It was a lifestyle, a dangerous wave one rode until beached, dead or alive.

I most certainly did not have any business with the West Siders; yet, hearing of big trouble in the works twice in the same week had me paying attention. First, it had been Dino's brother Mario at Uncle Mike's viewing who had voiced the incredulous prophecy, and it was precisely because it had been Mario that I had initially disregarded the information. Even should the rumor prove true, I would never be so desperate as to throw in with Mario.

Then it had been Tony F. that same night saying the rumors may be true. So, it was all the more surprising that the third time I caught wind of hard times brewing for the Boys came from Dino himself. My new lieutenant was over at my place.

In a two-man army, Dino could be a general if he wanted to be one; I didn't care. He had dropped by because he was bored and hadn't seen my new place yet. Hell, he didn't look any worse for wear and tear following his abduction by the redhead last night.

"What would a party girl from Queens know about the cops setting up a major takedown on the West Side?" I asked my cousin.

We were standing in the front room as the building super and a helper were replacing my hallway door. Occasionally they would give us a look, no doubt wondering what kind of lunatic visitors I got who could do that amount of damage to a steel door.

Dino spread his smile to the max, looking like a toothpaste ad. He had to have his teeth whitened every six months to mitigate the tobacco staining. He opened the balcony door to step outside for fresh air and a smoke.

"Her father's a cop," Dino said, wallowing with relish in such a punchline.

Ye gads, I had cops falling out of my ears.

"Her dad's a cop who goes around the house with nothing better to do than blab about a pending takedown?" I asked with a great amount of skepticism. And that was wrong of me. "Never say never" applied to everything, whether coincidence was stoically acknowledged or not.

"Well, her father is a lonely drunk who likes an audience, and the only one around to listen is Trish."

A powerful gust of wind blew Dino's smoke in my face, along with an unexpected soft burst of ash.

"What happened?" Dino queried about the goosey way I'd flinched.

I repositioned my cuz to a less dangerous position.

"Nothing," I said, using a shirttail to clean my eye. "So. We've got a drunk cop and his pretty daughter spending depressing evenings conversing about the West Side Boys. What, it's either that or watch *Wheel of Fortune*? In that case I can see the appeal."

Ah—there came the sounds of tools being packed away. "Hold on one minute," I told Dino, rushing back inside to surprise the super about the doorjamb that Paulie's forehead beat up.

When I returned, Dino was hipshot against the railing, looking out toward Manhattan and the gray clouds scudding low over the spiked skyline. We were caught up in a pattern in which rain could be expected every other day, or so it seemed. I was paying attention because I had it in mind to catch the big fireworks display this coming Fourth of July weekend from this very spot.

After I apologized for the interruption, Dino commented, "Paulie Pet's a one-man wrecking crew."

"With a little help from Officer Friendly," I said, the scene fresh in my mind. Hopefully, after the repairs, there would be no lingering visual reminder, which made me recall that I still had a bloodstained white carpet. You know, I was real close to torching this place and collecting on my renter's insurance.

Dino's smile got crooked. "You really think your neighbor's a psycho?" He was obviously impressed by the tag team of natural chaos imitating men.

Facing west and enjoying the breeze, I wondered what it would be like living up here during a hurricane. With the glass door all taped up I could throw a hell of a party.

Alfred Clarence Eddy a psycho? I felt as if I could pick his name out of a psycho lineup. "Yeah, I do," I told Dino. "He's the lunatic fringe side of gung-ho. But he's efficient; I'll give him that."

We tracked a flock of pigeons crossing the sky in blurring formation, going about a hundred miles an hour.

"Back to your new girlfriend, Dino. You believe this is on the level? A raid is definitely in the pipeline?" The damn cops had a death wish if they were anxious to root out that snake hole in which the Boys bellied up to the bar.

Dino was biting his lips. "Um, about Trish? Don't say anything to Vivi."

"Perish the thought," I said, without necessity I would have thought.

"Well, look. She's the one brought it up. Besides her old man, I think it had something to do with her being a criminal justice major at NYU."

I gave Dino a sorrowful look. "You sure know how to pick 'em," I said.

Dino shrugged. "Yeah, well, she's great in the sack, and if I ever need to know about what makes a guy like you tick I'll have the inside scoop. Besides, this could be worth somethin', right?"

"You been talking to Mario about this?"

Dino was offended. "Mario. What's Mario got to do with anything?"

I told him.

"No shit? Okay. Well, right off hand I'd say this is legit. No way you get three different confirmations that far apart."

"Exactly what I'm thinking. You want to take a ride?" I said, stepping back inside, with Dino on my heels.

"Sure. Where we goin'?"

"Oh. No place much. Take a cruise up by the Hudson."

"West Side, eh?" Dino said, working on his general/lieutenant look.

"It's a nice day. Why not?"

"What about them?" Dino asked, referring to the super and his man.

"I'll get them to lock up."

"You wanna beer for the road, Vinnie?"

My lieutenant was a bad influence.

"Sure. What the hell."

* * *

Dino and I took the Williamsburg Bridge, carrying over to Fourth Avenue, then south to Canal, just a couple of blocks from our warehouse or, I should say, Mr. Renaldi's warehouse.

Neither of us mentioned this happenstance proximity to Dino's previous nearly-legit place of employment, though I did see him cast his eyes in that direction as I wheeled the Nova the opposite way, heading west.

Catching glimpses of the docks and the water beyond, I began slipping lower in my seat as we neared Aces, the bar claimed by the West Side Boys as their own.

My cousin and I had shades on and, in maintaining a minimum profile, I had my left arm resting on the ledge of the open window, forearm making a picket in the frame. Coming up on my left along the street side curb, I saw what should be typically expected this early in the afternoon: three Harleys side by side and one car belonging to the bartender or someone's old lady. Not that any gal running with the Boys would be old, mind you, the Boys trending young, and just as likely to die that way.

The building itself wasn't all that wide, but rather deep, the length extending long toward the river end. An old-fashioned steeply pitched roof crowned the aged structure, a clue to its long-ago purpose as a residence, back in the days when the gangs controlled these streets. Since those days, the joint had possibly been reconfigured into a rooming house before coming into the current owner's hands as a dockside bar. The establishment's dark reputation had been well-established prior to the arrival of the West Side Boys in the late 1960s.

We stayed with the flow of traffic, riding on to circle back on Greenwich Street to kill a few minutes as I considered what I had seen.

Dino was let off to grab some cold beers as I circled the block, jumping back in a few minutes later, getting the eye from a foot patrolman. I began making my way toward the docks, coming up behind the bar this time. Traffic was spare and the timing right for a weekday afternoon snap decision.

Leaving Dino with the car parked along a row of warehouses, I set off on foot under the shadow of the El, coming up at a brisk walk behind Aces. Looking all around without seeming to look at all, I stopped at the dumpster behind the bar.

I had borrowed a cigarette and lighter from Dino, now used them as props to surveil anyone paying attention to me, quartering my body this way and that as if the wind was my greatest enemy. The breeze was swirling, making the trick that much easier to sell.

Spotting no one about, I dropped low behind the dumpster, ready to move on should I hear the rear door of the bar opening, or movement from either of the side alleys that ran parallel to the building's length.

On my right there was the rear of a fish wholesaler's business, and to my left what appeared to be nothing more than a superannuated warehouse, closed for some time. The fish wholesaler could not care less about the rowdy nighttime crowd at Aces, as their business was conducted during the day.

This entire area had an exposed feel to it. I could easily imagine the icy cut of the wind through these alleys come January, and smell the faint odor of fish overcoming any below-freezing days.

There stood a lone security light pole centered into the crumbling asphalt of the rear area between the back of the bar and the street, some ten paces from where I crouched, a strategic problem for what was developing in my mind, but one that was surmountable.

Though I have never been inside Aces, I had heard tales. People such as my dad believed in banks, loved banks as a matter of fact, not to rob them, but to use them as yet another secure way to make and squirrel away money.

The Boys, on the other hand, were said to favor keeping their loot close. I supposed that this lore meant the existence of a safe within the bar, probably in back if at all. Yet there was no way I could know for sure. I was currently operating on rumors, hearsay, and bloody legend. I needed better intel and I wasn't going to get that from outside.

For now, all I wanted was to eye the exterior layout and aid my memory with a few pictures. I set about snapping one picture after another from a low angle, keeping out of sight as much as possible, my back turned to the occasional passing vehicle on the dockside street behind me.

A creaking sounded—such as that created by a door weighted too heavy for its hinges. It had to be the bar's rear door. I could either take off and be seen, or ride it out. One crouched step brought me fully around to the street end of the rust-scaled dumpster, and thus farther away from the opening door of Aces.

Footsteps were nearing, dragging heels scuffing the pavement. An audible intake of breath prefaced a load thudding against the bottom of what would appear to be a recently emptied dumpster. Seconds ticked by.

"Hey! You!"

It was not until that moment I realized I had neglected to duck out the burning cigarette, not even having considered the giveaway odor, let alone the incriminating smoke. There was nothing to do but play it out.

When the guy rounded the corner, I was hunched over and shivering, hugging both shoulders, the cigarette in my mouth. I purposefully paid zero attention to the intruder hovering over me until he spoke again.

"Go on now! Clean outta here, ya damn spike!"

I struggled to a standing position and began to lurch away, committed to playing the role of a junkie having a bad day, still hugging my shoulders against a chill supposedly only I could feel, counting each step distancing myself as precious. My gun nested in its accustomed place in the small of my back, insurance I had no intention of using.

"Hey!"

I froze, halfway to the sidewalk, facing away from the guy, but prepared to spin around quickly if called for.

"Go one block over. Ask for Haddie. He'll fix ya up," the good Samaritan said.

I turned obliquely to wave a shaky thank you, my hand concealing my face. I got moving.

"The other way, moron!"

My second wave told the guy all he needed to know about this junkie—out of dope, out of money, and out of here just as fast as my role would allow. A quick look over my shoulder showed the guy remaining by the dumpster, hands empty, watching me. He was a large gentleman with an ample gut straining the surprisingly white apron covering it, either a very low-level member or hired help.

As soon as I was out of sight of my big-bellied admirer, I discarded the wretched cigarette and hightailed it back to where I had left Dino.

"That was quick," Dino said, another admirer.

"Not quick enough," I breathed.

"What?"

"Nothing. I got what I wanted. Now I need to take a look around inside."

Dino was staring a hole through me.

"Just a quick in and out," I said smoothly.

"You're gonna just waltz into Aces? Just like that?" Dino said, snapping his fingers very near my face.

"They might suspect something if I send a robot cam inside."

"Well, yeah," Dino agreed, "but a robot is expendable."

"Hm. There is a slight, calculated risk involved," I admitted, my eyes on my mirror, waiting on a pair of trucks to pass before I could pull away from the curb.

"Slight?"

I grinned at my sidekick, saying, "I'll be sure to read my horoscope before I go in."

"What? Alone?"

"Why? You want to go, too?" I had fun asking.

"I do what I'm told," Dino stated, and from the way he sounded he was hoping his answer was brave enough to qualify as an exemption.

It was. As greenhorn leader of my own gang I had to lead by example. And, if nothing else, this would be an excellent jump in promotion for Dino if I got myself killed.

Chapter 23

With anticipation, I removed the leftovers of Sandra's home-away-from-home cooking, shutting the refrigerator door with my elbow because I had both hands full with the heavy covered dish. I spied a mess, using my imagination to envision what the congealed food would look like warmed up. And not in the microwave—I remembered that much.

Preheating the oven, I set myself to the task of printing out the pictures taken earlier at the Boys' hangout. I had driven Dino home, wanting a quiet evening to myself to process what limited information I possessed.

As I waited on my meal to reheat, I spread my photos atop the kitchen table, satisfied with the resolution, though I would have preferred more angles.

It became evident that a possibility existed to ride out any police raid on Aces, and still be in position to rifle the premises once it had been cleared. Only theoretical at this point, my nascent scheme's feasibility warranted further investigation. Yet none of the beginning stages of this plan was worth the effort I was already investing unless I could accurately forecast when the rumored takedown would occur.

I put the problem aside as I uncovered Sandra's creation hot from the oven, the aroma filling the kitchen. Oh, my. Scallopine Buongustaia, with tomatoes that had been fresh. Now, a couple of days later, the juices from the veal, and the chicken livers, had all combined to make my mouth water. Not wanting to wreck the flavors, I poured myself a glass of water to accompany the feast and be my means of quenching my ridiculous moaning over the superb tastes. Damn, this kid could cook.

Washing up, I was ready to view the surveillance photos a second time when my phone chimed. I stared at the unfamiliar number before cautiously answering.

"Hello?"

"Is this Vinnie?"

"And who is calling, please?"

"This is Cara Beely. Social Services? This is Vinnie, right?"

"Oh, hi. Sorry, I didn't recognize your number. What can I do for you, Ms. Beely?"

"Cara. Ms. Beely sounds like an old maid librarian."

I chuckled politely. "Okay, Cara. What gives?"

"Did you get my earlier calls?"

"I'm afraid I only recently got in and never checked. Was there something important?" This could not be good.

"It seems that Paulie's mother is missing not only him, but her eldest daughter as well. There's an Amber Alert out for the both of them. Because of Paulie's recent run-ins with the law, the police contacted me. And the only other person I know of having any dealings in this matter is you."

"I see. I'm sorry that I can't tell you anything. Is their mother sure they've run away?"

"I didn't say anything about them running away, Vinnie. They could have been abducted."

"Oh. Right. Sorry. I didn't mean to be insensitive. I simply assumed . . . what with Paulie's beating and everything . . ."

"What does that mean—'and everything'? What do you know that you're not telling me?" Beely said, her voice hardening.

"Hold on, Cara. I'm afraid I wasn't making myself clear. I meant nothing by saying 'and everything'. It's just an expression, a way of referring to whatever else may be associated with the beating and other problems that Paulie seemed to have suffered. As you and I talked about earlier." Crap, I was close to babbling.

A somewhat mollified Beely said, "Okay. So, you're saying you do not know where the children are?"

Trying to ensnare me in linguistic circles of repetitive queries. Beely wasn't a cop, but she would make a decent detective.

"I'm not only saying it, Cara, I'm telling you they're not here. They could be anywhere," I said, and it was true. Paulie could be poolside depositing money in the soda machine, and Sandra could be out shopping, and Chis could be somewhere else entirely. Anywhere.

"Well, all right. I had to check. If you do hear from Paulie or his sister, would you please let me know? And tell them their mother is worried sick?"

"Sure, no problem. I'll help all I can, Cara. What, are you still at work?"

A disparaging laugh was not belittling of self but of a demanding job, Cara saying, "Devoted, huh?"

"Sounds like it. Look, I just finished eating," and wouldn't you love to know who the cook was, "but I know this little place that serves great bar food if you would like to compare notes and unwind."

"You're not drunk, are you?"

I laughed. "Not even close, or I should say, not at all. I'm sober."

"Oh. Good. In that case I'm going to have to ask where you have in mind, because honestly, Vinnie, it's—"

"Been a long day," I concluded for her, getting that same tired laugh I remembered for my less than stellar effort to be cute.

"Better yet," I said, "you tell me the general area you live in and I'll recommend a suitable place, and see if I can beat you there. That way there'll be no extra travel for you. Sound good?"

"And you're buying?"

Well, Cara was not shy, was she?

"Absolutely. I wouldn't have it any other way."

She named a place only a mile away, making my first choice a winner. I gave her the name of the bar and was not surprised when she said that she knew it.

We got off the phone. I freshened up and was out of my new dingless door in no time, wanting to beat Beely to the bar and get good seats. I was looking forward to picking her brain, finding out just how distraught the kids' mom pretended to be. I know Paulie Pet had put her up to this, I just didn't think he was genuinely that stupid.

Really, I could not say why stupid people should not do other than stupid things. I guess I would have to label myself an optimist, which, in times of stress, may very well be the world's worst kind of stupid to be.

* * *

I had forgot, for some stupid reason, just how bottomless were Cara Beely's eyes. If there were real witches, not the neo-pagan wannabes, but the spooky ones of lore and imagination, I would consider Beely's orbs to be Plato's ideal realized. The soft baby-blue bar light only seemed to tease hints of existing pathways into their depths.

"What are you looking at?" Cara asked.

"You've got some terribly dark eyes," I answered unguardedly, unable to pull myself back in time to make a joke of it.

"'Terribly'? I've got terrible eyes?" Cara said, one dimpled corner of her mouth curling.

"I probably could have put that better."

"Hell, I would hope so. Did I keep you waiting long?"

Upon Beely's entering the bar, I had stood from my stool to receive her and, for some reason, had reached out for her with both hands without saying more than hello. Or maybe it had been "Hi." And then I was bewitched. I planned on keeping a careful eye on her nose lest it twitch.

"Not at all. Please, have a seat. I'm afraid all the tables are full right now," I said.

For a gal who had been at work for what had to have been a seriously long day, all kidding aside, Beely looked to be in exceptionally good form.

"This is fine," she said, gazing around the bustling bar, ignoring my continued search into what I found so mysterious in this petite woman.

If you have ever seen anyone beautiful and on LSD, this, Beely's, was that look, the haunting eyes all black, all pupil. Yet I knew that her eyes were actually a very dark brown. Blame it on the odd lighting, and the fact that even with her eyes shut Cara Beely would be attractive. Terribly.

I caught the bartender's eye while simultaneously asking Beely what would suit her mood.

"A mai tai, please."

That made my day. I had feared that she was going to be a ballbuster, proving she could hang out with the big boys and knock back shots of whiskey.

"Make that two, please," I said, turning to find Beely pleasantly smiling at me.

"I'm surprised," she said.

"The mai tai?" I shrugged. "I haven't had one in years. It'll be a nice change."

"Oh? And what do you normally drink?"

"I'm more of a beer guy. A little whiskey and whatnot out with friends. What would you like to eat? As you know, they've got a pretty good blooming onion."

I caught the grimace. "Club sandwich?" I tried.

A smile. "I could go for that," Cara said, adding, "And maybe some wings?"

"Now you're talking," I said lightly.

I placed the order and nodded my thanks as our drinks were placed before us, Beely laughing at the look on my face as I inspected my tiny paper umbrella sheltering my drink.

"Mm, I believe I'll just set this to the side," I said.

When I looked back up I found my date, or my source of information on two legs, or whatever Beely actually was to me, looking deeper than ever at me.

Honestly, it was a bit disconcerting. In some far out way I found myself wishing she was an actual witch. One who worked for Social Services, a most unlikely place to begin a search for the real or the imagined. Pretty sure she was about to speak, I was unaccountably surprised when she raised her tall glass, quenching her thirst, her pleasure obvious.

I believe the ball had been served with understated style.

"It's a damn shame about Paulie," I said, knowing that sooner or later we would have to talk about our known common interest. It couldn't all be fruity drinks and chicken wings.

"Depends on how you look at it," Beely said enigmatically, catching me off balance.

"Um, how do you mean?"

Cara waited until the guy on the adjacent stool stopped braying his laughter, the increased decibel level too great for the setting, the bartender giving the fellow the once-over, with an eye to cutting him off. I rolled my eyes to lessen the jaggedness of the moment, watching as Beely copied, making me smile. I was sober. What was happening to me? I realized that I needed to ask the question concerning Paulie again.

"It depends on where Paulie actually is, wouldn't you say? Do you believe it's possible that he and his sister are together somewhere?"

And before I could respond, she tacked on, "Safe?"

"As opposed to a darker alternative? Sure. If that is the case, that they're safe, then I would have to consider his or possibly their position, as being beneficial. Being bullied as a kid is something a lot of kids go through. And live through. But when it's the father, or stepfather anyway, it has got to really hurt. And I don't mean just physical pain."

Beely's questioning looked zipped from one eye to the other. "Right," she acknowledged, "but you just said 'their' position more beneficial. Why would his sister's position be more beneficial by being away from her home?"

Well, crap. I was going to have to monitor my words more carefully. It wasn't hard to figure that Beely suspected me of aiding the kids. Hell, it was at her suggestion that I had become involved in the first place. At least that's the way I remembered it.

"Ah, we can assume that in a home in which Paulie is abused, that the family dynamic must be out of whack, correct?" I tried, covering my tiny slip.

Beely nodded, her dark searchlight all over me.

"So," I continued, in for a penny, "it's hardly a stretch of the imagination to say that if that is the case, then she, too, could be adversely affected from—"

My pseudo date was holding up one hand, palm out. I ceased my yapping and reached for my drink, tempted to reinsert the umbrella so I could poke myself good and hard in the eye. I knew how I must sound, as if I were the Petralucci kids' paid apologist. Perhaps this tête-à-tête wasn't such a terrific idea after all.

"But that's just it, Vinnie. You seem to have a wonderful clairvoyance, because this afternoon, just hours ago, Sandra Petralucci called my office and informed me that she was indeed safe but was not coming back home. She had seen the Amber Alert, she said, and was worried that a lot of trouble and expense would go to waste. What do you think of that?"

I think that it was a noble thing for Sandra to do. What I did not know was how this may affect my own position as protector and outlaw.

"Well, that's something," I said to prevent dead air. "Um, what else did she have to say? Are they fine?"

"There you go again assuming they're together, Vinnie. Why?"

It was far too late to declare a mulligan and tee off again. I had to think fast. "I thought that was what you meant," I said, turning the accusation around.

"No, you didn't."

"I—"

Beely held up a finger as the party animal one stool over roared in a fit of hilarity. I tilted myself back to get an unobstructed view of the joker's companion, another suit unwinding or, from the sounds of it, fully unwound already.

I tried again. "It would just seem to make sense that they're together, that's all."

The expression Beely wore said that was not all, at all. Oh boy.

"So, the Amber Alert is still on?" I asked, hoping the answer was no.

"Of course. The phone call could have been coerced from a kidnapper. We have no way of knowing. Do we?"

This last was underscored with a lean toward me. Beely said, "Drink up."

As accusations were apt to go, Beely's was subtle. Was this her way of asking me to give up my pretenses? For a guy who had been meaning to get around to seeing a lawyer, any lawyer, I had been slack, no excuses.

How could I trust Beely? She was on Their side. No, she wasn't police, yet she was on their side no matter how thin this baloney got sliced. I raised a silent toast and sipped, grateful to see our food order's timely arrival.

"You want half?" Beely said of her sandwich.

"No, thank you. Like I said, I had just finished my dinner when you called, though I do believe I could fit in a hot wing. Please, eat. I'm sure you're famished."

"Been a long day."

This time, and really every time she voiced the phrase, she did so with an unconscious sense of keeping score, her quietly kept litany of woes condensing into one easily choked-on pill per day-of-unvarying-length. It wasn't just an expression; for Beely it was the truth. Maybe she would like to take a break and hide out with the kids, have a spot of fun, nosh on some good Italian grub, and watch some sleepy daytime TV.

I made sure to look busy nibbling a wing, as I could tell that Beely would feel uncomfortable eating alone. She had perfect teeth that flashed into each bite, her full lips capturing my attention. She caught me staring and I innocently pointed to the corner of her mouth.

There was no blemish there, no speck of mayonnaise. I was covering my bewitched rudeness, nodding at the expressed question presented by Beely's finely raised eyebrows that, indeed, the spot was now cleared by her napkin.

"Let's have another mai tai," I said.

"Okay. One more."

I ordered. Shutting out the hubbub, I asked what she liked to do in her free time.

"What free time?"

"Weekends?"

"Oh. Those. A lot of paperwork, phone calls, and visits. But I do enjoy playing the tuba with a local chamber orchestra," Beely said, looking away at something over my shoulder.

Uh huh. I gave the nonsense several seconds of unnatural life, waiting for Beely's big eyes to land on mine, in the dark depths of which I detected a definite sparkle.

"Yeah, right. Tuba? In a chamber orchestra?" I said.

Beely smiled at her own quirky sense of humor. "Okay. The truth. I like to exercise. There's a fitness center down my block, but I don't get there as often as I'd like. There are a few things I like to watch on TV which I record and then hardly ever get to watch. I like difficult crossword puzzles I never finish, and I have a cat."

I knew it!

As casually as I could manage, I turned fully toward Beely to best gauge her reaction to my next question.

"Oh? What kind of cat?"

"A rescue."

"No. I meant—"

Beely giggled nicely. Perhaps the mai tais were more potent than I thought. She said, "I know what you meant; is she Persian, is she calico, is she--"

"Black?" I supplied.

"What! No, she's not black. She's a tiger."

When I did not respond to the tuba-like answer, she registered the incredulous blankness of my face, correctly judging me ignorant of cats in general.

"Tiger. Gray and black? Stripes? About yea big?" she said, holding her hands far too close together for a real tiger, and much too far apart for a housecat, or so I would assume and probably shouldn't.

"She's a monster," I said.

"Yep," Beely said, nodding in earnest, "she is. And what about you? You jog? Work out? You appear to be fit."

Luck of the genes. Whose genes I had no idea, but it didn't take much for me to stay in shape. I ran when I had to, mainly from bullets and not for pleasure. I've been known to scale all manner of tough obstacles, sprint across rooftops, and climb the occasional tall fence. To me a gym was just a guy's name badly spelled.

"Well, thank you. But, no, nothing like that. I don't have any real hobbies. I shoot pool every now and then. I like to eat. Does that count?"

"I'm afraid not. What about music?" Beely asked.

"What about it?"

"What kind do you like, silly?"

Silly? Hey, two drinks and Cara Beely had loosened up. Darned ol' DeeDee usually cost me an amount roughly equal to two limbs before she was feeling frisky. Then again, maybe Beely really did think I was silly.

"Music? Retro, I guess. As far as new stuff goes I like indie bands until they make it big, and I generally despise club music."

"Oh? Me, too."

"I've got some cool stuff downloaded at my place. I never record entire albums, or hardly ever. Something has to be solid, in my humble opinion, or I don't want it around."

Conversing, I had been facing Beely who remained facing the bartender's area. Now she swiveled on her stool until our knees touched, reaching out to return the favor of wiping sauce from the corner of my mouth, real or not. Her touch was not unexpectedly electric, but when Beely's finger glided back to her lips to vanish the evidence or lack thereof, I was 98.6% certain she had accomplished magic.

"Ah, would you like to hear some of it? And I've got some premium beer," I said, smiling, putting pressure against her knees, feeling the return signal.

"What about my car?"

"I've got some space for it beneath the building," which would be a much better use of the slot than a dairy cow for the kids.

"Oh?"

"Sure. What do you say? And, if you want, we can stop by and I'll get whatever it takes to make mai tais."

"Be ready to leave when I return from the restroom," Beely said, one hand brushing across my knee on her way.

I, entranced, watched her go. She was so short she was adorable and had a backside perfectly proportioned.

Turning, I discovered the smiling bartender at my elbow, already lifting the tab as I removed cash from my wallet. She accepted the bills with a sly wink.

No kidding.

Chapter 24

I could really get to like mai tais. That was what I was thinking as I watched Cara rummage through my mixed tapes of indie rock. We had been trying to outdo each other in music trivia, moving closer and closer together until I had pulled her atop myself in a passion that still had my heart racing.

Beely's reaction to the apartment had been favorable. Her question concerning my employment had been met with so vague a description that I believe I had detected a small look of uncertainty on her face, though I may have imagined it. We had discovered that if mai tais were made a bit stronger we did not have to make as many or spend as much time recycling them. How clever of us.

Vampire Weekend crept through the speakers and I was delighted with Beely's latest choice, especially when she asked what I thought the lyrics were about on this track.

"It's about lonely guys in seventh-floor apartments who find themselves falling deeply under the spells of beautiful witches."

"You know, I believe that's the second time you've called me a witch tonight."

"You? No, no, no. The lyrics," I insisted, lifting the sides of Beely's dark hair, letting it drift gently down to frame her oval face, the eyes so large and, absorbing light as they do, making Beely wonderfully angelic, otherworldly.

It was only fair my "calling" Beely a witch for the second time, and her return of a second "silly." We were definitely through chopping fruit and playing who's who. My hands were full when she whispered, "Not here."

Beely led me by hand down the hall, motioning me to keep going while she made a slight detour into the bathroom.

I had just enough time to run my electric shaver and blow my nose before Beely was with me, wearing only a bra and panties. She helped me undress, and I helped blow her mind. By the time we were finished with each other, we both knew we weren't really finished at all.

Spent a second time, I held Cara in my arms, unwilling to vocalize any concerns over her having to work come daylight, and whether either of us needed to pee again. The room was quite dark, the numeric green glow from my bedside clock turned away lest any reality intrude.

Had I really been as lonely as it now seemed? Or was it, as I thrilled to fear, that I had found someone I enjoyed so thoroughly that it would be a crime to pin a label on what I was feeling, for doing so would reduce the experience, and lessen its worth if not its appeal?

Did I normally sift through thoughts such as these?

That would be one large Hell No! Man, I was in trouble.

"Vinnie?"

I snuggled in closer, impossibly so, kissing those full lips lightly. "Hmm?" Ah, this was witchy heaven. I could feel myself closing in on sleep.

"Got another report of a missing child today. Would you believe this kid lives right down the hall from you?"

Why, you sneaky rascal. Holding out on me until now. And why? Beely, right at this moment wanted information. Bad timing? Or was it maybe a case of being afraid that broaching the subject earlier would ruin her jollies?

Yet, Beely wasn't squirming. Her respiration was restful and steady. She was not rushing to explain herself, her motive, or her lack of candor, not at all. If I was reading this correctly, she was appealing to me to be honest with her and her voice, soft, yet direct, was a connection between the puzzle which was her case load, and the greater mystery of whose arms she found herself within.

She already knew that I knew Chris Lewis, of course, just not that before today the likable kid lived at the end of the hall. So, what to do . . . what to say . . .

"I'm not real surprised from what Chris had related to me. His home life is less than ideal. Can you imagine being sixteen and made to stand in the equivalent of a corner as punishment?" I said, slightly evading the question.

"That's demeaning. Dehumanizing."

"Exactly," I said, lying still, the darkness a horribly excellent backdrop for the imagery in my mind and, I was sure, Beely's as well.

"And he had that black eye."

"Stepdad," I said.

"Vinnie?"

I ran my hands all over Cara Beely, loving the soft, yet firm, touch of her, and the way she rolled so easily onto me, her small frame taking my breath away.

"Vinnie?"

"Mm?"

"Where are the kids, do you think?"

Expecting the question, and not wanting to fib to this woman who only meant well, I said, "Hopefully all together. That would be for the best, wouldn't it?"

"And safe."

"Right. And safe," I asserted, confirming it to myself that between us we had just crossed a line, the truth there, yet not in the way.

"Vinnie."

Not a question.

"Cara."

* * *

I kept my landline phone all but muted, the ring reduced to the smallest burr. My cell was in the bedroom, along with a sleeping Cara. Up to use the toilet and brush my teeth, I had put on a pot of coffee, and was now rummaging around in the kitchen cabinets for some delectable I could offer Cara for breakfast, when I made out the distinctive alert of my safe phone.

"Hello?"

"What the hell are you whispering for?"

"Sorry, Dino. I've got company."

"Ah ha. You and DeeDee made up."

"Nope."

"You dog! Never mind. I just called to see what's up."

"Let me call you back later."

"All right, bye," Dino whispered, mocking me.

I was smiling as I hung up and began hurrying about my modest preparations. When I peeked into the bedroom, Beely was still asleep, which was unusual in my book—a strange apartment, strange bed, possibly a strange bed partner. Ha.

Damn, I was in a fine mood, all the drama and recent worries swept away. Such trouble seemed light, airy, and conquerable, with hardly any effort worth mentioning.

I had managed a stack of buttered toast, kept warm in the oven, and had a small dish of strawberry preserves on a funky Christmas tray Mom had sent one year with an assortment of snacks. It was almost the fourth of July and therefore perfect.

When I tiptoed into the bedroom again, Cara stirred and turned over. Her face, eyes closed, looked peaceful, sweet and delicate, appealing strongly to me.

I wanted to please this woman. I might get called "Silly" but I didn't care. Suddenly, for myself, this was important; this had meaning.

I eased atop the covers and turned to watch the eyes shoot open wide, then wider. Cara faced me, and the look softened. She had scared me, thinking she was going to bolt.

"Morning," I said, touching a shoulder.

"Mmm. What time is it?"

"It's early," I lied, worth getting fussed at if I could prolong the moment.

A look of knowing skepticism crossed Cara's face. She reached the bedside clock and turned it toward herself.

"Francine," she moaned.

Perhaps I had misheard. "Beg pardon?"

"My cat. She'll be meowing, wondering why I've abandoned her."

"Hold that thought," I said, rising, dressed quite casually in slacks, open shirt and bare feet. "Please don't get up yet."

"I have to go," she said.

Bathroom. "That's different. Meet you back here."

And did, totally surprising her with the aromatic coffee, and the nearly incredulous display of unburnt buttered toast and unburnt preserves, thereby rescuing the lesser known attributes of chivalry from the immemorable and tasteless cold ashes of the 21st century.

"You made this yourself?"

"Smarty-pants," I said in a most flattering way.

"Good coffee," Beely ceded.

"Grew it myself."

Cara smiled.

When we had completely and thoroughly embedded every nook, cranny, and tiniest crease of bedsheets with crumbs, Beely said she really did have to go.

"But it's still early," I tried, all things in life being comparative.

"Francine can't read a clock, but her tummy says it's breakfast time."

Ah. I could deduce that now was not the time to come between a witch and her familiar.

"Darn it," I said, before going on to say how much I really liked her and wanted to see her again.

"Write down my cell number."

I did and called it. Beely laughed, and said her phone was in her purse, locked in the trunk of her car downstairs. Not at all like her to leave it behind, she made sure I understood. She had spilled perfume inside, and to my surprise blushed.

"I'll walk you down."

Parking garages are very unromantic venues. I kissed Cara goodbye as well as I could, lingering on those soulful eyes, everything about her testing my resolve not to play the fool. I put on a grand smile waving goodbye, seeing one hand fluttering as she drove up the ramp.

Well, cats gotta eat and Vinnie's gotta get back to the duller real world. It had been nice while it lasted, but there was more, much more, to look forward to in this new relationship. It was with that attitude that I got on with my day.

I straightened the apartment, took a shower, and called "my" kids, a good gangster's responsibilities never ending.

"Hey. I heard you phoned Cara Beely yesterday," I said to Sandra.

"I hope that was okay. I didn't tell her where we are."

"No, it was a good thing. It put her mind at ease." Well, mostly. "Anyway, you guys are now officially in danger of being spotted and called in anytime you step outside. I would advise, for the time being, for you three to lie low and ride this out. I'll try to talk to your dad if you want me to."

"What in the world for?" Sandra asked quite seriously.

Excellent question. "Leave that to me, and don't worry. Trust me. I am not forcing anything."

"I do trust you. It's just that . . ."

"What?" I asked, then waited for Sandra's sigh to dissipate which took some time. Teens were great sighers.

"I don't know. I, I guess I'd just really like to know how this all turns out," Sandra said.

"I know it's tough, kiddo, but I don't know what else to do that wouldn't be even harder on you. Look, like I said, stay inside. You need anything? Large or small, tell me."

"Um, maybe some bread and sandwich stuff. And some tomatoes and milk. Oh, and some—"

"Tell you what I'll do," I said, interrupting. "I'll go to the store later today and call you from there. Okay?"

"Okay, Vinnie. You're the best."

Aw. "Well, you're welcome. Tell the boys hi. See you."

"Bye."

Sweet kid. Now, if I could just get Cara Beely to say the same thing.

Chapter 25

Dino was like I could imagine an annoying little sister would be—on the edge of his seat, leaning forward with his hands on his knees, and wearing a big sappy grin and expectant eyes. I was over at his place being grilled.

"So, tell me what she's like. Give DeeDee a run for her money or what? Huh? Look at you! She must be smokin' hot! Huh? Huh?"

"Damn, Dino, down, boy!" I now knew what Fred must have gone through.

My cousin walked a full circle around me, inspecting. Sniffing. I suppose being my lieutenant was a major hoot.

"Oh, yuck, she's old! Tell me she's not old, Vinnie!"

"She's not old, Vinnie. Seriously, Dino, it's no big deal," I said, and the way I'd said it had Dino narrowing his eyes almost shut.

"No big deal, huh? What's her name?" my inquisitor demanded, hands behind his back now, and on another circuit of yours truly.

Heck. It could be worse. It could be Mom sweating details out of me. "Her name is Cara Beely, and she's Paulie Jr.'s Social Services contact."

Dino looked mortified. "Why didn't you say something, man? I mean, shit, you know I'll hook you up. You ain't gotta go around bonin' ugly-ass Social Services bitches!"

"Dino? Shut up. Cara really is hot, and she's a nice girl, too."

"Nice girl? What's that supposed to mean? What'd you two do last night? Lay on top of the covers and hold hands?"

"We held everything, wise guy. Now, please shut the hell up and get me a beer."

"I bet she's got beaver teeth."

Dino loved to play. He would also love to fix me up with one of his party girls, girls even dumber than Dee. I got handed a beer and sarcasm.

"Probably no teeth at all is what I'm thinkin'. 42-42-42. And that includes her neck size."

I looked up into that marvelous smile and let it go. Dino had to run out of steam before I ran out of patience. I was mucho mellow.

"What kind of street clothes have you got, sport? I need something that says 'white trash and proud of it'. But with money."

"Damn, Vinnie, I wish you could hear yourself talk, man. How about somethin' that says 'wealthy Italian slummin'?"

"I haven't got time for a tanning bed and contact lenses. I know you've got some old jeans. And you used to have that old leather jacket. You still got it?"

"Yeah. I got it. And we could poke some needle holes in your arms, and maybe use the blood to stain a blade stickin' out of these boots I've got. And, hey! We can go get a really bad tattoo on your neck. Won't take no time at all!"

"I appreciate all the stellar advice, but I'll stick with a change of clothes. I'm going in Aces as someone from out of town looking to score. In and out," I said, working on the beer and planning on getting a few more under my belt before walking into the biker bar. I should never have shaved this morning, but hindsight's a—I've got to quit saying "bitch" all the time, Dino's fault.

"With that haircut? Damn, Vinnie, the Boys are gonna look at you hard, man. You know?"

"I'm not wearing a wig. That would be suicide. Damn thing could get twisted and fall off. It would be all over but the shouting."

"And the stabbin' and the bleedin'," Dino added with justification.

"Them too. C'mon, let's see what you have. I've got miles to go before I sleep tonight. Oh, yeah, do not let me forget that I've got to make a food run for the kids."

"All in a day's work," Dino mumbled on his way to the bedroom.

I put on some music at a quarter Dino-volume, and swept garbage off the sofa for a clean place to sit. In his previous incarnation Dino was a pig. In his present life he was still a pig, Karma being a tough nut to crack.

The jeans Dino brought me were just right, worn without being trendy-ripped. And the jacket would work. It had a decent quality of dullness, the black leather scuffed and frayed at the cuffs and collar. There were enough zippers to mimic authentic indie biker wear, and a lack of any "colors" helped advertise me as just an ordinary joe, no affiliations and looking for no trouble, even though the role I would be playing also included that my "look" says that if there was trouble, I wasn't running.

"Perfect. You want to sell it?"

"Geez, man, I don't think so. It's got a lot of sentimental value, you know?"

"Uh-huh. And if you lend it to me and get it back all ripped with cuts and bullet holes, then what have you got?"

Dino just laughed at me and said, "A damn good reason to draw unemployment, I guess."

"Let's see the boots. Have they really got a place to fit a knife?"

"Yeah. Hold on, I'll show you."

I grabbed another brew and rooted around the place until I came up with a box of Pop-tarts that I doubt Dino remembered he had. The expiration date was January, pre-civil war. I needed something to buffer the beer, no matter if it was stale cardboard smeared with a thin layer of colored glue that some marketing genius labeled as fruit.

Dino had the boots in hand. "I was savin' these for a special occasion."

"You're kidding," I said halfway into choking one shingle down.

"Yes. I am. Here ya go. See if they fit."

I already knew they would. Dino and I were able to share most anything clothes-wise.

"See that little sleeve thing? That's for a knife."

"Scabbard," I said, ignoring Dino's "Huh?"

"How does it look?" I asked, marching to the bathroom to use a mirror.

"It'd look better with a bike."

"A bike I can rent."

Dino posed as if he were seriously thinking. "Well, sure, unless you wanna buy one for our newly formed company. In case your employees need to use it."

"Nice try, Dino, but I believe I'll just rent one for the day. It'll be a few dollars cheaper."

My cousin shrugged it off. "You're the boss."

"And don't you forget it. Now I need a tee shirt and a belt. Whatcha got?"

"Damn, Vinnie. When you go slummin' you sure know where to get outfitted. What color tee? Black?"

"Preferably with holes, too."

The tee shirt was made to order, but the belt selection was disappointing.

"I'll just buy one," I told Dino.

"Or go without. Make a statement," Dino remarked, shooting me with a look and a cocked finger-pistol. Point taken, the waistband was tight enough to grip my gun.

"All right. Let's go," I said, taking a last look in the mirror.

"What! It's way early. The Boys' crib won't be rockin' till dark, man."

"Exactly. I want to get there while the sun's still up. Besides, I still have to rent a horse and get the feel of it. I'm going to take a leak, then we'll ride. You're driving."

"Your car?"

"If you want," I said.

Dino grinned. My support team grabbed a couple of beers, an historic Pop-tart, and my keys.

* * *

I rented a hog. The paperwork took forever. The fellow I was doing business with was sincere and well-meaning, but careful to the point of i-dotting madness. By the time Dino and I got out of the place, my orchestrated beer buzz had detuned and I could really have used a nap.

But, no time. We hit a bar on the outskirts of Brooklyn that pretty much looked like your typical bar on the inskirts of Brooklyn.

We had fun for an hour or so shooting pool and chugging beer, plenty of daylight remaining. The truth of it was that I was chugging beer, and Dino was doing a lot of grumbling about losing at pool because he was sober. I agreed, said it was a shame. When I reminded my lieutenant that he was now on the payroll he cheered right up, being paid to play pool sober.

Dino followed me in the Nova as I got acquainted with the Harley. Kids: never drink and ride motorcycles. It was needlessly risky, and after about eight beers totally against the law.

On the other hand, however, it was great fun, and no true imitation biker goes through life without wrecking occasionally. The only thing I could manufacture more authentically in my favor, other than being a stranger reeking of beer and fresh off a hog, would be to do so walking into Aces while ignoring fresh roadrash.

Willing as I was to take one for the team, I wasn't beyond the point of complete irrationality. I had the kids to think about. And my semi good looks.

The hour was creeping toward 7 o'clock when we stopped to down one last tall beer, and by "we" I mean Dino got to watch.

"Ready!" I announced and belched long enough to bracket a prize-winning bull ride.

"Whoopee," Dino deadpanned.

I told Dino not to mess with me 'cause I was a badass loco lobo, hitching up my borrowed pants leg to reveal the tang end of a truly vicious piece of cutlery I had picked up thirty minutes earlier at a pawnshop for five bucks.

Dino pretended fear. I flipped him off, in character, as we stepped outside. Grinning, I cranked the bike to hear the pipes burbling sweetly, the Harley in tune, making fine street music.

Pulling up in front of Aces, I was alarmed at how the last beer stop had cost me as much time as it had. The sun was lowering across the river, and the number of bikes out front by the curb were at least three times the count I'd had in mind when planning this reconnaissance/suicide mission.

In for a dime, in for a holler. What was the worst that could happen here? I shut the bike down and tried not to think about that.

The most important thing to remember concerning crazy-as-hell biker gangsters was that the thing that mattered most in their lives was to have fun. Sadly, this included the possibility of using some poor fool's head to play biker polo with. Other than that, I walked with the angels, as good a fantasy as any.

I took a minute to gawk at the exterior of the bar in my role as out-of-town tourist, just a good ol' boy figuring he had run across common ground out here in the wilds of lower Manhattan. The regulars might even conclude that I was some kind of dumbass from Jersey or Philly. I hadn't made up my mind, but I was leaning toward a fictional past out west. I did not talk like my parents or my cousin Dino. I is educated. I could fake this shit. My internal pep talk was allowing the sun to sink even lower.

Two guys outside the door to Aces were shooting me glances, nothing openly hostile, just smoking cigarettes and enjoying the city fumes and whatnot. They might have had to fart and politely stepped outdoors. You never knew.

From where I stood on the sidewalk, it seemed that the old building's wood and plaster walls were pulsing with the strong beat of music inside the bar. Dino would feel right at home, maybe, if he was also wearing a suit of armor and wielding a functional light saber.

I torched a bummed Marlboro and tucked the box back into a recessed sleeve pocket, the damn jacket about to roast me alive. Couldn't leave it out here. Screw it. I blew out a small iron lungful of crappy smoke and all but coughed. I was going to need to take it easy on these things or I would surely get sick.

"Saw the bikes. Looks like a good place. I ain't intruding, am I?" I intoned civilly, showing respect to the two Boys loitering, or farting.

"What da fuck do I care?" the closest young man replied.

He was maybe 23, probably on a cocktail of drugs, and almost certainly homicidal. I saw myself give a very slight nod to his warm hospitality via his mirrored shades, letting it ride. I reached for the door.

It was like stepping into a hurricane, punishing sonic waves of fairly good music turned up far too loud assaulted me and would be liable to push me backward unless I leaned into it. One thing was hazily clear—I wouldn't need the Marlboros. I could smoke free all night just by being in the thick cloud that hung in Aces.

I stepped back outside as a giant warlock with no shirt and an open blue jean vest propelled a frizzy-haired drunken girl out the door, the girl squealing with delight. I would call it delight and put it out of mind.

Letting my burning eyes adjust, I registered pool tables on my right, all occupied, with people lining the wall behind them, some looking my way. Lots of longnecked bottles of beer. Lots of rough-knuckled hands holding them.

To my left was a line of tables. Farther down the same side was a jukebox where a girl in short-shorts was bending over the selection, half-moon ass-cheeks firm and off limits. I looked away before I got busted, literally.

The bar proper was in the back and ran the width of the building. Access was from swing-up bar tops on either end. I needed a look behind there.

Getting closer to the bar itself, I kept my face impassive, receiving more interest, not a lost soul here recognizing this blond stranger. I was sure it happened all the time. The thing was, I wasn't privy to such outcomes, and I've got too vivid an imagination to give the nightmare full play right now. This was business.

Smoke stained drop-tile acoustical ceiling—check. One empty bar stool second from the left—double check.

"Taken," snarled the grand fellow on the end.

The guy had a ponytail down to his large ass, and biceps wide as my stomach. I nodded that I had heard, and so backed off, stepping to one side, trying to catch the bartender's eye, a potbellied guy wearing an apron that . . . oh, no.

The dude tossing something heavy into the dumpster yesterday had been the effing bartender. I quit trying to draw his attention and began avoiding it in earnest. I tore the shades from my face and stuffed them into a pocket. I'd had them on yesterday. But I had been wearing casual clothes and shivering in the heat.

I used what little time I still had left to inspect behind the bar, covering my surveillance by going through an elaborate process of first finding a cigarette, then a lighter.

There were two doors in the wall behind the bar, far left and far right. I figured one to be an office, and the other used for storage, etc. Restrooms were up front in the corner, and of which I had urgent need.

No one had yet bothered with any attempt at conversation to determine that I was, in fact, a bona fide, beer swilling, bike riding son of a gun. I needed to recycle some of my method acting in the worst way, and did not have the luxury of time to do so.

There were locks on both doors behind the bar, but the door on the right had twin deadbolt locks that appeared to be of good quality. I had not spied any cameras, nor did I expect to find any. Cameras were witnesses, and the Boys didn't care for witnesses. Didn't like snoops all that much either.

"Whatcha lookin' at, blondie?"

I had two big guys on either side of me, pressing close, keeping my arms all but pinned, the rising smoke from my cigarette damn near choking me in the confined space. Half those at the bar were now turned around watching the floor show—me.

"Nothin', man. I'm new here."

The towering construction on my left, my immediate left, possibly my age or younger but with a face of leather causing him to appear older, said over the top of my head, "Says he's new here!"

"No shit?" the other mountain answered back in mock surprise.

"Buy you guys a beer?" I shouted over the din.

"Where you from, blondie?" the first Boy asked, looking down on me.

I could smell carnivore, and alcohol, and some sickly-sweetish-burnt plastic odor I was unable to identify and didn't need to. These boys had been smoking something potent.

"Denver!" I shouted to be heard.

"Fucking Denver!" the second Boy said and went on to assert that there wasn't but two things ever to come out of Colorado, and that was steers and queers, asking me which one I was.

I managed to lever my right hand up to take a drag on the fumigator.

The first speaker, the big bully on my left said, "Answer the man! You a steer or a queer?" leering, having himself a winner no matter what I said, which was the point.

"They've got one more thing in Colorado," I yelled, smiling and feeling slightly out of joint for the good folk down in Texas at whom I had always heard the steer/queer joke directed. The two Boys were looking at me like I was a bug past its extermination date.

"One more thing! What's dat?" Meatbreath asked.

"Bike riders. You sure I can't buy y'all a beer?"

"Bike riders!" the second Boy roared, smiling I thought—hard to tell through the thick beard and moustache. "He called us 'y'all'! Ain't that cute!"

Hellfire, I was winging it. If I still had an unbroken finger afterward, I'd get on the net to find out what Coloradans called each other. At the moment it had sounded good. Now—not so much.

I hit the cigarette hard, hotboxing it, tensing my torso, readying, coiling. These two clowns weren't about to give me a pass. I was a new toy to be used roughly and tossed out back when they were finished. I had done the best that I could pouring oil on these playful waters.

The big guy on my left crowded closer, bumping me.

"We've got one more thing in Colorado," I said quite loudly to break their focus. I raised my eyes to see the two Boys eyeing each other over the top of my head, their shared look saying they were getting far greater entertainment value than they had bargained for, and were loving it, prolonging the inevitable beating.

"Yeah," the second Boy, the one on my right, said. "What's dat?" And, in superb form, showcasing his wit, added, "y'all."

I had been on the verge of delivering my punchline of, "Jackrabbits!" and making my break for the door, when they both cracked up over number two's "y'all."

Even better.

Stepping quickly forward from between them, I spun, planting the hotboxed cigarette's coals in the left eye of number one Boy, now on my right, and slipping behind his back as he howled. I drew my gun from behind my back to fire point blank into number two's thigh. Racing for the door amid screams of pain and howls of laughter, I was grateful to hear that my audience of onlookers along the bar considered my actions worthy of ovation.

No matter. I was almost to the impossibly far away door when I was blocked by a gentleman with an appalling lack of good sense and even worse timing. What, he thought I wouldn't shoot him, too?

Blam!

Another one bit the dust, another thigh wound. I wasn't out to kill anyone, dammit. I just wanted out. I leapt over this last guy even as he was clawing at Dino's boots while he was hitting the floor. I slammed into the front door with my shoulder as I twisted the knob, switching the gun to my left hand as I raced out onto the sidewalk, fishing the Harley's key out of my right pants pocket. Dino's right pants pocket.

I sprang across the Harley's seat as a crowd burst through Ace's door, friends and neighbors every one. Lefthanded, I fired purposefully low, and the knot of angry Boys surged back inside. Mostly. I got the bike started as a shot whistled past my head so close I heard it, and felt its threatening passage like a hot kiss of death. I aimed for a hit, having little to no choice, the gunman going down as I backed away from the curb, kicking hard with my right foot at the row of bikes to see three hogs topple before I was able to gun my rental, racing down the street as more shots rang out, sparks flying off the pavement around me.

I was topping out in third gear through the near intersection and flashing past Dino's position, hoping like hell that he was paying attention, because this was his cue to pull out to "innocently" create a block if my hurried exit indicated that I would want one. Highly occupied, I did not bother using my mirrors to check, all my focus invested in avoiding new dangers, the traffic light against me, and nothing saving my hide except a fraction of one second and pure dumb luck.

Our escape plan further stated that if I chose plan Bat-Outta-Hell, then we would meet back at Dino's. I would bet on my beating Dino there even if I wrecked and had to run on foot the whole way. I had left a lot of angry dudes behind me.

I zigzagged to stay clear of the worst of traffic, having picked a fine time for a getaway. Friday evening of a holiday weekend, the streets and avenues still clogged with taxis and tourists.

There was only one point during which I had a motorcycle behind me on the way back to Queens, and that was some guy on a crotch rocket who had zero business with me, though he weaved in and out just as impatiently as did I.

At Dino's I shut the bike down, with the Harley's exhaust still ringing in my ears. I let myself into the garage apartment, and finally had that piss I had been holding in forever. Nothing ever felt so good.

Calmed, I grabbed a fresh beer and waited on my cousin, hoping my number one lieutenant wasn't still back on the West Side, parked and looking stupid.

CHAPTER 26

Are you kidding me?" I asked Sandra. As I listened over the phone, Dino was doing his usual imitation of a lazy dragon, blowing smoke out of the Nova's open window while slumped riding shotgun.

When he had arrived at his place I had already been there for thirty-five minutes. Dino had obeyed all traffic laws in the wake of my mad flight. Pretty darned sober after my run-in with the West Side Boys, I offered Dino the chance to relax and drink beer now that the party was over.

I was chuckling while adding Sandra's latest request to my grocery list. Dino could no longer stand hearing my mirth without an explanation.

"She says Paulie is losing weight. Too much healthy food and almost zero junk food, and he can't go out and get it," I said.

"Doin' the kid a favor," Dino remarked as he examined the broad length of brightly illuminated storefront thirty feet ahead of us. There were still plenty of shoppers inside this time of night.

"Not the way Paulie sees things from what I hear," I said. "You want to come inside or sit here?"

"I'm comin'. I'm out of junk food, too." Dino polished off his beer. Denting the can, he opened his door to slide it under the car beside us. "Out of beer, too."

We got the groceries Sandra asked for, and several items that she was not expecting, taking pity on Jr. with some junk from the store's deli. I would leave it up to Sandra to ride herd on its allocation. Dino and I chose for our separate purchases those items that would not be in danger of spoiling by the time each of us made it home. For Dino that wasn't a big stretch. The crap he consumed was so preservative-laden that when he croaked all the mortician would need do would be spackle over any bullet holes and prop up the smile.

The kids were happy to see us, going stir crazy as they likely were. Altogether, they were taking the isolation in stride, which was tough to do at their age, and it was summertime to boot. We crowded around the dinette table as Sandra put groceries away.

"Tell you what. If nothing comes up, I'll see if I can get you guys out of here to watch the fireworks," I said. I had originally planned to have the kids catch the display from my balcony, but with Chris's stepdad down the hall, that wasn't such a great idea.

I removed my stupid smartphone from my pocket to check the weather for the Fourth, showing the kids the big fat chance for thunderstorms, and explaining why I couldn't have them over to my place.

Chris said his people (his term) would probably not be home that night. "We usually go up to Staten Island to my stepmom's sister's house and go out along the water there to watch them. Have the last two years, anyway."

"Well. If you're sure," I said to Chris, and even then, I was thinking that this wasn't such a great idea, the exposure, but they were innocent and could use some fun.

"I can double check to be positive," Chris said. His black eye had an awful green and yellow halo upon healing.

Waiting on Chris's confirmation, I spun their new plastic chess set around to see what Paulie had learned. Instead of chess, Paulie sought to enlighten me in another area. He pointed, "Watch this, Vinnie, it's pretty neat."

Paulie was indicating Chris on the sofa, with my cell phone on the coffee table. Beside my phone was a small device I did not recognize. Chris was looking at a small readout display on the device and talking softly to himself.

"What's he doin'?" Dino asked, not waiting for an answer, sitting down beside the boy genius on the sofa to observe.

"Paulie?" I asked, waiting on an explanation.

It was Sandra who answered. "I guess he's resetting his 'thing' for a different voice."

Game over before it began, I abandoned the chessboard to join the Petralucci kids behind Chris who looked up in surprise, unused to spectators. Before I could ask what was that he was doing, he took the time, and courtesy, to explain.

"It's an automatic digital voice mimicry synthesizer, slash, converter. I made it from some scraps I traded for. I adjust the controls to correct modality, then tweak it for pitch, intonation, and resonance. It helps to have a recording of the voice you want to imitate, but I've got a decent ear, so . . ."

Chris had been doing fine describing the strange-looking device until it came to patting himself on the back, allowing that part of the equation to fade away. The boy genius had received little to no recognition at home. His step-this and step-thats must be fools. And psychotic—couldn't forget that. Socially functioning foolish psychotics.

Sandra was smiling up at me like a proud sister. Good. Chris could use one. I took a second look.

Oh no. I had been afraid of this and quickly looked away as if I did not know what that look meant. It seemed that Sandra was suffering from a not-too-distant variation of Stockholm Syndrome, in which a "captive" transfers their feelings of insecurity toward the "abductor" in a twisted, yet understandable attempt to gain favor, and form a relationship enabling security, find familiarity, and even, gulp, love.

Now what did I do? Yikes. I eased away from Sandra for a better look at the science project.

As Chris continued to speak into a built-in mike, the device converted his voice into that of another—an older, deeper voice. There could be heard no mechanical effect, the generated voice sounding quite natural.

"That's your stepdad's voice?" I asked.

Chris Lewis was turning crimson out of a combination of pride and shyness. The redhead said, "Yeah. It's close. But when you get close, people can't tell the difference over the phone. So, now I just dial up my Aunt's number. . . ."

We could only hear Chris's half of the conversation, but it was very convincing.

"Billie? Al. Hope I'm not calling too late. I just wanted to ask if there was anything special we could bring for the show."

A few seconds passed before Chris said, "Are you sure? Fine. I will. See you then."

The whiz kid hung up. "By inference, they will be gone from the apartment."

Dino was handling the small unit—maybe 6" x 4" x 2"—an irregular rectangle, the product of cobbling "scraps I traded for." When Dino's eyes met mine, his shone as those of a prospector looking up from his pan after discovering a huge nugget he truly never expected. My eyes must have been just as large.

"Where did you—" I began to ask, and was rushed over by Chris, totally misunderstanding the direction I was taking.

"I'm sorry, Vinnie. But all my best stuff was there at the apartment, and I was really, really, careful when I went back and wore a disguise and everything."

"What?" I said.

"No, it's true, Vinnie," Paulie said, also misunderstanding, compounding Chris's error by taking up for his new friend. "He wore my bandanna and his sunglasses, and really, no one would have recognized him."

Okay. Chris had snuck back to the psycho's lair, obviously timing his return for when no one was home, and done so incognito. As interesting and dangerous as that was, my question had been, was about to have been, about where Chris had come up with everything to make the gizmo work.

Seemingly embarrassed, Chris left the room, saying he needed to use the restroom. When he rejoined us after quite a long stretch, I questioned him concerning his prowess with electronics.

"I'll assume your proficiency with innovations led you to conceive your own design?" I said in a voice that I tried hard to keep free of my rising enthusiasm.

"Not totally, no. Well, yes, in a way. The technology the big mixing studios use is way too clunky," Chris stated.

Clunky. Multi-billion-dollar industry to this kid is clunky. I felt as if I needed a seat. How about one beside my new discovery? I helped myself, scooting into place on the sofa, and taking the gee-whiz device from Dino's clunky hands.

"It can be made much smaller," Chris said. "You think I ought to patent it?"

This kid wasn't as dumb as I look. I cleared my throat. "Chris, the short answer is yes. The long answer is, that to do that, we have a few hurdles to clear first. Be patient a little while longer. In the meantime, I'll get in touch with a patent attorney on your behalf."

"You'll do that for me? Man! Vinnie, if you can do that, you and I can be partners, fifty-fifty!" Chris exclaimed, about to burst with joy.

I unhesitatingly extended my hand to shake, sealing the deal and feeling dizzy. "You think, ah, that you could use our little friend here to say, ah, maybe, I don't know . . . " (yes, I did) "like, fool someone in the police department into handing out certain, ah, information?"

Chris's answer was almost instant. "Well, I guess I could, but it would take time to record voices and learn individual speech patterns. See, like with Al, I know his voice, so I can, by ear, approximate a fair imitation of it. But a stranger's voice, well, there are a lot of variables. Am I making sense?"

"Absolutely," I said, a bit disappointed, sharing a look with Dino.

"Which is why it would be so much easier just to hack into their computer. What is it you want to know?" Chris asked, rising from the sofa to return seconds later with a laptop, I was assuming from his clandestine trip back to his apartment.

"You can do that?" I asked, poleaxed.

"Do it all the time," was Chris's answer, one so frigging nonchalant I was blown away.

"See, I've already hacked Al's passwords for at home and work. So, I can surf through the NYPDs database. Any particular file you want to take a look at?"

I felt like Dr. Frankenstein, movie version, wanting to proclaim, "It's alive!" minus insane chortling. But, how to answer the question when I—

"Begin a search parameter using 'West Side Boys' and 'Aces'," Dino said, earning his first paycheck.

"Four-hundred-seventy-two hits," Chris announced.

No fooling. The Boys had a history.

"Try adding 'Raid'," I said. "And 'Dates', question mark, together with the rest."

"Three hits," Chris said as I leaned in to see, reading "July fifth." Two days from now. Dino and I looked to each other. We tried for extra info, but besides a meaningless roster of names taking part in the raid, we had all we were likely to get. The rumors were true, and our recent legwork was now invaluable.

Thanking Chris for a most enlightening "demonstration," an "example" we called it, of what his abilities could achieve, we bid the kids goodnight with a genteel warning to remain tucked out of sight.

* * *

As soon as Dino and I got to my apartment we started planning. Dino's groceries stayed in the Nova's trunk, and we stayed with the problem solving half the night. I was good at this, comfortable in the planning stage of an operation.

If a problem was viewed in light of a worst-case scenario, there was a natural lessening of the probability of being surprised. Of course, survivability dropped at a rate proportionate to any realized level of "worst" in such cases, adequate preparation unable to account for X factors that were not unenvisioned, just unseeable.

But I was a career criminal, not a seer.

I had laid out several sheets of paper, each with a separate heading. One sheet was labeled Clothing, another Hardware, then Food & Water, on and on, each and every category covered that would enable me to secure the best odds of success in outfitting a two-man team for this job.

Some items listed I already had on hand. Some gear I would need to procure. My time for tying up loose ends was severely limited. By 3:00 a.m. I had completed the lists. I then set my alarm for 7:00 a.m. to grab a few hours of shuteye, Dino taking himself home to wait for my arrival.

Up with the rising sun, I raced through my ablutions before securing all items on my lists found within the apartment, ticking them off one by one, thorough yet fast. I headed out, hitting a hardware store, a supermarket, and an outdoor sportsman shop. The weight of necessary gear was adding up fast, but I did not see any solution other than putting our backs into it. This was work, not a lark.

Even so, Dino had a swell time playing with all the new equipment at his place. This was after I had cleared off all the crap from his counter that had reaccumulated like stubborn fungus.

Into the two new backpacks I began loading what would be needed last first and first last, figuring the middle could damn well take care of itself. The packs were frameless, the hike being short, and the bulk of a frame, space that I needed, and the rigidity of a frame, liabilities I could do without.

I had purchased the smallest battery-powered saw that the hardware store carried, not knowing if it would even be needed. What I did need was to slap Dino's hands away from it, the nut wanting to "crank it up" and play with it. If there ever should be a community college course of Gangsterism 101, one of the subjects covered should be on aggressively controlling stubborn subordinates.

"Ow!" Dino cried out for the second time, thinking I was kidding or something.

"Can't let you drain the power, Dino. Put it down."

"Aww!"

Being a good boss often meant overlooking childish behavior. I put Dino to work fashioning caps to protect the points of my grapnel's three sharp hooks. Naturally, he wanted to play with that, too, whistling it overhead inside the apartment, darn near taking me out.

"Dino. Behave. If you are good, once this is over I'll take you to Disney World."

"Fuck you, Vinnie."

It was lonely at the top. My head still attached, I triple-checked spare clips for our guns, flashlights and batteries, hand spikes, rope and bungee cords, all details inspected. I fashioned loops for any tools I was fearful of dropping. I cut away excess ounces here and there, reducing weight wherever possible. I calculated the minimum of water that we could bring, water being crucial to success, and quite problematic in carrying.

"Dino. Do not take this the wrong way, but you need to evacuate your bowels to the best of your ability if you haven't done so already."

Seeing that I was not having fun with him, Dino shrugged and traipsed off to the bathroom to give it what he called "the ol' junior high try." It was cooperation, and it was the one task I could not help him with. He was gone a long time, but that was not a problem as we were just about ready and still had daylight.

When Dino came out I went in, straining to bust a gut, wanting nothing to do with cramping and gas in a confined space. Back in the living room, I saw that Dino had changed clothes, now dressed all in black.

"Put on a different shirt until we get there. Anything but black," I strongly suggested.

"Good idea," Dino agreed.

No doubt. The same ensemble went for me: black cords, black socks and sneakers, my black watch cap in my back pocket, and also pocketed was a tiny square of black fabric that would unfold into a very large sheet, super thin and weighing practically nothing.

I pored over my lists a final time, beginning to feel the surge of excitement building now that the sun was lowering. Today was the Fourth of July. In celebration, we had decided to ignore the extra weight of a frozen six-pack of beer, nestled in its own, thin thermal carrying case. Now we were ready.

"You got everything?" I asked Dino.

"Unless you want me to tote my portable jacuzzi."

"Tempting. But, no. Got your piece?"

"Check," Dino said, patting his secreted gun, then saluting, the nut.

"Cigarettes?" I had to ask as a point of thoroughness. I couldn't comprehend being stuck with my cousin going through nicotine withdrawal for two days.

"Check."

"Lighter?"

"Check."

"Cell?" I asked, in case I busted mine, a real risk.

"Check."

I looked my trusty lieutenant over and could not resist brushing off one speck of nonexistent lint from one shoulder.

"Perfect," I declared.

"Check," Dino said, grinning like a 'possum.

"Let's go make some money."

Dino was down with that. "Checkeroo."

Chapter 27

The nearest public parking garage was four blocks from Aces, which I had taken to calling Ground Zero for the level of mayhem to come if the police stuck to their unadvertised schedule. Dino liked that name, whistling, off and on, during the wet ride over, a fucked-up version of the theme from *Mission, Impossible.*

Simply stated, there were uncertainties that I had not investigated, due to both a lack of time and opportunity. Planning under harsh time constraints had major drawbacks but, as with Chris Lewis's imagination, I, too, considered myself an innovator.

I seriously doubted that I would encounter any difficulty I could not overcome. I even had an off-the-wall Plan B that I hoped not to put into play. Plan B was iffy as hell.

Backing the Nova into a parking space, I then called a taxi before stepping out to temporarily raise the car's hood. Mechanical gremlins was the story, and what a pair of young urban types were doing lugging backpacks around was none of any cabbie's business.

We climbed in for the short ride through the light rain, talking about the chances of a soggy fireworks show, and little else in the way of information which might stick in the driver's head.

I had our driver let us out half a block from Aces, coming in from the dockside street behind the bar. Quickly, we shouldered our packs and fast-walked to the near side of the old warehouse, this side of Aces.

Over the patter of rain, the growl of a Harley-Davidson bike was heard pulling up out front of the bar, the sound traveling unimpeded through the alleys on either side of the old building we were behind. I easily imagined Aces to be a packed house tonight, an advantage.

The noise of the crowd inside the bar, and the decibel level of the jukebox, would help cover our operation. Yet, even with the aid of falling rain, the advantage of ambient noise amounted to a two-edged sword. Anyone walking through the alleys, or out Aces' back door, would be masked by the same noise, a danger I could do little about other than guard against surprises by being attentive and vigilant.

Dino's black ball cap did its job as camouflage, but as a guard against rain it had quickly reached its saturation point, as had mine. There was no cure but to bear up under the onslaught of the storm as the rainfall picked up.

Traffic was sparse on the street that separated Aces from the docks, most area workers home for the weekend or off for the holiday. Our position behind the warehouse was good, yet, as with so much of my hastily worked plan, luck had its proper role to play, start to finish.

A patrolling cruiser; a motorist with a curious eye; a passing drunk with a passable memory; any unaccountable collection of inquisitiveness and civil heroism, combined with at least one bar on a cell phone, any of these and more could easily trip us up.

Luck—that was what I ought to patent.

And that reminded me—I had been so busy that I never did call a patent lawyer for Chris. Just as well—I could not remember to get in touch with any lawyer this past week following my initial failure to connect with our family mouthpiece.

Dino and I were both wearing our fashionable crime noir tees, and both of us were now unfashionably drenched head to toe. This was fun. I removed the padding that guarded the claw points of my lethal-looking grapnel.

Carefully recoiling the knotted rope into my left hand, I backed up until I had as much free space about me as possible, vulnerable as I was in the exposed center of the alley. I built up the speed of the tool's revolutions until the line was a blur of motion, the grapnel's claws scarcely clearing the pavement.

Whispering, "We good?" through gritted teeth, I heard Dino whisper back that we were clear on both ends of the alley. I timed my release, momentum carrying the bright steel upward and away to glint briefly in the city-glow before descending across the shuttered warehouse's ridge line.

With Dino pressed against the near corner of the old building and providing lookout, I drew in the rope's slack until I felt the hooks bite into the far side of the roof. Increasing the tension, I tugged hard, then harder, until I was supporting my full weight upon the rope.

Not wasting time, I ascended, my feet locking onto the rope's small knots as I positioned my hands upward one knot at a time, but quickly. I would rather fall and reclimb than spend any more time than necessary exposed like this.

Once atop the warehouse roof, I had Dino tie our backpacks to the rope, one at a time. I hauled each up and secured them below the apex of the roof by means of short handspikes. Then it was Dino's turn, my cousin performing above par, grunting quietly while struggling over the lip of the roof, the hardest part. We made it up to our packs where we flattened out, listening as rain pelted us.

Noise from the bar next door was greatly increased with our new location, the jukebox wide open, and the general din one continuous roar, dulled only by distance, walls, and rain. Occasionally, a voice would drift up from the front of Aces, some hundred-plus feet to our east.

We flowed over the top of the roof, keeping flat as possible, re-spiking our packs several feet below the ridgeline. Recoiling the rope, I then rocked loose the grapnel's hooks. Crumbling shingles parted to slip away before I could catch them. I froze, listening to their slide, followed by a brief second of free fall, and their landing. Not tragic, yet it was evidence. Thankfully, it was dark in that alley, and it was raining. The building we were atop of was old, its roof in derelict status. Anyone seeing the debris should think nothing about it.

The space between this old warehouse and Aces was maybe eight feet wide, nothing to sweat. The bar's roof was lower than the roof we now crouched on, its rain gutters some six feet lower than our roof's edge. If we leaped from as close to our own roof's edge as possible, we should land a quarter of the way up Ace's roof. Unless we fell.

Those same ancient shingles that had been a nuisance coming up the warehouse's opposite side had been negotiated by the stabilized, knotted rope attached to the grapnel. And the rope would still serve as a steady hold for the first man as he readied himself to cross over the alley to the bar's roof, but not the second man, me.

I could not leave the grapnel attached to its current repositioned placement for two reasons. Though it was nighttime, it was anything other than comfortably dark. The security light pole behind Aces, plus lower Manhattan's glow in general, served to profile the tool as a small, yet out of place bump along the ridgeline's more or less straight edge. Secondly, I needed the claws at least one more time to gain my targeted entry point into Aces.

Cautioning Dino to take his time, I fed him enough rope to get him to our roof's edge, signaling him to flatten out across the rain-slick roof as traffic passed on the street to my right.

Clear, I gave him the sign to cross. Three feet from the edge Dino dropped the rope and stood, lightly rocking himself steady. With one short and one medium-sized step of approach, he leapt through the intervening space to land in a forward crouch, arms spread and fingers splayed to break his fall and arrest any backward slide. With care, he turned to face me, testing Aces' shingles with his sneakers, as a bolt of lightning brightened the sky behind me, followed by thunder several seconds later. Dino nodded to me, letting me know that the roof beneath him appeared to be okay.

Un-spiking one pack, I eased myself down the treacherous roof via the anchored rope. Swinging the pack from a stable stance, I slung it across the gap, Dino trapping it across his chest.

The second pack proved just as easy; both packs were now securely spiked several feet below Aces' ridgeline. Back up top of the warehouse, I loosened the grapnel before lying back to safely recoil the rope. Waving to ensure that I had Dino's attention, I made several practice arcs with the weighted rope, gauging for accuracy before casting the hooks across the two roofs. The grapnel fell short of Ace's ridgeline, with Dino scrambling to lay a hand on the rope before the tumbling grapnel clattered to the alleyway.

He was successful, looking like a cat attempting to pin a flashlight's moving spot. He soon had the line coiled with the grapnel, stowed atop our packs. We now lacked a single item across the gulf—me.

I debated gentling wayward to the launch point. Should I start to slide, the deteriorating shingles beneath my soggy shoes would serve as miniature sleds. I would be, in that case, badly out of position, with little chance of orienting myself in time to safely jump.

Which left, as an option, going for broke, with a fair chance of depositing myself into the alley, a recoverable mishap, but one in which I would be dangerously exposed, forfeiting the game due to a broken ankle, or worse, a West Side Boy having a timely stroll through the alley.

Watching me prepare, Dino presented himself in a figure-four as if he were shaping up for a slide into second base, his left arm extended as a focal point I should try for if my landing was skewed.

Approximating the number of strides, I would reach before my launch, I made it out to be six. Maybe seven. Full strides, no pussyfooting. I could do this. On a mental count of three.

Upon take off everything was peachy, until my right foot, coming down on stride #4, landed on miniature sled #1, as if I had leaped atop a skateboard careening out of control down a 35° slope. My heart was in my throat as I had zero time to consider what to do, semi-planting my left foot for quasi-stability, and diving across the open space to land in a sprawl, my torso fully on the roof of Aces, and my pecker in the gutter.

Dino was scooting toward me quickly, a crabbing figure-four, bracing himself to lend me one slippery hand. I would have preferred that he had planted the grapnel and utilized the rope, but help at hand is not a point to argue.

My legs dangled above the alley for all to see, those who had nothing better to do than be outside in Aces' alley in the rain on the Fourth of July to witness my predicament. The bad news was that the above description applied to every mother's son currently in the bar, as likely to step outside to burn some dope as to take a whiz.

Dino was that sort who fooled most people, deceptively strong. In a few seconds he had hauled me completely onto the roof in a single, long tug. We hustled to our spiked backpacks, lying in the rain and quietly panting, raindrops striking inside my open mouth.

When I stole a look over the roof, I saw nothing untoward from the darkened fish wholesaler's building. Easing to the rear of Aces, soaked watch cap pulled low, I was mindful of the security light's illumination of my face. Not surprising, there could be seen no traffic, pedestrian or vehicular, and no loiterers. So far so good.

Then, as if a faucet had been turned, the rain cut off, its abrupt cessation startling and oddly missed.

Setting the grapnel's hooks ten feet from the western end of Aces' ridgeline, I pounded it secure with my heels, the points biting deeply into the plywood sheathing underneath the shingles and tarpaper. Satisfied, I gathered from my pack the tools I would need once I was over the edge.

From the photos taken, I had been able to make out screwheads to be removed, but not what type: slot, Phillips, or hex, so I now prepared for all three. Screwdrivers, mini-crowbar, and pliers were all secured by cords ending in loops to be worn on my wrist. My penlight was also on a lanyard around my neck and could be held in my mouth if necessary. I was all ready except for my camouflage.

Though I wore black, head to toe, fashionable as hell, the security light near the dumpster behind Aces would paint my outline onto the building's wall like a sharply defined silhouette. I removed the square of black fabric from my back pocket. The unfolded sheet was ten square feet. I draped it over my head before pinning it into place on my shoulders. I then cut two slits, left and right, above each shoulder so I could look behind myself if need be.

Should anyone look my way, they would see what appeared to be a tarp covering the ventilation louvre inset of the building's attic space, imperfectly draped, sure, but it beat seeing me hanging there in plain sight.

I had considered taking out the security light, but it was small things that could bring the caper to a halt. Why was the light out? Our light? A light that had been serviced recently? Same with any direct attempt at gaining entry, such as with a ladder, or hooking up to the roof directly from beneath the ventilation frame—you never knew what X-factor was lurking to bite you in the ass. The avoidance of stacking unknown variables against yourself was always my preferred approach to problem solving.

The knotted rope was belayed around my waist, and under one thigh and back across my shoulder. I had the balance fed back up to Dino, who lay prone on a slant near the roof's edge, prepared to assist while acting as lookout.

Now, hanging just below the ridgeline, I found that all screws securing the ventilation frame were Phillips. I handed up the tools not needed. The first screw I attempted to back out was a son of a bitch, stubborn. I was about to go to another and return to wrestle with it later when it finally gave in its rain-swollen bed and began to cooperate.

Rejecting the use of a battery powered drill due to the awful whine one would emit, even the quietest ones, I had understood the possibility of encountering rusted and impossibly locked-in screws. If I had to, I would prize them out with my lever, the mini-crowbar being small but effective.

Working clockwise, I had all screws out but two. Wresting one corner of the old wooden framework loose, I had Dino hand me the end of the rope, to lash it to the frame, to prevent it from falling. Prizing against the lowest of the two remaining screws, I began to produce a nail-biting groan of rusted metal protesting its parting from the old wooden bed.

Dino kept admonishing my effort by going, "Shh! Shh!" until I stopped, hanging midair, listening, waiting. The damn screw which I had taken a personal hatred for, wasn't even halfway out. I started in again after a full minute had passed. My arms were tiring, and the unforgiving rope was about to bite me in half. Finally, the screw came loose with a few hardy twists with the pliers. One to go.

Top left-hand corner. Prize, prize, twist, stop and listen. Apply screwdriver. Nothing. I prized harder. Applied pliers. Dammit.

"Shhhh!"

I wanted to use the crowbar on Dino until he informed me, using the quietest whisper, that, "Someone's coming!"

There wasn't time for me to make it back up top. To do so rapidly would create all manner of unmistakable noise. I lightly gripped the fabric and spread my arms to the top slat of the ventilation frame, reducing the chance of the black fabric calling attention as the cover for a B & E.

Right. There were footsteps heard in the alley to my left. Two pair. Voices now, starting softly, but growing upon approach. Dino's hearing was admirably acute for a guy who believed there was a 10 on volume knobs for a reason.

I found myself peeking through the left hand slit in the fabric. Two young women stalked into view at a severely oblique angle to my position. They stopped just within my sight without my neck snapping, having arrived here via the alley that Dino and I had kangarooed, and in which ripped shingles rested.

Two words—"Fuck Sam"—were the growl of a tigress, a longhaired busty blonde, her hands caressing the breasts of a second young woman whose own hands were gripping the blonde's ass, massaging hard. They kissed and writhed, and if it were not for my awkward situation, I might otherwise have been highly entertained. As it was, I had no idea how far these gals were going to take their interlude of lust between rain showers.

Above me, I heard Dino whisper, "Wow!" I would have shushed him but I didn't dare. The rope was killing me, and rain was again beginning to patter. The second gal, a curly-headed brunette, had one hand all inside the blonde's jeans now. I could only hope they were fast workers.

They were, but if I had been worried about the sounds that I had been making getting this last screw loose, this pair, mere yards away, made all that screeching tame by comparison, crying out rough and loud and long. One thing was for certain—just as soon as this job was finished I was calling up Cara Beely.

Crap! All the lists, all the stuff I had checked off, I had forgotten to call Cara. Well, I could remedy that shortly once we were inside and safely hidden.

As soon as the wet lovebirds had flown away, I had Dino follow their progress from his position on the roof. When he was back to give me the all clear, I went for broke, giving the stubborn screw a violent yank. It came free upon one sharp bark of release, something the Aces gals would have no doubt considered weak.

Turning the frame cattycorner released all manner of desiccated insect husks and other ancient debris, causing me to hold my breath and whip my head side to side to rid my face of the worst of it. Muttering like Popeye, I slipped the frame into the dark attic space blindly, easing it down until it settled noiselessly. The packs followed, then myself.

Dino unhooked the grapnel and handed it down to me. Lowering his legs over the peak of the roof, I guided his feet onto the frame opening's edge. I gripped his waistband and belt with one hand, and placed my other hand high behind his back as he released his hold, and scraped over the roof and into the attic.

We quickly fitted the ventilation hatch back into place with the judicious use of a muted flashlight and bungee cords.

The rain was coming down in buckets, with lightning wild in the sky, nature providing her own fireworks, even as she put a damper on the pyro guys set up atop barges in the East River.

We had done it; we were in. We celebrated with fist bumps and an ice-cold beer apiece. Careful of our lights, we could now hang up our wrung-out clothes from cobweb-festooned rafters, and begin to reconnoiter our new home for the next day, day-and-a-half.

Chapter 28

Our exertions had exacerbated the clamminess of the night air. Now that we were without the breezes mere feet away, Dino and I were perspiring heavily, me more so than Dino. I had wrung out my pants and put them back on, unwilling to be literally caught with my pants down. Besides, my body heat and my movement would dry them quicker than would hanging them on a rusty nail.

"We do nothing further until our bodies cool down," I said in a low voice in case more partygoers lurked outside. "When you finish wringing out your shirt and socks, hang them on a nail but be careful.

Whoever had last contracted the roofing job had used unnecessarily long nails. Dino and I were fine in the center portion of the attic's length, able to stand upright, but if we went a step or two toward either the north or south eaves we were in grave danger of poking an extra hole in our heads. The darkness made our maneuvering even more claustrophobic and dangerous.

"Ow! Damn!" exclaimed Dino after a slight impalement.

"Move slowly," I said quietly, leading by example in all categories except bleeding.

Other than infrequent passers in the night out back of the bar, I was concerned with any sound created by us being overhead in the two rooms beneath us here at the western end, the rear, of Aces. With a door each between the rooms and the bar, they would be relatively quieter.

The attic was crossed in its width by ceiling joists that were, in turn, lapped lengthwise by walking planks. These planks were not uniformly distributed, here for inspection and maintenance purposes. Roughly, as far as my small flashlight's low-angled beam reached, the central run of planks extended along the entire length of the attic. A subset, not as numerous, halved the remaining widths, intended to be dragged about as needed.

What I had in mind upon this discovery was to determine which side of this western end we would operate from, and then form a working floor made from the superfluous planks. But, first, another cold beer.

"Thanks," Dino said as I handed him one. "Damn spiderwebs."

The thanks was for the beer. As far as the spiderwebs went, I wasn't a fan, and cared even less for their builders. I had already noticed plenty of movement, causing me to wonder how both predator and prey bypassed the fine wire mesh screen backing the two ventilation frames. But if we ran round trying to annihilate spiders we would risk crashing through the unprotected spaces between joists, and in short order end up so much dead meat. If the Boys found us up here, death would be painful and slow.

We enjoyed our beer as lightning crashed outside, electing to save the remaining two cans for later. Playing our flashlights along the interior, we kept the beams low to prevent any splash of light from nearing the ventilation openings of either end.

We also had the headache entertainment from the jukebox, the constant bass thump irritating. There was nothing to be done about it; earplugs would be futile. I brought out my cell and called Beely after checking my watch, wondering what she was up to on a Saturday night.

"That you, Vinnie? I hear music. You at a bar?"

"Yeah, outside. Me and my cousin are out in Jersey shooting pool. Say hello, Dino."

I held the phone at arm's length. The smartass said, "Hey! How youse doin'?" I jerked the phone back before he could say more.

"Dino's retarded. He can't help it. So, how are you? Doing any crosswords? Starving any cats?"

"I'm watching TV, and Francine is so obese she could probably go a week without eating, but boy would she be mad. She's got a wicked meow."

And suddenly the reception was poor, Cara making baby-talk to the damn cat. If she was trying to get it to meow for my pleasure she seemed to be going about it all wrong, as well as needlessly, I must add, for I cared not. I was interested in a single kitty connection at this number, and it was not with Francine the Fatass.

"Let's get together this coming week, Cara. You name something you would like to do and we'll do it. Anything you say."

I had to push Dino out of my face, the bum making kissy noises about three inches away.

"Anything?" Cara disturbingly clarified.

If "anything" turned out to be spectacularly stupid, I could figure a way to get out of my promise later. This was about making a second date, not setting limits.

"Ab-so-lute-ly," I affirmed. "You need time to think about it, fine. You can let me know when you're—"

"It would have to be next weekend, but I'd like to go sailing," Cara answered as if she'd had nothing else on her mind all day.

Well. I was sure that under ideal conditions I could probably coax a rowboat to reach a limited destination, though I wouldn't be thrilled doing so. I didn't know sailing from Shinola. I would assume that one did not speedread *Sailing for Dummies* and then instantly weigh anchor. I would further assume that sailing was tricky as hell.

"And there's no doubt in my mind we're going to have fun doing it. Is next Saturday good for you? Or, wait a minute . . . you probably have to work, don't you? I—"

"No, no, no! Saturday is great! And the seven-day forecast has it as perfect! Wow! Don't tell me you have a boat!"

Okay, I won't. I didn't even have a toy boat as a kid. I was an inner-city-almost-all-American kid. We played with cap guns and real guns. I wasn't some damn Yankee yacht club kid who played with radio-controlled boats, and went to Harvard, and never had trouble with hemorrhoids because all those kids were perfect assholes. Boats. Crap.

"Ah, I'm afraid not. We'll be renting," I said, threatening to backhand Dino who was now making ludicrous obscene finger and fist gestures I had not seen since the fifth grade, now dusted off and presented for my sole annoyance.

"Oh. Okay! Shit, I'm excited! Where?"

In the frigging water, what did I know? Me and my big mouth. Oh, yes, I could see that right about next Friday evening I was going to have to break my arm. Cara would be disappointed, but I would be in a cast, safely eating pain pills on dry land.

"I'll let that be a surprise," I said, and no one will be more surprised than myself if I actually went through with this madness.

"All right. Hey, what are you doing tomorrow?" Cara asked ever so spritely.

"Tomorrow?" Man, I just had to call, didn't I? "Ah, tomorrow I've got a cookout thing with my parents. I gave my word that I'd be there. But, for sure, next Saturday, you and me, Cara."

Again, the phone was undermined with a muffled confusion of rustling fabric and fragmented sentences from a million miles away, followed by the damnedest, loudest purring I have ever heard outside a cartoon. Cara came back on the phone laughing.

"That was Francine."

"Rats. I was hoping that was you."

"It can be, sailor. Call me. Bye."

Hoo-hoo! Now all I had to do was rip off a vicious biker gang, master knot tying by next weekend, and Google whether starboard meant left or right. Piece of cake. The good news was that once I inevitably sank us, I could rescue Cara, because I was a fair swimmer, and Cara would reward me by making her kitty purr.

"You wanna tell ol' Dino just what in the hell that was all about? Cats? And rentin'? What are you gonna be rentin' to impress this social studies lady?"

Dino was shining his light through his palm, freaking us both out. Not.

"Social services, dunderhead," I corrected and, no, I believe I would keep the whole sailing thing close to the life vest for now. I had already given my snarky cousin enough ammunition for one night.

More good news was that I was no longer sweating. It was time to go exploring. Rules first.

"All right, Dino, we're going to check this joint out thoroughly. Go slow. We've got plenty of time now that we're here. We'll plan on sleeping during the day tomorrow when it's going to be hot up here. We have to stay on the boards or the joists. One foot through the ceiling and we're dead men. Got it?"

"Got it."

"Keep yourself braced at all times when standing. Keep your head low and your flashlight pointed downward."

"Check."

"Let's start by taking a look out front."

"I'm right behind you, boss."

We tested every board's integrity, traversing the length of the building with the nightly party going strong under our feet. At the eastern ventilation louvres, we could make out a small area of sidewalk, curb, and street. In newer buildings, or older buildings whose owners were conscious of heating and cooling costs, automatic electric fans were installed at these openings to draw out excess heat in hot weather.

I considered it safe to assume that the owner of Aces was annually gratified just to know that the Boys had not burned down or blown the place up.

* * *

In one extreme far corner at the west end of the attic, I used one of the handspikes to gently probe into the acoustical ceiling beneath the joists. Working amid the hanging framework of suspension wires, I blew away the dusty material as I wanted to prevent any debris from falling below.

Using the same infrared camera housed within the tip of the flexible snake I had employed at the disastrous mini-storage heist, I waited until I was certain there was no sound from below, other than the ambient noise filtering into the room from the bar. I eased the probe into the snug fit.

As I had surmised during my nearly foiled recon, the southwest room was stacked with cases of beer. An old-fashioned mop sink and cleaning supplies were centered next to a small door that I took to be the employee restroom. I brought the snake up and took time to moisten a bit of tissue paper rubbing it into a pinch of dust. This clot was carefully fitted into the small hole I had created, fairly matching the old discolored tile.

In the northwest corner I repeated the procedure, though this time I worked even slower due to the very real possibility that the office, if that was what the room now beneath me was, could be occupied. However, it was now late enough that I figured the possibility to be slim.

After all but scraping through the soft cellulose material, and softly blowing away the resultant debris, and learning the answer to how spiders and insects came to be in the attic, I made the tiniest pinprick through the remaining skin of material. There was light. I slowly, quietly backed off.

There wasn't much further I could accomplish at this point. The light below meant I must assume that the room was occupied, though I had not detected a trace of movement or voice. Better safe than tortured.

Removing myself back toward the center of the attic, closer to the ongoing party, I checked the time. It was almost 12:30 a.m., July the fifth.

The bar probably closed at 2:00 a.m., not that Aces' closing time was intrinsic to my plan. It was curiosity that held me in its grip. I wanted a look at that last room to get an idea if my hunch was on target. Hearing rumors concerning the West Side Boys banking methods, and closing in on empirical evidence, were two different things.

Dino and I had already witnessed the vertical steel bars covering every window of the building, in itself good security, but no big deal. Plenty of businesses guarded their property in a like manner.

But there had been something I had noticed about the bars guarding the northwest room's window that was telling, the steel appearing thicker and less weathered, as of a stronger, more recent installation, as in a replacement job, as in circa late 1960s when the Boys had decided to make Aces their very own fully stocked spider hole.

There was no way their gang would have ownership on paper. The Boys didn't operate like that, leaving nothing that the feds could easily point to, most everyone having learned the lesson taught to Al Capone.

Even if half the rumors were true, I could expect two facts to hold sway around twenty-four hours from now. One, the corner room I was interested in was likely as good as finding a gold mine. And two, chances were around a thousand percent that the Boys would go out with a bang attempting to defend it.

And that became an excellent reason why Dino and I spent a productive hour transferring all but the central planks to our planned point of entry, stacking the old dusty lumber five deep. Come tomorrow night this was where we would stretch out, protecting our backs from stray lead.

I did bring earplugs to preserve our hearing to some degree from the expected gunfire, and filter masks to protect us from inhaling atomized spider legs, and sunglasses to save our eyes from splinters, and because we were cool.

1:48 a.m. I asked Dino to hand me a protein bar. My lieutenant had a cigarette. Whatever got us through the night was all right.

* * *

The rain had ended. Bikes were cranking up, the loud reverberations sounding off local buildings as if the area was one giant echo chamber. Good-natured insults were traded as the Boys called it a night at this address, quitting Aces to resume the eternal party wherever they chose.

From our eastern post up front, Dino and I watched the last stragglers leave and weave. We made our way along our attic boardwalk to the rear of the space, listening as the bartender, we assumed, and whatever help he employed this night, cleaned up below our hideaway.

We listened from our western lookout point as, eventually, the back door opened with a remembered groan of stressed hinges. As we watched, bags of refuse were walked to the dumpster. The sound of clanking glass a few minutes later was reasoned out to be longneck beer bottles being cased for recycling. As entertainment and active oversight, we followed the course of cleanup, listening to water running for the mop bucket and for rinsing bar towels, all easily heard now that the infernal jukebox had been silenced.

My ears were ringing. They were likely to continue to do so for days, and might affect my apprentice seamanship. A broken flipper by Friday night was looking better and better all the time.

That the cleanup of the bar consumed a fair amount of time was understandable, considering the brutish affectations that all West Siders practiced. But what had me baffled was what kept the cleanup crew lingering, until the odor of marijuana smoke reached our lofty position. It seemed that a spot of downtime was at hand.

I had considered making my raid on the office tonight rather than waiting, but that speculation fell by the wayside as I checked the time. It was too close to sunrise to mount an assault below. I was not tempting fate by forcing myself to believe that I was invisible.

A pickup and a car finally left from the curb out front. The building was now totally quiet, save for the ever-present background hum of the city. If there were mice, and there almost certainly were, they were well-behaved.

Erring on the side of caution, Dino and I remained stealthy as ghosts, careful of each footfall and exhalation. I had earlier taught Dino the art of stifling any sneeze, with no excuses for failure. Hovering over our projected point of entry, I enlarged the earlier pinprick hole I had made. I held still, listening, my flashlight's beam averted. There was no answering light below as there was before.

I dipped the snake through the ceiling and viewed the image brought to my small screen, the red tints familiarly interpreted. I could see a desk and chair, a closed closet door and a small table that upon scrutiny resolved into a mini bar stocked with decorative bottles--a touch of class for discriminating wild-asses. There was a large gun cabinet that put a chill into me, the Boys unable to resist what they damn well knew better they shouldn't do. They were counting on no one being either bold, or stupid, enough to actually come knocking and dictate to them what they could and could not do with an arsenal. Silly wabbits.

Oho! Now, what I found here in one corner of the room was either Cara Beely's purse or a good old-timey safe. Even red-tinted and slightly fuzzy, I knew what I had on hand. I didn't know if I could for sure open it, but I could darn sure give it a try, junior high or full-blown collegiate.

And the closet was interesting. Could be anything inside there, including Jimmy Hoffa and/or unrelated skeletons. I let Dino have a look so he would quit pestering me. Satisfied, he backed away, both of us now less skittish of rousing someone's attention, pretty certain that we had the joint to ourselves.

Another plug was fashioned for the second spyhole before I eased down atop my pile of planks to consider all I had seen. Dino was chomping on a snack, and starting a yawning contagion.

Not a bad idea, I told him. It might be too hot to sleep once the sun fully rose. We would get what sleep we could this morning. Using our spare shirts for ground cover, and our backpacks for lumpy pillows, we made our nests.

After pissing into our own empty beer cans, I capped them with empty food wrappers and set them far aside.

Dino farted and excused himself as if he had sneezed, which he had best not.

"Night, Dino."

"Night, Vinnie."

Dino and I used to camp out in each other's backyards as kids. He used to fart all the time then as well.

"Damn, Dino!"

"Sorry, man."

Pretty soon my cousin was snoring. Not too bad. Nothing that would get him kicked off the job. I checked my watch, unable to sleep. I thought of Cara, and of fatassed cats named Francine. I thought about the prospect of a huge payday that I didn't have to split with family and the big bosses.

4:35 a.m. I yawned.

And must have slept.

Daylight was streaming through the slant of the louvres at the far end of the attic. Otherworldly in its majesty, the bars of light were solid and soft at the same time, rich in mystery and form, haunting in distance traveled, yet seemingly still as death.

It was a beautiful capture for memory. I kept watch over its angled creep in reverent awe.

Chapter 29

There was a slow increase in traffic heard outside our attic H.Q. as the morning progressed, reduced from its usual bustle due to the holiday weekend, as well as its being Sunday.

Our weather pattern of late, showers and thunderstorms every couple of days, was currently embracing the sunny half. As a result, it was as I had feared, the attic steadily growing warmer.

Following a non-nutritious breakfast of prepackaged cinnamon Danish downed with sips of tepid water, Dino said that he really needed to use the bathroom. I asked him if he needed to take a bath.

Answering in the negative, Dino made it clear that he had to poot. Harking back to several hours earlier as we had been turning in atop our back-breaking berths, I could clearly see the progression, all that breaking wind having a traumatic source.

"All right. I'm going to remove the ventilation frame, and let down the rope. When you're done, just climb back up and set everything back in place," I said, looking at my cousin the way I used to when we were little and I could talk Dino into doing just about anything.

"You're kiddin'."

"You're damn right I'm kidding."

Dino chuckled at my nonsense, saying, "But I ain't. I really gotta go."

"You really got to hold it," I said. "Try lying back down. It'll go away."

Dubious, but compliant, Dino gave it a whirl, and not without complaint. I told the shitass to shut up about the same time I felt my own gut rumble. Uh-oh.

"What are you doin'?" Dino asked with suspicion as I resumed my own reserved space on the lumber.

"Killing time, bro, killing time."

A short while later Dino was up again, pacing the length of the attic, seemingly out of boredom, though I suspected the ambling to be of a highly righteous purpose—gassing the far end.

As a mental exercise, I calculated square footage, dispersal rates of gas in a known volume of air, factoring in a nearly zero wind vector, and came to the alarming conclusion that I was doomed to asphyxiate like a poisoned rodent.

"Damn, it's gettin' hot," Dino felt a need to inform me minutes later.

I checked the time. 10:43. I have got to quit looking at my watch.

"The best thing to do is either to sit very still, or put your face up to the slats of one of the frames. Constant movement is the worst thing you can do right now, Dino. And we've got a limited supply of water," I said, catching Dino going for a pint.

"Just a sip," he said, each time he tipped the bottle up, over and over.

"Think of it as if we were in the desert, and if the heat doesn't kill you, I will."

Dino recapped the bottle.

"Seriously," I said, "all we have to do is make it through this one day, cuz. One frigging day. No matter how hot it gets up here, it's still only for one day. Tough it out man, okay?"

"All right, Vinnie. I can do this. It's just that it's so damn hot."

Of course, I was going to play all this back to him in the very near future as we relaxed in a chilly air-conditioned bar downing ice-cold beer.

"It's the humidity," I said.

"Da fuck it is," Dino replied with some heat.

"Settle down, dude! I'm kidding," even though I really wasn't. Last night's thunderstorms had made the humidity today only slightly less than 100%.

East Coast Summertime Blues, for attic in A minor.

Hit it, boys.

* * *

Early afternoon, I heard movement downstairs. I hoped that the Boys were paying this bartender handsomely, because as far as I could tell all the fellow did was work and sleep, with the latter only a guess. If the guy was a meth head, then the hours amounted to chump change, because, for a tweaker, sleep was not only overrated, it was darn near nonexistent.

I made the mistake of looking at my watch, again. I thought of myself as just a regular guy with an irregular job. The only thing I was addicted to was breathing and, for me, the day was inching by like a fat man pushing a heavy load uphill. Dino caught me sweating my watch and asked what time it was, irrepressible and contagious, like the urge to mock fat politicians.

"Quarter after one," I muttered, jinxing time to slow even further, subjectively, by calling aloud one of its many names.

"You're kiddin'."

"I wish," I said, exaggerating my whisper as a reminder to Dino of who else was about the premises.

Dino nodded.

I had called the kids an hour ago, as much out of boredom as to keep in touch. They told me that the fireworks show had been rescheduled for tonight. I hated having to inform them that I would be busy tonight, possibly the understatement of the year.

As an unsolicited bonus, Chris informed me that the raid I had been curious about was still on for tonight. Being no dummy, I was positive that he had connected the two as being greater than a test of his considerable computer skills. He also made a rather enigmatic remark concerning combination locks, a subject he claimed we had been talking about the other day.

Though not recalling this, I had to conclude that Chris's comment was not a random stab at casual conversation. If so, the synchronicity was uncanny. In my line of work coincidences were to be picked apart to find what connection was being overlooked.

And Sandra, Sandra felt a need to fill me in on the fact that of all the city's boroughs, Manhattan was on track to be the hottest today. This was not unusual with all the concrete, pavement, steel and glass, yet not a very Sandra-like comment at all.

But it was when Paulie wished me luck that I had to ask what he meant. He fumbled with his answer before saying he, "didn't mean nothing by it," and I had to quickly assure the big kid that was okay and, um, thanks.

What the hell were those kids up to? I suspected Chris to be at the center of some hi-tech wizardry, but as long as they stayed put playing digital reindeer games, I was satisfied.

Not that I didn't already know it, but Sandra had been on target concerning the heat. I kept hoping to get some small breeze off the Hudson River behind us. I looked between the ventilation slats to see nothing stirring, no tiniest scrap of litter moving on the pavement. The air in the attic was stale and getting worse.

I forced myself not to drink more than a sip of water every thirty minutes. This was necessary to offset Dino's consumption. For all my hard talk, I didn't have the heart to tell my pal he could not have a little water.

We would be just fine, but by gum neither of us would forget this ordeal. The damn attic had to be 120°, and we still had nearly seven hours to go 'til sunset.

After another hour, Dino was stationed at one end of the attic and I at the other, our faces pressed to the frames' screens to better gulp at the proportionately cooler air outside—which had to be in the low nineties. It promised to be another smoker of a summer.

When I saw Dino light up a cigarette right next to his vent, I had to quickly reach him to say that was a no-no, too great a risk of detection. But he knew that. The heat was getting to him, affecting his judgement.

By now we had our socks and shoes off, and our pants legs rolled up. Our hair was mopping wet with sweat, as were our waistlines.

I took to giving Dino updates every half hour, encouraging him to recognize that the afternoon's length was finite, and that sundown would be here soon. It helped, Dino uncomplaining past the morning's initial spike in temperature, our remaining time in the attic now simply a shared burden to endure.

It was something of a torture to listen to the thump of the jukebox, and the occasional clink of a beer bottle, knowing that an ice-cold beer was mere feet away, and might as well have been a thousand miles distant.

Six o'clock rolled around, and it was as deadly hot as ever. But six o'clock was good. Six o'clock was real progress. Six-thirty was a milestone.

Seven o'clock arrived and the heat had us by the throats, the lowering sun's baking rays making a direct assault on our position. At seven-thirty Dino and I were both stationed at the attic's eastern end, sipping water and using our palms to cup the vent's air toward us, gathering a small amount of relief.

And when eight o'clock came we were veterans, cooked, done to a turn, but grinning, bumping sweaty fists, counting down. "Come on night," we told each other. Come on you beautiful, dark sonofabitching nighttime.

Eight-thirty was a long goodbye, and as the shadows lengthened, and the day came to a close, a rising breeze could be felt. We drank it in like the grateful survivors we were.

9:00 p.m.

We began preparing for the worst.

And the best.

Chapter 30

Flashlights in hand, Dino and I stood watch, fully clothed, at either end of the attic. I took the rear, the western end, where I strongly expected any staging and/or initial assault on Aces to occur. At the first sign of trouble, or opportunity arising I should plainly say, we were to flash our light on and off a total of three times, the signaling directed downward along our legs. The extra vigilance gave us something to do, saving us from sitting atop a stack of lumber hour after hour.

When a series of bangs sounded I froze, the noise coming from Dino's east end, the front of the bar, but his downward pointing flashes were two in number, then twice flashed again. False alarm, West Side Boys with frigging fireworks.

Minutes later I heard faraway *whumps*. The city's fireworks show postponed from last night was late, but finally under way. Anchored barges in the East River served as pyrotechnic platforms, this second delay likely due to last night's soaking.

I felt a pang of loss that the kids couldn't see the show. Who doesn't like fireworks, besides pets and fire departments? I hoped Dino was paying attention to the street and not the miniscule slice of sky available to him, though I seriously doubted it, my cousin probably doing both, lulled by a false feeling of security in the attic, however miserable he was, however drained.

Ah, but I must not confuse what was at hand here with what the truth was. Dino's probable lack of strict attention was not an issue as much as the case of me wanting to feel in control, when in fact nearly all my control had ended in setting the ventilation frame back in place last night.

I did know that I pitied the cops who had point on this operation, where control would largely be a willed state of mind in a fluid and volatile situation.

It was just as I was having these thoughts, and considering what strategy I would take if it were me in charge of the raid, that I had my answer. Dark helmeted figures dressed in tactical black bullet-resistant body armor, and carrying everything from riot control pump shotguns to assault rifles, came slipping toward the rear of the bar in ones and twos. The security light switched off as if on cue, which I was sure was the result of a set arrangement.

I flashed my light down alongside my leg, three times and was about to repeat, when I saw Dino's head in silhouette turn. I went ahead and repeated the signal. Dino came to me at a brisk walk, his light directed at his footing.

We wasted no time situating ourselves atop our protective barrier of planks. Gear in readiness, we donned our shades and plugged our ears, face masks in place. As an additional precaution I had held aside our two shortest planks to be used as cover.

Balanced on the toes of our shoes was one end of our boards, with the other end swung in place above our faces, gripped on either edge by fingers prepared to swivel the cover as needed. Taking stray rounds and ricochets into account was good, yet any round deflected toward our sides could be lethal, not to mention the danger to our exposed fingers. Unless I had banged together a coffin apiece, this improvisation would have to suffice.

"A bunch of 'em?" Dino asked beside me. There was no fear of being overheard with the music banging below us, and fireworks popping and booming.

"At least two dozen before I looked away. So, count on twice that many. Should be any second now," I said, finding myself both calm and thrilled. Prepared.

It was a no-brainer that the cops would have taken into account the large number of West Siders who would be drawn out front where they could catch sky-bursts from the highest lobbed fireworks a couple of miles away.

If the cops could corral a sizeable number of the crowd who had beer in one hand and a cigarette in the other, while also gawking up into the northeastern sky, then the casualties might be halved or better.

The fireworks postponement was a fortuitous break for the cops. But the NYPD wasn't going up against bassackward chapter members of the local gun-totin' wannabe militia out here. No, sir. No ma'am. They were fixing to squirt a garden hose at a big hornet's nest from point blank range, and hornets were naturally hotheaded to begin with, before they got all stirred up.

Beneath us came the sound of the rear door of Aces splintering under the driving force of a two-man battering ram. At the same instant was heard a coordinated, loud series of attention-getting rounds fired overhead. All the bullets exploded upward through the near-nothingness of acoustical tile in the storage room, peppering the attic's ceiling a few feet to my right. Some rounds deflected wildly off protruding nails, one scoring across the center of my covering board at gut level. I gripped the board tighter as a bullhorn's amplification came directly on the heels of the blistering wake-up call.

"This is the police! Everyone put your hands in the air! I repea—"

Whoever this clown was, he could repeat all he damn well wanted. The Boys had heard enough.

A bright splash from tactical searchlights lit up both ventilation frames as shouts and heavy gunfire erupted from the east end of the bar, drowning out the jukebox. In my mind's eye I saw the partiers out front scatter, with the majority pushing their way back inside Aces to seek cover. Fireworks watchers on the perimeter would have flown down the alleys as the big lights popped on.

Both outside and inside, the boom of shotguns roared. Individual blasts from a wealth of handguns were punctuated by the heavy stutter of automatic rifle fire, all of the warring parties' efforts drowning out the cheerful explosions of the ongoing fireworks show.

Directly under Dino and me a large volley of gunfire was loosed, upward angled, a swarm of bullets punching holes through our floor and smacking into and through the roof overhead, every shot mere feet from our feet.

I glanced to my left to make sure Dino had his wooden, all-purpose bullet-deflection device in place over his soft head. He did, looking back at me, eyes wide. My small flashlight was turned on by my side as a reassuring point of reference.

It sounded as if the prepared cops had been surprised, in that a wicked firefight was taking place directly below our position above the office. The situation led me to believe that several high ranking West Siders had been conducting business in the office when the raid had begun, and were either making a stand or attempting a breakout. The Boys were a long way from being at a total disadvantage. The arsenal I had seen crammed into that gun cabinet below was the same weaponry as that of the cops, or better.

Not only around the office behind the bar, but a pitched battle was taking place in the long room of the bar itself. I could imagine individual members of the gang firing from behind overturned tables, keeping the cops attempting entry through the front from making a grand sweep of the joint, with the cops now paying dearly for the open assault, body armor or not. The death toll from this night was going to be very high.

The bullet-riddled ceiling of the bar, our floor, suddenly went brilliant white with the explosive fury of flash-bang grenades. Even hidden away as we were, I was grateful to be wearing shades.

But there was more. "Gas!" I hissed at Dino, though there was little we could do. "Press your mask close!" I nearly yelled at my cousin, using one hand to steady the plank against my forehead and the other hand to press my cheap filter mask firmly in place. Even so, I fought not to gag as the gas drifted up from the battle-produced ventilation.

"Keep your eyes closed, Dino!"

"I am!"

"You doing okay?"

"Just fine!"

Damn, Dino was a bit jumpy. He was also funny.

"Not hit, are you?"

"No! You?"

"I'm good," I said one second before a line of lead stitched itself into the undersides of the stacked planks we were atop of.

"You feel that!" Dino said shrilly. "Shit!"

"Yeah. Hold on, cuz, it's almost over!"

And it was true, the raid's brutal surge winding down, the grenades and tear gas taking much of the fight out of the resisters. It was down to shots loosed from individual holdouts now as the bullhorn unceasingly blared instructions for both sides to hold their fire.

Still more stubborn gunfire erupted as if teased into life by the latest orders, the Boys never ones to be told what to do. The renewed fight competed with choking, yelling, and frantic calls for medical assistance. As the last pocket of gang members unwilling to surrender were quelled, there came to my ears the grinding of debris under bootheels and the harsh barking of commands issuing orders for ambulances.

Radio transmissions squawked all over the building, and distant sirens sounded. Anything and everything necessary to begin urgent triage was being called out amid screamed, furious orders for all remaining West Side Boys to comply or be shot.

* * *

The evacuation of the dead and wounded began. Sirens filled the night that only minutes earlier had been all gunfire and chaos. Despite the top-grade earplugs, my ears were ringing big-time.

I slowly, gingerly, set my top board aside. Dino copied without error. We stood, trying not to choke on the lingering tear-gas atmosphere rising through the odd constellations that had appeared in splintered relief across the nail-studded ceiling of the attic. Around us, mote-filled light was repeatedly broken by the passage of cops and paramedics below carrying out the casualties.

Now that the expected confrontation had ended, I entered a time I dreaded even more than when an earlier chance stumble, or loud-ass sneeze, could have alerted the Boys to our presence.

I had taken a gamble on there being no interest by either side in the attic. The first priority after securing the ventilation frame back in place had been to discover if the attic had an access hatch from the bar. It did not. The gamble had paid off for our successful seclusion. And with the attic being inconvenient, the Boys had no use for it. I was certain the cops viewed it much the same way, if they considered it at all.

"You take that end," I whispered to Dino. "And be absolutely quiet. Listen for any talk of the attic. If you hear of anything, come back here fast. Okay?"

"Gotcha," Dino whispered back, a serious look on his face. He knew we had just witnessed, by dint of hearing, a score of deaths. That knowledge was enhanced by his imagination and registered as a thoughtful scowl.

"All right. Get going," I said before easing myself into position directly over the office where I could now spot the occasional cop's movements via the still dangerous bullet holes. Fortunately, anyone looking up would see only darkness. We no longer needed our flashlights, though it was imperative we remain quieter than ever.

Nothing other than rescue work was at hand beneath our positions. There were too many cops around for any single one to take it into their heads to rifle the contents of the desk or anything else in the office.

I feared a long night ahead. In my imagined best-case scenario, the Boys would have collectively given up like a puppy rolling over to have its belly scratched. What I got was a heavy dose of reality, in other words—pretty much how I had figured it would go down. The biggest headache had been the gang members holed up in the office, though this too, could work to my advantage, for now there was no pristine aspect to the crime scene.

The forensic people would not waste much time with a riotously chaotic layout as they would find here. If they attempted planting markers for each shell casing found, they would better use their time by broadcasting the markers at random by the bagful, allowing them to land where they may, and still be no further from any ideal of science.

The same went for blood evidence, fingerprints, you name it; a supercomputer could not piece this scene together with accuracy. There were far too many variables having occurred simultaneously, with no chance of untangling microsecond's worth of confusion.

After two more hours, during which I knew Dino had to be getting weary, the last of the ambulances were leaving, as were the majority of law enforcement. The crackle of radios went from an overlapping constant squawk to an intermittent code and response, the drama definitely winding down. During this period, I had been catching segments of radio traffic calling for the balance of investigative work to wait for daylight, leaving in place perimeter patrols.

I waved my arms until I knew Dino had seen me, then motioned him over. In a whisper I said, "They're rolling out crime scene tape. Give it maybe another hour and we should be ready."

"All right. Vinnie?"

"Yeah, man?"

"That was wild as hell," Dino breathed out.

"You got that right," I whispered, patting him on the shoulder, asking, "You want something to eat?"

"No, thanks."

"Okay. Keep up a watch out this end for a minute, all right?" Man, I was tired. I sounded like a dunce. Maybe Dino wouldn't notice.

"Okay."

I lowered myself carefully atop the planks, easing through my pack until I found a protein bar. Next, I spent two full minutes teasing the damn noisy-ass wrapper off and about thirty seconds chewing . . . my appetite sharp. Dino gave me a weird look.

Sitting there, I remembered our cans of piss and the food wrappers covering them. Fingerprints.

I tiptoed to where I had left them. One can had laid down its life, spilling piss everywhere. Due to the tear gas I could not smell it. I found the wrapper some fifteen feet away. Collecting that trash, I inspected the entire area, being careful not to cause any dust to sift through one of the many bullet holes.

Time slowed again. I worked my way to the east end of the attic, neither hearing nor seeing anyone below. Parked at the curb sat two patrol cars, with two cops apiece lounging inside. Front guard duty, or was this the entirety of perimeter enforcement?

Back to the west end and Dino, listening for movement. All lights were off now, due either to visibly exposed shot-up electrical wiring or, more likely, some competent someone taking the precaution against a belated fire because of that possibility. Excellent.

Tapping Dino, I whispered for him to keep a sharp lookout as I made my way back to our plank base. I began the awkward task of navigating supporting wires to remove several of the office's ceiling tiles, sliding them atop adjacent tiles for easy replacement. The spacing between joists was tight, the original construction having been engineered for strength, far surpassing requirements for the then modern-day building codes.

It would be a tight fit, but neither Dino nor I had spare fat to get in the way. My superfluous battery-operated saw would remain at rest—a very good thing. Maybe I could get a refund on it. That, or I could give it to Dino as a toy. Ready, I pulled on a pair of gloves.

Negotiating the wires, and with an ear out for trouble, I lowered myself and what gear I would need through the ceiling, dropping lightly upon the desk, making almost no noise. I took Dino's continued quiet as a good sign.

First, the closet. Debris littered the office's hardwood floor. I found it best to slowly glide my feet to keep from rolling on spent shell casings. The closet door was partially open; cops clearing the room of threat had required that minimum of security. I ignored the bullet-gouged door frame and one highly suspect stain along the door's edge, black in the room's near-darkness. Suffused light entered the office's barred window, its curtain hanging askew, ragged as a battle flag.

I entered the closet and eased the door shut behind myself. Turning on my small flashlight, I kept two fingers of my hand across the lens, allowing only a sliver of light to guide my search. Even with the door closed I had to be mindful of the quarter-inch gap at its bottom.

Shelves were installed the width of the closet, and extended floor to ceiling. Here were no loose articles; all shelves housed boxes of different sizes. I picked a shelf at random, chest high, finding guns and ammunition. Quality goods.

Higher—baggies of powder, either heroin, cocaine, or meth, I didn't know. I kept going. Top shelves—shoeboxes.

I had to pocket my flashlight to pull one down, working as fast and as quiet as I could. The night was muggy, and the stench of cordite, tear gas, sweat, blood, and busted liquor bottles was strong. The combination of smells was making me slightly nauseous, and the confines of the closet had me sweating heavily. I lifted the box's top and shone my light.

Cash, stacks of it, all secured with rubber bands, all $100 bills. I reached for a second box. It was the same, each box stuffed with hundreds. Eight boxes in total.

I carried the boxes, four at a time, to the desk, climbed atop, and whispered through the ceiling for Dino. When he was in sight I handed him the shoeboxes, one by one, telling him to stack the bundles into his backpack.

Our reduced load of water, beer, and food would provide space for the loot. "Keep a lookout," I whispered to Dino before returning to the floor. The office door connecting the bartender's area was almost, but not quite shut, as if in methodically clearing the place someone had failed to go the extra mile, or, in this case, the last inch. I took the time now to ease it shut, feeling both better and worse for the action. Its closure would mask any noise I inadvertently created. It also meant that I would not be as alert to any cop's stealthy approach.

I did not have the luxury of time to be a worrywart. I canvassed the closet again, this time taking two bags of powder, two kilos. Normally, for me, it was hands off dope, but this was strictly business. What I did not sell I could plant on the Dezzes—a little payback for Uncle Mike. I didn't know why I disliked them so much, I just did, a legacy inherited from my dad.

There was nothing else of importance to be found. I wasn't about to take any guns with us.

The desk provided several interesting surprises: small quantities of dope, some really hardcore porn, more guns and ammo, and a cache of munchies along with several bags of weed.

I took the weed.

A cautious sweep of the office's perimeter yielded nothing of consequence, my progress slower than I was comfortable with, broken glass and broken everything else conspiring to crunch and crackle with my slightest movements. I gave it up and went straight to the safe, kneeling, frowning at the surfaces' scarring from bullets.

Suddenly—"Psst! There's a cop right outside the back door!" Dino hissed through the ceiling.

Locked into place by circumstance, I was hidden by the desk from any casual incursion into the office. Just then, I, too, heard the intruder's footsteps coming through the storage room, crunching amongst the splinters and shell casings on the bare concrete floor. The footfalls halted, then came on again, right next door with only the one wall dividing us.

Closer now, the cop was working his way with care. There came the abrupt squelch of a radio transmission, quickly dialed down. A few more steps. The guy, or gal, was being super cautious, knowing that the radio had blown his approach.

"Freeze!"

I froze!

"Do not move! Let me see those hands in the air! Now!" the cop bellowed.

Well, thank goodness he wasn't talking to me. And he couldn't be talking to

Dino unless Dino had made his own path down, and I couldn't see Dino doing something that stupid.

Voice tensed, the cop called for backup. Seconds later came the sound of running footsteps, followed closely by the unmistakable sound of handcuffs ratcheting into place on someone's wrists.

Apprehension was slaying me, but I was dying to know what the hell was going on that did not concern me. Had someone been knocked out earlier and covered with debris, and was only now reviving? Whoever it was that had been found was now being hauled away.

Seconds later the door to the office opened. I held my breath, gun in hand. If it came to a gunfight I could probably get away, but I wasn't sure about Dino.

No. I was sure. We would both get missing. I wouldn't have it any other way. If it came to a shootout, I had the willpower and the firepower.

All the same, I remained low as the door eased open.

Chapter 31

Adarkened silhouette, a human form black against the all-but-black depth of the bartending area behind him, the cop moved slowly through the office door. An instant later a dazzling beam of light stabbed across the room, sweeping left and right over the walls and furnishings.

When I saw the light land on the ceiling above me I felt my heart knock. I readied myself, gun in hand, sweating out the seconds before I would have to counter the cop's approach.

The sharp ring of hollow brass casings colliding reached my ears as the cop moved even closer. By sound, he could be no more than three feet from the desk. The beam, directly over my head, flashed down to the desktop before crisscrossing the room once more and lowering. More brass rolled and skittered. The door closed. A brief radioed report jarred the stillness as the cop could be heard touring the rest of the shot-up bar.

I had to think that in his mind the cop had seen the missing ceiling tiles above the desk as collateral damage, as nothing more interesting than a part of the multiple wounds that the ceiling as a whole had sustained.

Whoa. I tried to breathe normally again. My hands were not their steadiest as I turned toward the safe. Pressing my ear against the safe's face, up near the locking wheel, I willed myself to keep my back to the door.

This freestanding wheeled safe had to be a hundred years old at the very least. It was a sturdy, old Wells Fargo model about two and a half feet tall. If the Boys had kept shoeboxes of hundred-dollar bills in an unlocked closet, albeit within a locked office, just what might they keep in an old safe, I wondered. Not dope, that was pretty much a given. I had to know what was in there.

The building was absolutely still. There was one wailing siren to be heard blocks away, someone else's drama.

Concentrating fiercely, I eased the combination dial clockwise, listening for the slightest sound indicative of a released pin, unsure, but stopping at what I thought was a tell-tale internal something. Now I spun the dial in the opposite direction, all the way around past my initial guess, and slowing, listening closely. Ah. Now clockwise again. Stop.

I was either on the money or way off. I yanked on the lever.

Nothing. Locked up tighter than a penny-pincher's purse.

I tried again and failed again, alarmed at how much time I was spending. In my consideration were the boxes of one hundred-dollar bills already secured. I should leave. Now.

But, crap, it had to be something valuable in the safe, more valuable than cash or dope. If I finally got the damn thing open, and it turned out that the safe was used to house some West Side Boy's spotless collection of Easy Rider magazines, I was going to be highly pissed.

I should not do what I was thinking about doing, but indecision was a crisis that could be avoided, so I did. I got my dumb smartphone out and punched in the preset number.

"Hey, Vinnie! How's it going?"

I looked at my watch. 3:40 a.m. What the hell?

"Um, hi, Sandra. Is, ah, Chris up too?" I whispered.

"Right here. Hold on."

Right-here-hold-on's ass! What were these guys doing up? Not that at this par-tick-u-lar moment I wasn't grateful; it was just that—

"Vinnie."

"Chris. We talked about locks, right?"

"Send me a picture."

There had been no, "We did?" no, "Yeah, what about it?" No. The smart kid intuited a need and disregarded any hypothetical. I reeled my tongue back into my head.

"Hold on," I responded, everyone holding on. I imagined that Dino was holding on, about to go nuts.

I held my breath as I shielded the coming flash as best I could, snapping the picture and freaking out, expecting the cops back in the next five seconds, four, three, two—I sent the picture after verifying how great a photographer I was, something I could brag about in jail.

Chris said, "A relic. Okay. I need you to put the phone flush to the left of the handle. When I say 'Go!', loud enough for you to hear, turn the dial clockwise until I say 'Stop,' and we move on from there. Ready?"

Blank on a jet ski! "Ready," I breathed, and complied with the sixteen-year-old's instructions, placing the phone where, and how I was told, waiting on Chris's tiny bark of, "Go!"

I could only imagine what all the whiz kid had hooked up on his end, but it didn't matter. I was already a believer, and a mightily impressed one at that.

"Go!" came the redhead's disembodied voice, making me wince. He must be nearly shouting inside the apartment.

Slowly, I turned the dial. I listened for Chris, certainly, but I still had to be alert for the cops coming back as well. My paranoia was building, and there was no dialing it back the other way.

"Stop!"

Man, I hoped I had not spun past the point, the precise point.

"Go!"

Sweating, glancing over my shoulder to ascertain that the office door was still closed, and not closed because a cop had eased it shut behind him and was reaching for my collar, I dialed the combination the other way, the seconds stretching.

"Stop!"

And have a nice heart attack.

"Go!"

Almost instantly as I was turning the dial, Chris barked out, "Stop!"

I pulled on the lever and, feeling as if I were in a dream, the door swung open. I stared open-mouthed in astonishment as a tiny voice was calling me back to a closer reality.

"Vinnie? Vinnie?"

"Shh. Here," I whispered.

"Did it work?"

"Yes!"

"Great! You okay?"

"Fine. A little busy, so I'll talk to you later. Thanks, Chris."

"No problem. Be careful coming back. Look for a tail," Chris said and hung up.

What! Look for a tail! When? What tail!?

Seriously freaking out about half a dozen different ways, I almost forgot to search the safe that was right in front of me and open to the world.

Velvet jewelry sacks. I looked into the first one my hand landed on. Darn near put my eyes out with the low light sparkle. Man! I took them all, all the velvet sacks.

Papers? I ran my light quickly over them. Freaking bearer bonds. A stack of them. I took all those as well, then eased the door shut and spun the dial.

Holding my breath, I climbed atop the desk, eyes hard on the office door, welding it shut with my will. Carefully, I made my way back up into the attic, handing the backpack to Dino. I wanted to replace the ceiling tiles as I had originally planned, but now I did not dare. The cop had seen a vacancy, and that was what they would find should they grow suspicious and search the attic—a vacancy. "What happened?" Dino hissed.

"No time," I answered, silently scrambling to make sure that we were not leaving any gear behind, any evidence of our visit, other than a few ounces of blasted piss and a quart or three of dried sweat.

Shoe boxes. Crap. We had been wearing gloves. Okay, cool, but leave them? No. I began ripping them flat, Dino helping, making awful faces at the slight noises we made.

"That was Mario in there!" Dino whispered.

"What? Mario? In the bar?"

"Yes! He came out of nowhere, the idiot! The cop was almost right behind him!"

"No shit?" Huh. Well, Mario, that wasn't the way to do it. Maybe I would buy him something if we got out of here. Something useful, like a supply of tissue to dry his tears and his runny nose. The putz would be charged with trespassing. Maybe disturbing a crime scene. In other words, nothing at all.

We were done with the boxes, nice and flat and thin enough not to take up too much space in our packs.

"The cop still out there?"

"He comes and goes," Dino whispered. "He's walking a beat around the building. It takes him about a minute and a half, but every now and then he slows down and it's more like two minutes."

I patted my cousin on the back for the excellent intel.

Triple-checking that we were leaving the attic clean, we waited for the patrolling cop to pass our bolt hole. When he did, I noted the time. We removed the bungee cords from the frame and packed them away. Everything I needed from this point forward was at the top of one pack.

Ninety-seven seconds later the cop rounded into view and was gone again. With speed, my hands already on the frame, I placed it aside, and stepped upon the sill in a crouch. Standing, with Dino securing my waist, I leaned out and found a purchase on the roof, and was up, adrenaline a huge aid.

As Dino set the frame in place below, I flattened out up top, waiting on the cop's next circuit.

When the cop was again around the corner, Dino lifted out the frame and handed up both packs, which I quickly spiked to the roof.

I had thought of simply bolting from the attic in one move, but we did not know what waited around any corner out there. Could be Mario's accomplices, if any. Could be cops on an outer perimeter. On the roofs we had options.

This go round, the cop's patrol was extended. After a full two minutes elapsed without hearing his approaching footfalls in the alley below, I began to conjure up too many plausibilities, none of them good.

Then I smelled tobacco smoke, and was so relieved that I could have wept. It wasn't Dino smoking, but the cop who was stopping to introduce a cigarette into his dull routine. He had to be feeling relaxed by now. Another Mario event unlikely to liven up the remaining bit of his night.

As he rounded the building again I had the end of the knotted rope waiting for Dino's use. The worst part of his exit was having to wrest the frame back into place one-handed.

Footsteps were nearing our end of the alley. I could hear Dino whispering curses at the unwieldy frame. With time running out I gave Dino a successful hand up as he scraped over the edge of the roof with a hurried sound impossible to miss.

We lay beyond the line of sight grown used to by the cop in his unending courses, just beyond the security light's glow which had been on again some time now since Mario's capture, the cops wanting no more surprises. The cop's flashlight beam searched along the roof's edge and, finding nothing related to the heard sound, flickered away.

Very close to having synchronized heart attacks, Dino and I listened for the cop to move along. What we heard was radio chatter—the cop discussing possible movement inside the bar.

I smiled at Dino and whispered, "Let's go!"

As the cops made a renewed investigation of the bar, I slung my hook across the alley, connecting on the far side of the derelict warehouse, tugging hard on the rope for confirmation of a firm seat, and for peace of mind. Now being a rotten time to slip.

Taking up all slack in the line, I secured an unshakeable grip on the knots and leapt, knees bent. I impacted lightly with the side of the warehouse, absorbing the shock easily before hauling myself onto the roof in seconds.

One hand on the rope, all potential problematic slack taken up, and careful of my footing, I waited on Dino's toss. Both backpacks were quickly spiked on the far side before Dino's hiss. The cop was back.

We both flattened out, me with the coil of rope clutched to my chest. Dino, atop Aces, was about to make me bust out laughing. He lay on his back, knees up, head adjusted forward, with his right hand held up to catch the light. He inspected the hand bent toward him, eyebrows raised, then returned to mime filing his frigging fingernails, the nut.

Cop gone, Dino made his crossing. On the warehouse roof a shingle popped loose and went sliding off the edge as we scrambled out of sight. The shingle landing was clearly audible in the absence of the jukebox's covering noise. Nothing to be done about it, we used our time wisely by sticking to the game plan, changing out our black tee shirts for our less suspicious ones.

At the roof's edge, with all gear packed away, I eased over the questionably-secure gutter and released my grip, landing with a bone-jarring roll, not too bad. I picked myself up to catch the packs and encourage Dino.

Dino came down all wrong. Just like when we were kids. I saw it going bad right from the get-go, Dino leaning to one side before letting go, with no way to correct. He landed with an involuntary, "Oof!"

I shushed him and listened. Dino was on his side, with me bending over him. We were exposed in an alley not nearly dark enough.

"You okay?"

"Not really," Dino said through gritted teeth. "My ankle."

Figured. As a kid jumping out of trees, Dino had always been more concerned with being able to see the spot where he was going to land. Instead of looking straight down, he would always look over one shoulder, always not a good idea. It was my fault. I should have remembered. Hell, I could have scrounged up an old mattress to place here for him to break his foot on.

"Get up!" I said, hauling on both arms.

"Ow!"

"Shh. Wait here!" I said, leaving both packs and racing to the corner. We were only the one building over from the cops at Aces. And we were subject to discovery by any random police cruiser and its searchlight. Up and down the street I detected no movement. Racing light-footed back to Dino, I asked if he could walk.

"I'll try," he said, which, to my ears, sounded anything but good.

Dino put weight on his right foot in a small step that nearly resulted in the collapse of both of us. Sweat had broken out across my cousin's forehead. His jaw was clenched.

"Okay. Chill and let me think." To be caught in the alley would be disastrous.

My plan had been to cover several blocks before calling a taxi, or just hoofing it all the way to the parking garage, whatever seemed best at putting distance between ourselves and Aces the quickest. Whatever I did, it had to be quick.

"Okay. Listen up. I'm going to take one pack a block away, and come back for the other. I'll make it fast, all right?"

"Right. Go on. I'll be okay," Dino said, the pain evident on his face.

"Stay low and against the wall," I said. "If the cops find you, say you were out drinking and got rolled, that's all you know. If you have any cash on you, hide it."

And with those few instructions delivered, I sprinted to the corner. The pack on my back, besides about to flog me to death, felt like I was wearing a blinking beacon. I was tempted to spike the packs to another building's roof and retrieve them later, but that was nighttime thinking. In the city, from the air in daylight, the packs would draw attention. Our move was now or never.

Scanning for traffic, I ran, ready to brake to a walk at the first sign of headlights. Even being early Monday following the Fourth, traffic would be picking up any time now.

I crossed a narrow street, and found another alley that would have to suffice. The alley wasn't dark enough by half, but the pack was, and situated in shadow. I felt strong now that I was out of the stuffy attic and pumped with fear and excitement. Spying nothing other than a couple of small passenger cars, I ran.

As I ran I revised my new plan, with a sense that we were running out of time. Into the ally I raced, braking as I unexpectedly met Dino who had felt the need of expediency in saving us both extra steps.

I shouldered the pack he thrust at me. Between great lungfuls of air I told Dino that this was it, that we were going for broke. Dino grimaced, then chuckled.

Letting me know what to expect, Dino said, "I think it's already broke." His smile was as painful as his joke.

Rather than correcting Dino's grammar, I compounded it. "I ain't real worried about that now, Dino. We'll get you to a doctor soon, I promise. Right? First things first. I want you to hop on your good foot. I'm guessing that's how you made it this far. Lean on me as hard as you have to, but move."

Dino, grinning, hopped unaided, and fast, to the corner. Hell, I had to trot to catch up to him.

Looking to my left, back toward Aces, I spotted no cops, and wanted to keep it that way. Turning right, Dino race-hopped ahead of me. I kept one pace back in case he faltered. We made it past the first intersection, early commuters giving us funny looks.

Two blocks ahead, a patrol car rounded the corner.

"Stop! Light a cigarette, Dino, and be cool about it. Take your time," I said, cutting my eyes to the cops coming up on us without turning my head. They were slowing.

"Give me one, too," I said, slowly turning as Dino stood in place with his back against the wall of some old redbrick building. His right foot was touching the sidewalk as light as he could make it and still allow his stance to appear natural.

Dino's lighter in hand, and a Marlboro hanging from my lips, I stared down the cops as they braked to a stop one lane over from us. The driver's window was already down. I waited for them to speak first. We weren't guilty of shit, my look said, so why should I say anything?

"Where you guys headed?" the driver asked, eyeballing us hard, his partner leaning forward for a better look.

I held the lighter inches away from the cigarette as an advertisement of the cop's interruption, and held the pose as I answered, "Down to the docks. Supposed to be a job waiting on us." Now I lighted the cigarette.

"Yeah? Who with?" the cop asked, needing only a moment of hesitation for reasonable cause to be suspicious.

"Solomon Brothers Imports," I said, a firm dad's business dealt with, legit.

"Doing what?"

"Whatever they want," I said, the cigarette bouncing with my speech. "Be unloading's all I know."

"Yeah?" the skeptic said. "Kinda early."

True. "It's our first day an' we ain't gonna be taking no chance of being late, see? We need the dough. It's honest work, officer."

And, really, what could a cop say to that? It wasn't against the law to walk down the street because it was early.

"All right. Keep it clean," the driver said, pulling away.

I took my time, letting the cop get a good look at me handing Dino his lighter before adjusting my pack. When the cops were out of sight I said, "Run!"

Or, in Dino's situation, run one-legged. We made the next intersection and across. As we did so I was on my phone calling a taxi. We were in a bad position if the cop circled back. A little further along, I told Dino to wait as I dashed down the alley to grab the second pack.

The eastern sky was showing an early morning glow as our taxi arrived a long two minutes later. I hid Dino's awkwardness with my body, getting him into position before I climbed into the taxi first, tossing my backpack onto the far floorboard, and Dino's where his feet would momentarily be. Dino pivoted, and was dropping in, just as headlights came around the corner. It was the same patrol. On that instant, Dino slammed his door shut.

I had already slipped my black watch cap from by back pocket and jammed it onto my head as disguise before the driver could get out his, "Where to?"

Dino, and here I really had to hand him deserved praise, had ducked low the second he had spotted the cops going with an award-winning mutter about his "damned shoelaces," tossing a toasty red herring the driver's way.

"Take a right," I said, getting us going, meeting the driver's eyes and watching how they cut to the cops.

I kept myself half-turned from the window as the taxi got rolling. I knew without looking that the cops were looking, but they were checking for two guys, one with blond hair.

All clear, I gave Dino a tap on the shoulder so he could rise from the contortion that had cost him pain. I gave him a low, heartfelt fist bump while directing our cabbie to the parking garage and my waiting Nova. That car had never looked better in its entire history, I guarantee it.

I paid the cabbie as Dino scooted out to stand one short step away, prudently waiting for the taxi to disappear before hopping to my car. He was really using his head. I have always liked my cousin, but I was really starting to respect my new lieutenant as well.

Backpacks in the trunk, I ripped off a quick prayer to the patron saint of criminals and thieves, ol' whatshisface, and turned the ignition key. The Nova didn't let me down.

And Dino, grinning from ear to ear, and wincing from ear to ear as I gave my baby gas, ol' Dino, he had not let me down either. I was so damn excited I was vibrating.

Dino fired up a victory cigarette.

I asked for one, too. I wasn't going to smoke it. I was going to savor it.

Chapter 32

For a certainty, I was running the speed limit. I was also paying more attention to my mirrors than anything in front of me on the streets. Plenty of cars still had their headlights on, even though I was currently squinting against the morning sun sending blinding rays above the top of a neatly straight-edged cloud.

Chris's mysterious warning of a couple of hours ago to watch for a tail was tarnishing my celebration. There were so many vehicles behind me that they could all be tailing me, and I couldn't prove otherwise.

When I came off the Brooklyn Bridge I continued east, until I chose to swing north into Queens. From there I began executing random lefts and rights, swift enough to foil all but the likes of Batman.

Satisfied that we were safe, but hating how it felt wasting time zigzagging with all this loot in the trunk, I briefly considered stashing it all at Dino's. I rejected that idea. Dino's security was only acceptable if I spiked the packs to his roof, and there was no way I was leaving this amount of wealth in the open, period.

But I did not want to keep the stuff with me. The dope alone would net me scads of time, and there was simply no way to explain my possession of the diamonds and jewels.

What I had an itch for, above and beyond my need to safely stash the loot, was answers. I wanted to know why and how Chris could have been knowledgeable enough to be concerned about a tail. And I wanted to know how he seemed to be so on top of the situation of the safe. Those were just for starters. Questions—I had about a million of them.

"We're going to see the kids," I told Dino.

"What! Why?"

"Because something ain't kosher," I said, back to checking my mirrors, uneasy, maybe due to this getaway going smoothly, or maybe I was spooking myself for no good reason. Yet I trusted my instincts, and something didn't feel right.

There was no way to connect me with the heist at Aces. And I was sure the surviving West Side Boys had already written off their stash. Logically, the Nova's trunk should be okay as a temporary cache.

"When we get there keep your eyes peeled."

"What's wrong?" Dino asked, transitioning from relaxed with a broken ankle, to agitated and feeling the pain increase because of it.

Yes, I had nearly forgot, dammit. The foot really should at least be iced and elevated, and here I was driving around playing Spy vs. Spy. I told Dino about Chris's warning, and the kids' inexplicable behavior over the phone.

"They're up to something," Dino said.

I agreed.

A check of the mirror was followed by a check of Dino firing up yet another cigarette. His nerves were a bit ragged. We needed rest and rehydration. We could get at least one of the two at the kids' place that I was pulling into now.

Yeah, the kids were up to something. But what? I liked to fool myself that I was up to date with computers and what was new, but being around Chris made me feel like a knowledgeably happy idiot in the Dark Ages admiring the shiny beads on his new abacus.

"That kid's hi-tekking something. Count on it."

"You ever call him a lawyer?" Dino asked, grimacing as I took a speed bump too hard.

"Ah, no. Been a little busy," I admitted.

Dino chuckled through clenched jaws. I pulled into a parking space in front of the kids' apartment. Before anything else, I called a taxi for Dino to take him to the doctor's right now; and then I had to ask Dino if he had a doctor.

"Hell, no. What for? I don't get sick."

Well, that much was true. Dino may fall out of trees and off buildings all wrong, but even as a kid he never got sick. Hardly ever. Eating Coney Island crap, smoking cigarettes, and then riding rides and puking didn't really count.

"Stay right there. Do not go anywhere," I said after climbing from the car. Looking up, I could see Sandra's face at a gap in the partially opened front door.

"Ha. Ha. Real funny," Dino said, tossing a finger wave to Sandra and seeing forms behind her.

I took the steps two at a time up to the second-floor apartment, the door opening wide to admit me.

"Hi, guys. Sorry about the fireworks," I said, suddenly snapping to how I must smell. Regardless, Sandra insisted on a hug which I kept chaste as possible.

Chris was peering out the window, one edge of the curtain eased furtively aside. Paulie was looking over his shoulder.

"Okay, guys. What gives? What's with all the cloak-and-dagger bullshit?" I asked.

While the boys were attempting to formulate a response, I turned back to Sandra and said, "Dino needs something to drink. Got any soda or juice?"

"Orange juice," she answered, walking quickly into the small kitchen.

I remained where I stood, looking at Chris. "Thanks, with the, uh, thing," I said lamely. It didn't seem right to be openly discussing safecracking with a sixteen-year-old.

"You're welcome, Vinnie. Everything good?"

Damn, this kid was cool, showing his usual reserve, but moxie? The kid had that in spades.

Paulie was eyeing me as if I were unconsciously late in announcing the fact that I had tickets to see a major jam band and everyone knew it. Yep—it was a conspiracy, all right.

Sandra returned from the kitchen carrying two glasses of juice on ice, a glass for me unasked for but, hey, one look at me should constitute an automatic request I would think.

"I'm going to run this out to Dino," she said.

"I appreciate it. And when a taxi comes for him, don't be surprised at his limp," I named what would be Dino's hop, delivering the information as casually as I could get away with.

"Limp?"

"Yeah," I assured her. "It's okay."

I was not going to use the words "broken ankle," too many complications already. There would be time enough for broader explanations. Right now, I was engaged in overtime-thinking to come up with a lesser truth to deliver to my wards. It might not help, but I did not want them possibly labeled coconspirators after the fact, a very real danger should something unforeseen arise.

Sandra was closing the door behind her as I turned to Chris. Paulie looked to be about six and a half feet of wished invisibility.

"Well?"

"It's simple, really," Chris began. "We could tell that you were about to enter into something risky. From there it was reasonable to assume a likelihood of your encountering a safe at some point, and that's something I'd been studying since I discovered Al's safe. And it only took a few minutes to put a chip in your phone."

What! I stared at Chris, my comprehension just fine. It was my credulity that was taking a beating.

"Whoa, whoa. When would you have had time to—"

"Two nights ago. You were showing us updates about the weather and the fireworks show, and then, after I showed you the voice converter, I excused myself to use the bathroom and opened your smartphone. The connection was fairly easy. We were able to track you and access your location for local weather, and read your biometrics as long as you had your cell in your pocket."

I asked for an explanation of when, and got a rundown on how the kids knew precisely where I was, and how much I was sweating and having heart attacks.

"So. You knew where I was." There goes my good intention to protect the kids from guilt by association, etc. Chris had jumped in with both feet before I was ever in that attic.

"The raid made the news nationwide. Reports we heard spoke of a major shootout. You must have done an excellent job of infiltration," Chris said.

"Thank you?" I tried, getting a large grin from both boys. I noticed that my hand was freezing, the iced O.J. doing no good where it was. I lifted the glass and speedily drained it, my throat raw with thirst.

"The taxi already come?" Paulie asked.

"What?" I saw that Paulie was looking through the curtains. He repeated the question.

"I don't know. I wouldn't have thought so this quick. Are you—"

"There's no one out there," Paulie said.

"Where's Sandra?" I asked, puzzled. She would not have accompanied Dino without saying something. And she really shouldn't be outside at all, risking exposure and identification on the Amber Alert.

No sooner had I asked than Sandra was at the door.

"There you are. Dino's gone?" I said, freezing as I saw Dino right behind her, his face pale, stricken with pain and something else. He should not be on his feet—

And that was when I noticed that the two were not alone. Both were crowded from behind, and now pushed forward into the apartment. I went for my gun. Went, but did not get.

"Put that away unless you want your friends hurt, Mr. Renaldi."

"Imagine my surprise," I said, and looked to Chris who wore an open look of astonishment as he watched his stepfather shove Dino into the apartment at gunpoint.

Okay, this would explain the who to watch tailing me, but not how Chris knew, and if he did, why the show of surprise.

"Hands up, Renaldi."

Rats. I brought them up. Halfway.

"You two, on the couch," Eddy said, giving Dino another push to send him in the desired direction.

Dino was out of control. He voiced his feelings as the broken ankle sent lightning bolts of pain searing through his flesh. Trying to help him, Sandra's face was ghostly under her naturally darker skin tone.

"Chris, you and your pal crowd in. Everyone on the couch except for Renaldi, here," the cop said, voice even and gun unwavering.

I inspected Al Eddy—the rumpled clothes, lines on his face, the bloodshot eyes, as Paulie sat between his sister and Dino, with Chris on the far end of the sofa, or "couch" to Eddy.

"You look worn out, officer. Up late?" I said, moving to one side.

"Take one more step and you're a statistic, Renaldi."

I swayed to a stop, putting more distance between myself and those on the sofa, needing to make it harder for Eddy to cover all of us.

"Okay," I said to the tough guy. "What's up? You in the neighborhood and thought you'd drop by and say hello to Chris? That it?"

"Shut up, wise guy. Lie down on the floor, and put your hands behind your head. I've already got your pal's piece, so don't even think about making a move for yours. You got a problem with that?"

"No. No problem, officer. Nice and slow, everyone is cooperating," I said, easing down to my knees, hands midlevel in the air.

If it was me alone I'd make a plan and take my chances, but with the kids here, there wasn't a lot I could do except wait for Eddy to make a mistake. Already he had failed to investigate the bathroom and bedroom. The kitchen he could see into from where he stood in full psycho glory. I caught Dino's eye and winked, seeing the steely resolve in his own eyes that said all he needed, broken ankle or not, was half a chance.

Prone, I placed my hands atop my head. Eddy quickly relieved me of my gun. Because he had not expressly stated that "Mother, may I?" was a rule, I rolled over onto my back, even farther away, and sat up, as, alarmed, Eddy startled and backed away, pocketing my gun in a front pants pocket.

I was guessing that he already had Dino's piece at the small of his back. Getting rather cumbersome, was it? A heavy gun in a pants pocket is a nuisance.

"Now, then," Eddy said, "Where's the goods?"

"What goods?" I said, and couldn't help adding—"You mean you're not here for your kid?"

Al Eddy's harsh laughter set my teeth on edge. If I didn't already know that the guy was a real bastard before this confrontation, I would have now by that sarcastic laugh alone. This was a nasty dude, a real peach.

"You kidding me? I ought to pay you for taking Peabody off my hands."

I looked at Chris whose face was furiously red. He met my eyes and said, "It's what he calls me."

That and nothing more, past cruelties were evident in Chris's terse explanation. The teen was on the sofa's end nearest the kitchen, squeezed in. Even so, I noticed his peculiar slump, his right hand crossed over his stomach, out of sight to his left side, and his left hand completely hidden.

Dino had his broken right ankle propped upon the coffee table. His left knee was up, his heel hooked on the sofa's edge just under the cushion, instinctively helping to shield Chris's activity from Eddy.

Paulie was glaring at the big cop, knowing a bully when he saw one. He look prepared to take another beating if freedom demanded it, even as the results from the last one were prominently visible, though fading. His sister looked her age for now, a scared young girl in more trouble than she had ever dreamed.

"You're a real piece of work," I said to our captor, maybe not the wisest move on my part, but I certainly didn't care for Eddy's company. Besides, I did believe that he was planning to kill us all.

"Flatterer," Eddy said. From his left pants pocket he came up with a wicked looking, professional-grade noise suppressor, long and ominously well tooled. He screwed the device to the barrel of his .45 automatic, with the barrel holding steady on those seated upon the sofa.

"Oh, come on, man. You can't be serious. You're willing to murder five people? For what?" I said. I mean, the nerve of some people. Rent at the building we lived in was ridiculous, but hey, there were other ways to make ends meet.

"Do I not look serious?" Eddy asked.

Damn! Had to give him that one. Guy looked as if he could take first prize in a rebar eating contest.

Eddy took a long step forward, out of range of anyone's possible lunge, yet still close enough to us all that any shot taken was a guaranteed winner. He pointed the gun at Sandra, but was looking at me.

"Renaldi? I know all about you. I had you checked out the day I met you. Ronnie rucking Renaldi's son."

Eddy laughed pretty damned evilly.

"If you know that, you also know that if you kill me you're a walking dead man. So why don't you do everyone a favor and admit you made a mistake, apologize to Chris, and then take an extended vacation down in Mexico. I'll chip in for gas."

"Last chance, Renaldi. Don't push it."

When I winked at Sandra she looked at me as if to say that should Eddy fail to kill me, she would, the crush quickly fading. Certainly, I knew how she could easily be misled by my seeming to ignore her peril—but, not so! I was merely getting Eddy wound up, increasing his heart rate, and shifting his psychotic thinking off center so he would be more susceptible to error. The man's physical strength was well-remembered, and there was no way I could take him in a fair fight, so I would have to take him any way I could, including getting into his cancerous mind.

"All right, all right. You got me. But you are not going to get me to tell you where anything is by threatening these kids," I said, with nothing to lose by reminding him that he had everything to gain.

"You talk too much, Renaldi. The goods. Where are they?"

"I left everything in Manhattan. You don't think I'd try to haul all that crap right out from under you guys' noses, do you?"

"Bullshit," Eddy said, and before he could tell me why it was bullshit, he barked at Dino. "Hands up, asshole!"

"Ma-an, I'm just gettin' a smoke. Fuck. I got a busted foot and I need a smoke. Geez!"

That Dino. Giving Eddy a hard time, Dino chanced a bullet over a nicotine fit. Mostly it was the pain talking. That, and Eddy was a jerk.

"I followed you from the bridge, Renaldi. Try again. And before you do, let me also tell you I know you didn't stop anywhere on your way here. So, the stuff is probably in your car, and douchebag here didn't have the key."

Dino blew out a cloud of smoke and half-shouted, "Hey! Who you callin' douchebag, douchebag?"

"I'm running out of patience here, Renaldi."

"And I already told you, officer. I left the stuff in Manhattan. No way I was hauling around that much dope."

"Dope, huh? How much?" Alfred Clarence Eddy asked with greed in his eyes.

Well, this let me understand how much intel he had received concerning the contents of the office—zip. But . . .

"How did you follow me. I—" And it hit me. "You bugged my car. Didn't you?" What was it with this family? Everyone got a starter espionage kit for Christmas? Ah: this had been Chris's suspicion, that a strong possibility existed for this scenario to develop.

"That's right, pal. And I caught you going into the attic at Aces. Better you than me."

Son of a bitch. This turd had me pegged from square one. But he did not know if the heisted goods were in my car or not. He had slipped, fallen behind when Dino and I grabbed a taxi. He could not be sure if I was lying.

I shrugged. "Bully for you. So, what? A fat lot of good it does you."

Outraged, Eddy flashed to the end of the sofa, grabbing Sandra roughly by the hair, yanking her partially off her seat, the end of the silencer jammed hard under her chin. Not good.

"All right? Enough already! I—" Eddy started to say.

"Let her go, Al," Chris said.

I twisted to see Chris rise several inches from his seat. In his hand was the device he had used for the voice magic. I didn't know what he had been doing fiddling with it as Eddy and I had played our game, but I figured that whatever it was had to beat my desperate badgering and delaying tactic.

"Peabody? You looking for another black eye to match the one you already got?" Eddy snarled.

"No."

"No, what?"

Hell, the ex-marine psycho cop expected Chris to weakly amend his answer to "No, sir!" but I had a feeling that the muscular idiot didn't know the youth as well as he thought he did.

"No, you overblown, egotistical steroid freak psycho. You see this?" Chris asked coolly.

What I saw was Al Eddy about to blow a 50-amp fuse, the gun digging so hard into Sandra's throat that she was choking from the pressure.

"Ease up, officer," I inserted, mad but forcing calm into every word.

"Shut up, you! Yeah, Peabody, I fucking see you've got one of your little toys. So, what? You want me to shove it up your ass? Sit down!"

"No," Chris said, his composure maddening Eddy even further, the cop now shaking with rage.

"What!" Eddy said before he burst.

"This controls the cameras I've set up in here. While you have been talking, I've uplinked to my computer and had it dial 911. Not only are responders not getting a reply from the emergency call dialup, they're receiving a live stream from the cameras. You probably want to leave now. And you damn sure don't want to shoot anyone because that would make it first-degree murder, as you well know. And one other thing."

Al Eddy looked as if the whole world had just turned into the biggest lie possible, because in his world he was in control, not a . . . not Peabody.

I watched Eddy lick his lips.

"You're bluffin'!" He tried.

"No," Chris said with the trace of a smile. "But, you, on the other hand, are wasting time. They'll catch you, but it's your choice of what you're charged with."

I didn't know if Chris Lewis was playing Al or not. Strong emotions warred on Eddy's face. There had to be a large part of the cop that knew of, and feared, his stepson's genius. That same aspect of Eddy's self-awareness also recognized the trauma and cruelty that he had imposed on the redheaded stepchild. In Eddy's world retribution was a driving factor. Comprehending how the boy naturally had to loathe him, the threats by Chris carried the full weight of years of payback. If I were Eddy I know what I would do.

I thanked my lucky stars that I was not an overblown, egotistical steroid freak psycho and Chris's enemy. As soon as I remembered to get a darn patent lawyer, I and the kid would be partners, full blown, not overblown, there being a huge difference. I got to my feet—for me it was all in, or fold.

The look on Eddy's face intensified into a mark of panicked insanity. If Chris was right, then the steroid abuse was a major contributor in Al Eddy's house of cards imminent downfall. I believed that we were witnessing the weak foundations that had been propping him up collapsing right now.

I presented my hands, palms out in a gesture of reasonableness. "You're hurting the girl, officer," I said, reminding Eddy again that some time ago he had sworn to protect people, not try to poke holes in them with silencer barrels.

The cop's eyes were wide and wild, cutting from me to Chris, everywhere but at his latest victim. He had actually been quite clever, and I could see where Chris got some of his earliest inspiration from, possibly before Eddy crossed some delicate tipping point.

"Step back, Renaldi! I'll do it!"

I froze in place, one step away from being able to be one second too late, no matter what I did, if this guy decided to go through with pulling the trigger.

A knock sounded. To my ears it seemed to have landed at the apartment next door. To Al Eddy it must have sounded like Chris's prophesy come true. I began to lean into my move, judging the angle and the superhuman force I would need to prize the gun's silencer away from Sandra's jawline.

To my horror, Eddy's torso twisted in his investigation of the knock, exposing his back to Sandra. Her eyes fell on Dino's gun tucked into Eddy's waistband.

But it was Paulie's long arm that had been resting atop the sofa behind Sandra, that in one flawless move enabled the teen to reach for and purchase a solid grip on the gun, the barrel on the rise and the trigger pulled faster than anything I could have imagined.

I have never been considered slow, though even as I was reacting I knew that I would be too late to prevent Eddy from squeezing the trigger and blowing out Sandra's brains.

But that did not happen. Eddy's eyes widened, impossibly so. His gun hand flew outward in alarm as his gaze traveled to his midsection where the gunshot had ripped a hole in his belly.

I completed my lunge, tearing Eddy's gun from unresisting fingers. Paulie was pulling Sandra away as Dino was leaning left into the space Chris was vacating, the lineup on the sofa tumbling like dominoes at high speed.

As we all backed off, with Dino now in possession of his gun, having taken it from Paulie's slackened hand, the scene was all but completely silent. It was so still, so quiet, that it was a horrible atmosphere, all watching Eddy's mouth wordlessly gape open and close as blood welled over his waistline and painted his thighs. Having emitted no sound, Al Eddy toppled over face first onto the carpet.

"I'm on it," Chris announced, dialing 911, meaning he had been bluffing.

A horn sounded outside. I jumped to the window.

"Dino! Taxi!" I ordered.

"But I can't leave now!" Dino said, looking nervous.

Growling, I yanked him to his feet, and together with Paulie, we shot Dino out the door, down the stairs, and into the taxi. I told the driver to get him to the emergency room, handing him a Benjamin.

I gave Dino my best 'Bossman' look and said, "Call me when you're all set." Despite his shocked expression I knew that he would be fine. And Dino knew that I did everything for a reason.

Inside, Sandra was pressing a towel to Eddy's exit wound. There was a big ugly bruise on her neck that looked rather painful, and here she was trying to save the life of the creep who had been threatening to kill her.

Chris was loosening clothing and elevating his stepfather's feet, his black eye shining like a badge of honor, his actions those of a man with integrity, not a sixteen-year-old boy forced to stand at attention in front of an apartment door as punishment for imagined slights.

I asked Paulie to stand outside and direct the paramedics to the right door so no time would be wasted. The big kid nodded, his young face hardened with the knowledge that life, as bad as it had been, was over as he had known it, and the looming future now one giant question mark.

"It's going to be okay, Paulie. You hear me?"

The teen produced a nod for my benefit, slow and sad.

"Paulie—listen to me. You are not in trouble. Okay? You're a hero. Get the ambulance guys in here, pronto."

That seemed to snap him out of his funk. I rushed back inside. Eddy's eyes were closed, but as I felt his neck there was a pulse, weak, but there. The main concern now was loss of blood.

I asked Sandra if she needed relief from the tiring job of keeping pressure placed on the exit wound.

"Can't risk it, Vinnie. I'm fine," she said and seemed to want to say more, but instead of more talk she redoubled her strength to hold the saturated towel in place.

A siren grew louder and abruptly cut off in the parking lot below. Paramedics rushed through the apartment's open door and took over. Before they had loaded Eddy into the waiting ambulance the cops were pulling up outside.

Oh, brother.

I had always taught Dino to wipe his brass and his clip when loading. The gun I had disassembled and tossed following the mini storage fiasco was done as security against matching ballistics, and for thoroughness. Today, Dino's gun had been handled by himself, Al Eddy, and Paulie. I quickly wiped down Dino's piece but not for erasure; my intent was to smear all the prints together.

Then, before the cops entered, I pulled the kids aside and sped through what must be clear: "The gun in Eddy's pants pocket is mine"—bloody and no time to fool with it—"the one with the silencer is his, and the gun Paulie pulled from Eddy's waistband we don't know about, other than it was damned convenient. Got it? No matter what the cops throw at you, you know nothing of that gun except that it was taken off Eddy. Understand?"

Without even a chance to answer me, the kids watched the cops march inside, taking charge. I met the three teens eyes, receiving from each these grownup nods acknowledging that they all were aboard with the reality I had laid out.

I still had to catch up to Dino to make certain he did not say anything stupid in case his name came into play, such as the kids slipping, or a neighbor noticing his earlier presence. I figured he was safe, but, hey, shit happened. Dino did not have a gun permit, and I needed my lieutenant to have a clean start to his career.

"All right. Who can tell me what happened here?" said the cop in charge, briefly glancing to the very large bloodstain on the floor. His gaze then traveled to Sandra's bloodied hands, the bruised neck, the black eyes. And me.

Placing the most sincere, been-to-hell-and-back look on my face as I could come up with on short notice, and being honestly exhausted to help paint my act as authentic, I stepped forward and said, "I can, officer."

The tale I wove was 90 percent truth, and so shitty in rendering the kids as innocent victims and Alfred Clarence Eddy as woefully deranged, that I knew I had him, the cop nodding when I nodded, and shaking his head sympathetically when I did so in relaying the children's stoic bravery.

I gave him the name of Cara Beely as corroboration, and offered myself up as a sacrifice to justice if that was what society demanded be the price to be paid to maintain the kids' safety.

Statements were taken of all involved. Parents were called and facts checked, and when next time the Academy Awards were handed out, film or no film, if I did not win something for my outstanding performance, I would have learned one thing for sure: there wasn't any justice.

CHAPTER 33

I awoke in a dimension removed from time, my mind displaced and my subconscious bearings all wrong. Eyes closed, I felt a great pressure upon my chest, as was said to be felt by victims of heart attack.

Easing my eyelashes half a millimeter apart, I found that I had an 800 lb. gorilla sitting atop my chest like an incarnation of Buddha, that is if Buddha came back as an overfed female tiger housecat.

Francine was squinting back at me, what Cara told me was the feline equivalent of a smile. The tiger cat's big fat paws were tucked under her as her immense body was a furry, weighted puddle pooled atop my chest. Her face was close enough that she may have been attempting to steal my breath, or my soul, through my nostrils. About the time I had this alarming thought she licked the tip of my nose.

"Awwww, look at that. She really likes you!" Cara Beely declared, impressed with my ability to attract giant housecats even while totally asleep.

I checked my watch, having to crane my neck to see beyond Catzilla. Dammit, I had planned on staying asleep a couple of hours more.

Cara was stroking the cat's back, resulting in the monster purring so resonantly that the thrum threatened to send my heart into arrhythmia. What precisely was wrong with this picture? Thought and resolution took two seconds.

I raised up, spilling cat, claiming I had to pee which might even be true. I smiled innocently at Cara who relaxed back against a brace of pillows, pulling the bedsheets over the top of her breasts. Last evening had been fun. My undaunting contribution to the social welfare of our city's children had been rewarded in numerous ways, multiple times. Cara Beely had been unstinting in her wordless praise. I was a little sore.

"Hurry back, big boy," Cara said, and it might have been my imagination, but I thought I heard her purr.

I didn't hurry back. Instead, I stepped into Cara's shower, sticky all over, and I had cat hair on my chest. Cara joined me shortly and I got a little sorer, all for a good cause, being selflessly noble.

"The grand jury presents their indictment today?" Cara asked as I toweled her dry, taking my time, lingering one might accuse.

"Yeah. My lawyer says they're likely to throw the book at Eddy," I said, speaking of my new lawyer, the one I had hired the day that Paulie Jr. plugged the crooked cop.

"You have to be there?" Cara asked, rushing now that she was up, getting ready to go into work.

"Nah. Eddy's still in the hospital, and there's no reason any of the kids need to have anything to do with it."

Everyone's story had jibed, with only understandable minor variances. Initially, the law had frowned on my setting the kids up with their own apartment, but when the facts came out about Paulie Pet's "alleged" abuse, and Al Eddy's bullying and erratic behavior, the cops were unwilling to charge me, especially as no one else was pressing charges. For damn sure not Paulie Pet. And Eddy had enough problems without worrying about dicking with me.

The psycho cop had survived his wounds thanks to the kids' help, and the speedy arrival of the paramedics. To keep our case solid, Eddy's private stash of stolen goods had been exposed, and Chris's negligent stepmother arrested as a co-conspirator. Unfortunately, Chris himself had been temporarily remanded to the care of the state. Cara and I assured him that we were working to bust him out.

"Are you going in to work today?" I was asked by Cara.

Dressing, in no big hurry because I was now my own boss and did not have a teaspoon's worth of worries, I still found it prudent to maintain the fiction that I was employed as a paper pusher for my dad. Soon, I would work Cara close enough to me so that I could begin to trust her more. Until then, why should I ruin a beautiful thing?

"Yeah," I said in answer, "you know how it is. Work, work, work."

Cara sighed, taking a break from her minimal makeup. "Yeah, tell me about it. My caseload gets bigger and bigger, and the days get—"

"Longer and longer," I finished for her, completing her old tried and true saw. I met her big beautiful eyes in the mirror and smiled at the poor thing.

Actually, I did have a job to do today, several, as a matter of fact. All were of the non-paying variety, yet I expected to find this day's tasks sweetly gratifying.

Cara puckered up for a kiss. I was physically tempted to wreck her career. Certainly, I was growing attached to this warmhearted gal with the big eyes, and the fat pussy, Francine.

She was in gear now, zooming around her apartment, with Tubbybutt weaving between her ankles, making really bad coffee and burning toast, highly efficient to the point of me dying to hire her a maid or something, but that was a no-can-do on my fictitious salary.

The truth was that I could hire said maid, buy the apartment building or the whole damn block, and still have dough running out of my ears. The total take from the heist at Aces was in the millions, and I was in no rush to fence the jewels. The longer I waited, the better a price I would get. Already shed of the dope, I still had the stack of bearer bonds, the jewels, and my share of the cash in several safety deposit boxes scattered throughout the city. I could live off the cash alone for quite some time. Plus, Dino and I finally got paid our cut from the Great Diaper Robbery.

Dino was still living in his garage apartment, though I was trying to get him to take the unit vacated by the Eddys down the hall from me.

He said that he was considering it, but I believe his reluctance stemmed from his misplaced fear that I was a bad influence. And how could that be? What other boss promoted a warehouse flunkie to top lieutenant so fast it made the dizzy guy dizzy all over again, huh?

"I couldn't talk you into scooping out Francine's box, could I?" Cara asked as she rinsed burnt crumbs down the sink.

Ah. A true test of our compatibility. I was currently trying to picture how Francine would look in concrete galoshes. But, fantasies aside, a stupid cat wasn't the worst thing a fellow had ever put up with for remaining in the good graces of a fine woman.

And yet I told Cara, "No way, no how, never."

"Aw! Vinnie! There's nothing to it!"

Cara promptly led by efficient example, as all good bosses tended to do, showing how very easy it was to play butler to a fat cat. She finished the chore in around fifteen seconds with a celebratory, "Ta da!"

I applauded while smiling and left it at that. If we do end up keeping house one day and, gulp, even have a rugrat together, I planned on leaving that litterbox in her capable hands as well. I've said it before: I am a young, old-fashioned kind of guy.

What I was thinking of doing to simplify matters between Cara and myself, was to invent a dearly departed rich relative who had left me a ton of money, and buy for Cara the services of a cat nanny.

We parted in her apartment building's parking lot. I waved goodbye before pulling out my dinosaur smartphone.

"Yo! Dino's bar and grill. Dis is da proprietor speakin'."

"Yo, ho!"

"Vinnie, what's up?"

"Me. How about you? You taking it easy? Eating plenty of pain pills?"

"Oh, yeah. They're great with beer."

For crying out loud. "You might want to be careful with that," I said, never knowing when Dino's logic circuits got too hot and needed some downtime to cool off. My cousin was like the little brother I never had, and I wouldn't let him kill himself until he was ninety.

"You wanna take a ride?" I asked.

"Where to? I can still beat you in pool, cast or no cast."

"In your dreams," I lied. He could. "I want to tie up some loose ends. Beginning with a certain Mr. Paulie Petralucci. You game?"

Dino laughed. "Wouldn't miss it for the world. Just let me pop another couple of these pills and I'll take him mano-a-mano."

Paulie Pet would wad-up Dino like used tissue.

"I hear you, tiger, but do me a favor, and let's keep our heads on straight today, all right?"

"You're the boss, boss."

Bingo. That's the way the help should talk. Dino and I would do just fine. "I'm on my way," I said, and hung up before dialing another number.

"Hello?"

It was a high sweet voice, one of Sandra's little sisters answering the phone.

"Hello," I said, "Is Paulie Jr. home?"

"Yes, he is. Who's calling please?"

The kids had manners despite being sired by an ogre. Paulie's wife wasn't a bad person, just a coward, and I disliked her for that reason alone. But, while I was out doing everyone else a favor, I figured I would help her out as well.

"Tell him Vinnie's on the phone."

"All right. One moment, please. Hey, Paulie! Telephone!"

Loud as hell. Manners only went so far when you were ten. I waited a few seconds, amused.

"Vinnie?"

"Yeah. You okay?"

Paulie lowered his voice. "The air's so thick with tension around here you could cut it with a knife."

"I can imagine," I said, intending to change all that.

The kids had been sent home, otherwise too many questions would have been asked. As it was, the kids had not been AWOL all that long, and had called home every day.

"Is he there?" I asked.

"Yeah."

"I'm coming over to pay a visit. Tell Sandra, but no one else. *Capiche?*"

"Sure, Vinnie."

"And I'm bringing Dino."

"All right. Now?"

"Soon. Hang in there. *Ciao.*"

"Bye."

I hung up and climbed aboard the Nova, thinking. Thinking of how best to, well, traumatize the Petraluccis without destroying them. If not an actor, perhaps I should have been a surgeon, because this upcoming operation called for a bit of fine cutting, excising the cancer and leaving the body healthy.

I figured that Paulie Pet would see things differently. As Cara Beely would have no second thoughts declaring, this promised to be a long day.

* * *

Dino was getting to be quite good with crutches, taking his outside stairs like a champ, showing off and coming within a whisker of breaking his other foot. The break suffered in his less than stellar descent from the old warehouse roof was actually a multiple, with the doctor telling him he could not walk on it for at least two months.

"No problemo," Dino had said that day I picked him up from the emergency room. "I'll take a vacation."

Today he looked the part.

"Where in holy hell did you get that shirt?" I asked, dividing my time between looking where I was driving and the freaking glow that was my cousin's shirt. It was a Hawaiian number featuring truly kitschy art: outrageously colored parrots, and outrigger canoes and canoeists, and hula dancers, and palm trees, and if all that weren't enough, there was an awesomely gaudy erupting volcano.

Following my second and third observations concerning Dino's garment, he explained that, "Back in the day they didn't have kitchen sinks," excusing the one item the shirt lacked. It turned out that the shirt was an authentic pre-WWII silk produced by a master, and the price was well over two grand. Dino could easily afford it.

What the heck. It was summertime and the living was easy. If my cousin wanted to look like a plugged-in fruitcake, fine, what did it matter to me?

To be fair, I had to admit that Dino, wearing the loud, buttoned statement, and wearing dark shades and smoking a cigarette, looked to have something going on. The closest I ever came to flashy dress, or flashy anything, was wearing argyle socks.

Dino turned up the radio, and then turned it back down, not needing a tutorial on love this morning. "With Paulie, you're gonna do what? Give him an ultimatum?"

"Yep," I said.

Dino lowered his glasses, peering at me. "You're kiddin'."

"Nope. Not kidding." I enjoyed being tight-lipped about what I had in mind, let Dino learn to appreciate being employed by a smooth operator. I had peeled away one set of rotten parents, and now all I had to do was to get Paulie Pet to see the light of my righteous fire.

The Petralucci abode was a suburban haven, the joint looking nothing like one would expect to be the home of a beast like Paulie Pet. The two-story wood frame house was in excellent repair—roof, shutters, paint, etc. all looking good. The yard was neat, and the mature shade trees front and back lent an idyllic passivity to a neighborhood of such lots. Absent were any signs proclaiming: Here there be monsters. Should, but weren't.

I pulled in beside Paulie's big Suburban and shut off the engine. Dino and I sat there for a minute for those within to become aware of our presence before I made my way to the front door. Dino crabbed up beside me, every other crutch placement missing the stepping stones, with Dino going, "Dammit!"

As I reached to engage the doorbell, Paulie Jr. opened the door, a serious look on his colorful face. The bruising was fading, and if I had my way the kid would never again look this way unless he took up hockey or joined Dino in climbing stuff.

"Where is he?" I asked, not pussyfooting around.

"Who's this 'he'?" Paulie Pet barked, shouldering Jr. out of the way to fill the doorframe.

"Just the person I wanted to see," I said, meeting the giant's downward glare, slightly lower than normal due to the hunched shoulders, Paulie Pet's crutches bearing a significant strain. Dino might not be able to take Paulie in a fight, but I would put my money on him in a head-to-head crutch sprint. Paulie Pet on crutches was as graceful as an upright tortoise.

"Aren't you going to invite us in?" I said, pushing my way past a startled Sr. who let out a weak, "Hey!" but quashed any further protest because I was inside now.

Uncrutchified, I pivoted smartly. "Long time no see, Paulie. What's up?"

"You feelin' all right, Vinnie? 'Cause you're sure as shit actin' stupid," Paulie sneered.

I kept the smile on my face, just old friends here, no reason to get excited. I gave a nod to Paulie Jr., and then extended this friendly recognition to his adoptive mother, Doreen, having come from the kitchen and now standing in the open archway connecting the living room and dining room.

"Doreen, how are you?" I asked, making a point of staring at her hard enough to inform her that it might be best if she found some activity to busy herself with for the next few minutes.

Hair prematurely graying, and worried eyes set in an otherwise attractive oval face, gave Doreen the look of one who set about the day's tasks with the knowledge that no matter how good a job she made of it, that life would just throw it all right back in her face tomorrow, undone and mocking the coming effort.

"I'm just fine, Vinnie," Doreen said in a voice that was anything but sure. "It's good to see you."

"Is it?" I couldn't help but say, reinforcing my message to lay low in case it had not registered with her the first time.

A nervous smile was followed by her retreat. Okay, one problem solved. I glanced up to see Sandra and her two sisters at the top of the stairs, side by side by side and silent, watching me, all clutching at the landing's balustrade.

"You all right, Sandra?"

"What's with you, Vinnie? Comin' in here like da fuckin' Welcome Wagon. Whatchu want?" Paulie Pet growled, his hunched attitude an apt portrayal of his encumbered belligerence as a whole.

"A glass of iced tea would hit the spot," I said, turning up the wattage of my smile, beaming it free and wide. Behind me I heard Dino's suppressed snort holding back a laugh.

"If I give you a glass of tea, then will you leave? I got nothin' to say to you, Vinnie. I promised your father that I wouldn't pay you back for takin' off with my kids, but I think he'd understand. You bustin' in here changes things."

He pronounced it "tings."

"You know, I'm getting some hostile vibes here, like you really don't want me in your house. I mean, we go way back, you and I, Paulie," I said, glancing around like an offended health inspector. I took a moment to twiddle my fingers at the girls above looking on.

"Hi, girls."

A quiet, "Hi" came from the little one, cute, all the kids taking after Doreen, a big slice of karmic justice right there. Sandra appeared worried, as if she was taking a mental "before" picture of all the nice furniture soon to become a pile of splinters.

"It's a nice day, Paulie. What say we take this civil conversation out in the ol' backyard, hm?" I suggested, moving in that direction with Dino clumping behind me and Paulie Jr. bringing up the rear.

"You. Stay," Paulie Pet said, pointing a big finger at Jr. We all stopped moving.

I turned to Paulie Jr. "Probably a good idea. We've got grownup stuff to discuss."

Frowning, Jr. clearly wasn't happy about being treated like a kid, but then I winked and made it okay. Paulie Jr. nodded as I waited for Paulie Pet to precede Dino and myself to the rear of the house, Sr. huffing like a locomotive going uphill.

I really did not think that Paulie did his own yardwork, but whoever he hired did a nice job. The lush borders presented a jungle look, yet remained tidy, with lots of broadleaf plantings for young children to play around—a deceptive paradise.

Paulie Pet shut the back door hard enough to rattle the panes in the top half of the frame.

"Say what you gotta say and den get da hell outta here, Vinnie. You done been kicked outta da boss's house, so whatchu want, to get kicked outta everybody's house you used ta know?"

This was supposed to get under my skin. It didn't even come close. My old man was hardheaded, but he wasn't a fool. Loyalty was his problem, and Paulie Pet was that, loyal, but he was more loyal to his beastly ways than he was to any old-fashioned code.

"For a guy who beats his oldest kid and rapes his daughter, you sure talk big, Paulie. You're a piece of shit, and if you didn't work for my old man I'd take you out of here right now and shoot you like the dog you are," I said, saying what I had to say, like the man wanted.

The look on Paulie's face was priceless, that same maniacal rage I had seen on Al Eddy's face, but with a no-nonsense murderous intent that Paulie had perfected over the course of his lifetime. He went for his gun, but he had nothing on me.

Even without his crutches I could outdraw Paulie on my worst day and half asleep. I had him dead to rights while his hand was still reaching. My barrel was level with his gut, and my hand was steady as ever.

"Go ahead, Paulie. It's called self-defense. You pull, I shoot, no biggie. You feeling lucky?"

"Fuck you, Vinnie," Paulie said as he returned his right hand to its position on the crutch's grip.

I put my piece away. There was no need to further frighten the kids who I could feel watching out of sight. There were five pairs of eyes on us right now, and I could not afford to look like the aggressor, even though that was exactly what I was in this situation, and exactly what Paulie Pet needed.

"You're playin' with fire, Vinnie. You ain't got da old man to protect you no more."

"Did I say I did? But you're wrong, Paulie. You see, my dad's problem is that he never was good at expressing his love. He always saw it as a weakness. It doesn't mean he doesn't love me, it's just the way he was brought up. Kind of like you.

"But, whereas Ronnie Renaldi knows right from wrong, he chooses the right way every chance he gets. Sometimes the job gets in the way, eh? But the man never punched me, Paulie. And if he ever raped a thirteen-year-old girl my mom would shoot him in the face."

Paulie wanted to go for his gun, thinking maybe this time he would outdraw me. So far, Dino had not said a word. With the flick of a finger from me Dino moved apart to create a triangle, making Paulie nervous, watching the two of us only by keeping his eyes constantly on the move.

"You want to know why I'm here, Paulie? I'll tell you. It's like this—I'm not willing to allow you to live one more day around those kids. You're not fit, Paulie. You're a fucking animal, and like an animal you need to be somewhere you can't get at them. If a dog mauls someone, what happens, what do they do? Hm? Answer me, Paulie."

The big chest was heaving with his hatred of me. I watched Paulie's eyes travel to the windows of the rear of the house.

My back was to the house for a reason. I wanted those inside to see Paulie's face, see the bully backed down, see the beast at bay in its own lair. I wanted them to see myth shrink, become less larger than life, much less.

Paulie remained silent for the moment, itching to pull the gun. And me? It didn't matter. This was a showdown, with the odds on my side. If Paulie did draw I was going to kill him.

"Nothing to say? Fine. Then listen up, Paulie. Since you're not denying beating one kid and raping the other, I'm taking that as your confession of guilt."

"Fuck you, Vinnie. You can't prove shit."

"Aren't you listening? I just said . . . oh, forget it. Paulie? You're an idiot."

"Fuck you, Vinnie."

"No, fuck you, Paulie. Fuck you!"

I took every step but one to put myself directly in front of the big guy. If he swung on me, so be it.

"You think you're tough, Paulie? Hm? How tough? You want to play, big boy? You want to come looking for me, all the time not knowing if that noise you hear is me right behind you? Yeah, you're a regular tough guy that can pound on a fifteen-year-old, right? I mean, damn, Paulie, a fifteen-year-old? Geez!

"And rape his own kid? You are seriously one disturbed, disease-minded sick fuck, Paulie. But what are you going to do now that you know I'm your enemy, huh? You think I don't have this figured out, Paulie? You think I'm so stupid I'm going to waltz in here and start a fucking war?"

He was so ready to swing, and by gum, as hot as I had worked myself up to be, I wanted him to swing. We stood glaring at each other.

"You don't know nothin', Vinnie. You're a punk! That's right, a punk! In my day a skinny little prick like you would never have made da cut! Never! And what you're so quick to call rape—it ain't like dat. Dat girl—"

And here Paulie jabbed a finger at the house.

"—was beggin' for it. You hear me? I ain't lyin', she was beggin' for it. Walkin' 'round with practically no clothes on, always teasin'. She wanted it, you dumbass, and I gave it to her! And dat shit-for-brains Junior, damn! I never woulda adopted the puke if I'da knew Doreen coulda finally got prego! You want him, you take him again for all I care. You two's probably queer for each other anyway!"

I backed away, giving Dino a brief look, Dino appearing ready to shoot the bastard himself.

"Paulie," I said quietly, getting his attention. "Paulie, she's thirteen. Thirteen-year-old girls are all about teasing. It's how they experiment, how they learn. It does not mean they are asking to be raped, and for damned sure not by their father."

"Fuck you, Mr. know-it-all."

I shook my head. "Paulie, I'm going to hang around for one hour. In that time, you are going to pack whatever you want, and I'll see that it gets put in your vehicle, and then you are going to leave, and you're never coming back. And if you do, you're a dead man. You listening to me?"

"Get outta here, Vinnie! I've had about enough of your mouth!"

My eyes were steady on his hands. Don't do it, dumbass. Not here in front of your family.

"I'm not going anywhere. And your hour has already started. What time is it, Dino?"

In a flat voice, Dino said, "10:33."

"10:33, Paulie. Which means that at 11:30 you are either pulling out of that driveway or already gone. Clock's ticking."

"You think you're so fuckin' smart. I'm callin' the cops."

Paulie Pet began stabbing at the moist lawn with his crutches. I let him get a couple of feet beyond me before letting him know how effing smart I was.

"Before you do that, there's someone I want you to talk to," I said, reaching into my shirt pocket and removing my phone.

Into the truly smartphone I said, "You there?" I grunted once and held out the phone to Paulie.

The panicked look on Petralucci's face let me know that as dumb as he acted, he knew he had been had. He did not move. He was locked up, frozen.

"Go on," I said. "It's for you," I said in a firm voice. I placed the phone on the grass and moved away, watching Paulie's face, his curiosity and his ego having to play this out in case I was bluffing. Me, I only bluff when all else fails. And I wasn't bluffing.

Paulie picked up the phone after splaying out his crutches like a stout giraffe at a watering hole. He laid his big head to one side. "Who's dis?"

I watched the bully's eyes grow big, rounding in shocked awareness. The scarred face paled. Paulie's dazed look came around slowly to find my face, looking stunned, looking for all the world like Al Eddy had the moment he was gut shot. But this wounding was otherwise invisible, though a head wound for sure, and fatal if the warning encased therein was left unheeded.

After listening for less than a minute, Paulie Pet numbly held out my phone for me to take. My eyes on Paulie lest he do something crazy, I brought the phone closer to my face.

"I'm here," I said. "Yes, sir," I said, listening. "Yes, sir," I said after another half minute.

"No, sir, I won't . . . yes, sir," I said and closed up shop, my dad having said all that was needed to be said to both Paulie Pet and me.

Bless his heart, Dino needed to close his mouth.

"We're right there with you until you're out the door, Paulie. Just one more thing," I said, holding out my left hand.

Paulie meekly handed over his gun, all fight gone out of the bully.

In much less than an hour Paulie Pet was gone. Forever if he knew what was best for him.

* * *

I sat Doreen down and explained that she didn't have to worry about a thing. She would have plenty of money in her bank account, and her kids would not lack anything in their lives except fresh bad memories. But, before I left, I also strongly advised Doreen that her next choice of soulmate should be a friendly milksop.

In the front yard Sandra hugged me, and Paulie almost did, stopped himself, and shook my hand before both brother and sister broke down and cried all over me. It should have been Dino because that frigging shirt he had on would never show tear stains or paint stains.

"Yes, you can repay me," I said in reply to Sandra's lament that such a thing could never be done. "You can grow up remaining the good person that you are, and go on to college. And, in the meantime, take care of this guy and your sisters. Okay?"

The poor girl was leaking like a rusty bucket, but I smiled through it, knowing better days were ahead.

"I thought you were gonna shoot him," Paulie said.

For the life of me, he sounded wistful. On this one point Jr. had a bit of bloodlust in him. The kid had showed me he had guts, hanging tough when I had asked him to move back home, at least temporarily.

There just may be a place for the kid in my gang when he was grown, but I was not going to push for that to happen. It would be his decision. Me, I would be encouraging all these kids to go to college, but the Paulie Jr.'s of this world, who did not feel as if they fit into academia, weren't bitter by leaving the worrying about grades and school to smarter kids, kids who came to their love of learning naturally. Their understanding of what came "naturally" to other kids was in their definition—kids who got the chance, the right breaks. There was nothing natural, nothing lucky, about a kid getting degraded and beat up on a regular basis.

I would give Paulie his chance, encourage him to live up to his potential. And if that didn't work out, school, there was always room for a big goon in the families, albeit one with a little sensitivity training under his wide belt.

"Nah," I told the kids about how close I had been to drilling their dearly departed pig, "it was never even close, trust me."

I smiled real big as if my words were true. The truth was that it had been touch and go. Paulie Pet could have easily tempted fate and tried me. And lost.

The only reason Paulie was still breathing was because of the deal I had made with dad. Paulie Pet, for all his evil ways, had saved my life, and I figured to return that favor, period. Had it not been for that one mitigating factor, Ronnie Renaldi would not have suffered to allow a known, that is, proven, child molester in his gang to live.

I had tricked Paulie into incriminating himself because my old man's code demanded it. Fine. I did not make all the rules in this world, but I could damn sure come up with ways to circumvent some of the dumber ones.

Dino and I left the kids after I had slipped them each a few hundred bucks in spending money. I had given Doreen five grand to keep her going until we worked out a way to stuff her bank account that wouldn't draw the attention of Big Brother. Doreen had been caught up in a nasty situation, and had not been strong enough to deal with it. There was no need to punish her further. Her own conscience would see to that.

"That felt good," I told my lieutenant as we drove away. The windows were down, all of them, forgoing the A/C. It was going to be another hot day, but I didn't care. It was summertime. It was supposed to be hot.

"Think he'll come back?" Dino asked, lighting a cigarette and sitting sort of sideways to allow his cast some liberty.

"No," I had to say, but there was of course a realistic fear that Paulie Pet would show his mug if only to go out in a blaze of infamy.

Dino looked thoughtful as he began fiddling with the radio, turning it up too loud and, at the same time asking, "What now?"

I cut the music down a notch, still loud. "We go see the don," I said.

"Oh, yeah? Cool," was all Dino said concerning that upcoming stretch of rocky road.

I asked Dino if he would like a beer for the short ride and he didn't say no. When we pulled up at Rancho Renaldi we were on our second.

Mom opened the front door and pulled me in, dragging me inside, smiling and chattering away a hundred miles an hour as if our recent estrangement had been years instead of days. Mom's got her emotional side.

She sat Dino and me at the kitchen table and rustled us up some grub whether we wanted some or not, and gave us both a beer without us asking. While she was busy at the counter, still talking, I looked down at my beer, supremely arching one eyebrow for Dino's amusement, Dino grinning hugely.

Mom was saying something about Dad being down in a minute, she was sure.

It would not do for Dad to be waiting on the doorstep to welcome home the anti-prodigal son. Way too emotional.

When Dad did enter the kitchen some time later, it was as if he were mildly surprised, glancing from our faces to the honking big slices of pie Dino and I were working on. "Apple pie and beer," the look said. I badly wanted to crack up but, no, that would not do either.

"Vinnie. Dino," Ronnie Renaldi said as if he had last seen us yesterday, and there wasn't a whole lot to say that did not get addressed yesterday or the day before.

"Hi, Dad. How's tricks?"

Dad blew out a breath, a huff of disregard, my airy utterance beneath any worthy response. Instead of deconstructing "tricks," Mr. Renaldi got right to whatever point he wanted to make, and it had nothing to do with Paulie Pet, that being finished business, done and done.

"I heard the West Siders got knocked off. I heard they got hit hard," Dad said, briefly looking between me and Dino before saying, "Coffee fresh?" to mom.

"Coming up!" Mom answered cheerfully.

Mom was seriously freaking me out. Emotional now and then, yeh. But today she had animated into a merry cartoon chipmunk. I'd keep that observation to myself.

Dad looked back to me. I acted as if this-here par-TICK-u-lar bite of pie was extra work as I formed a response.

"Yeah, I heard the same. The cops hit them hard, I understand." I glanced across to Dino who was wisely absorbed with the workings of his fork.

I pretended that I wasn't being stared at, then looked up innocently at my dad. If my old man wanted a slice of the pie he would have to get it from Mom, because my score was mine, and that was the way that ball bounced, brother. Dino and I had worked for what we got, taking a huge risk, and then keeping our mouths shut like the pros we were—except to take another bite of the pie before us that was absolutely delicious. I chugged half my beer and stifled a belch with my hand. I smiled.

"Dom's got a score coming up," the don mentioned out of the clear blue.

And here was what I had been waiting on, an invitation to return to the fold, being offered my place back in the gang. It was gratifying, and at the same time it smacked of ancient history. Sitting at my parent's table, eating their food, drinking their beer, it felt as if I were being offered a step backward, rewarded with the status quo.

I caught Dino's eye. He was watching me closely. There was no doubt in my mind about what he was thinking, what he was silently voting for, and what he secretly feared I was about to say.

Believe me, I was torn. I had been taught that loyalty was everything, yet I had seen how blind loyalty was crippling. Others' rules, society's, were what we broke, and what rules we forced upon ourselves should not become so rigid that we could not break them as well.

There was no need to be callous and, certainly, no reason for me to forget everything the Renaldis had done for an orphaned baby. Flawed as they were, they were still my parents. And though Ronnie Renaldi would go to his grave without once saying, "I love you, son." I knew that he did, and it was enough for me.

But this, this was my life. As much as I appreciated the fine start, this was my time. This talk around this table was not about selfishness. It was about being in control. I wanted to do things my way.

I said, "Dom's got something going on, huh?"

I believed quite firmly that Dad got it, right there, right then. He was no dummy. The first words out of my mouth following the informal invitation had not been issued in favor of coming aboard Dom's gravy train.

Ronnie Renaldi shrugged and sipped his coffee. Mom was leaning against the counter by the sink, watching.

"Says it looks good. A payday shop that hasn't wised up yet," Dad said. And just in case he was wrong and my mind wasn't made up, he looked at me with eyebrows raised just enough to ask if I was in. Or out.

"Me and Dino are laying low until his foot heals," I said, and then asked Dino if he would like another beer.

My dad was nodding his head slowly in understanding. He didn't feel a need to discuss anything. What was there to discuss?

"But as soon as that cast comes off we can talk," I said, leaving everyone an out, relieving the tension, except for maybe Dino's, and I would straighten him out on the ride away from here.

"Right. Sounds good then," Dad said, perking up, the future again looking any way he chose to see it. He had his son back and he was still the boss.

Just not of me.

We finished our pie, chatting about Mom's garden and Dad's problem with a touch of arthritis which he pooh-poohed. I got a hug and a handshake, and Dino got the same.

In the Nova I let out a burp and a sigh. Dino farted.

"Geez, Louise!" I exclaimed, climbing back out to allow the aerosol bomb to disperse.

"Sorry," Dino said, though it didn't sound like he was sorry as he laughed at my expense.

I sighed again and climbed back in, Dino now gassing me with a Marlboro.

"Where we headin', Boss?"

Ah. Dino had not been fooled.

"My place to change clothes, then your place where we're going to call a taxi after we get primed. Tonight, we're going to see how many bars we can get kicked out of."

Dino laughed. "They wouldn't dare pick on a cripple."

"Don't count on it," was my advice. I gave the Nova some gas, not worried about a ticket. I could afford it.

"Almost forgot," I said, punching numbers into my cell and waiting. And waiting.

"Chris Lewis, please. I'm his social worker contact," I said, fudging just a little. This wait was shorter.

"Hey, Vinnie."

Ha. He knew it was me calling. Who else?

"Afternoon, sport. How are they treating you?"

The pause was too long. I could read between those absent lines all day.

I cleared my throat. "Never mind. Me and Dino are coming by to pick you up," I said, glancing over at Dino who was nodding, accepting.

"I'm not supposed to go anywhere," Chris said.

"From here on you go anywhere you choose, Chris." I was on my cell and would not incriminate myself except to say, "Be ready when we roll yup. It's your last day there."

The kid actually said, "Ha ha!" which I found amusing. I didn't think anyone actually said that. I disconnected and smiled, explaining to Dino that from this day Chris Lewis was now eighteen and able to have his own apartment, his own car, pay his own bills, and very soon his name would no longer be Chris Lewis. I would show him how to change his identity. At his age it would be a cinch.

When it came to forming a new gang Paulie Jr. was a longshot, but Chris Lewis was in for the asking. Screw social services. They meant well, but they could not do what I was prepared to accomplish.

One way or another, Chris was free. I would keep him so far removed from anything that could lead back to him it would be as if the teen were growing up playing a full-time game. He would grow wealthy without the possibility of doing time.

And that basically was my new business plan. The Joker in that okay Batman flick, had it right when he said that what this town deserved was a better class of criminal. My point was that you didn't have to be a psycho to make that happen.

"I wonder if the kid can shoot pool," Dino pondered.

"I'm wondering if he can hold his beer," I said.

"You ain't never gonna work for your old man again, are you, Vinnie?"

"Might help him out every now and then, but, no, Dino. I'm the boss now. And you're my lieutenant. We recruit smart and we keep our mouths shut. *Capiche?*"

Bumped fists on that.

Dino cranked up the radio and eased back in his seat, smiling.

ABOUT THE AUTHOR

M. G. Akins has lived in NC, TX, AL, and currently resides in Virginia. His love of literature and writing began when he was five.

His own passion for writing began later, when the stories in his head sought release in a years-long burst of creativity. Intrigued by mysteries involving UFOs, ancient civilizations, the paranormal, and what makes people tick, those tales are now mainstream story lines minus undertones of whispered stigma.

When not writing, he enjoys freestyle frisbee, the outdoors, creating unique art, and embracing unapologetic humor.

About Pisgah Press

Pisgah Press was established in 2011 in Asheville, NC to publish works of quality offering original ideas and insight into the human condition and the world around us. To support the tradition of publishing for the pleasure of the reader and the benefit of the author, please encourage your friends and colleagues to visit www.PisgahPress.com. All Pisgah Press releases are available on Amazon.com, BarnesandNoble.com, on our website, or through your local bookstore. For more information, or to submit a book for consideration, please contact us at pisgahpress@gmail.com.

www.ingramcontent.com/pod-product-compliance
Lightning Source LLC
Chambersburg PA
CBHW071727190726
48292CB00003B/645